Praise for *Mists of Parac*

"Golus spins another page-turning, fantasy adventure in this sequel to *Escape to Vindor*. Why do the mists destroy memories in Vindor, and who controls them? This fantasy, with its well-crafted world building and lovable characters, offers a clean, thought-provoking, and memorable story readers of all ages will enjoy."

— **Kristen Hogrefe,** author of the award-winning *Rogues* trilogy and the *Wings of Dawn* trilogy

* * *

"*Mists of Paracosmia* is a beautifully crafted story with vivid description and lifelike, relatable characters. Emily does an excellent job portraying the hopes and struggles of the characters, incorporating humor, and crafting a creative fantasy world. I wish I could visit Vindor someday!"

— **Carrie Looper Stephens,** author of *The Xenia Wood*

* * *

"Emily Golus brings back the thrill, mystery, and danger of Vindor and its people in this engaging sequel! I couldn't wait for any chance I could find to dive back into this thrilling story with its diversity and powerful messages of heroism."

— **Laura A. Grace,** book blogger at UnicornQuester.com

* * *

"Emily Golus is the voice Tolkien fans have been waiting for. *Escape to Vindor* had me begging for more, and *Mists of Paracosmia* does not disappoint! Golus's attention to detail, character building, and fantastical worlds take you on a journey you won't soon forget. A book that stays with you long after you've put it down."

— **Alice Pennington,** Assistant Librarian, Pacolet Public Library, Spartanburg Co. Public Libraries

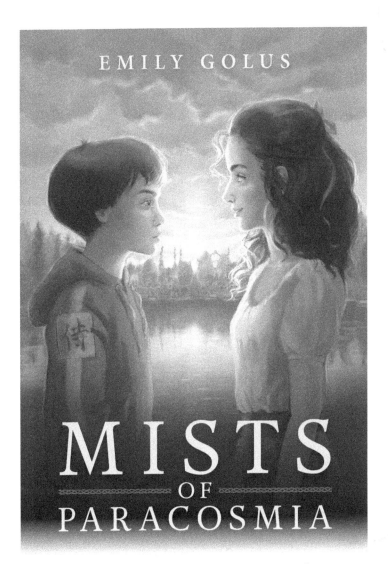

EMILY GOLUS

MISTS
OF
PARACOSMIA

The sequel to *Escape to Vindor*

TABERAH PRESS
GALAX, VIRGINIA

Mists of Paracosmia

Published by Taberah Press
An Imprint of Sonfire Media, LLC

PO Box 6
Galax, VA 24333 USA

Cover design: Michael Golus
Cover Illustration: Jessica Ellen Lindsey, www.jessicaellen.com

ISBN No. 978-0-9845515-0-7

Dedication

To my own son, David,

born between *Vindor* and *Paracosmia*:

Stand tall as the pine,

be fearless,

be kind.

Acknowledgments

To my true love, Michael: I cannot say how much it means that you continue to support my dream, even in the midst of moving, changing jobs, and becoming parents. You are my very, very favorite, and I love you more every step we take.

To Mom Park and to Mom and Dad Golus: You have been my most enthusiastic cheerleaders and you make me feel very loved. Thank you so much.

To Vie and Mary Beth: Thank you for tightening the story, asking hard questions, and helping me catch all those *-ing* words. Most importantly, thank you for believing in Vindor and in me.

And finally, to my enthusiastic fans: I am honored that you have entered into Vindor and love it as fiercely as I do. It means the world to me.

Table of Contents

Mists of Paracosmia

Prologue

The mist was like none they had ever seen—thick and heavy, with a dull sheen like nickel. It seemed to sense the company's presence and withdrew a little, revealing the dark silhouettes of round tents.

A young woman with straight, red-brown hair dismounted her horse. Tendrils of mist reached out for her silk slippers, then pulled back.

"Selena, be careful." An old warrior with a deeply creased face and a wispy beard leaned over his horse. "That's no normal fog. I would not touch it."

"Don't breathe it in," added the bald lieutenant beside him.

The young woman nodded. She covered her nose and mouth with the sleeve of her white gown and stepped forward. "Is anyone in there?"

Silence. No sound of human life. Even the birds in the forest around them had gone quiet.

She stepped closer, shuddering as the cold mist touched her feet. "Is anyone in there?" Selena called again, her voice trembling. "Anybody? Is everyone all right?"

"There!" called a soldier. A dark shape appeared in the mist, beginning as a small, blurred shadow and taking form as it came closer. Several of the horses nickered and drew back.

The shadow now had a definite shape. A boy of about six appeared on the edge of the village.

"A child," Selena called back to the company. She turned to him. "Are you all right?"

The boy, his face still obscured by the mist, nodded slowly.

"What's your name?"

"Caldwell." The voice was startlingly clear.

"Caldwell," Selena repeated. "Are your mother and father all right? Is anyone hurt in there?"

"Get away from there." A hulking shadow appeared behind the boy, and an arm pulled him back into the nickel-colored fog. "Go back home, Caldwell."

"Boath?" Selena called.

The large figure stepped forward, and the mist pulled back to reveal a heavyset man with a reddish beard.

Selena sighed in relief. "Boath. You had us worried."

The man raised a longbow and pointed an arrow at Selena. She opened her mouth but made no sound.

A cry came from one of the soldiers behind her. "We're surrounded!"

Selena turned to see Greyhawk Huntsmen stepping out from between trees with their bows drawn, leaving no escape route for the small company of horsemen. She raised her hands into the air. "Drop your weapons," she commanded her men, and swords and arrows clattered to the ground as she turned back to the leader.

Boath did not lower his arrow.

"Boath, what is this?"

"How do you know my name?" he demanded. "And what business does a strange company like yours have with our village?"

"What do you mean? It's me! Don't you recognize us?"

Boath frowned.

"We spoke a fortnight ago." Selena's voice broke. "Don't you remember? I was there at the council with the Otterclaw and Deerfoot, and with the Houndsfang the week before that."

"What are you talking about?" Boath lowered his bow, and the other Greyhawks did likewise. "Who are the Otterclaw and Deerfeet?"

Selena hesitated, trying to understand if she'd heard right. "The Greyhawks' allies. The other Huntsmen clans in these woods, united against the threat of the Ravensblood."

"Other clans in these woods?" repeated one of the Huntsmen behind her.

"What are Greyhawks?" asked another.

Selena's hands trembled. "I-I don't understand. Is this some sort of joke?"

"You're the one speaking nonsense," Boath said. "And you still haven't told us *who* you are. Are you Otterclaws?"

"No, I'm Selena."

"Selena who?"

She swallowed. "Selena, Guardian of Vindor. I've been here before."

"Vindor?" Boath chuckled, and some of the Huntsmen did likewise. "I've never heard of such a place. What is Vindor?"

chapter 1

A Vindor Dream

"Every human who has been here has learned something that could be learned only here, and returned to his own world a changed person."
– The Neverending Story

"Megan ... Megan Bradshaw."

The nickel-colored fog began to clear, and Megan sensed something important slipping through her fingers.

"Mehhh-gan. Hey."

She opened an eye and made out the form of Rosalind Williams leaning above her, wearing running clothes and smelling of cold air.

"Sorry to wake you, Meg, but don't you have a nine o'clock class?"

Megan opened both eyes and turned toward her alarm clock.

8:41.

"Oh no!" She threw back her silky, purple comforter. "But I never sleep through my alarm."

"Sorry, girl." Rosalind sat on her own bed and unlaced her worn Adidas. "You get first dibs on the bathroom—I'll stay out of your way."

"I owe you one, Roz." Megan stumbled into the bathroom, plugged in her hair straightener, splashed water on her face, then rushed toward her closet. Despite the adrenaline surge that allowed her to pull on her plaid skirt, cardigan, and tights in record time, she still had that funny feeling from when she first woke up—the sense that something important had gotten away.

"Hey, Meg, want a breakfast bar?"

Megan glanced over at Roz, who sat on her rough, brown bedspread—

woven of bamboo or something eco-friendly—and unwrapped a rectangle that looked like twigs compressed with sand. Roz held it out. "I've got a bunch of them. It's quinoa."

As though that made it better.

"Uh, thanks, but I think I'll grab something after class." Megan swiped on some mascara, then took the straightener to tame the unruly bits of her long red-brown hair.

Roz laughed.

"What?" Megan asked, not taking her eyes from the mirror.

"Nothing," Roz said. "It's interesting that when you've got nine minutes to get ready, you still have to use the straightener."

"Force of habit, I guess," Megan said, unplugging it and then hurrying to her bookshelf. "I used to be self-conscious about my hair flipping out in random directions."

"That's funny." Roz leaned back on her bed. "You don't strike me as the self-conscious type."

"Oh, you have no idea." Megan laughed. "It was bad." As she said it, something inside her brushed against that lonely place again, but only for a second. She grabbed her psychology book and shoved it into her book satchel.

"Gotta go." Megan whipped on her wool coat and violet scarf and then dashed out the door. "Later, Roz!"

She clattered down the rickety wooden steps of the Grace Palmer Girls' Dormitory and rushed out into the sunlight. The cold, salty air stung her nostrils and lungs as she inhaled. Megan pulled her scarf over her nose as she jogged down the cobblestone sidewalk toward the center of campus.

Cove College was a tiny liberal arts school run by an old Christian denomination that didn't do much now besides run the college. The campus stood a stone's throw from the Connecticut shoreline, tucked between the historic towns of Mystic and Stonington. Some of the longtime residents didn't even know it was there.

Megan had first learned about Cove through a classmate at the Academy, and when she found out it had one of the best counseling programs in the state, she'd been sold.

Now she passed beneath the sprawling boughs of the old Captain's Oak. The sea breeze loosened a few of its remaining rust-colored leaves and swirled them past Megan's ear.

The feeling she'd had when she first woke up returned. What had she been trying to remember?

"Madame President!"

On a bench outside the Edmund Fanning—a sagging, three-hundred-year-old house that had been converted into the college library—three other freshmen sat, eating hot bagels. The steam rose in the chilly air, and Megan's stomach rumbled.

"Madame President," repeated Ellie Johnson, waving in Megan's direction. "Are we still having the Foster Care Advocates meeting at four o'clock?"

Megan slowed. "No, I have to pick up my brother at four. Besides, it's the Friday before Thanksgiving break. Go on vacation already."

She turned, then glanced over her shoulder. "Oh, but tell the group if they have any more toys for the Christmas drive to drop them off in Lab 201—the door will be unlocked until five." She glanced up at the old clock tower and resumed her jog. "Sorry—running late!"

Only a few students milled outside the Miner classroom building—not a good sign. Megan jogged faster—okay, she was running now—and dashed through the double doors and down the hall. She made it to Room 117 and slid into her seat only two seconds before the bell rang.

Success.

Megan covered her mouth with her hand and inhaled through her nose, trying to muffle the sound of her panting as she pulled out her Psych 101 book and her laptop. As Professor DeBois began his lecture in his thick, Boston accent, Megan remembered.

A Vindor dream. She'd had a Vindor dream, and a vivid one at that.

In fact, it was that one with the fog and the Huntsmen again. She'd had that same dream for three nights now—noteworthy, since Vindor dreams came more rarely now that she'd started college.

Part of her wanted to close her eyes and relive the dream, savoring every detail and comparing it to the real Vindor she remembered, like she'd done for years now. But Professor DeBois had already moved onto the next point of his lecture, and Megan's notes page remained blank. She typed quickly to copy the words DeBois had scrawled on the whiteboard.

Megan pushed thoughts of Vindor from her mind. She had to concentrate on class.

*   *   *

Concentrate!

Arden Nakamura Bradshaw stood in the center of the school ice rink, trying to block out the fifty other boys chasing and whacking each other with battered hockey sticks. He took a calming breath to regain his focus. The gym's fluorescent lights sparkled on the ice, highlighting the intricate crisscross patterns and spirals the boys' skates left on its surface. Each time they skated by, the pattern changed slightly, and—

Stop it, Arden scolded himself. Warriors didn't come to ponder the beauty of the ice. They came to dominate it.

He exhaled and inched his skates closer to each other, trying to stand taller—not easy to do in skates that were a size too large and that stayed loose around his ankles. All the borrowed school equipment was too big—especially the helmet, which he had to adjust every few minutes.

On the other side of the Edith Wharton Academy rink, the coaches stood with their heads close together, discussing something. *Deciding our fates*, Arden thought grimly. He swallowed and readjusted his helmet.

A distinctive three-note laugh came from the bleachers, and without turning, Arden knew Evan had come to watch the tryouts with his friends.

Senior Evan Okamoto was everything Arden wished to be: tall, popular, the MVP of at least two of Edith Wharton's varsity sports, and a black belt in martial arts. Also, fully Japanese.

Only a handful of Asian students attended Edith Wharton Academy, and the coolest of them sat at Evan's lunch table: Jiang Chen and Teddy

Park (who played bass and drums respectively in Evan's band), popular girls like cheerleader Ashlee Park (no relation to Teddy), and occasionally some of the boys from Arden's homeroom.

Arden, painfully aware that he was only half-Asian and not cool by most people's definitions, had worked up the courage a couple of times to try to sit at Evan's table. But each time Evan's girlfriend, Hitomi, told him the empty seats were saved for someone else.

But this could be his chance to change that.

The coaches came forward on the ice and waved their arms for attention. The boys' chaos subsided, mostly.

"We're gonna finish with a scrimmage," Coach Kent barked. "Team One—Patel on goal, then Fernandez, Johnson, Steadman, Jackson, and Bradshaw."

"What?" Roger Steadman yelled. "Why do we get stuck with the pipsqueak?"

C.J. Jackson turned to Arden. "I think you're at the wrong tryouts. The kindergarten tryouts are next week." He elbowed Steadman.

"Yeah, next week when there's no school." Steadman guffawed.

The two of them skated toward the other side of the rink. Arden watched them, his fists clenched around his hockey stick.

He'd show them. Maybe he stood a head shorter than the rest of the boys, but he was fast and had good control. And he'd spent all last winter practicing his puck-handling skills on the icy patches behind the science building. His hard work would finally pay off.

He was glad to have Steadman and Jackson on his team, in a way—better than them being against him. As the old samurai saying went, "Keep your friends close and your enemies closer." At least, he thought that was a samurai saying.

"Steadman! Miller!" Coach Kent shouted. "You, over here for face-off. The rest of you boys find a position."

Arden skated to the right of center to take the wing position, a few seconds before Jackson got there. But that didn't stop Jackson from elbowing Arden in the chest hard enough to send his eighty-nine-pound frame toward the wall.

"My spot, runt." Jackson spat onto the ice.

Arden regained control of his skates quickly and glared at the back of Jackson's helmet. He wanted to shove the big, blond dolt back, but Jackson weighed probably thirty pounds more than he, and the raw physics weren't on Arden's side. Besides, the coaches were watching. Arden skated into the right defenseman position, farther away from the action.

Focus. Breathe, he told himself over the clatter of skates and the impatient thumping of hockey sticks against the ice. *You can do this.*

Coach Kent stood between Steadman and Dante Miller, holding the puck high.

The blast of the whistle. The click of the puck hitting the ice.

And the frenzy began.

Within seconds, positions were irrelevant as every boy on the ice sped to the center, whacking at the puck in a confused clatter of hockey sticks.

But Arden knew better. He watched the melee intently, but from a distance, skating toward the opponents' goal.

Finally, Jimmy Fernandez broke free from the tangle of boys, his stick guiding the puck in the direction of the goal. Immediately the other team blocked him.

"Here!" Arden cried, his voice higher than normal. Ugh. "Jimmy, I have a clear shot. Pass it here!"

Jimmy glanced up in Arden's direction for a second, then took the shot himself. Miller intercepted the puck halfway toward the goal and sent it to the other end of the rink.

But Arden was already on it. He sped down the ice effortlessly, at one point weaving right between two of the bigger boys on the other team.

He hoped Evan could see him.

Steadman and Miller squabbled over the puck now. Neither had good control, so they shoved one another more than they made contact with the puck. Miller finally pushed the puck away. It sped down the ice—right to Arden.

Arden caught it with his stick, spun it around deftly, and saw he had a clear path all the way down the rink toward the goal. He doubled his speed, keeping the puck neatly in front of him.

One hundred feet to the goal.

Eighty feet.

Sixty feet.

And then, faster than he could register, a tremendous force hit him on his left side. Arden lost control of the puck and went sprawling. He hit the Plexiglas wall hard. As soon as he regained control, he twisted back to see who had hit him.

Jackson.

"We're on the same team!" Arden shouted, his voice cracking over the clatter of sticks and skates. Jackson, of course, had lost the puck, launching both teams back into a mad scramble.

Arden got back on his feet, ready to speed toward the fray when Steadman—all 140 pounds of him—crunched him against the wall, his elbow driving into Arden's collarbone.

Arden's loose skate slipped out from under him, and as he tumbled, he received a second blow. Jimmy Fernandez practically kicked him in the chest.

The back of Arden's head hit the wall, and the oversized helmet shifted, the metal from the cage digging into his lip.

Arden tasted blood, but he peeled himself up off the ice. He steadied himself for a moment—ready to race back into the game—when he heard a cheer from Miller's team. They'd taken possession and scored.

Coach Kent skated into the center. "Steadman, Jackson, Miller, and Fernandez—you guys stay in. Everyone else, clear out and let the rest take a turn."

And just like that, Arden's chances for making the junior varsity team ended.

There was no use sticking around. Arden pulled off his skates and made his way to the locker room, hoping to change before the other boys got there. He paused at the mirror and pressed a rough paper towel into his lip to mop up some of the blood. Yeah, an injury wasn't cool if you got it by getting crushed.

He glared at his reflection with its not-quite-Asian eyes. He took a calming breath and recited something he'd read in a samurai book from the library: "It does not matter how slowly you go, so long as you do not stop."

The words didn't make him feel better.

He exhaled and brushed his red-brown bangs from his face. His mom would make him cut them soon, but right now they were long, the way he liked them.

Arden stepped onto the locker room scale, closing his eyes and concentrating, as though by sheer force of will he could make the number bigger. He opened an eye.

Eighty-eight. He'd lost a pound.

Arden wadded up the borrowed school jersey and flung it into the laundry basket by the door. He grabbed his backpack and stepped out to a cold and grey November afternoon.

Pulling his black nylon coat closer, he made his way across the Wharton campus—his school and home all in one. His mom had been the principal of Wharton for nearly as long as he could remember, which for no good reason counted against—not for—Arden's popularity with the boys.

A muffled electric guitar riff came from his backpack. He pulled out his cell phone and answered, cutting off the *Dragon Ball Z* theme song. He needed a new ringtone.

"Hi, what?"

"Hey Arden."

"Hey Joe, what's up?" Arden slowed his pace and pushed his phone into his ear. He was mostly used to Jozef Grzeksiewicz's accent by now—his family had recently moved from Warsaw—but understanding him over the phone posed more of a challenge.

"Me and Shonda and Davey are here in the Quad," Joe said in his signature monotone. "We have our cards. Do you want to bring your deck? We can have a tournament."

"Well—" Arden hesitated. "I can't today. Sorry."

He heard Shonda's voice in the background: "Joe, ask him how tryouts went."

"How did tryouts went?" Joe asked. "I mean, go. Shonda, is my telephone—let go."

Arden winced. "I don't want to talk about it. Look, tell everybody to have a good Thanksgiving, okay? I gotta pack for my trip. Bye."

He shoved his phone back into his bookbag pocket. Hanging out with his three closest friends would probably have been a good release for him right now. But being seen playing nerdy card games in the middle of campus had caused him ... well, other problems.

And as Arden turned onto the sidewalk that cut between the elementary gym and the science lab, his other problems appeared.

"Hey Arden."

Arden's stomach tightened.

"Nice work on the ice out there."

It was Eric, Roger Steadman's older and nastier brother, with a thick neck, broad chest, and square jaw—like someone had tried to squeeze a bullmastiff into the Wharton cardigan and khakis. Puberty had gotten carried away with this one.

Big Steadman was flanked, as always, by younger students—sort of thugs-in-training. This time it was Tyler Cross and Jay Feliciano from Arden's homeroom. They reminded Arden of those tiny fish that hung around sharks.

Arden clenched his jaw but kept walking at a steady pace, resisting the urge to run. Running always made it worse.

Big Steadman stomped toward Arden—apparently, he couldn't *not* stomp—and cut Arden off in his tracks.

"I think you tried out for the wrong sport." Big Steadman towered over Arden, standing a foot or so too close for comfort. "You're more cut out for figure skating. Maybe that prissy Polack you hang out with can lend you a tutu."

Arden couldn't stop himself. "You leave Joe alone," he barked. "Don't you ever call him that again!"

"Oh yeah?" Big Steadman stepped closer, forcing Arden to back into the wall. Jay and Tyler pressed in too, surrounding him. "You gonna make me?"

Arden could barely stop himself from socking Steadman in the gut. But clearly outnumbered and outmuscled, he knew how badly that would end. He dropped his head. "No," he said quietly.

"No, what?" Big Steadman pressed.

A tremor of rage moved up Arden's spine. "No, sir," he muttered.

"Good." Steadman stepped back, and his henchmen did the same.

It wasn't fair. Only a biological accident let Steadman and his thugs push him around. One day Arden would catch up, and then they'd pay.

"Hey, what's that?" Apparently, Arden had left one of his backpack zippers open. Jay grabbed at it and pulled something out.

No, no! Arden felt a wave of panic as Jay opened his battered sketchbook and flipped a few pages.

Studies of leaves, trees, flowers, birds. Sketches of faces—including some of the Wharton professors. And then a whole section of samurai warriors, complete with armor that Arden had designed himself. No one was supposed to see that, especially not these guys.

Steadman frowned over Jay's shoulder. "Did you draw all that?"

Tyler guffawed. "He's drawing his people."

Jay looked up at Arden. "You're a good artist," he said.

"For a little girl!" Tyler added.

Big Steadman smirked. "Don't you know art is for pansies? We're going to start calling you Pansy Arden from now on."

In a sing-song voice, Tyler added, "Pansy Garden Arden."

Big Steadman took the sketchbook. "You know what I think of this?"

Please don't, Arden silently pleaded.

"Heads up," hissed Tyler.

The boys glanced up the sidewalk. Mr. Gupta, the chemistry teacher, had turned the corner and now walked in their direction.

Steadman took a step back. "I think it's great," he said, his tone suddenly friendly.

Tyler smirked. "Yeah, thanks for showing it to us."

Big Steadman held the book out. Arden's fingers shook as he took it back.

"Boys," Mr. Gupta said, crossing his arms. "Shouldn't you be heading home now?"

"Yes sir," Big Steadman said cheerfully. "We were just on our way. See you later, Garden—I mean, Arden."

Tyler suppressed a snort of laughter as he followed Steadman down the sidewalk. Jay glanced back, looking almost apologetic.

"Everything all right, Arden?" Mr. Gupta asked.

Arden nodded, not trusting himself to speak without his voice breaking.

Mr. Gupta leaned closer. "Are you sure? If anything's wrong, you can tell me."

"I'm fine, sir. I'd better get going—my mom's waiting for me. Have a good Thanksgiving."

Still shaking, Arden made his way back toward the principal's residence. He hated being weak. For once he wanted to be the strong one. The hero.

And he wanted to get away from this place. Nine days wasn't going to be nearly long enough.

chapter 2

The Incident at the Bridge

"Nine days isn't going to be nearly long enough." Celia Amiens sighed. "We'll probably only see a fraction of Montreal before we have to turn around and come back here."

Celia sat across the cafeteria table from Megan and was engaged in her favorite pastime, complain-bragging. Adam, her latest boyfriend, hung onto her every word.

"I'm sure it will be fine," Megan said, glancing at Roz who didn't try to mask her boredom. "Plus, after all that time speaking French, I'm sure you'll be relieved to be able to order a sandwich in English again."

"Hey, anyone want ice cream?" Orlando Ruiz appeared at the table, holding out a tray of soft-serve. "I got enough for everyone."

"That's sweet, Orlando. Thanks," Megan said, glad for the interruption. She didn't know much about Orlando, except he was Adam's longtime friend and a sophomore science major of some sort. He was tall and heavyset and typically stayed quiet—especially when casting shy glances toward Roz.

He set the tray down on the table and held out one of the soft-serve cups to Roz. "Want some?"

"Sorry, can't have dairy," Roz said.

Orlando's smile faded. "I thought vegetarians could have milk."

"They can," Roz answered. "But I'm vegan on Fridays. It's kind of an experimental thing."

"Oh." Orlando put the soft-serve down. "That's okay. You can have my red Jell-O."

Roz looked up in horror. "Do you know what they put in Jell-O?"

Orlando took his place at the end of the table, rubbing his thin chinstrap beard with his knuckles and regarding the bowl of gelatin with suspicion.

Adam slapped him on the shoulder. "Where are you going for Thanksgiving break, mi amigo?"

Orlando shrugged. "I live like an hour from here, so I'm going to drive home and back on Thursday. The rest of the week I'm staying on campus to catch up on lab work." He glanced up at Roz shyly. "What about you"—he quickly shifted his gaze—"Megan?"

Megan smiled. "Well, my brother's coming here this afternoon. We're going to do some of the touristy stuff around Mystic tonight, and tomorrow we're heading off to go camping with Roz's family."

"Yep," Roz said. "We're gonna rough it for a whole week at Mount Greylock State Forest. You can't drive to your campsite—you have to hike. We'll climb the mountain, check out part of the Appalachian Trail, and try to roast a turkey outdoors. It's going to be transformational."

Celia cocked an eyebrow. "Megan is going camping?"

"Yeah," Roz said, "and knowing Megan she'll probably get all the birds and squirrels to tell her their life stories, then organize them into support groups and committees."

Megan laughed.

"No, but seriously," Celia persisted. "Megan? It makes sense for Miss Greenpeace, but Megan's like the prep school princess." Celia glanced at Megan's cardigan and Mary Janes. "You know they don't have like hairdryers and stuff out there."

"Celia," Megan said, forcing a chuckle. "I'm not that girly. I can hold my own out in the wilderness."

"Megan, we went to school together for how many years? I've never seen you spend more than thirty minutes in the woods."

"Now hold on, I—" And Megan stopped. She wanted to point out that she'd spent weeks out in uncharted woods with nothing more than a blanket for a tent and had crossed a barren mountain range besides.

But all of that had happened in Vindor, and she couldn't tell them that. She had never told anyone about it, because the whole thing seemed crazy.

"You what?" Celia pushed.

Megan sighed. "I went camping before I left Georgia, but it doesn't matter now."

And that old loneliness came back—the loneliness of having a life-changing secret, an adventure she longed to share with someone, anyone, but never could. Burying it inside herself had always been hard.

She changed the subject. "So Adam, what was that running record you set last week?"

Adam beamed and launched into a description of last week's track meet. Megan's pocket buzzed. She glanced at her phone under the table. A text from Mom.

Train arrives 4pm. Plz pick A up then. Love Mom

"Hey, Orlando," Celia said. "You didn't eat your Jell-O."

Orlando rubbed the back of his neck. "Yeah, I kind of changed my mind." He looked up at Roz as though hoping for her approval, but she wasn't paying attention.

Megan began to say something about the left-over soft-serve when she felt it—a prickling, tingling feeling on the back of her neck and shoulders.

She'd felt that once before, many years ago.

She stood abruptly. "Excuse me." She turned, almost tripping on the chair leg, and hurried through the small cafeteria, scanning the crowd.

Nothing there.

She pushed her way through the wooden doors and outside onto the plaza steps. A chilly gust of wind spun oak leaves in a spiral, and there it was—the smell of sea salt.

Her heart leapt, then she caught herself. Mystic always smelled of the sea.

She scurried down the plaza steps toward the main sidewalk where other Cove students braced themselves against the cold and darted to class. "I'm here!" she said aloud. But among the moving crowd she saw no figure in white.

The tingling feeling stopped abruptly.

Megan's heart sank.

But what did she expect? It had been years. She'd grown up now.

"Megan!"

She suppressed a sad ache and turned. Orlando jogged toward her, holding her leather book satchel. "You okay? I thought maybe you were sick or something."

"Sorry. I didn't mean to worry you."

"Here's your bag. I thought you might need it."

"Thanks, Orlando." Megan took hold of the leather strap. "You didn't have to do that."

"Look, don't let Celia bother you," Orlando said. "I'll bet you'll be like the wilderness queen out there. Kill a bear and everything." His face fell. "Don't tell Roz I said that, okay?"

Megan smiled. "I won't. You know, she *is* vegan on Fridays. She wasn't making that up."

"Really?" His face brightened.

"I'm her roommate, I should know. She also—"

And then in the crowd, a girl in white appeared. Megan stepped forward so quickly she nearly tripped over her own feet.

But it was only a blonde girl in a white sweater-dress.

"You okay?" Orlando sounded concerned.

"Yeah, I'm fine." Megan exhaled. "I thought I saw someone I recognized. But it was only my imagination."

* * *

Arden hoisted his overstuffed backpack into the trunk of his mother's white Volvo, next to the sack that contained his pillow, sleeping bag, and extra sweatshirts.

"Are you sure you have everything?" Arden's mom wore a navy-blue dress suit and no-nonsense pumps—typical of her attire as principal of one of Hartford County's top private schools. Her red hair came down in gentle waves, in stark contrast to the sharp, decisive angles of her face. She frowned, adding more stern lines to her forehead. "That doesn't look like a lot of gear for a week of camping."

Arden shrugged. "Megan's roommate said her family had all the tents and food and stuff. They do this kind of thing all the time."

Mom's face relaxed a little. "Well, the Williamses do seem to know what they're doing. All right, let's go."

Arden waited until the Volvo merged onto the highway before he brought it up.

"Hey, Mom," he said, trying to sound casual. "Do you think that maybe I can take that martial arts class after all?" He held his breath.

Mom paused for a long moment. "Driving you all the way across town for a four o'clock class will be hard when I still have meetings going on. Edith Wharton has plenty of after-school activities. Why don't you pick one of those?"

Arden exhaled. Yeah, but none of those activities would teach him how to stand up to guys like Steadman. Even if Mom did know about the humiliation Arden went through every week, he doubted she would understand.

He wondered if his dad would have understood. He could only wonder, because he knew virtually nothing about Jonas Nakamura, the man who'd walked out when Arden was only four months old. There were no pictures of him anywhere in the house—Arden had searched—so he didn't even know what he looked like. Most of the time he imagined his father looked like Jackie Chan, and he sometimes daydreamed that he'd return home one day to teach him the basics of a roundhouse kick and the perfectly timed punch.

"Besides," Mom said after a few minutes of silent driving, "I thought you were going to go out for hockey. Aren't tryouts coming up?"

Arden didn't say anything for a moment. "Nah," he finally managed with a forced casualness. "Hockey's not my thing."

"After all the practice you did last year? You should at least give it a try."

"Okay, I will."

Mom pulled the Volvo into the Amtrak station parking lot and maneuvered into a space. But before she cut the engine off, she turned to Arden. "I got a phone call from Miss Robinson this morning."

The art teacher. Arden had been doing fine in art class and hadn't been called out for talking or anything. Maybe she had confused him with the kids at the noisier table behind him. But that wasn't his fault, he—

Apparently, his worry showed on his face, because Mom laughed. "A good phone call, Arden. Miss Robinson's been impressed by your last few projects. She says your eye for lines and detail is excellent, and you've got good control with the pencil and brush. She wants you to enter the state art competition in the spring."

"Oh." Arden wasn't sure how to respond. "Okay. Cool."

"There *is* an art club at Wharton, you know."

"Right." Like that would protect him from Steadman and his henchmen. "I guess I can think about it," he said, determining not to give it any thought at all.

Riding on a train wasn't nearly as exciting as the Hogwarts Express made it out to be. The real-world train had no smoke stack, no chugging sound, no private booths, and was almost like riding a big bus, and a boring one at that.

Arden entertained himself by watching the few other passengers in his car. A man three seats ahead of him had a nose like a russet potato. Arden's fingers itched to draw. He wanted to study that face, to capture it and unlock its mysteries. He reached toward the overhead storage compartment for his backpack.

No. Art is for pansies.

What would the other passengers think if they saw him completely absorbed in his sketchbook with that intense, in-the-zone drawing face, as Shonda called it? Better to look out the window like everyone else.

He shouldn't have brought the sketchbook with him—it only took up space.

But he thought he'd want it with all those mountaintop views he'd be seeing. Breaking things down, stroke by stroke, allowed Arden to remember things in a way a photograph couldn't. Drawing helped him see the way one tree's branches interplayed with another's, to notice the way sunlight and shadow revealed the three-dimensional shape of a tree trunk, to pay attention not only to real objects, but the negative spaces in between them, and—

No.

If he was going to spend a week in the wilderness, he should be using it to get stronger. He would sleep in the cold with as few blankets as possible, jog the trails instead of walking them, chop and carry logs for the fire, learn to survive off the land. He would search for ways to prove his strength, to be a hero—maybe kill a bear or cougar or something.

And then, when the Williamses weren't listening, maybe he could ask Megan for advice.

He wouldn't tell anyone that last part, of course, with his sister being a somewhat prissy girl and all. But if anyone would understand him, it would be Megan. She listened to him—really listened, not just waited for him to finish so she could jump in with what she wanted to say. And besides some gentle teasing growing up (sisters were required by law to do that), Megan never made Arden feel like a stupid little kid.

She kept telling him things would get better, and Arden wanted to believe it. He once told her that it was easy for her to say, since she'd always been Miss Popularity and Miss Class President.

And she'd laughed. "You don't remember what I was like, do you? Before we left Georgia? I practically threw up every time I had to talk in front of class, and I spent lunch praying that the popular girls wouldn't look my direction."

"What changed?" Arden had asked.

And Megan got that distant sad look again—the one that came out at the strangest times, and Arden was never sure why.

"You know," she said at last. "Growing up. Anyway, it gets better."

Arden closed his eyes and leaned back against his seat. How much better would it get? He tried to remember Megan during her awkward stage, before they came to Edith Wharton, so he'd have something to compare to. But he'd been so young that he didn't remember much, and he'd never seen her at school. Only a few odd things stuck in his memory, like the encounter with the toaster.

They must have just started the process of moving, because he had been in the old kitchen and empty brown boxes sat all over the table.

He remembered coming into the kitchen to see Megan standing at the toaster, gazing at it as though it were the most curious invention in the world.

"What are you doing?" he had asked.

Megan turned to him with a look of wonder, like she'd never seen him before. "Arden Bradshaw?" she asked.

"Uh, yeah," Arden had said, feeling weirded out. "If you're not using the toaster, can I?"

"The what?"

Arden pointed. "That. The toaster."

"Oh, I wasn't touching it. I was merely looking."

"Uh, okay." Arden tore the silver wrapping off a toaster pastry and pushed past her. Megan watched him carefully as he dropped the pastries in with a clunk and pressed down the lever.

"Wow!" Megan appeared to be fascinated with the toaster's glowing red wires. And a moment later when the pastries popped up, she literally gasped and jumped back.

Arden stared at her. "You're acting weird. And aren't you supposed to be on the school bus now?"

"Oh!" Megan cried. "School—I forgot that she had to go to school!"

And Megan ran out the door, without a backpack or lunch box or anything.

His sister had more bizarre moments like that over the next few weeks—acting surprised at everyday things like TVs and zippers. Arden had tried to point out Megan's weirdness to Mom, but she told Arden it was only the stress of moving.

Once they got up to Connecticut, Megan's strange behavior stopped suddenly. She had no trouble making friends when school started, and by Christmas her classmates put her in charge of organizing the food drive.

Is that what Megan meant by "growing up"? Did you have to go through a bizarre stage and then suddenly you turned normal and popular?

Great. Like Arden could afford to get any weirder in front of Steadman and his gang.

The cadence of the train changed, and it now sped over a metal bridge that spanned the broad Connecticut River. White boats raced across the water, leaving churning, ever-changing lines in their wake. And beyond the boats, Arden could see where the river water flowed out into the blurred outline of the sea.

Not too much longer before he reached Mystic Station, then. Good. He was looking forward to his adventure.

* * *

Megan usually didn't put much stock into hunches or premonitions. But an unsettled feeling crept over her during her three o'clock history class, and it had only gotten worse.

As soon as the bell rang, she jumped out of her seat and rushed out the Miner building door toward the student parking lot, hardly noticing the cold November breeze.

Once I pick up Arden, I'll be fine, she told herself. *Look at me, worrying like a mom.*

She unlocked the door of the ancient blue Toyota—a rusty, temperamental thing her friends had taken to calling the Millennium Falcon for its habit of quitting when it counted.

She plopped onto the torn driver's seat and turned the key in the ignition.

The Toyota clicked and groaned.

She turned the key again. "Come *on*, Falcon. You can do it."

The car groaned some more, but the engine would not start. She tried again. And again.

Nothing.

Megan dropped back in her seat, her stomach churning. "Piece of junk." She'd have to ask someone to jump it later, but right now she didn't have time.

She pulled the keys from the ignition and locked the Toyota door behind her, though she didn't know who in their right mind would steal this car. Megan stood, rocking on and off her tiptoes to warm herself against the cold.

Roz had a four o'clock class, and most of Megan's other friends would be halfway home for vacation now. She didn't know who else could give her a lift.

She pulled her scarf closer and dropped her car keys into her satchel. The train station stood just over the Pequotsepos River bridge, and it would probably be faster to walk than to try to find a ride.

And that churning feeling inside her told her the sooner she got there, the better.

She readjusted her satchel over her shoulder and began a brisk walk toward the campus gate.

She dialed Arden's number as she walked, pressing the phone against her ear. Why didn't he answer? *It's fine,* Megan told herself. *Maybe his phone is with his luggage, or he has it on silent. No need to panic.*

A click on the other end. "Hi, you've reached Arden's phone. I'm not here right now, but you are. So leave me a message so when I'm here and you're not, I can hear it … I think."

"Arden," Megan said. "I'm going to be a bit late—I'm having car trouble. But stay at the station and wait—"

The blast of a train whistle cut her off.

You could always hear two things at Cove College: trains and the sea. But this time the sound startled her. She checked her watch. That had to be Arden's train, and she'd underestimated the distance to the station.

"Don't go anywhere, okay? I'm coming!" She jabbed the "end call" button and broke into a strained walk down Stonington Road.

She slowed when a sharp pain in her shins got too much to bear. She had reached the car dealership but couldn't even see the bridge over the Pequotsepos River yet. And the short November day was already drawing to a close, the sun dipping closer to the horizon every minute.

She grimaced and resumed her painful pace, hoping she wouldn't be too late.

* * *

The Mystic train station was much smaller than Arden had expected. At first, he thought someone had built their house too close to the tracks, but nope, the building with the red trim was the station.

Photos of local attractions cluttered the walls of the station, and a few people milled around the tiny lobby—a man with an unruly beard, a girl with a book, and a lady with a fur coat that looked like it came from a whole bear. But no sign of Megan. Arden sat down on a hard, wooden bench and waited.

And waited. He looked up at the clock on the wall. 4:09. Where could she be?

Someone sat down beside him on the bench. He turned to look—and suddenly no one was there.

He glanced back up at the clock.

4:16.

Arden sat up straight, a shiver running through him. What happened? He glanced around the station. The bearded man and the woman with the bear coat were gone and different people stood in their place. But he hadn't heard a train go by, hadn't seen anyone open the door.

Had he really skipped seven minutes?

Rattled, he picked up his backpack and the navy sack with his sleeping bag and went over to the station window, looking for his sister's old blue jalopy of a car. *Come on, Megan. Where are you?*

Someone tapped him on the shoulder. "Excuse me—"

Arden turned toward the voice. No one. He glanced again at the clock. 4:25.

Heart pounding, he pushed his way out the station door. Maybe he needed fresh air.

The sky had turned a dusty rose as the sun sank toward the distant tree line. He stood for a minute, trying to slow his breath as he watched cars pass on the road. He readjusted his backpack and his grip on the sack.

Another tap on the shoulder. "Excuse me—"

But this time Arden didn't turn. He dashed through the parking lot and across the road. He slowed when he reached the sidewalk on the other side. Only then did he glance back.

No one, of course.

Heart pounding, he power-walked down the sidewalk. Hopefully, Megan would see him from her car on her way to the station, but he had to keep moving.

Up ahead flowed a river with grassy slopes leading down to its banks. The road and sidewalk before him formed a bridge over it.

That's when he felt a hand grab his elbow. "Excuse me—"

Arden abandoned his pride, dropped the sleeping bag on the sidewalk, and ran. His sneaker hit a stone, and he pitched forward, tumbling down the grassy slope toward the river below.

* * *

Megan pulled off her glove and grabbed her phone. 4:35. With fingers trembling and not just from the cold, she dialed Arden's number again.

The phone rang six times, then went to voicemail.

"Arden, I'm on my way. Stay where you are," she called into the phone. She had reached the Pequotsepos River bridge now. On the sidewalk ahead, someone had left a big navy-blue sack.

Megan's stomach dropped as she approached the familiar bag. Written on it in marker was a single word: *Bradshaw.*

Megan froze. "Arden? Arden, where are you?"

She whipped out her phone again and fumbled as she redialed.

From somewhere below the bridge came a muted electric guitar riff. Arden's ringtone.

"Don't go to voicemail yet!" Megan cried. She scrambled off the sidewalk, her Mary Janes slipping down the grassy slope as she followed the sound.

Megan stopped in her tracks. A red backpack with Japanese characters drawn onto it lay neatly by the water's edge. She knew that backpack well.

"Arden!" she cried, her voice breaking. "Where are you?"

She dropped her bag and pulled off her shoes, ready to wade into the waters of the Pequotsepos, when a twig snapped behind her.

"Arden," she exhaled, turning.

But it wasn't Arden.

Faster than she could take it in, the stranger leapt at her.

chapter 3

Bradshaw

Arden opened his eyes. He lay on the ground, looking up at a blue sky and tall, yellow grass all around him. He sat up, rubbing his neck. What had happened? He felt like he'd been in a wrestling match.

He reached for his backpack—but it was gone. He stood and searched the tall grass around him. No backpack or sleeping bag sack or anything.

I've been robbed!

Arden tried to fight back panic. He vaguely remembered being followed and running into the grass. It seemed that something else had happened after that, but he couldn't recall. A black place filled his memory.

Okay, so someone had chased him down and stolen his backpack. Not cool. Really not cool.

One problem at a time, though. First, he had to figure out where he was and how he could find Megan, who might be freaking out over him now. Arden patted his pockets. No phone—that had been in his backpack.

He patted his coat pocket again and looked down.

This wasn't his coat. His coat was made of black nylon, with zippers down the front and over each of the pockets. He now wore a wool coat, also black, but with wooden buttons instead of zippers.

Arden's skin prickled. Was this some sort of practical joke?

A bead of sweat ran down his forehead, and he realized he felt warm. He pulled off the impostor coat and dropped it in the grass.

His hoodie zipper had also been replaced by buttons. He looked at the left sleeve, where he had ironed on a patch with the Japanese kanji for "samurai." Here, the exact same patch was stitched on instead of glued.

Why would someone take the time to do this?

He peeled off the impostor hoodie too. The sun was far too intense for November—in fact, it felt like summer here.

But where was here?

No road or sidewalk interrupted the expanse of tall grass around him, but he could still smell the sea, so he couldn't be far from the train station.

He had to find a phone and call the police. No—Megan first, then the police.

Arden turned around. "No way," he muttered.

Sure, he'd heard of rich people building fancy houses by the coast, but this—this was ridiculous.

This house looked like an actual castle—white towers, fluttering pennants, and a big, white spire reaching into the sky. A nine-foot wall surrounded its huge yard. Some people had *way* too much money.

Since Arden couldn't see any other houses anywhere, he guessed this must be all one guy's land. The only road in sight, probably a driveway, led up to the castle property.

He sighed. This was the only option, then. He hoped Mr. Rich-Fancy-Pants wouldn't chase him away.

Arden stepped onto the dirt driveway and made his way toward the huge, wooden doorway in the wall. It didn't look like many people drove on this—all the dirt was soft, without the usual hard lines compressed by tires. Maybe the guy didn't have many visitors or didn't leave his house much.

The door set into the wall was also ridiculous. The wood was painted *purple* of all colors, with a silver paisley design all over it. It looked like a little girl had designed it.

Arden paused, then knocked hard. "Hello?" he called. "Can someone help me? I've been robbed, and I don't know where I am. Can I use your phone?"

No answer.

He waited for a moment, then knocked harder. Still nothing. Maybe they couldn't hear. He turned his fist and whacked the door with the side of his hand, as hard as he could bear.

The door swung inward on silent hinges, revealing a huge, carefully manicured garden beyond.

No one was there.

Arden hesitated. The last thing he wanted was to trespass and have the police called on *him*. But he needed help.

I guess I have to find the front door and knock there, he thought. *I hope they don't have guard dogs.*

He carefully followed a cobblestone path into a garden of rosebushes and other flowering shrubs. Tall evergreen hedges, cut into perfect rectangles, formed looming walls.

The owner had to hire at least sixteen people to keep this place up. Maybe Arden could find a gardener.

"Is anyone here?" he called, following a path that led to a marble fountain. "Hello?"

"Hello!" The voice came from around a corner of the hedge.

"Hey," Arden called. "Sorry for trespassing, but I need someone's help. Do you have a—" And his words died in his throat, because a monster appeared around the corner.

From the waist up, the creature looked like a dark-haired child, but he was nearly five feet tall. Where he should have had normal legs, the giant boy had the knobby, black legs of a horse. As the thing turned the corner, Arden saw the giant had all *four* legs of a horse.

Arden squeezed his eyes shut. *They drugged me. Whoever stole all my stuff gave me a drug to knock me out, and now I'm hallucinating.*

"Hey," said the horse-boy. His voice was childlike but rather low.

Arden pretended not to hear it.

"Hey," the horse-boy said again. "Wanna play?"

"No." Arden tried to keep his voice calm. "No, I want you to go away."

"Aw. Why?"

Arden heard hoof steps—hoof steps, not footsteps—moving toward him. *This is not happening.*

Then another voice—a low female one. "Bradshaw, where are you?"

"I'm here," Arden cried. "I'm over here!" Someone had been sent to look for him.

"Mommy," the horse-boy called.

And around the hedge corner came what had to be the horse-boy's mother, standing at seven or eight feet tall. Below her waist she had a muscular horse's body, with her coat, tail, and four hooves raven-black. Above the waist she appeared human, wearing a swath of red cloth like a toga that left her arms bare. Her long, black hair was tied in a simple braid, and her skin was a cinnamon color. Arden briefly wondered if she were Indian like his friend Andy Patel or his teacher Mr. Gupta—before remembering that Andy and Mr. Gupta were not, nor ever had been, part horse.

"Bradshaw, where have you been?" the monster woman asked. Her face was fully human and all sharp lines—an angular nose, a well-defined jaw—but her dark eyes were kind.

"I don't know where I am now," Arden said. "I need to find my sister."

The horse-woman paused and looked at him. "Are you okay, kid? Who are you?"

"What do you mean? You said my name."

"Your name?"

"Yes, Bradshaw."

She raised a dark eyebrow. "*Your* name is Bradshaw?"

"Yes," Arden said. What was so hard about this? "And I'm trying to find my sister Megan. Someone drugged me and stole all my stuff, and now I'm seeing trippy things."

The horse-woman started. "Your sister is ... Megan Bradshaw?"

"Yeah, do you know her?"

She ignored the question, looking around. "*How* did you get here?"

"I don't know. I was walking from the station and someone was behind me and ... and then I woke up here."

The horse-woman turned to her giant child. "Bradshaw, go find your daddy and tell him that Mommy has some business to take care of."

The giant boy nodded and trotted down the hedge corridor.

"Wait a minute," Arden said, "*His* name is Bradshaw too?"

"Yes," the horse-woman said. "I named him after your sister."

Arden stared at her.

"What is your first name?" she asked, gently.

"Arden."

"Arden Bradshaw. I'm Nikterra. Your sister and I are old friends." She cocked her head. "You've ... never seen a centaur before, have you?"

Arden put his face in his hands. "I'm seeing a bunch of stuff I've never seen before."

"Poor thing—you must be confused. Here." Arden looked up to see Nikterra the horse-woman extending a giant hand. "Come with me. I think we can get this all sorted out, and hopefully send you back home."

Arden had to practically stand on his tiptoes to reach her hand. It was three times the size of his, but gentle. He not only saw but felt the long fingers close around his entire hand. Could you feel hallucinations too?

Nikterra led Arden through a maze of garden pathways to the tall wooden doors of the castle house, also painted purple. She pushed them open and cantered right in like she owned the place.

The interior of the mansion was designed like a castle, too—high, arched ceilings; silver chandeliers; huge, white columns; and long hallways lined with solemn sculptures. He wondered how much of this was real and what came from the drugs.

Nikterra started down one of the hallways, pulling Arden along. He had trouble keeping up with her long strides, and oddly enough, he could *hear* her hooves clacking against the marble floor.

She stopped at a large, rectangular door and pushed it slightly ajar. Muffled voices came from inside.

"They remember family histories," a familiar voice said, "every great-grandparent who passed away, and yet they have no recollection they were ever called the Greyhawks. How is that possible?"

"Selena, the mist isn't the only threat," said a second voice, a man's. "Moriana made her intentions clear with this latest attack. The merfolk are officially at war. And the Ravensblood threat in the east is—"

"Stay right here a moment," Nikterra whispered to Arden. She pushed the heavy door open enough to stick her head through.

"Yes, I know, I know I'm breaking all sorts of protocol." Nikterra spoke over several voices of protest. "Throw the book at me later—but Selena, I've got something you need to see right now."

She pushed open the door fully, and now Arden could see the people in the room: a bald, muscular, black man in medieval armor, and a solemn, white-haired Asian man in a green robe.

A young woman with red-brown hair sat between the men.

"Megan!" Arden dashed across the room. The men rose as if to stop him, but the girl stood abruptly and motioned for them to stay back.

Arden wrapped his arms around his sister, relief washing over him. He rested his head against the collar of her white gown and didn't care who watched.

Megan pulled away and held him at arm's length, studying his face.

"Arden Bradshaw?" She said his name as though it were foreign to her.

"Megan, this is the weirdest college I've ever seen. Does Mom know it looks like this?"

His sister didn't answer, her forehead creased with concern. And for a second, Arden had a strange misgiving. The face was definitely his sister's, but that particular expression didn't look familiar.

"I found him in the gardens," Nikterra said. "He has no idea where he is or how he got here. He says he's looking for his sister."

"Impossible," Megan whispered.

"Look, Megan, someone stole my stuff," Arden said. "I think they gave me some sort of drug because I'm seeing some weird things."

The girl addressed the horse-woman and the two men. "Can you give us a minute here?" She took Arden by the hand and led him to the back of the room, her long gown swishing against the stone floor.

"Megan, what's going on?"

She ignored the question. "How did you get here?"

"I don't know. I know I was supposed to meet you at the station, but someone chased me, so I went down the road, and then I woke up outside of this crazy house. I think I—"

She bent over slightly to look him right in the eye. "What happened in between?"

"I don't know. I can't remember."

"Are you sure?"

"There's like this empty place in my memory. I literally can't remember anything past running away from the bridge."

She straightened and didn't respond for a moment. She clasped her hands by her heart, wringing them. Another mannerism Arden didn't remember his sister having. At length she spoke.

"Arden, I am sorry for all of this. It seems there's been a terrible mistake."

"Am I having a dream?" Arden asked. "Because if I'm having a dream, you can tell me now and maybe that will wake me up."

"I'm afraid not," she said. "Everything you're seeing right now is completely real."

"Um, your friend back there has horse legs."

"I know," she said. "It's real. It's all real—the centaurs, the white castle, the gardens, the gate, everything."

Arden stared at her. How could she know he'd hallucinated about a white castle and a gate, unless …?

"No," he said, fighting the urge to freak out. How could Megan be so calm? "And you're okay with all of this? What kind of college *is* this?"

"Arden." Megan paused, as though weighing her words carefully. "This place isn't called college. I don't know where you think you are, but … you're not in your world anymore. You're in Paracosmia, and this land is Vindor."

Arden stared at her, then forced a laugh. "Okay, okay. Wow, you had me going there. Where are the hidden cameras? Because for a moment I believed that."

But Megan didn't laugh back. "I wish I could tell you this were all some sort of trick." She sighed. "It's a lot for anyone to take in."

Arden felt his stomach dropping. "Megan …"

"That's the other thing. I know I look and sound like your sister, but I'm not Megan. My name is Selena."

"But—but that doesn't make sense," he said, immediately recalling the unfamiliar mannerisms. "Are you like a, a twin that Mom never talks about?"

"No, it's more complicated than that." Megan, or Selena, or whoever she was, now paced in a circle. "I don't quite understand it myself, but Vindor is part of the world of Paracosmia, a real place. But from what I understand, every land's history and makeup in Paracosmia is guided by the imagination of a person in the Mirror World and—" She stopped. "No, that's too confusing. Let me say it this way—Vindor, as you know, is a world that your sister imagined over many years. But here it exists for real, with independent—"

"Hold on." None of this made an iota of sense to Arden. "What's Vindor?"

Selena looked at him. "Megan never told you about Vindor?"

"Uh … no."

"But she *came* here. Physically came here, a few years ago. She saved Vindor from destruction by a monster called the Shadow. She stayed here for twenty-eight days. She has never mentioned this?"

He stared at her. "No, no she hasn't. And—wait—and Megan? Megan, no offense, is just a normal girl who goes to preppy schools and likes volunteering. She's never talked about a friend with horse legs and space travel and saving worlds from monsters!" The absurdity of it all both annoyed and frightened him. "Besides, if Megan were here for a month, don't you think we would have noticed she was missing?"

Selena nodded. "That's why Eira sent me to take her place in your world for a while. You were a lot younger then, so you probably don't remember. I arrived right before your family changed homes, and …"

"You didn't know how to use the toaster." A chill ran down Arden's spine. "You were confused by cars and zippers and stuff, and you nearly got run over by a school bus."

"In my defense, your world is as baffling to me as Vindor must be for you."

Arden leaned his back against a wall and held his head, trying to sort out all this preposterous information. He wanted to spit the whole thing out, but there were parts that he couldn't dismiss. Like being in a castle with a horse-woman and his sister's twin. "Can I go home now?"

"We'll do our best to send you home," Selena said. "Only—"

"Only what?"

She exhaled. "Only we're not entirely sure how you got here in the first place. That makes sending you back a bit more … complicated."

"You don't know how?"

"We'll figure something out," Selena said quickly. "Don't worry." She smiled, but Arden noticed it was with her mouth only, not her eyes. "Come."

Arden followed her back to the center of the room, where Nikterra the horse-woman was talking with the two men.

"I'm still not following," the bald soldier said.

"It's not complicated." Nikterra tossed her black braid. "Eira went to the Mirror World to bring Megan back, probably to save us from the fog this time. But somehow she made a mistake and pulled in her brother instead."

"That's no simple error," said the old man with the wispy beard. "That doesn't seem like her at all."

"Meh, even guardian spirits have their off days, I suppose," Nikterra said. "We just need to let Eira know, and she'll get this sorted out right away."

"But," Selena said, rejoining the circle, "we don't know where Eira is. No one's seen her in over a year." She motioned to Arden. "This doesn't make sense—anyone coming from the Mirror World to Vindor doesn't make sense."

"There's no way to pass between worlds without Eira, is there?" asked the old man.

"Not that I know of." Selena paused. "There's one person who might know, though—Korvin."

"The Rikean girl?"

Selena nodded. "She seems to have done a lot of reading on that topic, among many others. She may be able to tell us how to access Eira."

"But she's been away in N'gozi for months now," the soldier observed.

"Ah, yes," Selena said. She paused for a moment, then turned to Arden.

"We'll find a way back, Arden," she said, "though it may take a little longer than we'd like. In the meantime, you are welcome to stay here at Alavar as my honored guest."

Arden nodded, wondering exactly how long "a little longer" would be.

"I thought of something," said Nikterra. "If Arden's now here in our world … who from Vindor is in his place?"

chapter 4

Meeting Again

Megan's attacker had her by the arm, dragging her toward a clump of bushes. She resisted, pulling herself the other direction. The guy wasn't very big, but she had taken her shoes off and had trouble getting traction in the marsh grass in only her tights.

With a surge of adrenaline coursing through her, Megan did something she had never done before—she tried as hard as she could to hurt another person. She stomped on the guy's bare foot, then socked him in the gut, with more speed and power than she knew she had.

Her punch hit its mark. He let go of her arm and clutched his stomach, and Megan broke away. She scrambled up the incline toward the road.

Then she stopped.

Every nerve in her body told her to run for it. But Arden's backpack still lay by the water, and he could be in danger.

"Do not go up there!" her attacker gasped. From the strained sound of his voice, it seemed Megan had knocked the wind out of him.

"Where's my brother?" she demanded.

The guy didn't answer, still clutching his ribs. He was a scrawny kid who didn't look more than sixteen. He had dark ebony skin, and a perfectly bald head—in fact, he didn't even seem to have eyebrows.

"But the monsters!" he cried.

"Monsters? What are you talking about?"

The strange guy pointed up toward the bridge. A car drove by, but nothing else.

Megan squared her shoulders, ready to fight if she had to. The guy looked smaller than her, so she might have a chance. "Where's Arden?

What have you done to him?"

The skinny kid straightened and looked right at Megan. His pale, ice-blue eyes startled her.

And though she felt certain she'd never seen this guy before, something deep inside her recognized him.

His ice-blue eyes studied her in return, and he took a halting step forward.

"LadySelena?"

Megan's skin prickled. "What did you call me?"

"LadySelena," he repeated.

"Where did you hear that name?"

The guy drew closer. "Is me—Shahck-re-ahck of Ipktu!"

"That's not possible." She trembled. "You're not him. You can't possibly know all these names—how are you doing this?"

"You do not remember me?" The blue eyes searched hers. "You cannot remember Shahck-re-ahck the goblin king, LadySelena?"

"I'm not Selena."

The face fell into confusion, it seemed—Megan struggled to read his face in the dim light, and the guy's lack of eyebrows really threw her off. But then his eyes opened wide.

It was a different face, but she'd recognize that expression anywhere.

"No," he said slowly. "You are not LadySelena. You are *my* Selena, who comed with me and FriendNikterra all the way to Elnat and back, and you fighted off the Shadow with stars. We called you Megan, who goed away to another world after. You did not call me Shahck-re-ahck, then. You called me—"

"Bat?" Megan stumbled toward him in the grass. She threw her arms around him, and he wrapped his bony arms around her to return the embrace.

Not him, but definitely him at the same time.

Tears trickled down Megan's face—happy and achingly sad at once.

She hadn't allowed herself to feel this—how much she'd missed the little goblin all these years. Parting from him and Nikterra had been the hardest part of leaving Vindor.

She squeezed him tighter. "I can't believe this."

The guy who was also Bat sniffed. "My heart hurted when you leaved. But I always knowed you would come back to Vindor."

Megan pulled away, wiping an eye. "Wait, what?"

She scanned her surroundings. The Pequotsepos River flowed beside them and she could hear cars going over the bridge, and beyond that the faint waves of Long Island Sound.

The guy who was also Bat didn't seem to notice. "Now you can keep your promise to see Ipktu. We have growed so, so much."

"Bat ... do you know where you are?"

The blue eyes glanced around the riverbank. He wrinkled his dark nose—a proper human nose now. "No." Bat sounded puzzled. "I have never been to this part of the River Plains."

Megan regarded him for a moment. "You know," she said carefully, "you, uh, look a little different then the last time I saw you."

Bat puffed out his chest. "Yes, I growed taller."

He didn't know.

"Bat." Megan weighed her words. "Yes, you're taller, but ... Bat, why don't you take a deep breath and look at your hands?"

"My hands?" He held them out, and the blue eyes grew huge. He scrubbed his hands together, as though trying to rub the dark brown off to get back to his natural green, but to no avail. Bat then seemed to catch sight of his human feet, which were bare in the long grass, and began stomping them erratically. He ran his hands over his face and bald head. His fingers paused as they ran over his ears, no longer pointed, and his nose, no longer flat. "How? *How?*" He seemed to be on the verge of panic.

"Bat, sit down."

Bat obeyed and clutched his dark feet. "But—but—I am man! How is this?"

Megan knelt in the long grass beside him. "I don't know."

"But I don't want to be man! I want to be me!"

"We'll get you changed back to a goblin," Megan said firmly. She had no idea how she would deliver on that promise, but Bat seemed to calm a little. He shivered. He wore only a pair of light shorts and a dark purple hoodie that reminded Megan of the cloak he once wore years ago.

"You must be freezing." Megan pulled off her wool peacoat and wrapped it around Bat's small frame. He stopped shivering, though Megan could now feel the cold breeze through her cardigan. It was growing dark, and they'd have to get somewhere inside soon. Which added in a new complication.

"Uh, Bat?"

He sniffed and looked up at her with that not-Bat, yet very-much-Bat face.

"There's something else you need to know. We aren't in the River Plains. I didn't come to Vindor."

He wrinkled his nose. "Then how are you here?"

"*Here* isn't Vindor, Bat. We're in the Mirror World. My world."

"*What?*" The blue eyes opened wider than Megan realized possible.

"I don't understand it either, but you're in my world." She pointed up to the bridge. "Those noisy things up there that scared you—those aren't monsters. They're cars. Machines that are normal here in my world. And look—those buildings up there." She pointed to the restaurants and inn beside the road, built in the sturdy New England style with white siding. "Those aren't Tsuru construction."

"But, but ..." Bat stammered, "How did I get here?"

"That's what I was going to ask you! Did Selena send you?"

"I know not." Bat held his head in his hands. "I remember no thing."

"Well, what do you remember?"

Bat squeezed his eyes shut, apparently thinking hard. After a moment he raised his head. "Friends. From Elnat. I meeted with Rikean friends, and then ..." He scrunched his face, as though working hard to dredge up the memory. "And then there were monsters. And I hided, and then I seed a lady in danger, a lady full of scared, and the lady was you." He looked up at her. "If the monsters are not scareful, why were you full of scared, FriendMegan?"

And the churning feeling in her stomach, which had never quite gone away, returned at full force. She looked over at the backpack still by the water.

"Arden," she gasped. "I still have to find Arden." She'd been so distracted by Bat that she'd lost precious time. She didn't know where to start looking, unless—

"Bat—did you see a boy down here? You said you were hiding. Did you see other people by the water?"

He shook his head slowly. "I seed things, but I cannot remember the things. It is like a black place in my mind, and things keep falling into it."

"Wait." Megan hurried to her book satchel and fished out a small change purse. Between her debit card and some store loyalty cards her shaking fingers found a wallet-size photo. She still had it.

"Bat, look at this."

She handed the photo to him. In it Megan stood in a white graduation robe. Mom had her arm around her, and beside her grinned Arden.

Bat squinted at it in the failing light—apparently, his goblin night vision was gone, too.

"Is a very good drawing," Bat said.

"It's not a—never mind. Did you see this boy at all?" Megan leaned over him and pointed at her brother's image.

Bat stared at the picture for a long moment, frowning.

"Yes," he said at length. "Out of the blackness, his face comes back to me."

"What happened? Was he hurt? Where did he go?"

The blue eyes darted back and forth as though searching the darkening sky. "Black places keep coming back. But I standed close to him. And he was full of scared, for some thing I don't know. And I was full of scared too, but I sorried for him. I grabbed his hand."

Megan could hardly breathe. "Then what?"

Bat paused longer than Megan thought she could stand. "Oh," he said suddenly. "I remember—so very odd. I holded his hand, and then I was not. But I never letted go—his hand just goed away. And then I heared monsters. I mean, cars."

"No." Megan fell to her knees, the cold moisture of the grass seeping through her tights. "*No.*"

"FriendMegan, what is wrong?"

"You were in Vindor, then you saw Arden," she said slowly. "You touched his hand, he disappeared, and then suddenly you were here in my world. Is that what happened?"

"It all goes back into blackness now. But I think that, yes."

"That's what happened to me when ... I was right. Selena must have been coming for me—I didn't imagine it. But something must have gone wrong. Somehow they got the wrong two."

Bat tilted his head. "FriendMegan?"

"You and Arden switched places, Bat. You touched, and you ended up here in my world, and Arden ... Arden is in Vindor right now." She tried to let the concept sink in.

"FriendMegan?" Bat's voice was tentative. "FriendMegan, if I am switched with the full-of-scared boy, then ... we can switch back, yes? Can we do this?"

Megan picked up her brother's backpack. "We have to. Only ... I don't know how."

* * *

Arden circled the strange room for the umpteenth time. Each time he saw the exact same things: a table covered in hand-drawn parchment maps labeled with silly names. A purple flag with a white castle and star design. A globe with all the wrong continents on it.

If he were hallucinating or dreaming, the details would probably morph each time. But they didn't. Everything, somehow, was real.

This was a lot for a guy to take in.

He'd been alone in the room for several minutes now. His sister's impossible twin and the two men had some sort of important meeting they had to prepare for, and Nikterra went to find her kids before her husband went into the meeting too.

So that left Arden here, wandering around this room filled with maps and charts and a few decorative weapons on the wall.

He wasn't supposed to be here. He should have been visiting Mystic Aquarium, having dinner with his sister, and getting ready for his camping trip.

But somehow, he'd gotten stuck in this world where people lived in pretentious white castles and dressed like they worked at a Renaissance fair. And did anyone notice that the Nikterra lady was literally half horse or was he the only one bothered by that?

Arden passed the marble table with its disorganized piles of maps. Beside them lay a book Selena had given to him to look through—a thick tome bound in purple with silver swirls and a strange hole in its cover.

He stopped to open the book. The hole continued through the center of the yellowed pages, like someone had stabbed the book with a pocketknife. He leafed through pages filled with journal entries, written in elegant calligraphy.

He paused at a page marked with a white ribbon. Here the handwriting changed abruptly—an uneven cursive with some parts barely scratched in, other parts splotchy, as though the writer had struggled controlling the flow of ink. The beginning of this section read:

Day One

~~*Megan's*~~

~~*Sel*~~

My adventures in Vindor

The next twenty or so pages contained entries in the same struggling script. A bit of an epilogue followed, and the rest of the book remained blank.

This is what Selena had wanted him to see. Megan's handwriting.

Megan had been here before. That was the hardest part of this whole thing for Arden to wrap his mind around. Megan lived in this world once and had been important.

But she'd never breathed a word of it. She had said that she'd grown up and things got better.

"I thought you were talking about puberty," he said aloud. He pushed the book away and scowled. "Not killing monsters in another dimension!"

Why hadn't she told him? Sure, it was hard to swallow, but if she'd told him he would have trusted her.

I would have believed you, Megan. But he wasn't sure he believed it now that he saw it.

Arden paced again.

As he neared the room's large wooden doors, voices floated in from the hall—a lot of them. He opened a door a crack and peeked out.

A slow-moving crowd, wearing bizarre and elaborate costumes, choked the hallway. Men and women dressed like Robin Hood and Maid Marian chatted with people with long, white hair and dark veils over their faces. Several more giant horse-people—some dark-skinned like Nikterra, others with lighter skin—stood a head or two taller than everyone else. Things that Arden initially thought were hummingbirds flitted through the air above them. Then one flew closer and he saw its face and arms.

Fairies.

Seriously?

As a group of ebony-skinned people wearing brightly patterned robes passed, a small *thing* darted out from among their legs, nearly tripping them. The short green creature had pointed ears and sharp claws and looked like something from Joe's fantasy card game—a goblin or orc or something.

This was all too much for Arden. He began to close the door but stopped when he saw the samurai.

Real samurai, with ornate kabuto helmets filed down the hall toward him. They wore leather-and-iron dou breastplates, the kote gauntlets— everything Arden had read about in the books from the public library. One warrior stood taller than the rest, wearing a helmet with a golden trident shape on the front, and the other samurai followed him.

As they passed the door, one of the younger samurai stopped and looked directly at Arden. "What are you doing there?" he demanded.

"S-sir?" Arden asked, opening the door wider.

"Oh," the samurai said. "You're not Akihiro. Sorry, I thought you were one of our trainees."

"Really? Me?" The words came out much more eagerly than Arden meant them to.

A few strands of the warrior's hair peeked out from beneath the helmet. The hair was red-brown, not black. Arden caught his breath. Now that he saw the samurai's face closer, he noticed the shape of the eyes, the in-between complexion of the skin ... Arden was looking at an adult who shared his mixed Asian-Caucasian features.

The soldier smiled. "What is your name, son?"

Arden bowed. "Uh ... Nakamura, sir."

"Well, Nakamura," the samurai said. "Are you interested in being a warrior?"

Arden nodded dumbly.

"Then that's the man you need to train under." He motioned to the tall samurai who had nearly reached the door at the end of the hall. "Yashi-Ito is the most skilled teacher out of any Tsuru settlement. He's been my teacher since I was smaller than you. When you return to your village, seek him out for training. He won't turn you away. Now scurry back to your quarters—your father is probably wondering where you are."

The samurai tousled Arden's hair, then rejoined the last of the crowd. Women in blue and green kimonos walked near the samurai, and many of them had red-brown hair as well. The people filtered through an ornate door at the end of the hall and were gone.

Arden stood staring after the doors had closed.

The samurai thought I was one of them. They thought I belonged.

chapter 5

Andmerica

As Megan stood shivering, her mind circled from problem to problem but never came upon any solutions.

"FriendMegan, you are cold." Bat pulled off the peacoat and put it around Megan's shoulders. He pulled up his own sweatshirt hood, though Megan doubted it would do much against the steady cold breeze.

Megan sighed. "We're gonna have to go inside somewhere before it gets too dark." She stepped forward and stumbled over something in the grass—her shoe. "Ugh, where's the other one?"

"I help!" Bat held out his hand, fingers stretched to the sky.

Nothing happened.

"But …?" He pulled his hand back and studied the palm.

"You're human now, Bat. You can't make light."

Bat looked toward her in the darkness and had to squint. "Why am I not a goblin anymore?"

Megan found her other shoe and slipped it on. "I'm not sure. Maybe it's because there's no such thing as goblins in my world. Maybe when you come here you have to play by our rules."

"Why not make me an elf? Or a griffin? I like griffins."

"Because we don't have those, either." Megan hoisted her book satchel strap over her shoulder, then picked up Arden's backpack. "Humans are the only kind of people in our world, now that I think of it. We don't have any other creatures that talk or build civilizations. I guess you have to be human by default."

She headed up the grassy incline toward the bridge, then stopped. Bat plowed right into her back.

"Sorry," she said as Bat rubbed his new nose. "I just realized …

uh, don't tell anyone about being a goblin, or coming from Vindor or anything."

"Why not? It is real."

"Yeah, but it will sound completely nuts. No one will ever believe it." Wasn't that the reason she'd never breathed a word about Vindor to anyone, not even her family and best friends? "Pretend you've always been here, and try to blend in."

A train horn blasted, and a thousand feet away an Amtrak sped over the rail bridge. Bat cried out, covered his head, and hit the ground.

Maybe blending in wasn't going to work.

"It's fine, Bat." She took his hand and helped him back to his feet. "It's a train."

"Is it alive?"

"No, it's like a car, only faster and louder. A machine." A blank stare. Megan sighed. "Okay, it's like … in Elnat, the vendors push around those carts with wheels on them, right? Cars and trains are like those carts only bigger, and the people are on the inside."

"Who pushes?"

"They push themselves. Well, they've technically got engines—okay, that doesn't mean anything to you—but the people inside the cars are controlling them."

"So they're not dangerful." Bat looked relieved.

"Right. Well, yes, they are because the people inside aren't always paying attention. Never walk in front of them—they can hit you hard and hurt you badly."

"So they *are* monsters."

"No. Well. Look, they stay on their tracks, or on the black roads. Stay away from train tracks and the black roads and you'll be fine." She shifted the weight of her satchel and started up the incline again, and Bat followed.

Arden's navy sack still lay on the sidewalk. Megan swallowed and grabbed it with her free hand.

Bat crouched down, pressing his palms against the sidewalk. "This is a thing! This stone is so flat, and so strange!"

"It's cement. It's like … I don't know what it's made of." Megan's brain was simply too tired. "Look, Bat, if anyone asks, let's tell people you are new to America."

"I thought this is the Mirror World?"

"It is, only no one here calls it that. America is the name of this country—uh, this land—here. Don't mention coming from a different world, just say you're new to America. Pretend you've come from another land in this world. Does that make sense?"

"Oh, like crossing under mountains from one land in Paracosmia to another land."

"Right," Megan said. She paused. "You can do that?"

Bat shrugged. "Is how goblins came to Skraggs long ago. Nobody remembers when or why for."

A pair of headlights coming around the bend nearly blinded them. Megan dropped the navy bag and grabbed Bat's hand. "It's fine."

Bat, to his credit, stood his ground, though Megan could tell by the way his fingers practically crushed hers that he wanted to bolt.

The headlights slowed as they approached. A white car, unfamiliar to Megan, had its window rolled down and its radio blasted something in rapid-fire Spanish. The car slowed to a stop and the driver poked his head out.

"Megan? Is that you?"

"Orlando?"

Orlando Ruiz leaned out the window, wearing a bulky white coat with a ballcap crammed over his short-cropped hair.

"Megan, what are you doing out here?" He frowned toward Bat. "Who's that guy? Is he giving you trouble?" Orlando swung open his car door.

"No, Orlando, he's fine. He's an old friend."

Orlando relaxed, and Bat stepped forward. "I am Bat! I am new to Andmerica!"

Ugh. Not the introduction Megan had been hoping for. She should have given him a regular-sounding name of some sort, but now it was too late.

Orlando raised an eyebrow. "Bat, huh? Okay, cool. What are you guys doing out in the cold?"

"Shivering," Bat answered.

Orlando laughed. "I like this guy. You two need a ride somewhere?"

"Orlando, that would be wonderful," Megan said.

He reached back and popped the lock on the back door, and Megan opened it. Warm air spilled out, and it felt heavenly as she slid the navy sack, Arden's backpack, and her own book satchel onto the back seat.

Bat stared at the door but didn't move from the sidewalk.

"Don't be shy, Mr. Bat," Orlando said.

"It's okay, Bat," Megan said. "You can get in."

"But I can't step on the black road," he said in a loud whisper. "You said it is dangerful."

Megan glanced at Orlando nervously. "One moment." She leaned close to Bat's ear. "It's fine. You can step on it to get into the car. Please don't make a big deal about this—it will look strange."

She finally coaxed him into the back seat, got him situated, and fastened his seatbelt.

"You ready?" Orlando asked as Megan climbed into the passenger seat.

"We're good," Megan said. "Sorry."

Orlando put the car in drive and hit the accelerator, maybe a bit too hard.

"Yaow!" Bat cried, clutching the door handle.

Orlando glanced at Megan.

"He's, uh, not used to cars where he comes from," Megan said.

"Oh," said Orlando. "I got it, I got it. Hey, did you guys eat yet?"

Food had been the last thing from Megan's mind, but as soon as Orlando said it, her stomach gurgled.

"I have not," Bat said. "I have not eated since ..." He paused. "I don't know when I eated last."

"Well." Orlando grinned. "With that kind of appetite, I know exactly where to go."

Mistuxet Valley Pizza didn't look like much from the outside, with a laundromat on one side and a rundown loan office on the other. A bell suspended from the ceiling clanged as Orlando opened the door and let Megan and Bat pass through. Faded movie posters hung over tables and booths crammed closely together—but it was warm and cozy and smelled wonderful.

A portly man in an apron looked up from the cash register and smiled. "Orlando! Aren't you going home for Thanksgiving?"

"Nah, man. I wouldn't give up Friday pizza night for something like that. I even brought friends this time."

"Welcome, welcome," the portly man said. "Hey, Maya, get 'em a table."

A waitress nodded at them, and they followed her to an unoccupied booth in the corner. Megan saw Bat's eyes ricochet around the room, looking at everything from the electric lights to other diners, but he said nothing.

"Gracias, Maya." Orlando motioned to the booth. "After you two." Megan slid on the pew-like seat to the wall, and Bat sat beside her. Orlando sat on the other side of the table and pushed away the laminated menu. "I already know what I want. Pick whatever you like, my treat. Nope," he said, answering Megan's look. "I insist! It is in honor of *Mr. Bat Comes to America*."

"That's kind of you," Megan said. She opened her menu, and Bat mimicked her. Only he held his upside down. She took the menu from him and set it down. "We'll have whatever you're having," she told Orlando.

"Okay, I get their Mega Supreme. I hope you like olives."

"Anything sounds good right now." Megan leaned back onto the hard, wooden seat, her exhaustion catching up with her.

"Maya," Orlando called to the waitress. "Extra-large Mega Supreme and a pitcher of root beer." He turned to Bat. "So Bat. You have a second name?"

"Shahck-re-ahck," Bat answered before Megan could think of something more normal.

"Bat Shahck-re-ahck?" Orlando echoed. "Sounds like a rapper name. That's cool."

Megan relaxed slightly. Of all her friends to introduce Bat to, laid-back Orlando was turning out to be the best possible person.

"So Mr. Bat Shahck-re-ahck, how long have you been in our fine country?"

"Oh, I just comed here today."

"He's here temporarily," Megan interjected. "He's only visiting. It's this weird … thing."

"Oh, I got it," Orlando said. "Like a foreign exchange student?"

"Yes, exactly," Megan said. Actually, that was a remarkably accurate way of looking at it—the exchange and everything.

Orlando ran his knuckles over his thin chinstrap beard—it seemed to be an unconscious habit of his. "So where you from, Mr. S.?"

"Ipktu," Bat said before Megan could stop him. "Is near Elnat. In the strong mountains of Vrith Emnar."

Orlando stared blankly for a moment, and Megan held her breath.

"Yeah," Orlando said at length. "So I was never good at geography. I'm more of a science person."

"Don't worry about it," Megan said with forced casualness. "It's kind of obscure."

"Then how did you two meet?" Orlando asked. "You said you were old friends."

"Uh, it was this ... travel visiting thing," Megan faltered. "Oh look, here's our root beer!"

The waitress clunked a sloshing plastic pitcher on the table, along with three cups with ice in them. Orlando poured a glass and handed it to Bat.

Before Megan could stop him, Bat threw his head back and took a giant gulp.

"Oh!" Bat spluttered and coughed, clutching at his nose. "Oh!"

"Is he okay?" Orlando asked.

"He's never had anything carbonated before." Megan grabbed a stack of paper napkins to mop up the soda sloshing out of the glass as Bat rubbed at his face.

Orlando grabbed another pile of napkins. "Bat, are you okay, amigo?"

Bat spluttered and looked at Orlando with wide blue eyes. "What kind of roots are those?"

"You mean in the root beer?" Orlando asked. "I dunno ... Never thought about it."

"You do not know what is in it and you drink it?"

Orlando shrugged. "Welcome to America."

Bat glared at the soda in his glass, swirling it around as though trying to make it tell its secrets.

"Watch out, this is hot." Maya, the waitress, set a pan of sizzling pizza on the table. Orlando said something to her in Spanish and she nodded, returning a moment later with a glass of water for Bat.

Orlando pulled out a steaming slice of pizza—piled high with veggies, sausage, and pepperoni—plopped it on a plate and handed it to Bat.

"You ever have pizza before, Bat?"

Bat shook his head, frowning uncertainly at the cheesy slice before him. Megan knew the Rikeans ate mostly root vegetables and wondered if the goblins of Ipktu did the same. She was sure they didn't have cheese or wheat dough, and certainly not pepperoni. She braced herself for another scene.

Bat raised the pizza slice to his mouth and took a bite. He closed his eyes, chewed deliberately, and swallowed. Finally, he opened his eyes and lowered the slice. He leaned forward and whispered, "That is the best thing I have ever eated."

And he wasn't kidding. Bat downed the rest of the slice, then proceeded to eat half of the extra-large pie over the course of dinner. That was fine with Megan—the more he ate, the less he talked, and the smaller the chance he'd say something too weird for Orlando to accept.

Megan, for her part, turned the conversation to Orlando—what he was studying, his classes, and so forth. Orlando was an engineering major, it turned out, with a minor in biology. "There's much we could do to make hospitals better." His eyes, the color of smooth espresso, shone as he spoke. "I mean, you have these little kids with like brain problems or something, and the only way the doctors can find out what's going wrong is to put them inside this MRI machine and make them lie there for a whole hour. I mean, that freaks grownups out, but kids—that's traumatic. If we could come up with a way to get those images with a small, portable machine, that would be better for everyone. Anyway, that's why I spend all those lab hours sitting in front of circuit boards and microscopes and stuff."

He looked over at the pizza tray, from which Bat pulled the last slice. Orlando grinned. "I guess we won't have to worry about leftovers. Did you eat enough?"

"I had plenty. Thank you so much." Megan folded her napkin and put it on top of her plate. "Where are the restrooms?"

"Back near the kitchen. Hey, Bat, put down the pizza for a second and let your lady friend out."

There was no one else in the women's restroom, which suited Megan fine. While washing her hands, she stared past her reflection for a long time.

Arden. Right now, he was in Vindor, a world he knew nothing about. Was he safe? If he happened to be in the company of people like Doctor

Resh, or Nikterra, or Boath the Huntsman, he'd be fine. But what if he ended up somewhere more dangerous, like Woodshea? Or among hostile goblins?

Megan had almost drowned in Vindor—at least twice—nearly fell to her death from a tower, was almost shot with an arrow, nearly froze to death …

And while she had always recalled those things as thrilling parts of her own adventure, now it was different. Arden could be hurt, or worse. Vindor was real, and it was dangerous.

She shivered despite the faucet's hot water still running over her hands. She had to get her brother back. But how? Last time Vindor had come for *her*, not vice-versa. How could she—?

The restroom door opened and in walked Bat.

"Bat! This is the women's restroom!" Megan pushed him back through the doorway with wet hands. "You can't come in here. See this symbol on the door? Never enter where you see the woman symbol. You have to look for the one with the two long legs, like the one on that door there."

"Oh," Bat said. "Why does the lady picture have fins?"

"Never mind, just go." She pushed him through the men's room door, breathing a tense sigh. At least no one had seen him.

A second later, Bat poked his head out of the men's room. "FriendMegan? What do I do in here?"

"Um … stay there a minute."

She could feel her face burning scarlet as she crossed the restaurant. Orlando still sat at the table, chatting with the waitress. He looked up at her. "You okay, Megan?"

"Um, Orlando … uh …" She dropped her voice to a mortified whisper, hoping the waitress couldn't hear. "Can you show Bat how to, uh, use the American facilities …?"

And Orlando laughed out loud—a genuine laugh that made Megan feel better.

"Sure," he said. "You're in over your head here, aren't you?"

"Well, a little. Okay, a lot."

"Don't worry, I'll take care of it. He's coming to visit Cove, right? Do you have a place for him to stay?"

"Well, no. His arrival was unexpected, and I haven't thought that far."

Orlando set cash on the table and slid out of the seat. "My roommate dropped out second week of school, so I've got an extra bed. Bat can be my roommate over Thanksgiving. Will be nice to talk to someone besides myself."

He turned toward the restrooms, and Megan could have hugged him.

Orlando looked back at her. "You look kinda stressed. Relax, Megan. Everything will work out fine—you'll see."

Boy, did Megan hope he was right.

chapter 6

The Girl with the Staff

Arden wasn't sure how long he'd been standing in the empty hallway.

It was such a strange feeling to him—to be mistaken for someone who belonged.

A whole group of men and women in Vindor looked just like him. And were samurai. There might even be a whole country of them. What were they called? The Sura?

When you return to your village, seek Yashi-Ito out for training. He won't turn you away.

Maybe being stuck in Vindor for a little while wouldn't be so bad after all. Training under a real samurai would beat lessons at the Hartford Martial Arts Academy any day.

And then …

Arden imagined the look on Big Steadman's face the next time he tried to push him around. He closed his eyes and imagined the scene—Steadman towering over him, Jay and Tyler leering on either side. Arden punched the air and did a forward kick.

Down went Tyler, no problem.

Here came Jay—Arden hopped forward, rotated, and let out a roundhouse kick.

And his foot made contact with someone.

"Oof!"

Arden heard a thud and the clatter of something wooden on the marble floor. He opened his eyes and saw a dark-haired girl in a tangle of flowing skirts, on her knees and clutching her ribs.

"Hey, what's the big idea?" she gasped.

Arden could feel his face burning scarlet. He had trouble making any sound come out when the girl spoke again.

"Hey, is someone there or not?"

"Uh ..."

The girl raised her head in the direction of Arden's fumbling voice. A dark eye looked past him, darting left and right in an unnatural pattern, not settling on anything. Thick waves of black hair swept over one side of her face, hiding most of it, but Arden caught a glimpse of her other eye—pale blue swirled with white, useless and still.

Arden hadn't kicked just a girl. He'd kicked a blind girl. He wanted to sink into the floor. Somehow, he resisted the urge to run back into the Map Room and hide.

"I'm so, so sorry," he said in almost a whisper. "I didn't mean to do that. I'm so sorry—I didn't know you were blind."

"So you normally kick girls who aren't?" A funny sideways smile played on the girl's lips while her eye continued darting back and forth.

Was that a joke? Or had he said something wrong? "I, I, uh ..."

The girl ran her hand along the floor methodically, her long fingers searching for something. Arden noticed a long wooden shepherd's staff just beyond her reach. He picked it up and held the end out toward her. "Uh, here's your stick."

The girl reached for it, but her hand was several inches too far to the right. Arden moved the staff into her palm, and she grabbed hold of it.

She planted the end of the staff on the floor and used it to help herself up. She was thin and lanky and stood a head taller than Arden.

The girl ran her hand over the long ruffles of a red and white skirt that reminded Arden of something a Spanish flamenco dancer would wear.

Her fingertips then surveyed her thick black hair, rearranging several wavy tresses over her pale blue eye. Her dark eye never stopped flitting back and forth in that rhythmic pattern, and Arden wondered if she had any control over it, or even knew it did that.

"Well, nice to run into you," she said.

Arden's ears burned again.

She paused as though waiting for a response, and that funny sideways smile came out again. "Please, I know you're very talkative, but I simply don't have time to listen to you chatter." She tossed her hair dramatically. "I must ask you to desist talking and direct me to the Council Room."

"Council Room?"

The smile grew mischievous. "Yes, it's the room with the huge council meeting in it."

"Oh, right." Was she making fun of him? Arden couldn't tell. "It's right there." Arden pointed toward the door. The girl raised an eyebrow, and Arden realized pointing probably wasn't helpful.

"It's at the end of this hall," he said. "You're facing it. Well, turn to the right."

The girl turned to the far wall, her back now to Arden.

"Uh, no, that's too far right." This was awkward. "A bit more to the left. Nope, too far, just a few inches … there, now you're facing it. But the door's closed now."

The sideways smile disappeared. "Closed?"

"Yeah, they've already started. You're like ten minutes too late."

"But—I was supposed to go in there."

She thrust the end of her long wooden staff out in front of her as she walked, clicking the tip against the marble floor until it made contact with the Council Room door.

Arden followed her.

The girl ran her hand up and down the wood panels, as though to confirm that it was shut. She turned and leaned her back against it. "I was supposed to go in there with Uncle Lokta. I came all this way because he said …" Her dark eye darted back and forth as though searching the air. "She promised she'd come and get me in time. But she never did."

"Who didn't?"

The dark-haired girl turned her head in Arden's direction, as though startled to hear his voice. "Oh—no one," she said, swiping at her still eye. "Doesn't matter now, I guess. I'll go wait in the garden."

She straightened herself and turned toward another corridor.

"But wait …" Arden started.

She didn't appear to hear him. Staff clicking briskly, she made her way down the hall.

"I think the gardens are the other direction," he finished quietly. He watched her disappear around a corner, going who-knows-where, embarrassed for her but mostly embarrassed for himself.

Could that have gone any worse? Kicking a blind girl and then making an idiot of himself—ugh.

He tried to shake off the uncomfortable encounter. He had some important reading to do, and he needed to find the library.

* * *

"You guys take as long as you need—I have like two months' worth of things to pick up." Orlando wrestled a shopping cart from the tangle of carts and kicked at the wheels. The front one spun wildly. "Not a real trip to Jerry's if you don't have a crazy wheel." He grinned. "Anyway, take your time and I'll find you somewhere in the aisles when I'm done."

Megan extracted a cart herself and headed for the entrance of Jerry's Supercenter. Bat stared as the doors slid open automatically, but he didn't panic the way he had in the busy parking lot.

"Sorry, Bat," Megan said as she pushed the wobbly cart over the carpeted entrance mats and onto the scuffed linoleum. "Jerry's has got to be one of the most overwhelming places I could take you, but we have to get you some of the basics. Follow close and save your questions for when I have time to explain them."

Bat followed obediently as Megan steered down one of the first aisles. She dropped a toothbrush and tube of Colgate into the cart. "Tonight, ask Orlando to show you how they use these in America," she said. She picked up some cheap shampoo, glanced at Bat's bald head, and put it back.

Bat's eyes were fixed on the twenty TV screens in the electronics department. The monitors flashed images of a rock concert with laser lights and crazy camera angles, and Bat swayed unsteadily.

Megan took his hand and pulled him toward the clearance clothes racks. "Come on. You're sure going to have stories to tell when you get home, aren't you?"

Bat nodded. "I do not know how I will explain it. Your world is so … bright. And noisy. And wiggly."

"Wiggly?"

He squinted under the fluorescent warehouse lights. "Yes. Everything here is nervous, moving, flashy lights, running along a road, making noise. No stillness and no peacefulness. How do you stand it?"

Megan shrugged and sorted through a pile of discount jeans. "It's what I'm used to, I guess. Here, do you think these will fit?" She held a pair up, frowned, chose a different size and dropped them in the cart. "I'll have you try these on in a minute. Now look through those sweaters and pick some out that you like."

They worked quietly for a few moments. Megan dropped a pack of socks and a cheap belt into the cart, then removed a sweater with sparkles and purple stripes.

"I liked that one," Bat protested as Megan put it back on the shelf.

"Yes, but here those colors are for girls only. Stick with red, blue, and black." She moved the cart and tackled a pile of shirts. She glanced around to make sure no one was in earshot.

"Okay, I've been dying to know," she said quietly. "How is everyone back in Vindor? How is Nikterra?"

"FriendNikterra and I only sometimes see each other, if she comes to the council with the yellow centaur when I am there too. But she is well. She has a little one, I think, maybe two."

"Really? Wow." Megan leaned back against the shelf and tried to imagine Nikterra as a mother. "Wow. Good for Nikterra." She took a pair of striped footed pajamas out of the cart and hung them back on the rack. "Some days I miss her so much. I've always wondered how she did in Mauritius."

"I think she makes trouble, but good trouble. That is all I know." Bat picked up a pair of tiny cutoff jean shorts, then put them back down when he caught Megan's expression. "Are those for only girls too?"

Megan wrinkled her nose. "Daisy Dukes aren't supposed to be worn by *anyone*. Anyway, what about you? You're going to the council now—does that mean Ipktu is an official nation?"

"Yes, we have growed so many! Which is good because we keeped our promise to Mriv and Krea."

"What promise?"

"They were right," he said. "Goblin Masters discover way to Elnat—but more ways than we knowed. Ipktu fighted them away. Now at least the Rikeans are having peacefulness."

Megan dropped the shirt she'd been holding. "What do you mean, at least?"

Bat seemed reluctant to say more, focusing hard on the argyle sweater in his hands.

"Tell me, Bat," Megan said. "I need to know."

He sighed. "Vindor is full of warring. All the mermaids are fighting in the sea. And in the forests, LadyDagger leads bad Huntsmen to attack other tribes."

Megan's mind went to Boath and Edgwyn, their children and their whole village. Were they safe?

"Do not be sadful," Bat said. "There is always hope to hope. We think Selena will send more warriors—from all over Vindor—to help."

Before Megan could ask anything else, a cart wheel squealed behind them.

"Are you guys buying the whole store?" Orlando asked.

And the conversation regarding Vindor ended for the evening.

chapter 7

Shadows of War

Arden found a library down the hall, and the small door, painted in swirls of silver, opened quietly at his touch. He stepped into a tiny, circular room lined with curving bookshelves that spiraled upward, like the ridges of a nautilus, meeting at some point hundreds of feet above him.

The first row of books he searched had been bound in leather of green and violet and burgundy, many with white ribbon bookmarks peeking out from the yellowed pages. Arden scanned the handwritten titles on the spines.

Elves and their Elements. A Rudimentary Guide to the Rikean Language. The Culture and Customs of the Tsuru People.

Tsuru! That's what the samurai had said.

Arden pulled out three books about the Tsuru, then returned to the Strategy Room and sat down at a table.

The first book contained several maps and surveyed major Tsuru settlements. According to the book's description, most Tsuru lived on large manors—either as nobles, samurai, or peasant-farmers—but there were some cities, including the port city of Shido.

Oddly enough, all the different settlement descriptions were written in present tense. Arden expected to read how long each city had been there, why people had chosen that spot in the first place, and so on. But none of the books contained a word of history. Weird.

The next book dealt with Tsuru culture, including the many subtleties of politeness. Arden busied himself memorizing these—just in case.

The door burst open behind him, and in clattered the giant horse-boy from the garden, laughing and galloping in circles.

"Bradshaw!" Nikterra stomped in after the boy and grabbed him by the arm.

A smaller centaur followed her—a girl, who wobbled on knobby, reddish legs like a newborn fawn. So this is what centaur toddlers looked like. She still stood at Arden's height.

The centaur boy laughed as he tried to struggle free from his mother's strong grip.

"Sorry," Nikterra grunted. "I don't know where he gets this wild streak from. We'll be out of your way in—" She looked up. "Oh, it's you, Arden. Good. Will it bother you if we stay a bit?"

"Uh, no problem. Go ahead."

Nikterra shoved what looked like fruitcake into the boy's hand before letting him go. He plopped down onto the floor, four legs splayed in every direction, and chewed it ravenously. His younger sister did the same, munching her own cake.

"Last time I stayed at Alavar, it was Korvin reading in this room," Nikterra explained. "She was a lot less, uh, patient with interruptions to her study. I mistook you for her—though of course you don't look like a Rikean."

"Why, what does a Rikean look like?"

"Oh, that's right." The centaur stepped closer to the table where Arden sat. "I keep forgetting you don't know these sorts of things. Rikeans have much darker skin than yours, and long, white flowing hair. And they prefer dim light." She tossed her hair. "This whole idea of crossing worlds is strange to me. I imagine your world is quite different?"

"You could say that."

"By the way, I've been dying to know. How is your sister? Is she happy?"

"I think so," Arden said. "She always seems to be."

"Oh, I'm glad to hear that. Is she a hero back in your world as well?"

Arden frowned, looking at the purple book on the table. "No. She never gave a hint of being a hero. She's just a regular girl, going to school, living a normal life."

"There's nothing wrong with a normal life, Arden." Nikterra glanced over at her giant children, who now entertained themselves with tiny wooden carts. "I've learned there's an extraordinary beauty in the everyday. I'm glad she's found happiness. What about you—are you happy in your world?"

Arden's thought immediately of the failed hockey tryouts and of Steadman and his cronies. "I ..." He hesitated. "I'm kind of looking forward to having an adventure here. Trying something different, learning something new."

Beyond the closed door came a rush of voices.

"Ah, council's let out," Nikterra said.

Arden rose to his feet.

"Where are you going?" the centaur asked.

"I, uh, wanted to talk to someone." Maybe if he caught that samurai again, he could ask—

Nikterra shook her head. "Listen."

The voices continued, but instead of the easy chatter from before, the voices were terse and strained.

"Doesn't sound like it went exceptionally well." Nikterra folded her dark arms, looking concerned. "This probably isn't a good time to start a conversation."

The great door opened with a shudder. The bald soldier and the man with the wispy beard entered, followed by Selena. Worry lines creased their faces, Selena's especially.

His sister's twin pulled a chain over her hair and dropped a stone pendant on the table with a careless clunk. Nikterra clicked a hoof in surprise.

"Selena—your pendant."

"It's a false one," Selena said. "The true Moonstone is missing."

"Moonstone?" Nikterra asked. "I thought it was purple, with a star reflection."

Selena shook her head. "The Starstone went back with Megan to her world and cannot be replaced. Since that time, I've had the Moonstone."

"But it's been stolen," said the bald officer, the one called Captain Okoro. "We still need to investigate how—"

"My pendant is the least of our worries at the moment." Selena sank into a chair.

"If you're about to have an official session, we can leave," Nikterra said.

"You can stay a while longer," Selena said. "We'll be discussing things that will be public knowledge soon enough, and I wouldn't mind having your perspective."

"Is it bad?" Nikterra asked.

Master Ryuu, the solemn older man, nodded. Now that Arden looked more closely at him, he realized Ryuu was a Tsuru as well. Perhaps he was a samurai in his day. Arden wondered if he had trained with the samurai master with the trident helmet.

Or, maybe Ryuu had trained the master—a kind of Qui-Gon Jinn to the master's Obi Wan. Had they fought off hordes of marauders together? Stood defending the walls of Shido for long nights in the rain?

As he tried to picture the scene, Selena and the others discussed an army in the woods led by someone called Dagger Ravensblood, which sounded like a name made up by a Goth who was trying too hard.

Nikterra cleared her throat. "What about the merfolk situation then?"

"They're officially at war," Ryuu said.

Arden almost laughed. Mermaids at war? He had a mental picture of dainty sea-girls throwing starfish at each other. But based on the looks on the faces around him, that's not how the others saw it. He stifled his amusement.

"It's the Selks," Okoro said. "King Harg has been pushing for war for—"

"The Selks are defending themselves," Selena interrupted. "The Loray have long been attacking them in secret. Queen Moriana is a madwoman. She doesn't want territory, she doesn't even want fishing rights. What she wants is an annihilation of all merfolk who are not Loray, and she hates the Selks most of all. And ... I don't know how to help them."

Arden hadn't seen Selena look genuinely scared until now.

"But the Selks and the Arions are united," Okoro said. "Together they'll hold the Loray off. We'll nail down the strategy tomorrow at the merfolk council."

"I suppose." Selena didn't sound convinced.

"And the Tsuru samurai stand ready to help if needed," Master Ryuu said.

Arden straightened, really listening now.

"The Selks have long been my people's allies," Ryuu continued. "Our warriors will protect them and our waterways."

"The Tsuru have also volunteered forces to help the Huntsmen on the Adræfan front," Captain Okoro said. "They may be the force that tips the scales against the Ravensblood clan's advance."

Arden grinned. His people were going to be heroes.

"We'll take all the help we can," Selena said. "Especially since the Greyhawks have dropped out of the alliance." Her expression darkened. "They don't know there ever was an alliance—and that's the most troublesome part."

"Selena," Captain Okoro said. "We know you're worried about the Greyhawks, but we can't lose sight of ..."

"No." Selena stood. "Don't you understand? What if the other clans lose their memories as well? We could lose Adræfan in a day, and then what?"

The men glanced at one another but didn't answer.

"It's that mist." Selena paced now. "And some reports are saying it's been spotted along the eastern border, too. How far will it go? What if it reaches N'gozi, or Shido? What if it reaches Kavanna in the east, and the centaurs forget their history and their loyalties—"

Nikterra snorted. Selena frowned up at her.

"Sorry," Nikterra said. "But my people would sooner give up their hind legs than the tiniest detail of Kavannan war history."

"The Greyhawks were the same way, Nikterra. You and Megan stayed with them for several days —you know it to be true."

Nikterra went quiet, and Arden guessed that Selena had made her point.

"This may all be so," Master Ryuu said. "But we can't plan military tactics to defeat mist."

"I know," Selena said. "That's what concerns me."

She was quiet for a moment, then glanced up at Arden. "Oh, Arden, I'm sorry. This isn't what I wanted you to hear—it's all heavy and meaningless to you. Look, we're going to get in contact with Korvin and send you home soon, and—"

"I want to fight." The words came out blunt and heavy, but Arden didn't care.

Selena looked startled. "What?"

"All of this war stuff—it isn't meaningless to me. There are people in trouble here. And I want to help."

"Arden—"

"I want to fight. And if I can't fight, at least let me train with the Tsuru. I want to do something, not just sit here."

"Out of the question. Arden, you are far too young to be getting involved."

The words came like a slap. *Too young. Too small.* The story of Arden's life. And to hear it in Megan's voice, even if it wasn't actually her, made it that much worse.

"Look," Selena said, more gently. "I know your heart's in the right place, but—"

"Arden." Nikterra trotted forward. "What is your family name again?"

Arden hesitated. "Bradshaw," he answered.

"Huh," Nikterra said. "Selena, didn't we know someone about his age named Bradshaw who—oh that's right—saved all of Vindor?"

Arden glanced up at the centaur. Was she doing what he thought she was?

"Megan is different," Selena said evenly.

"Was she now?" Nikterra tossed her braid casually. "If I recall correctly—since I traveled with her extensively, you know—I remember her as a small, timid girl. Well-meaning, but not exactly hero material. And look what she did."

Selena crossed her arms. "This isn't the same thing."

"Of course not. Because here we have a Bradshaw who *wants* to be a hero, with the same heroic blood flowing through his veins."

Arden felt something welling up deep inside him.

"Give him a chance, Selena," Nikterra said.

"But," Selena said. "I owe it to Megan to keep him safe. That's what she would want."

"You owe it to Vindor to let Arden prove himself," Nikterra retorted. "Who knows the tremendous good he can do? Maybe Vindor needs an outside hero again. And look, here he is."

Arden felt like he'd grown a foot taller. He locked eyes with Selena. "Let me help. Please."

Selena looked away, gazing once more toward the window. "I'll think about it."

chapter 8

Candles in the Dark

"Well, this is your stop." Orlando pulled into a parallel parking spot outside of Grace Palmer dormitory and put the car into idle. "This ride has been courtesy of Ruiz Taxi Service."

"Thank you." Megan lowered her voice and motioned to Bat in the back seat. "Are you sure you're going to be okay with him?" Bat now craned his head sideways and stared open-mouthed, apparently trying to get a better view of the street lamp.

"Relax! Mr. Bat and I are going to have lots of fun that is funny. Aren't we, Bat?"

"Very yes," Bat answered. He turned abruptly, staring wide-eyed at a passing moped.

"I'll take care of him," Orlando said quietly. "You quit worrying, okay?"

Megan sighed. "All right. I'll meet you guys at breakfast tomorrow at eight."

"Um, tomorrow's Saturday. *And* vacation," Orlando said. "Nine. Or later. No promises."

"Fair enough." Megan climbed out of the passenger seat and opened one of the back doors. As she reached into the back seat to retrieve her book satchel, the navy sack, and Arden's backpack, she tapped Bat on the shoulder to pull his attention away from the fire hydrant. "Listen, go with the flow and do what Orlando tells you," she whispered. "Don't … do anything weird."

"Weird like what?"

Megan thought back to when they had camped out in Vindor—it felt like a lifetime ago—and tried to remember if he'd had any especially strange bedtime habits. "Like, don't eat frogs or anything."

"Are there frogs?" Bat sounded hopeful.

"No," Megan whispered. "Just do whatever Orlando tells you." She pointed to the plastic shopping bags. "And be sure to put on your pajamas—the blue clothes—before you go to sleep, then put on the clothes in this bag tomorrow morning."

"Hey, the clock's still running on this thing." Orlando pointed to an imaginary meter with a wink. "I don't get paid for sitting here."

Megan pulled out her book satchel and Arden's two bags. "Good night, Orlando. And *thank you*."

Orlando tipped his ball cap. "No problem. See you tomorrow—not *too* bright and early."

Megan, exhausted physically and mentally, lugged the three heavy bags up the creaking, wooden steps of Grace Palmer. She shifted the bags with some difficulty to retrieve her key and then unlocked her door.

"So there you are." Roz sat on the floor, surrounded by empty coffee cans and veggie tins, trying to poke holes in them with a Swiss army knife.

"Hey Roz." Megan plopped Arden's backpack and navy sack on her purple comforter.

"You and your brother have a good time in Mystic?"

Megan mumbled something incoherent, and Roz seemed to accept it. "Cool. You don't happen to have a power drill, do you? Or even a screwdriver?"

"Sorry, Roz, I don't. What are you making this time?"

"A rocket stove. Super energy efficient and made from recycled materials. Only it would be easier to do if I had power tools, I'm discovering."

"Well, maybe you can stop by the carpentry shop tomorrow. I'm sure they have that kind of stuff there."

Roz stared at Megan.

"What?" Megan asked.

"You do remember we're leaving first thing tomorrow, right?"

The camping trip. Megan had forgotten all about it. "Roz …"

Roz put down the can. "Everything okay?"

"I can't go."

"What?"

"I have to stay here … Arden is …" How was she going to explain this? Megan exhaled. "We're kind of having a family emergency. I can't go into more details."

"Oh, Megan." Roz stood up and hugged her. "Is everyone okay?"

Megan returned the embrace. "Yeah …" She glanced at Arden's backpack and the sinking feeling returned. "I think."

"Is there anything I can do?"

Megan sat down on her bed. "No, I think this is something I—we—are going to have to handle. But I can't go camping. I know you've been planning this forever, and I was really looking forward to it. I'm so sorry to cancel."

Roz shook her head. "Nope. Family comes first, Megan. You do what you need to do. You want me to stay too?"

"No, go with your family. You guys have a good time."

To help convince Roz that Megan didn't mind if she had fun without her, Megan helped her finish the stove, feigning cheerfulness when all she really wanted to do was sleep. They stayed up packing and chatting until nearly midnight.

When the lights finally went out, Megan practically collapsed into bed.

And then couldn't sleep. Finally, alone with her thoughts, uninterrupted, she had a lot to process.

Arden.

He was in a completely different world, maybe even another dimension. How would she ever get him back?

Her own journey six years ago had been arranged by the ghostly, blue-eyed spirit Eira, whatever exactly she was. Eira seemed to have things under control.

Well, except for at the Battle of Alavar, when the Shadow had frozen everyone and Eira seemed to have a serious panic moment.

But surely she was in control again now. Eira had taken Arden instead of Megan on purpose, and left Bat in his place. On purpose.

Even though that made no sense whatsoever.

Megan exhaled. *Right.*

Last time, Eira had kept Megan in Vindor for a month, which hadn't been a problem since Selena had taken her place and no one had noticed. How that had worked out, Megan had never figured.

But I don't have a month, Megan realized. *I have what—nine days, tops?*

She might be able to hide the switch over Thanksgiving break. Roz and Orlando weren't asking questions about where Arden went. Mom assumed Megan and Arden would be off in the woods soon and didn't expect to have much contact with them.

But Mom would be coming to pick Arden up the Sunday after Thanksgiving. And she would *definitely* notice then. How would Megan ever begin to explain where Arden was, or why she hadn't reported him missing for over a week?

Megan stared at the dark ceiling for a long time. This was beyond her ability to fix. She slid out of bed and silently went over to her closet.

Roz stirred, mumbled something, and rolled over. Megan quietly pulled on a pair of jeans, her furry boots, a thick sweatshirt, and her coat. She grabbed her keys, a flashlight, and a box of matches, then stepped out into the dorm hallway, locking the door behind her. She tiptoed down the creaking dormitory stairs and out into the night.

A bitterly cold wind stung her nostrils. Megan shivered and followed the sidewalk, illuminated by the light of the half-moon, toward a part of Cove campus she knew well.

She reached a small building with a steeply angled roof. The white wooden siding reflected faintly in the moonlight as Megan followed the cobblestone path to the hundred-year-old door. She paused to shine her flashlight over the plaque:

You are not here to verify,

Instruct yourself, or inform curiosity

Or carry report. You are here to kneel

Where prayer has been valid.

—T.S. Eliot

The heavy wooden door opened easily—it was always unlocked. Megan fumbled along the wall for the light switch. The old electric chandeliers sprung to life, casting enough light for Megan to navigate past the four rows of pews to the front steps. The building smelled faintly of incense and old paper.

Two tall candelabras flanked the stairs. Megan struck one of her matches against its box and lit the tapers one by one, as she had many times before. The flickering light reflected off the building's single stained-glass window, its image currently invisible in the darkness.

Megan ascended the stairs and knelt at the top. In her mind's eye she could see the shadows of hundreds of other students who had climbed these steps over Cove's long history. The scene expanded to thousands of shadows on similar steps through the ages—altars of wood and stone and earth, altars in magnificent buildings and dark catacombs, transcending the boundaries of time and place and—as Megan knew firsthand—the boundaries of dimensions.

"World-Weaver," she whispered. "Creator of the stars and universes and life itself. I know You are here. And I know You are there, too, because anywhere that is or can be, there You are too." She paused. "Please, protect my brother in Vindor. Send a guardian angel to watch over him. And please—please—bring him back safely to me."

The words hung in the air. At length Megan rose and blew out the candles, watching the thin plumes of smoke rise toward the vaulted ceiling and vanish from sight.

She descended the steps and had reached the second row of pews when another thought struck her. She turned and scrambled back up the steps. "One more thing. You know there's trouble going on in Vindor, and great danger.

"Please, please, if Arden asks to join the war—tell Selena not to let him fight."

* * *

Arden wasn't the kind of guy who thought much about mermaids, not in the real world. So it surprised him how deeply disappointed he felt when he saw the Selks.

He saw his first one as he picked his way down the treacherous cliff stairs, following Selena and her advisors and pretending that the hundred-foot drop into the sea didn't faze him in the least. The uneven stairway, carved directly into the stone cliff, wound downward through a maze of rock. He had been so busy watching his footing that he didn't notice the figures pulling themselves up onto stone outcroppings until he practically walked into one.

She wasn't at all a graceful sea-maiden, singing and combing her flowing hair. The mermaid on the ledge before him was stockily built, with coarse dark hair and a thick furry tail. Claws on the end of her seal-like flippers dug into the cliff rock. She wore a ragged tunic made of some sort of grey skin, fastened with a broach made of shark teeth.

A second Selk slid out of a cave and joined her—a merman with an unruly beard, clutching a spear.

Arden felt a firm hand on his shoulder. "Don't stare," Captain Okoro said. "He'll take it as a challenge."

"Oh, uh—" Arden quickly looked back at the grey stairs and hurried down the next few. "Thanks."

Other Selks pulled themselves onto jagged outcroppings around him as he descended, scowling toward the breaking waves. They called warnings to one another in low, hoarse tones that reminded Arden of sea lions barking.

Three Selk girls reclined near the bottom of the stairway, giggling and plucking spiky cliff flowers and threading them in their tangled hair.

One of them grinned at Arden as he passed. He almost lost his footing for a moment—her pointed canines were larger than the rest of her teeth, making her smile more unnerving than friendly.

Now Arden balanced on a giant boulder at the bottom of the cliffs, feeling the spray of salt water on his skin. There was no beach, only an uneven wall of rocks that marked where the land ended and the sea began. The water churned several feet below him, drawing back and then smashing against the rocks in a spray of white foam.

He looked up again at the tall cliffs towering against the sky, dotted with hundreds of caves overcrowded with Selks.

Arden wrinkled his nose. High-rise apartments for cavemen.

They were awkward creatures, moving around on their bellies and pulling themselves with their arms, their tails dragging along. Arden saw one or two splay out their flippers like sea lions, using them for grip as they climbed to higher ground.

He shook his head. *You really could have done better with the mermaids, Megan.*

A few hundred yards down the rocky coast, Selena and her advisors stood on the shore chatting with an old Selk chieftain with a bushy beard, surrounded by dozens of other Selks.

Selena had to attend some sort of council meeting, and she had told him to wait here until they finished. After that she'd explain to Arden his assignment for helping Vindor.

Selena had been vague on this point, but that morning she'd provided him with an outfit that looked like something to practice karate in—loose trousers and a long-sleeved tunic that tied at the side, both in a deep garnet red. So that was a good sign.

And apparently, Arden would be traveling somewhere with her, otherwise why would she have dragged him along to wait during her meeting?

She's taking me to the Tsuru. He grinned, leaping from the big boulder to a smaller one. He almost lost his footing in his straw sandal, but he righted himself to avoid tumbling into the seawater several feet below.

He'd have to get used to moving in these if he was going to start martial arts training soon. He jumped down onto a smaller rock, soaking the woven straw in a salty puddle. Oops.

A Selk barked out a warning, and a hundred barking shouts took up the cry. Arden covered his ears and turned.

Rounding a distant sea cliff came a school of merfolk, leaping in and out of the water like dolphins. They had tails like dolphins, too, and wavy brown hair.

"Just Arions! False alarm!" cried a Selk merman, his voice somehow carrying over the din. The deafening shouts quieted.

One dolphin-tailed mermaid wearing a seashell crown pulled herself up onto the rocks next to Selena. The rest of her people crowded together in the water, keeping their heads and shoulders above the surface, and looking nervously toward the open sea.

Arden guessed there were two hundred of them there. Many had seaweed bandages tied around their heads and shoulders, and some had their arms bound in slings.

He looked toward the dolphin-tailed queen. The long wavy hair was right, but she looked like she could be his mom's age—too old to be a mermaid.

Didn't anyone around here understand what mermaids were supposed to look like?

Arden turned and leapt onto the next sea-boulder. His sandaled foot landed squarely on the rock surface, and he grinned at his improvement.

"It would be best not to advertise the name Bradshaw," Selena had told him that morning. "Just to be safe. Could you go by something different, temporarily?"

"Nakamura," Arden had said without hesitation. "I'll be Arden Nakamura."

It wouldn't be the first time. *Arden Zachariah Nakamura*, the name on his birth certificate, had been his name for six whole months before his mother changed it to her maiden name to expunge every trace of Jonas Nakamura from their lives. Arden didn't have a single photo of the man, but he did hold on to his name—secretly, of course. Until now.

"Arden Nakamura," he whispered to himself as he hoisted himself onto a taller rock. Waves hissed seven feet below. The top of the boulder was steeply angled, and the wet straw sandal began to slip. Arden felt himself falling. He leapt toward the next angled boulder and the rush of salty wind hit his ears—then the lurch of falling. His jump had been too short. He managed to grab onto the rock face, the sharp stone biting into his fingers.

A wave smashed against the boulder, soaking him. Arden blinked the foam from his eyes, then looked below him. Water, mostly—then an uneven pile of smaller rocks. His fingers tingled with pain, and his sandaled feet couldn't find any footholds.

He had nowhere to go but down.

Arden swallowed, braced himself for the drop, and let his aching fingers slip.

He landed with a splash and felt the waves pulling him back, away from land and into the restless sea. Arden's hand found a rock and he held onto it with all his strength. When the wave receded, he dragged himself onto the highest stone he could find, wet with seawater.

And that's when he saw her.

Three feet above him, perched in a crevice between two tall rocks, sat a *real* mermaid.

She was young and beautiful with porcelain skin. She had long, dark hair and a silver, fish tail that dazzled in the sunlight.

The mermaid leaned down to look at Arden, seemingly surprised by his presence. A perfect, dainty face. Dark eyes, so large and beautiful. He could lose himself in those eyes.

Arden knew he was staring, but he couldn't pull himself away. Now he knew what people meant when they say they met someone and immediately felt enchanted.

The mermaid regarded him for a moment. "Give me your name," she said in a silky voice.

It was a command, not a request. Before he could stop himself, he answered, "Arden Bradshaw. I mean—Arden Nakamura!"

A mysterious smile played on her lips, making her face even more alluring. And then without warning, she dove into a rising wave and vanished.

Arden stared after her, his heart pounding. Sea foam danced on the waves where she had disappeared.

Who was that lovely dark-eyed mermaid? And when could he see her again?

chapter 9

Shido

"So … where are we going?"

Arden sat behind Selena on the back of the sturdy white horse and had spent most of the ride trying not to fall off. He wanted to ask about their next stop ever since they left the Selk cliffs. But based on the glum looks Selena had exchanged with Master Ryuu and Captain Okoro, he guessed the meeting hadn't gone well, and held back his questions as long as he could.

The two men now rode their own horses behind them on the dusty road. Neither had said a word.

Selena turned to look at him. "We're going to Shido, the Tsuru riverport."

Shido! She *was* going to let him train with the samurai.

Arden wondered what his training would be like. How long would he work on form before sparring with other trainees? At what point would he get to use weapons? He tried to recall what he'd read about polite Tsuru greetings and silently rehearsed how he'd greet his samurai master when he met him.

Meanwhile, the land had grown more level since they'd left the cliffs. The horses' hooves occasionally clattered over wooden bridges that spanned slow-moving creeks and rivers. White cranes stood serenely in the long, river grass. In the distance Arden spied neat villages of wooden houses on short stilts.

Now they passed by low fields with standing water glistening in the afternoon sun. Tsuru men and women in stiff straw hats stood ankle-deep in the water, bent over what looked like long blades of grass.

Rice farms. Arden wanted to call out to the workers and greet them—after all, he was a Tsuru himself now—but they were engrossed in their work.

Up ahead, sunlight glared off a large body of water. As they drew closer, Arden recognized it as a river, probably a football field's length to the other side. There was no bridge here to cross; the road curved and followed the riverbank northward.

Arden watched the murmuring water for a minute and saw a tiny, white wave break in the surface.

The dark eyes and perfect face flashed in his mind's eye. *It could be her!*

The silver-tailed mermaid could be under the water, swimming upriver, ready to meet him at Shido. Arden didn't know why she'd be following him, but she *could*, if she wanted to.

He continued to watch the river for another little wave, anything that could indicate someone swimming under the surface.

Then he noticed it. The water in half of the river flowed clear and blue. But along the far bank, the river water was six shades darker, like a shadow had fallen over it. Arden squinted—it wasn't a trick of the light. Clear water and dark water flowed side by side, like two separate rivers, barely mixing where they touched.

"Uh, Selena? What's with the water?"

"Hmm?"

"The river—the water's two different colors."

"Oh, yes," Selena said. "The Ember and Blackwater rivers converge a few miles ahead. It takes a while for them to fully mix into one—it's something about the Blackwater being slower and colder."

"The Blackwater is literally black?"

"Not quite, but close. You'll see for yourself soon enough."

Arden watched the river as they continued along the road. The Blackwater half grew darker the farther upstream they traveled. A slender, wooden ship with a square sail floated down the center of the river. Arden turned to watch as it passed. In the boat's wake, dark and clear water joined together in lopsided swirls.

"There," Selena said at length, pointing. "That's where the two rivers meet."

Arden looked upriver. The black-colored water came from a narrow river to the west, and the clear water came from a broad, sparkling river to the east. Between them stood a small strip of land, a peninsula crowded with neat white buildings. The roofs, made of clay tiles in a dusty green, swept upward at each corner.

"That city between the rivers is Shido," Selena said, though Arden had already guessed. He couldn't help but grin—the city looked like something out of a samurai history book.

Boats of every kind congested the waters around the city. As they got closer, Arden saw wooden gondolas and rowboats maneuvering between large cargo ships piled high with barrels of rice, fish, and cloth. Several boats that looked like floating houses zipped along in the waters, though Arden didn't see oars or sails.

There were more people and horses on the road now, as well as many farmers leading ox-drawn carts. Neat, white buildings stood on either side.

The party dismounted their horses. Okoro spoke briefly with a Tsuru man who then led the three horses to a large stable, already crowded with other animals.

A bridge of five tall arches spanned the blue Ember River, connecting the Shido peninsula to the mainland. Selena climbed the steep staircase of the first arch, and Arden and her advisors followed. A large, narrow ship, a dozen oars swinging rhythmically on either side, passed under the second arch as the party ascended it. Arden leaned over the stone railing to get a better look and was surprised to find the sailors were fair-haired centaurs, their hooves clopping against the wooden deck.

"Shido is a major trading port for all of Vindor," Selena told him. "Even for those as far away as Mauritius. Come."

Arden's legs felt like jelly as he descended the steep stairway of the fifth arch, but he tried not to let it show. He held his breath as he stepped off the bridge and onto the streets of Shido—his new home-to-be.

The narrow streets, neatly paved with flat stones, bustled with people—elegant women in colorful kimonos, merchants in long robes, farmers with straw hats, samurai in full armor. His heart leapt.

On either side of the busy street tidy shops crowded together, their goods spilling out into the walkway: sacks of rice, colorful bolts of silk, fresh vegetables and fish, pots and pans, knives, and stirring spoons. Arden paused to gaze at a shop filled with ornate swords before noticing he'd nearly lost Selena and the others in the crowd. He squeezed between a shopkeeper and a farmer arguing loudly over the price of pruning hooks and hurried to catch up.

Master Ryuu led the way through the narrow tangle of streets. He paused as he came to an intersection congested with people and rice-carts. Through a gap in the white buildings, Arden caught a glimpse of several boats bobbing in the dark water.

Ryuu motioned to Okoro. "They'll try to overcharge you if they can, Captain, so be firm."

Okoro bowed his bald head toward Ryuu and then Selena, then turned and disappeared in the direction of the river.

"Where's he going?" Arden asked.

"We'll explain that later," Selena said. "Ryuu, where are we meeting them?"

"By the sakura tree. I see them now," Ryuu said.

Finally. Arden followed on his tiptoes, straining to see over the crowd. At the end of the street, tucked between two buildings, stood an elegant tree, reddening cherries peeking out among the green leaves. As they drew nearer, Arden held his breath.

But the samurai with the trident helmet wasn't there, nor were any samurai at all. The two people under the tree weren't even Tsuru. A barefoot man with dark, wavy hair, wearing loose red trousers and a dusty, woolen shirt, held a shepherd's staff from which dangled a long, white feather. Beside him stood a scowling old woman wrapped in a red shawl with intricate embroidery. She also held a shepherd's staff, hers with a fox's tail hanging by a red cord.

Who were these people? There had to be some mistake.

"Lokta," Selena said as she approached. "Chieftainess Taytum. Thank you for meeting us here."

The old woman's scowl deepened. "Well it's about time. I don't like having to stand in this human anthill a minute longer than we have to."

"Mother—" The wavy-haired man's voice broke slightly. "You're speaking with Selena, Guardian of Vindor, who—"

"I know who I'm talking with," the old woman snapped, snatching her arm away from the man's touch. "We go to the council meetings, I know her when I see her. Goat pox, boy."

Arden saw Selena and Ryuu exchange a glance.

Ryuu cleared his throat. "Lokta, where is your niece?"

"Talulaweyna should be here shortly," the man said. "She wanted to explore a bit."

"And the fool *let* her!" the old woman said. "Can you believe that?"

"She's perfectly capable if you give her a chance," Lokta said quietly. "She only went twenty steps to the end of the pier."

"Maybe she'll take twenty-one and rid us all of a lot of trouble." The old woman spat on the ground.

Did she say what Arden thought she did?

Lokta gave an apologetic look to Selena. "Please disregard my mother," he said in a low voice. "I think she is mistaken as to who is truly blind."

Wait … wavy dark hair, looking for her uncle in the Council Room—suddenly the pieces started to fall together. Arden's stomach sank. "Uh, your niece—she's not, uh, *literally* blind, is she?"

"Not completely," Lokta answered. Arden froze. "She still has some usable vision in her right eye."

"Uncle!"

Arden turned and saw her—the same lanky girl from the Alavar hallway. She waved and hurried toward them across the street, her shepherd's staff swinging in front of her and tapping against the stone. She almost bowled into a crowd of arguing merchants, and another merchant pulled his rice cart to a stop seconds before striking her. He hurled out several insults as the girl ran across the road, her bare feet slapping against the stone.

"Uncle Lokta," she called again, apparently oblivious.

"Over here, Talu," Lokta called. "Southeast." The girl altered her course, slowing only slightly when she tripped over a basket of dried beans beside a farmer's stand.

"She's used to the open plains," Lokta said. "There's nothing this crowded in Gavgal."

"There you are." Talu practically tackled her uncle, wrapping her long, brown arms around him in an embrace. She pulled back, readjusting a thick wave of dark hair over her pale eye, while her good eye danced with excitement.

"Uncle, you won't believe the things I have seen! First of all, there's not a wheel on a single house here. I asked a lady what happens if you have a house and you get tired of the spot it's in, and she says you're stuck there forever! Also, I kept hearing this sound like a squeaking wagon axle and I couldn't figure out what it was. The same Tsuru lady—she was very kind—said that birds that made that sound, big white birds that come from the sea."

The girl closed her eyes and sighed. "The *sea*. Oh! And the lady had this dog that had his face smushed in. It looked like if one of our wolf-dogs ran straight into a tree, but she said—"

"Goat pox, girl!" the old woman snapped.

The girl's sideways smile disappeared. "Grandmother?"

"It's bad enough you eat the food we labor for, but do you have to fill our ears with your meaningless chatter?"

Talu seemed to shrink three inches. She lowered her head.

"Sorry, Grandmother," she mumbled.

The girl probably hadn't seen the world's worst grandmother standing right there. She'd thought she was having a private conversation with her uncle. Arden felt embarrassed for her.

Lokta squeezed Talu's shoulder. "I want to hear all about it later," he said gently. "But for now, I'd like to introduce you to some important people."

Talu straightened, her good eye darting back and forth.

Please don't recognize me, Arden silently pleaded.

"Standing to the south is Master Ryuu, top advisor to Selena, the Guardian of Vindor. And directly in front of you is Selena herself."

The girl's mismatched eyes widened.

"Wow! Really? I mean, how do you do?" She pinched the edges of her flowing red skirt and gave a quick curtsy. Somehow her long legs tangled up in the process, though, and she stumbled, her face reddening.

She hadn't seemed like such an awkward person moments before.

Selena smiled warmly. "Talulaweyna," she said. "Your uncle has told me much about you. He says you're a bright girl with a bright future."

"He did? I mean—" Talu's blush deepened.

The old woman snorted.

Selena glanced at the girl's uncle, who nodded. "We have a subject of some importance we'd like to discuss with you, Talulaweyna—in private."

"W-with me? Sure, I mean, of course, that is—" Talu looked back toward her family.

Her grandmother waved dismissively. "Take her."

Lokta smiled. "Best of winds to you."

"Miss Talulaweyna," Master Ryuu said, offering his arm. "If you'd come this way."

Talu hesitated, then put her hand in the crook of Ryuu's elbow.

"You too, Arden," Selena said. She glanced to either side, then disappeared between two buildings. Ryuu and Talu followed her, and Arden trailed behind.

What was going on? Why would they need this girl as well as him? Surely, they weren't training *her* to be a samurai, too.

Selena led them through a long, narrow alley between the white buildings. Up ahead stood a tall, bamboo fence with hedges peeking over the top. Selena approached a square, wooden gate in the middle and rapped on it four times.

A pause, and then the gate swung open. Selena motioned for the others to follow.

They stepped into a garden of purple-leaved maples and weeping willows, passing a serene pond with white fish hiding beneath lily pads.

"Hey, why did it get quiet all of a sudden?" Talu still held Ryuu's arm and tilted her head at odd angles, as though trying to look out of the side of her moving eye. Arden wondered what exactly she could and couldn't see.

"We're in a walled garden," Ryuu explained. "And up ahead is a tea house."

Selena approached a simple thatch-roofed house in the center of the garden and slid open a door of bamboo and translucent paper. Arden stepped inside.

The room was nearly bare, without a single chair or other furniture. For decoration, the room had only a scroll with a simple kanji character and a bowl with a cluster of pink flowers. Selena sat down on a white floor mat, and Talu and Arden did the same.

Master Ryuu knelt and poured hot tea into four thin bowls, placing one before each person. Arden watched him, imitating the way the old samurai picked up his tea bowl.

Arden grimaced as he raised the green liquid, which smelled a lot like lawn clippings, to his mouth. Green tea was not his thing, but he'd have to get used to it.

"Well," Selena said, setting down her own bowl of tea, "I want to thank you both for following us out here. Talu, the young man to your right is Arden Nakamura."

Talu turned toward Arden, her dark eye searching him.

He stiffened. Don't recognize me, don't recognize me.

"Pleasure to meet you," Talu said politely.

Arden breathed a sigh of relief. "Nice to meet you too."

"Wait," Talu's eye darted over him again. "Didn't we run into each other before?"

"Uh …"

The girl's mischievous, sideways smile came out again. Arden wanted to sink into the floor.

"I'm sure you're both wondering why I've asked you here today," Selena said.

Arden leaned in closer. Here it was—his big break.

Selena continued. "Doubtless you've both heard about the wars between the merfolk and the Huntsmen clans. But Vindor also faces another threat—a strange mist is coming up over the mountains of our eastern border. We're not sure what it is, but it's affecting peoples' memories and seems to be gaining territory. It may have the potential to do great harm to our world if left unchecked."

She turned to Arden. "Arden, you have asked to help defend Vindor, to train as a warrior and fight."

"Yes." Arden held his breath.

"But I cannot let you do that. It is far too dangerous, and it's my responsibility to keep you safe. You can't fight."

Arden felt like he'd been punched in the stomach. *Too dangerous,* which was another way of saying *too small* and *too weak.*

Just like that, his path to becoming a hero ended.

He glared down into his tea, his face growing hot. Why bring him all the way out here and make him think she was going to let him train?

"But there's something important you *can* do to help Vindor," Selena continued. "In the great city of N'gozi, there is an ancient library. Take this letter to the head librarian, and ask to bring back Korvin, a young Rikean scholar who's been studying there for a few months now. She knows the history of Vindor better than anyone—if there's anyone who can solve the puzzle of the mist, she can."

So that was it. Instead of sending him into battle, she was sending him on an errand to the *library*. He half expected her to ask him to pick up some bread and eggs on the way back.

"There's a second part to this quest," Selena said.

The word *quest* was definitely an exaggeration.

"We've also lost communication with the westernmost tribes of the Nomads," Selena said. "Korvin will lead the expedition after N'gozi. We need someone to check and make sure they're safe—I don't want to lose track of anyone these days. Also, Korvin needs to talk with the people to discover whether there are any reports of the mist on the western borders as well.

"Keep in mind the various Nomad tribes can be hostile to outsiders. This is why Talulaweyna will be accompanying you."

The girl had just gotten the bowl of tea to her lips. She spluttered. "Me?"

"Yes, Talu," Selena said gently. "We need your help in speaking with the tribe leaders, to assure them that Korvin is worthy of their trust."

"Me? But Guardian Selena, my uncle's the Peace Talker, not me. The tribes won't listen unless I have the white feather, and ..."

"I understand," Selena said. "But your uncle tells me you aspire to be a Peace Talker yourself one day—is that right?"

Talu studied her tea. "I always talked about it when I was a little girl," she said quietly. "But I'm so young and nobody will—"

"Is it still your dream, Talu?"

Talu looked up, her dark eye solemnly scanning Selena's face. "The World-Weaver has put it into my heart, so yes."

"Your uncle seems to think you have great potential. Which is why he asked me to give you this. Hold out your hand."

Talu put down her bowl of tea and held her palm out. Selena drew out a stiff eagle feather and placed it gently over the girl's outstretched fingers. Talu started as it touched her.

"What?" She wrapped her fingers around it and pulled it an inch or two from her good eye.

"It's brown with a white tip," Selena explained. "Your uncle said this is the mark of a trainee Peace Talker."

"R-really? But—"

"I understand there is supposed to be a ceremony and everything in front of your people," Selena said, "But your uncle assured me that my giving it to you would be sufficient."

"I—" Talu held the feather close to her heart. "Wow. *Thank you!*"

"Talu will be the party's guide as you advance into Nomad territory," Selena continued. "But please, *please* be careful regarding the mist. Besides having an effect on memories, we don't yet know its full capabilities. If you see it, stay far away from it. I don't want either of you hurt.

"Once Talu reaches her own tribe, she is relieved of duty and may return home. Arden, we're hoping that Korvin will know how to ... ah, set things right with your situation."

"And if she doesn't?" Arden asked.

Selena hesitated. "Return downriver with Korvin and we'll figure out the next steps then."

Next steps. Maybe ... maybe if Arden could prove himself during the trip, and he ended up having to stay longer in Vindor, maybe then she would let him train. After all, he was in no hurry to get back home and face Steadman without at least a few fighting pointers.

"Do you have any questions?" Selena asked.

"Wait a minute," Arden said. "If we *return* downriver ... that means we'll be going *against* the current the whole way there? How does that work?" Vindor didn't seem to be the kind of place that had speedboats with motors.

Talu tossed her wavy hair. "We'll take a taxi, of course! What do you think?"

"What?"

Ryuu stood. "Captain Okoro should have arranged that by now. We'd better get to the docks."

chapter 10

Dark Morning

Megan sat on a bench outside the school cafeteria, hugging her peacoat to herself. The sun shone down warming the earth below, but the breeze rustling through the last of the autumn leaves nipped through her thick clothing.

Only a handful of students milled around on this frosty Saturday before Thanksgiving. Megan squinted down the sidewalk toward the guys' dorms. Where were Bat and Orlando?

She reached into the pocket of her wool skirt and pulled out her phone to check the time.

Her heart sank. A text from Mom:

Hi, did Arden get in okay? Hope you're having a great time.

Megan typed:

Yep

That was a complete lie. She deleted that and started over:

Everything's great

She paused and deleted that, too.

Having fun …

Nope. Her fingers paused above the phone, aching with the cold.

"FriendMegan!"

Megan looked up to see Bat and Orlando bundled up against the cold and heading down the walkway. Bat appeared to have his shoes on the wrong feet, but otherwise he almost passed for normal.

Bat stopped, picked up a stone from a flower bed and presented it to Orlando. Orlando, wrapped up in his puffy white coat, grinned at him.

"This is an indignant rock," Bat announced as he reached where Megan sat.

Orlando laughed. "It's *igneous*, I think. Been a while since I studied geology."

Bat put the mottled grey stone into the pocket of his jeans—only it was the back pocket, so it looked awkward. "Orlando is giving me a rock library."

"I said he could have my collection, and he got super excited," Orlando explained. "This kid really likes rocks." He pulled open the cafeteria door and motioned to Megan. "I smell bacon. We'd better get in there fast."

Megan slipped the phone back into her pocket, text unanswered, and stepped inside.

Bat covered his tray with a mountain of pancakes, hash browns, bacon, scrambled eggs, and twelve pats of butter. Megan bit her tongue as he proceeded to dump maple syrup over everything on his plate.

Orlando nodded at him as they set their trays down at the cafeteria table. "Kid's got a healthy appetite."

"Yeah," Megan mumbled, watching Bat pick up a dripping pancake with his hands and eat it like a slice of pizza. She picked up her fork and knife and tried to demonstrate how to cut up her own pancake, but Bat had now moved onto the pile of bacon, which he ate by the handful.

Megan turned away. "Orlando, uh, what's your plan for the day?"

"Oh, well, I have a big lab project due at the end of vacation, and I have major plans to procrastinate. So I'd better get the work out of the way first." He grinned. "How about you two? Weren't you going on a big camping trip or something?"

"Uh, plans kind of changed on that," Megan said. "We're ... probably going to explore the area a little bit." In reality, she planned to take Bat back to Pequotsepos Bridge. Hopefully, they'd figure out how Arden had gotten into Vindor, and then work out a way to reverse it.

"Need a ride again?"

"Nope, I can drive my car ... oh, wait, the battery's dead." She remembered battling with it before heading out to pick up Arden. Had that only been the evening before? A lifetime seemed to have passed since.

"I've got jumper cables in my trunk," Orlando said. "I'll get it running for you again—that is, once Mr. Bat finishes tackling Mount Baconmanjaro over here."

"Bacon's better than pizza!" Bat announced between swallows.

Orlando grinned. "This kid's a true American at heart. Mr. Bat, stay in our country as long as you like. You're going to fit in here fine."

* * *

Arden followed Ryuu and Selena down the narrow streets of Shido. Talu clicked her staff on the cobblestones as she walked beside Arden, turning her head in all directions as though trying to take in as many images and sounds as she could. The brown feather dangled from a scarlet cord on the end of her staff, swaying as she moved.

The paved street led them to a crowded riverside dock, where a neat row of wooden piers stretched out from the street into the water.

There could be no mistaking the Blackwater River. Where the waves lapped against the wood supports of the piers, the water was a rusty brown like tea, but as soon as it got any depth it became coffee-black and impossible to see through.

Dozens of what Arden initially thought were floating houses bobbed on the dark water. They turned out to be long boats, twice the length of a typical canoe and twice the width of a rowboat, with a pointed bow in the front and a blunt, square stern at the back. Each boat supported a wooden roof—shingled and swept up at each of its four corners in the Shido style. There were no walls beneath the roofs, just tall poles and occasional divider curtains.

How the bulky crafts were supposed to move against the current Arden had no idea. He didn't see any oars anywhere.

A single sailor manned each houseboat, bartering loudly over transport prices with the people on the piers. Most of the sailors were Tsuru, but Arden spied a few Nomads like Talu.

"There he is," Ryuu said. Captain Okoro carried a heavy sack of rice down one of the piers.

As they approached, Okoro put down the sack beside a houseboat with a red shingled roof. He waved to Ryuu and Selena.

"Whoa," Arden said as they drew closer.

Talu tilted her head toward him. "What?"

Arden pointed, forgetting for a moment that it wasn't helpful. "The sailor—she's a mermaid."

Talu's mismatched eyes widened. "A *real* mermaid? How lovely!"

"Uh ... she's probably not the kind of mermaid you're thinking of."

Sitting on the flat stern of the houseboat was a Selk, her furry tail dangling in the black water. Her long, brown hair was tangled into uneven dreadlocks, with the hair at her scalp grey-streaked. A plain, colorless garment covered her thick torso, and she crossed muscular arms as she scowled in Arden's direction.

The mermaid's dark eyes bored into Arden for a moment, and she frowned at Okoro on the dock.

"You didn't tell me they were *children*," she said in a gruff voice. "I'm a cabbie, not a nursemaid. That boy looks as though he's never been away from his mother."

Arden clenched his jaw.

Selena put her hand on his shoulder. "This boy is Arden Nakamura of Shido, who is a very capable young man," she told the scowling mermaid. "And the girl, Talulaweyna of the Windrose Tribe, will one day be a leader of her people. They are not children."

Okoro gestured to the Selk. "Arden, Talu, meet Dark Morning, who will be escorting you on your journey north."

"How do you do?" Talu said with a cheerful curtsy.

Dark Morning didn't answer, but instead turned her head and glared into the water.

Okoro picked up the bag of rice again, and Arden noticed several crates at the end of the dock.

"Are these coming with us?" Arden asked.

Okoro nodded as he stepped into the boat with the rice.

Arden hurried over to the crates and picked up one that contained a black pot, a frying pan, and a few other cooking instruments. He groaned as he struggled to lift it. *Are these pans made of lead?* Arden made a few laborious steps toward the boat, trying not to let the Selk see how difficult this was for him.

"Let me get that heavy one for you, son." Okoro lifted the crate out of Arden's arms before he could protest. "There are lighter ones back there."

The brawny captain carried off the crate with no sign of strain. Arden caught a glimpse of the Selk frowning in his direction, her forehead wrinkled.

Humiliated, he turned back to pick up a crate filled with fruit and bread.

Talu, meanwhile, had already boarded the boat, gingerly stepping over the wooden benches and tapping the end of her staff along the sides.

She's trying to figure out how big it is and how it's laid out, Arden realized.

Now she reached up toward the wooden roof, feeling along one of the support beams. "Ah," she said. She pulled a cord and a red curtain fell, dividing the space under the roof into two. "I get the front room!"

Arden carefully stepped from the dock into the boat, feeling it shift and bob under his foot. He put the crate down next to the one Okoro had loaded. Arden grasped the handle of the cooking pot to inspect it and was surprised at its heft—the one piece alone probably weighed twenty pounds.

No wonder the crate had been so heavy—everything was made of iron.

Talu breezed past Arden and made her way to the stern of the boat. Apparently, she had no trouble getting her sea legs.

"Ms. Dark Morning," she said to the Selk, "you have an interesting name. Is there a story behind it?"

The Selk scowled. "How many years old are you?" she demanded.

Talu paused. "Summers or winters?"

"Either, I don't care."

"Hmm." Talu tilted her head in thought. "Well, I was born in early summer, so that's one. And then—"

"Wait," Arden interrupted. "You don't count the first one."

"Huh?"

"You weren't *one* your first summer," Arden explained. "You were zero."

"That doesn't make any sense."

"Never mind." Arden got back on the dock and picked up another bag of rice, relieved to find he could at least handle that. No one seemed to be watching, though.

"I am sixteen summers and fourteen winters!" Talu announced as Arden stepped back onto the boat.

"How do you figure that?" he asked.

"Well, two winters ago was really warm—it never even snowed—so we don't count it."

Arden shook his head and slid the bag of rice under one of the benches. Then he did a doubletake. In the shadows under the bench a shriveled, skeletal leg poked out.

"Uh, guys, I think there's a dead animal under here!"

Dark Morning turned. "Not on my boat."

"It's under here." He nudged the bone with his foot, and to his surprise it drew back.

"Wait—it's alive," he said, peering under the bench.

A second later a skinny paw appeared, then another, and out stepped the ugliest cat Arden had ever seen.

The bony creature was white with a long body, impossibly thin legs, and a tail like a whip. Oversized, bat-like ears protruded unusually low on the sides of its head, and its sunken-in cheeks and narrow muzzle gave it a permanent sneer. Its eyes were slightly slanted and a painfully bright blue.

Arden figured that if you unwrapped one of those mummified cats from ancient Egypt, it would look something like this thing.

Dark Morning spat into the water. "Oh, the cat. He floated downriver a few days ago and won't leave our ships alone."

Talu crouched down, her good eye dancing. "Come here, sweet kitty."

The cat turned its sneering face and prowled toward her.

"Don't touch it!" Arden said.

"Why not?" She smiled as it rubbed against her skirt, and she reached down to stroke its bony back.

"Because I think it might actually be dead."

She tossed her hair. "You are such a strange boy." She scooped the cat into her arms. It fixed one blue eye on Arden and made a low growling sound.

Arden shuddered and went to pick up the last of the crates.

Ryuu and Selena stood on the end of the pier, deep in conversation. Selena looked up as Arden stepped onto the dock and motioned for him to come.

She was the last person he wanted to talk to at the moment, but he went anyway. He looked up at the girl who was identical to his sister, but so unlike her in many ways.

"Arden, I know this isn't what you expected," Selena said. "But your sister would want me to keep you safe."

Arden crossed his arms. "Megan would have believed in me."

Selena sighed. "Regardless," she said. "This is no fool's errand. We need Korvin's knowledge of Vindor's past to find answers regarding this destructive mist, and we do need to make sure the Nomad tribes are safe."

She glanced toward the boat where Talu tried, unsuccessfully, to strike up a casual conversation with the mermaid.

Selena lowered her voice. "The other part is that if there's anyone in this world who may know how to send you back home, it would be Korvin. Tell her everything—and her only. She's the only one you should trust with the information about you crossing worlds. As far as the rest of Vindor is concerned, you're a Tsuru from Shido."

Oh, how Arden wished that were true.

"Here's the letter you'll need to give to the head librarian in N'gozi. Oh, I almost forgot—the Book of Vindor." Selena pulled out the purple tome with the strange hole in its cover. "Technically only the Guardian of Vindor is supposed to write in these, but since this volume contains your sister's notes, I think it would be appropriate for you to document your journey here as well."

Arden took the heavy book from her hands. A *writing assignment,* too. Would the excitement ever end?

Okoro stepped out of the boat onto the dock. "Everything is loaded up. Arden, are you ready to depart?"

Arden exhaled. "Sure."

"Best of journeys to you," Selena said to him. "And if you do come across the mist, please stay away from it."

Arden stepped down into the houseboat and sat on one of the benches beneath the wooden roof. Something white darted out from under the bench, hissing as it went.

"Oh, there you are, kitty." Talu knelt on the floor of the boat. The skeletal cat leapt into her arms and purred. "What a little angel."

"Okay, that thing is definitely not an angel, and we are *not* bringing it with us," Arden said.

Talu cradled the creature like a baby and rubbed its chin. "Who made you the boss? Besides, you try to get rid of him."

"I'm not going to sleep with an undead cat prowling around. Besides, I'm sure it's got a Tim Burton movie to get to."

Talu shook her head, smirking. "It's *almost* like you're using real words."

Suddenly the boat rocked as Dark Morning jumped from the stern and dove into the water, disappearing under its dark surface. She re-emerged a few seconds later, climbing into the bow of the ship. The boat shifted under her weight. Dripping, she took a long pole and tapped at something under the water.

A set of ropes strung along the sides of the boat snapped taut, and the boat jerked forward, seemingly of its own accord.

"What's happening?" Arden leaned over the side of the boat but could see nothing in the opaque water. "How are we moving?"

"Um, *botos*, of course," Talu said. "What did you think?"

"Oh, sure." Arden had no idea what a boto was supposed to be, but apparently this was common knowledge in Vindor.

He glanced back at the dock where Selena, Ryuu, and Okoro shrank into the distance. Then he held on tight as the boat jerked along to join the dozens of other vessels in the congested Blackwater.

Arden hoped this trip would be more exciting than it promised.

chapter 11

River Waters

The engine of the blue Toyota wheezed to life as Megan turned the key for the sixth time.

Finally. She leaned out the window. "Thank you, Orlando."

"No problem, mi amiga. Jumping a car is super easy." He pretended to lick his fingers, then reached under the Toyota's hood to retrieve his cable. "I love electricity."

"Stop," Megan chided. "Bat's watching, and he might try that for real."

"Nah, he knows better." Orlando carefully disconnected his cables from Megan's Toyota and then from his own car. "They have batteries and electricity where he comes from, too."

"No they don't," Bat piped up from the back seat. "I have never seed such things as cars and batter-knees."

Orlando closed the hood with a clank. "What country are you from again?"

Megan quickly put the car in reverse. "We got to get going—thanks again for your help. I owe you big time."

Orlando waved dismissively. "It's nothing. Oh, hey, you wanna get tacos tomorrow for lunch?" He paused. "Both you and Bat, of course."

"That sounds great, only …" If everything went as planned, they should be in Vindor by this afternoon. She had no idea when they'd be back. "It depends on whether we're still around tomorrow."

"Still around? That sounds ominous. You guys like going skydiving or something?"

Megan laughed. "No, I mean whether we're around Mystic. We're not sure of our plans. But if we are, we'd love to join you."

"Okay. Let me know. You guys have fun doing your dangerous activities."

The drive to the bridge took no more than five minutes—the significance of which was not lost on Megan. If only the Toyota had the decency to start the day before, maybe she'd be with Arden right now.

She sighed and pulled into the train station parking lot. The tiny building looked abandoned.

"What are we doing, FriendMegan?"

"It seems that you and Arden switched places near that bridge. I want to see if we can find any clues on how it happened." She looked toward the train station and frowned. "That's strange. It looks like there's somebody …" She let the sentence trail off.

Bat climbed out of the back seat and closed the car door gingerly, using both hands. "Somebody where?"

Megan blinked and shook her head. "Weird—I don't remember what I was about to say. It must not have been important. Let's get over to the bridge."

They crossed the street and picked their way down the grassy incline toward the river. Megan had thought to wear boots today, and they had better traction than her dress shoes the day before.

She stopped by the water, watching where it ran underneath the bridge. Nothing seemed to be out of the ordinary.

Bat stood beside her. "FriendMegan, how do they get the Thillah in the little glasses?"

"The what?"

"The Thillah that does not flicker, in the glass circles."

She thought for a moment. "Oh, you mean light bulbs. That's not Thillah, it's electricity." She saw the next question forming in on his lips. "It's like … lightning," she said. "Only it runs through wires to go wherever we want."

His blue eyes widened. "A someone catched lightning and maked it obey?"

"I guess it is pretty amazing when you put it that way."

"How was such a thing done? With strong magic?"

"No, it's with … science."

"Science," Bat repeated with a tone of hushed awe.

Megan walked along the edge of the river, scanning the grass and mud for anything that might indicate something unusual had happened the day before.

Bat followed. "What about the box with the little man in it?"

"What little man?"

"The one that sings about snake shoes. I seed him in a little box, and he danced and singed."

Megan turned. "What on earth?"

"He singed the 'Blue Snake Shoes' song. And the 'Hug of Burning Love.' He has a white suit with little shiny rocks on it, and when he says, 'Thank you very much,' all the females scream."

She furrowed her brow. "Are you talking about Elvis Presley?"

"Yes, the King of Rocks that Roll. He was in a box, and he danced like *magic*."

"Okay, Orlando was showing you a video. On TV, or on his computer. It's not actually a little man."

"But I *seed* him."

Megan exhaled. "I know. It's not real, though. It's like a photograph of a person that moves. The man is not inside."

"What's a photo-grass?"

"It's like … drawings. Only not." She pointed to where the water went through the tunnel under the car bridge. "You like dark spaces, right? Could you check under there for anything odd?"

"Yes, I look." Bat scrambled eagerly into the shadows.

Megan continued scanning the grass along the bank. Nothing.

"Orlando was seriously showing you Elvis music videos?" she asked after a long pause.

"Oh yes." Bat's voice echoed from the tunnel. "He said it was the Andmerican culture." Bat poked his head out from the shadows. "He teached me his very important Andmerican dance, too—it goes like this."

Bat curled his upper lip, swung one arm in a windmill circle and pivoted his leg wildly. He lost his balance and tumbled onto the bank.

Megan tried to mask her laughter with her glove. "Are you all right?"

"I finded it!" he called.

"Found what?"

"The strange and odd thing that opened the Mirror World."

"What?" Megan rushed over to him, her boots splashing in the water. "What is it?"

Bat pulled an object from the river grass and held it out solemnly.

A crushed Pepsi can.

Megan sighed. It was going to be a long day.

* * *

An hour into the trip and already Arden was bored.

At first, he had been interested in the wide variety of other vessels going up and down the Blackwater—boats of all shapes and sizes, carrying everything from fat fish to rich people hidden behind curtained litters—but the farther upstream they went the fewer other ships there were to watch.

He did notice several other Selk cabbies, most of them mermen, who called out to one another with seal-like shouts. However, none of them called out to Dark Morning, who sat in silence, the breeze barely rippling through her tangled dreadlocks. Even other Selks didn't seem to like her.

Now he leaned over the side of the boat, watching the sunlight reflecting off the coffee-black water. He found it unsettling that he couldn't see anything more than a few inches below the surface.

He managed to get a few glimpses of the mysterious botos that pulled the ship along. He had hoped they were something cool, like Japanese water dragons, but no such luck. The best he could tell they were goofy dolphins, pinkish in color with oddly long snouts. They didn't seem to have any trouble navigating the murky water, and the boat clipped along at a decent speed.

Talu had been quiet during the trip, idling with the brown feather at the end of her staff and chanting something quietly under her breath. Arden wondered what it must be like for her, feeling the boat move under her but unable to see much going by.

Arden watched a small Tsuru village as they passed it, the simple wooden buildings featuring the signature upswept roofs. A handful of samurai stood chatting on the dock, a trainee around his age among them. Arden sighed. *That could have been me.*

Arden eyed the Book of Vindor and the vial of ink. His hands itched to draw. He carefully lifted the book and opened to the first blank page. Surely no one would notice a small doodle.

He dipped a quill into the ink and practiced a few strokes—rough at first, but gradually getting smoother as he learned to control the flow of ink. He sketched out the river village, the samurai on the docks, and the many types of ships he'd seen on the river. He'd almost filled an entire page when his skin prickled.

He looked up to see the ugly, white cat staring at him with unblinking blue eyes.

"What do you want?" Arden asked.

"Rrrrg," the cat sneered.

"Kitty?" Talu called. "There you are! Come here."

The cat whipped around and launched itself onto Talu's red skirt. She cooed and rubbed its creepy nose. Maybe she couldn't tell how ugly the thing was.

The creature's eyes fixated on one of Talu's dangling hoop earrings. He swiped at it, nearly scratching her face.

"Watch out!"

Talu turned toward Arden. "What?"

"That thing almost scratched you."

"He's only playing." She pulled a red ribbon from her wavy black hair and dangled it in front of the thing's shriveled paws. "You're a sweet boy, aren't you, Snow White?"

"Uh, what did you call him?"

"Snow White. That's the name I picked out."

"You do know this is a *boy* cat."

"Yeah. So?"

"Snow White is a princess name. You know, Snow White and the Seven Dwarfs? The fairest of them all?"

Talu frowned, clearly not understanding.

"Okay, I take it you've never heard that story before. Fine. But if I were to name that thing, I'd go for something like Jack Skellington. Or Gollum."

Talu wrinkled her nose. "Ick, that's a gross name."

"Exactly. That's what makes it perfect."

Talu hugged the cat near her face. "Aw, shush. You're hurting Snow White's feelings."

"The cat can't understand what I'm saying."

"Yes he can. And *I*, as a Nomad, would be able to tell."

Arden paused. "Wait, why?"

"You don't *know*?" Talu's mismatched eyes widened, her good eye darting back and forth. "About Nomads and cats?"

He hesitated. Was this something the Tsuru were supposed to know?

Talu sat up straighter. "Long ago," she said with the air of a storyteller, "the women of our grandmothers' generation had mystical connections to all sorts of birds and beasts. We've lost most of it now, but we still maintain a connection to the most mysterious of animals, the cat. We can tell simply by being near them what they're thinking and feeling."

"Wait." Arden raised an eyebrow. "You're a cat psychic?"

"If *psychic* means I can tell you what Snow White is thinking, then yes, I am that. Right now, he's debating whether he should stay here with me where it's comfortable, or whether he should pester Dark Morning for some of those treats she keeps for the botos."

The cat was indeed looking in the Selk's direction.

"On second thought," Talu continued, "she's never given him anything before, so he's probably better off staying here."

As if on cue, the creature butted his sneering face into Talu's empty palm.

"Oh, you'd like me to rub your nose, then?" Talu rubbed her finger along the snout, and the cat closed his eyes halfway, purring. "How about the chin?" More purring.

Suddenly the mummy cat straightened, staring right at Arden with his enormous ears pinned back.

"Oh dear," Talu said.

"What?" Arden shuddered slightly under the cat's intense stare. "What's he thinking now?"

"I'm sorry, but he thinks that you're the most gullible boy he's ever encountered."

Arden sat puzzled for a second, then felt his ears turning red. "Hey ..."

Talu broke into a snorting laugh.

He picked up a cushion from underneath the bench and threw it at her.

The cat dashed off, but Talu only giggled harder. "I had you *going*! You should have heard yourself. 'What's he thinking now, Talu?' You fell for that *way* too easy."

"Now just a minute, I ..." Arden found himself smiling despite himself. "Fine. You got me. But two can play at this game."

"What, a game of wit-strength?" Talu tossed her dark hair. "I seriously doubt you are equipped to battle me, Arden of Shido."

Arden grinned. "I'd watch my back if I were you, Talu of Windrose."

* * *

"I finded it!"

Megan sighed. Bat had found three more soda cans, two glass bottles, a plastic six-pack ring, a bicycle chain, and a waterlogged dictionary. She was growing tired of trying to explain each item, so she'd gently suggested he search through the grass farther away from the river.

"What is it this time?" She glanced at the sun sinking toward the horizon. How could it be getting dark already?

He held out his dark hand, the fingers covered with a grey powder.

"I finded ash."

She turned back to the bank. "Probably from someone smoking a cigarette or something."

"It is enough to cup in my hands," he said.

"Oh, don't touch it—it's gross."

He wiped his hands off on his jeans, leaving grey smears. "FriendMegan, we are not finding a way to Vindor, are we?"

"No." She sat down, the chill from the grass seeping through the fabric of her skirt. "You're sure you don't remember anything about how you got here?"

"No. It is all empty places in my head when I try." He rubbed his fingers together, studying the bit of ash that remained. "How did FriendMegan get in?"

"Huh?"

"You comed all those years ago."

Megan thought back to that moment, so long ago, when she saw Selena standing in a field in her neighborhood. She remembered her heart pounding, her disbelief in the possibility of the moment outweighed only by that wild stab of hope that it could be real.

"I remember," she said. "I just have no idea how to make that happen again."

"Were there passingwords?"

"What?"

"Did you say magic passingwords before?"

Megan closed her eyes, picturing the moment once again. She remembered how desperately unhappy she'd been, how terrified she was to switch schools and meet new classmates and move to a new state—things that now seemed more like an adventure than something to dread. She tried to remember what exactly she'd said before Selena appeared.

She stood and cleared her throat. "I can't do this. I wish I really were in Vindor."

The words felt hollow in her mouth. And besides the dull roar of a distant train, nothing changed.

Megan squeezed her eyes shut, trying to force the feeling. "I don't want to be here anymore. I'm tired of this world. I wish I could escape to Vindor!"

She stood there for a moment, her arms outstretched, then tentatively opened her eyes.

A figure in white stood up on the bridge. But a second glance told her it was only a girl in an oversized coat, clutching a book beneath her arm as she gazed out over the river. A man in a blue sweater passed her, walking a German Shepherd, and farther down the street a kid whizzed by on his bicycle.

Megan sighed and turned to Bat.

He gave her a sad half-smile. "We will find a way. You will see."

Megan folded her arms, and her stomach rumbled. They'd forgotten to eat lunch, and now it was growing dark.

Bat nodded knowingly. "You need pizza."

Megan glanced once more toward the darkening water. "All right, let's go."

chapter 12

Songs of Connecticut

Arden wasn't sure how many hours they'd been traveling upriver—after all, his watch had mysteriously disappeared when he arrived in Vindor. But by his best reckoning, it had been approximately a ridiculously long time. The river narrowed the farther they went, and the dark trees of the forest pressed in closer, some of them with tangled roots that plunged directly into the black water.

The chirring of frogs crescendoed as the sun sank closer to the horizon. Without warning, Dark Morning shouted something toward the black water.

The boat's forward motion stopped abruptly, and Arden felt the current pull it back the way they came.

Dark Morning thumped her furry flippers on the bow of the boat and launched herself into the water. She removed the leather harnesses from the lumpy pink botos.

They splashed away down the river, their tiny pig-like eyes winking happily.

"You're letting them go?" Arden asked.

"They need to hunt," Dark Morning said gruffly.

"But what if they don't come back?"

The Selk patted a leather pouch at her side. "They always come back for their treats. What, have you never traveled with botos, boy?" She yanked on a rope attached to the front of the houseboat and tugged it toward a sandy patch along the bank.

When Arden could see the river bottom through the tea-colored water, he leapt over the side of the houseboat, landing with a splash. He grabbed one of the ropes along the side and tried to help pull it toward the shore. It was far heavier than he expected it to be, and his bare feet sank into the mucky river bottom so that he barely gained traction.

Dark Morning grunted and wriggled onto the shore, the claws on her flippers digging into the sand. Clutching the rope, she pulled the boat shoreward with no help from Arden whatsoever.

"Here," Arden said, struggling onto the beach. "Give me the rope and I'll anchor—"

"Done." Dark Morning tightened the ends of the rope around a leaning tree trunk.

Ugh.

Dark Morning turned and dragged herself back into the dark water, where she disappeared again with hardly a splash.

"So I guess we're docking here for the night?" Arden asked.

"And making dinner," Talu called from the boat. "I just decided that part, because I'm ready for a hot meal. I'll get the pans." Talu turned her back to Arden and rifled through the crates.

"I'll start the fire," Arden announced. He took a couple of steps to where the tiny beach ended and the first thin trees of the dark forest began. He gathered as many loose, dry branches as he could find, bringing an armload back to the center of the beach. He found two exceptionally dry sticks and rubbed them together. The result was surprisingly underwhelming. Even after rigorous rubbing, they were barely warm.

Something fell into the water with a small *plunk* and a quiet *ugh*. Arden looked up to see Talu perched on the side of boat, dangling her feet over the water.

"You okay?" he asked.

"Oh, just dropped a skillet, that's all. I don't think it fell far."

She balanced there for another moment, squinting at the water nervously.

Arden stood. *She can't tell where the water is. She doesn't know how far of a jump it is, or if there are any rocks under her.* "Do you need some help?"

"I've got it." Talu gritted her teeth and slid feet-first into the water. She must have misjudged the depth, since her legs buckled when she hit the mucky bottom, and she went down with a splash. She struggled up, her long skirt soaked all the way to her stomach. Talu shuffled toward the shore. "Ow. Oh, I found the skillet." She leaned down and retrieved the iron pan, then stumbled onto the sand.

Arden saw the piece of driftwood in her path but didn't think of mentioning it until Talu had practically fallen over it. In fact, he had been sitting there, watching her struggle, without being the least bit helpful.

Fail.

"Talu, I'm sorry, I should have—"

"I've got it," Talu said firmly. She put down the pan and bent over to pick up the driftwood.

Water splashed beyond the boat.

"What was that?" she asked.

"Uh, I think that was our Grumpy Neighborhood Mermaid."

Talu suppressed a giggle. "Shh. She'll hear you!"

Arden smirked and turned back to the two dry sticks, rubbing them as intensely as he could. This is how everyone started fires in movies, right? After several minutes, his hands hurt, but the sticks were becoming smooth—and maybe a little warmer.

A burst of light came from Talu's driftwood stack. "Fire's ready," she announced.

It was a good fire, too, with pieces of driftwood precisely stacked and quickly blazing. How'd she light that so fast?

Arden kicked down his own wood pile. Could he not do *anything* right?

Something cold and slimy hit him in the back of the head, then flopped away on the sand.

Another flying object followed, coming from the direction of the river. This one hit Talu. "Ew, what is that?"

"They're fish." He glanced toward the river and dodged one speeding right toward his face. "Dark Morning is throwing fish at us."

"Oh, that's good," Talu said, as though this were a matter of course. "We'll clean the sand off and get them frying." She pulled a small knife from a pouch on her belt.

Moments later fish fillets sizzled in the iron pan. They were a bit scorched on one side—that had been Arden's fault—but the flavor was rather good.

The Selk reappeared from the water and pulled herself onto the sandy shore, holding two fish of her own.

"Here Ms. Morning," Talu said, "the skillet's still hot and we've got room for—"

"Uh, I think she's skipping the cooking step," Arden said.

Talu wrinkled her nose. "Oh."

Arden watched with disgust as the Selk took a bite out of the raw fish, skin and all, a few feet away from him. She paused, pulled out a small pouch and sprinkled something white all over it before taking another bite.

"Uh, is that—?"

"Salt," Dark Morning said between mouthfuls.

Arden watched her add another generous helping onto the next bite. "So … you like salty things?"

Dark Morning spat a bone into the water. "These fish are bland. Everything in this river is tasteless and bland."

"They taste fine to me," Talu whispered.

Arden shrugged. "Maybe she's used to sea water."

They ate quietly, and the growing darkness drew them closer to the firelight. Snow White, the cat, had made an appearance, mostly pacing along the shore and staring out at the river. Occasionally he'd come up to Talu and headbutt her until she petted him, but when she offered him scraps of fish, he turned up his bony nose.

Suddenly Dark Morning looked up at Arden and frowned.

"You, boy, where are you from?"

"Me?" Arden asked, nearly choking on a piece of hot fish.

"Is there another boy here?"

Arden wiped his mouth with the back of his hand. "My name's Arden Nakamura, and I'm from Shido."

Dark Morning shook her head. "No. You smell wrong."

"I'm sorry, what?"

"Every nation has a certain smell to them," Dark Morning said. "Comes from what they eat, where they live. Hard to disguise it. Dembeyans smell of earth and paper. Nomads smell of grass and beasts."

"Beasts?" Talu turned in the Selk's direction. "Oh, probably because of all our horses and goats, I guess."

Dark Morning ignored her. "Tsuru smell of bland water and pickled vegetables, but you, boy—you smell completely strange to me."

"Uh, thanks?"

"Wait, do I really smell like goats?" Talu looked concerned as she sniffed her own shoulder.

"So where are you from?" Dark Morning crossed her arms. "Don't lie to me."

Now what was Arden supposed to do? Selena had told him not to say anything about coming from the real world, but the Selk had put him on the spot.

"Well ... I'm not *exactly* from Vindor," Arden started, not sure what he was going to say next.

Talu gasped. "You mean, you're from Outer Paracosmia?"

"Uh ..."

"Oh, I've always wondered about the lands beyond the mountains!" Talu closed her eyes and sighed. "When I was younger, I wanted to run away and see. What's it like, your land?"

"Definitely different from here."

"What's it called?"

Arden hesitated. "Connecticut."

"Con-nee-cut?"

"Conn-ET-i-cut. Though there's an extra '*c*' in there somewhere."

"An extra sea?" Dark Morning cocked her head. "What makes it extra? Is your land an island?"

"Uh, no," Arden answered, not completely sure what she was talking about. "But it is on the ocean. Well, not actually the ocean, only the Long Island Sound."

"Oh, that sounds magical!" Talu leaned in toward the firelight.

"The Long Island Sound? It … isn't. Trust me."

Talu pulled out a bunch of red grapes from a sack and held a cluster out in his direction. "What does it look like, your land of Conn-eh-tut with the extra sea?"

Arden took the grapes and popped one into his mouth. "It looks like a rectangle with a little nub on the end. I don't know, it's not all that interesting."

"Oh, I get it." Talu smiled gently. "You're homesick and talking about it makes you sad. That's all right, we can talk of other things."

The funny thing was Arden didn't feel homesick at all. He'd almost forgotten his old life existed, even though he'd only been away a day.

They sat watching the fire crackle. Arden idly peeled the thin skin off one of the grapes and rolled it around in his fingers, feeling the slimy membrane underneath.

He remembered something Shonda's mom had once done at a Halloween party, and he got an idea. He grinned and slipped a few grapes into his pocket for later.

Abruptly Talu stood and drew a large circle in the sand with her staff. She kicked a few stones and pieces of driftwood out of the center.

"Time for songs," she announced.

"Uh, what?" Arden asked.

Dark Morning only glared.

"Come on, we've got a fire going, the meal's over, what else are we going to do?" Talu carefully set her staff down outside of the circle. "I go first because I called it. Hmm, I wish I'd brought a tambourine."

Arden shook his head. "Because that's totally a practical thing to pack."

"Well, I guess I'll have to make do." She pulled a long red ribbon from her hair. "All right, so I'm going to sing the story of Tattie Tall Pines, who is my second cousin."

"Wait, you're seriously going to do this?" Arden asked.

"Or maybe my third cousin. What's it called when it's your father's aunt's daughter?"

"You're not really going to sing, are you?"

"And dance." Talu cleared her throat.

Arden braced himself for the imminent awkwardness of having to watch Talu make a fool of herself, and then having to come up with nice, generic comments to say at the end, and …

And then Talu's dance began.

She moved like a flame of fire, as graceful as a willow in the wind—spinning, twirling, stepping, and jumping in a mesmerizing pattern that Arden couldn't follow. Her long, ruffled skirt flowed with her movements, becoming part of the choreography. In her hands the red ribbon sprung to life, swirling and turning back on itself, helping to tell the story.

And all the while Talu's strong alto voice sang something about a girl trying to climb an unclimbable mountain and outsmarting wolves, a bandit, and a griffin on the way.

Even the firelight seemed to flicker in time to her steps and her song.

Talu finished with a graceful twirl and paused, panting, with her arms outstretched to the stars. She held the pose for a moment, and then made a quick curtsy and flumped down into the sand.

Arden wasn't sure what to say. It had been so unlike anything he'd seen before, not at all like the staged folk dances at the cultural center back home, but more real somehow. "Wow, that was …"

"Yeah, I'm a little sloppy still," Talu interrupted. "Truth is, I have trouble, you know, following the other women, so sometimes I make my own stuff up. Plus, there was this stick in the sand I kept tripping over, so that threw me off." She tied the ribbon back into her thick wavy hair. "But the more you practice, the better you become. Well, Dark Morning's turn."

Arden had noticed that the Selk had watched Talu's performance with a stoic expression he couldn't read. Now she frowned again and only grunted in reply.

"All right," Talu said. "It looks like you're up, Arden."

"Me? Um, I don't dance."

Talu's mismatched eyes widened. "At all?"

"At all."

"But what do you do during your village dances? Didn't your father teach you the steps?"

Arden's face darkened. "No, my father never taught me anything." It was the understatement of the century. "Besides, dances in Connecticut are …" He thought of his school's dances with a shudder. "Well, they're lame. I avoid them when I can."

"Well, I guess it would be fine if you just sang. Sing us a song of Conn-et-i-tut!"

"I don't sing, either."

"Can't you do *anything*?" she asked, astonished. Then that mischievous smile played on her lips. "Oh, I get it. You're scared to. Well, in that case, that's fine. I won't make you."

Arden paused. "I'm not scared."

"Sure you are, and it's fine. Besides, I can understand you being intimidated, since my story was so much better. But I can't argue with performance jitters—I used to feel that as a tiny little girl, so I understand."

"I'm not scared."

"Of course you are. If you weren't, you'd be singing right now."

Arden stood. "I'm not going to sing, okay? But I can tell a story."

Talu leaned forward, stroking the skeleton cat. Dark Morning looked up at him, still slightly scowling.

He cleared his throat a few times, more nervous than he expected to be. Now what? After a minute, he launched into the first thing that popped into his head:

Listen, my children, and you shall hear

Of the midnight ride of Paul Revere,

On the eighteenth of April, in Seventy-Five:

Hardly a man is now alive

Who remembers that famous day and year.

His fifth-grade teacher had insisted the class memorize the entire Longfellow poem, all fourteen stanzas of it, saying it would come in useful someday. It looked like she'd been right—though probably not in the way she'd anticipated.

He continued through the story:

… One if by land, and two if by sea;

And I on the opposite shore will be,

Ready to ride and spread the alarm

Through every Middlesex village and farm,

For the country-folk to be up and to arm.

Arden was amazed he still remembered it all—had this really been taking up storage space in his brain? But this time around, it wasn't a list of dry historical facts, but a story, and an interesting one at that.

Talu listened with rapt attention, hugging the white cat to her chest. Even Dark Morning seemed to be listening, shuddering at the lines about the spooky graves on the hill.

Arden was rather enjoying this. He took his time with the descriptive parts of the poem to drag out the suspense, then sped it up when Paul Revere got his signal. He watched for their reactions at the part where the horse moved so fast its hooves ignited sparks on the cobblestone.

Dark Morning leaned forward.

Arden had hit his stride and was disappointed when the poem neared its end. He briefly considered making up another few stanzas about the battle, to make it last longer.

Instead he let the ending swell, trying to give it a dramatic air of prophecy:

> *Through all our history, to the last,*
> *In the hour of darkness and peril and need,*
> *The people will waken and listen to hear*
> *The hurrying hoof-beat of that steed,*
> *And the midnight-message of Paul Revere.*

He let the words linger for a moment before sitting down.

Dark Morning blinked, then went back to her normal scowl, but Talu burst into applause.

"That was fantastic. What a story! Did they win?"

"Did who win?"

"Paul Revere's side—the ones fighting the Red Coats."

"Oh, yeah. It was the Revolutionary War, and we won our independence and became our own country."

"The country of Conn-tet-cut?"

"Well, America." Arden said. "Connecticut is just one part."

"And do you still chase out the Red Coats?"

"Uh, no, we're friends with the British now. We, like, share TV shows and books about wizards. But we're still our own country."

Dark Morning cleared her throat. "What are musket balls?"

And Arden had to explain what a musket was, and how far away England was from America, and why the colonies wanted freedom in the first place. He had to admit—American history *was* fascinating when you paid attention to the people and stories. And no one once asked him for any of those dry dates he'd had to memorize.

Talu stretched out her legs, putting her feet close to the dying fire.

She sighed.

"Have you ever met him?"

"Met who?" Arden asked.

"Paul Revere!"

"Uh, no. He died hundreds of years ago."

Talu sat up straight. "*What?*"

"Yeah, all this stuff happened a long time ago. You didn't think I was talking about things that happened recently, did you?"

"That's such an *old* story. How does anyone remember it?"

He shrugged. "We wrote it down. Why? Doesn't your history go that far back?"

Talu shook her head. "Maybe a few legends, but not true stories. Wow!"

Arden was about to ask how that could be possible when a branch snapped in the woods.

"Shh," Dark Morning hissed. She tensed, looking toward the darkness creeping between the trees beyond the sand. The Selk closed her eyes, sniffed a few times, then turned.

"Clean this up and get back on the boat."

Talu picked up the iron pan and wiped out the crumbs. "I'll take care of the fire," Arden said.

"Leave it." Dark Morning still watched the woods.

"Leave it burning?" Arden asked. "But it could catch—"

"Leave it," she barked.

Arden followed Talu as she picked up her staff and headed in the general direction of the boat. He wondered if she could see where it was. Should he say something? He didn't want to insult her, but she was getting close now and looked like she might run right into the side of it.

Then he got an idea.

"Hey, Talu, do you need a boost?"

"Huh?"

"As in, I'll help you into the boat, so you don't get your skirt all wet. Here." He stepped in front of her and positioned himself beside the houseboat, his feet in the murky water. "Grab onto the side and step into my hands."

"Um, okay." Talu reached out her hand and found the boat's wooden side. She dropped her staff and the pan inside the boat with a heavy *clang*, and stepped toward him, hands still on the rail. He cupped his hands together around her foot and hoisted her in.

"What about you getting wet?" she asked.

"These sandals are straw, and they dry fast," he said. "And—"

He stopped. A pulse of water pushed toward him. A sudden surge of adrenaline rushed through him, and he leapt into the boat, nearly bowling Talu over in the process.

"What's wrong?"

Arden exhaled. "I don't know. I got this feeling like … like there was something coming toward me in the water."

"Hmm. It could have been one of the botos."

"Oh." Arden felt silly. "That's probably it. Only—"

The skeleton cat stared at the water and hissed, its whip-like tail flicking from one side to the other.

Arden shivered. "There aren't, like, alligators in this river, are there?"

"What's an ally-gator?"

"Good, that's the right answer to that question." Arden sat down on a bench. Talu reached up to the roof of the boat and released the red curtains, forming four makeshift walls around them. Talu then reached for the center beam, where a thick curtain fell between them and split the room in two.

"This is my side," she informed him. "You sleep on that side."

Arden reached into a crate and retrieved a straw-stuffed mattress pad and a few blankets. "Where does Dark Morning sleep?"

"I don't know," Talu said from the other side of the curtain. "Do Selks sleep under roofs? They seem like the type who would sleep beneath the stars."

At that moment, the Jack Skellington cat pushed its way through the red curtains and walked across Arden's room, glaring up at him as it passed. "Raaaauw," it said, and then slipped into Talu's room.

"Aww, kitty." she exclaimed.

Arden felt the grapes inside of his pocket and saw his opportunity.

"I wouldn't let that thing sleep in your room if I were you," he said casually, peeling the first grape. "Considering its condition."

"Condition?"

"Yeah. It's like I said when I first saw that thing—he's actually dead."

Talu scoffed from behind the curtain. "Then how is he moving around?"

"He's a zombie—it has a spirit or virus or something that keeps it animated. But his body is dead."

"Zombie? That's obviously not a real thing."

"Suit yourself," Arden said, peeling the thin skin off the second grape. "But you watch—parts of it are going to fall off. Tomorrow morning you'll probably wake up to find a toe, a claw, an eyeball …"

Grinning, he subtly raised the curtain an inch and rolled the two slimy grapes into her room. "Good night!"

chapter 13

Twelve Fathoms Deep

Although the mattress pad wasn't the most comfortable thing he'd ever slept on, Arden found the gentle rocking of the boat soothing. He had probably been asleep for some time when he awoke to growling.

He sat up abruptly, straining his eyes in the darkness. Another growl, and then a dog-like yelp of pain, from somewhere outside.

Arden crawled to the side of the boat and peeked out between the heavy curtains.

There, on the shore, several figures moved near the light of the dying fire. A pack of dog-like creatures with bushy fox tails, but built much heavier than foxes, slunk toward the imposing figure of Dark Morning. The mermaid sat on her thick furry tail as though kneeling in the sand— if one could kneel without knees. She held a long wooden pole out in front of her, daring the dogs to come closer.

Arden tried to shout out a warning as one of the dogs leapt toward the Selk. Fast as lightning, Dark Morning whipped the heavy pole around and sent the creature flying into the dark woods.

Now she spun the pole above her head at an amazing speed. Another dog lunged forward, and with a yelp it splashed into the water. Dark Morning smacked the staff down into the sand, pinning yet another dog, then thrust it back and jabbed one sneaking up from behind.

Several of the remaining fox-dogs regrouped and ran at her at full speed. Dark Morning sliced the pole through the air and took three out in one blow. The rest of the dogs fled whimpering into the woods.

All of this happened in mere seconds.

Arden couldn't believe it. The Selk wielded that staff faster and fiercer than any of the martial arts champions Arden had watched online. She was basically black belt in bōjutsu.

Dark Morning watched the woods, her pole held out at the ready, but the dogs weren't interested in another thrashing. The forest stayed quiet for a long time.

Arden must have dozed off while watching, because suddenly he jerked awake. Dark Morning still kneeled by the few remaining embers of the fire. She did not turn at the sound of the voice.

It was the most beautiful voice Arden had ever heard—a girl's voice, crystal clear but sweet and tremulous as it sang. He quietly made his way to the other side of the boat and looked out to the river but could see no one in the moonlight. Still the mesmerizing song continued:

> *Oh moon of pearl, I see your light,*
> *Dreaming while under this spell.*
> *Oh kindest moon in darkest night*
> *Dreaming while under this spell.*
> *Twelve fathoms deep*
> *I lie asleep*
> *Why am I dreaming of here?*

> *Oh tell me, moon, if you can hear,*
> *Dreaming while under this spell*
> *Is someone here my voice can hear,*
> *Dreaming while under this spell?*

"I can hear you," Arden called. "Where are you?"

At his voice, Talu stirred in the room beside him. From the shore, Dark Morning called, "Who are you talking to?"

"There was a—I heard—"

"You're dreaming. Go to sleep, boy."

Arden looked out over the moonlit river again. Still no one out there. Maybe he *had* been dreaming.

He lay down on his mat again, letting the river current rock him back to sleep. As he drifted off, he heard the voice, much quieter this time:

Twelve fathoms deep

I lie asleep

Who has drawn me here?

* * *

Megan pulled the creaking Toyota back onto Cove's campus, sympathizing with each of its weary groans. She pulled into her parking spot and cut the engine.

"Am I going to Orlando's house again?" Bat asked between bites of pizza crust.

"It's not his house, it's a dorm room, but yes." Megan climbed out of the car, shivering as the cold breeze fluttered through her hair. "Let's hurry up and get out of this cold."

She led him to an old two-story building. The faded lettering above the door read, *Captain Nathaniel B. Palmer Boys Dormitory.*

Bat pulled on the handle, but the door held fast. He tried again, yanking the door harder.

Megan pointed to the electronic card reader that looked out of place against the old stucco. "Didn't Orlando give you an access card?"

He blinked up at her, then went back to yanking on the door handle.

"Hold on. You can't open it without a key, no matter how hard you pull."

The old door clicked and swung open, and Orlando appeared.

"You guys trying to break down the door?" He grinned. "Mr. Bat, glad to see you're still in one piece after your day of dangerous activities."

"We eated pizza," Bat announced. "With bacons on it!"

"America is getting better and better for you, isn't it?" He slapped Bat on the shoulder playfully. "Hey, my door's unlocked—go ahead and warm up inside. I'll be there in a minute."

Bat disappeared down the hall as Orlando stood in the doorway and lowered his voice. "Can I ask you something about our friend here?"

Megan inhaled. "Uh, sure, what's up?"

Orlando frowned at something across the street. "That's weird— who's that?"

Megan turned. She couldn't see anyone on the darkening campus lawn. "Who?"

Orlando blinked. "What?"

"You asked who that was."

"Who?"

"I don't know."

"Weird. Vacation brain must be kicking in. Right on schedule." He shook his head. "Anyway, don't you think it's a bit strange that the school didn't assign Bat an official room? I mean, I'm happy to have him stay with me, but they must have arranged for him to come over here months ago."

"Huh." Megan tried to sound casual. "Strange."

"Also, I know they probably don't celebrate Thanksgiving in Iptukastan or wherever he's from, but why would the school have him arrive over break when everyone's gone? Why not wait until next semester starts?"

Megan shifted from one leg to the other. "Yeah, that is odd, isn't it." She cleared her throat. "So, uh, Bat says you've been listening to music together?"

Orlando grinned sheepishly. "Gotta educate him on the important aspects of American culture."

"You taught him 'Hunk of Burning Love.'"

"Hey, he needs to know the essentials."

Megan gave him a mischievous smile. "I never would have guessed that Orlando Ruiz was such a huge Elvis Presley fan."

"He is *the* King—undisputed." Orlando paused. "Uh ... don't tell Roz, though, please?"

Megan laughed. "Your secret is safe with me." She stopped. "The *safe*. Of course—what was I thinking?"

"Come again?" Orlando asked.

"Oh ... nothing. I gotta go."

Megan turned and practically sprinted back to Grace Palmer.

The key waited for her back in her dorm room, right where it had always been.

* * *

Arden woke up at the first light of dawn. He pulled back the curtain and looked out on the misty river. Talu breathed heavily on the other side of the curtain, but Dark Morning was nowhere to be seen.

Arden sat looking out onto the surface of the dark water for quite some time, wondering about the fox-dogs and the mysterious song it seemed only he could hear. It had all been too real to be a dream.

He watched the reflection of the treetops broken into an ever-shifting, mesmerizing pattern of waves. Suddenly the pattern went wild as the surface of the water bubbled. Arden drew back.

But it was only Dark Morning. She glanced at him briefly before pulling herself onto the boat without a word.

She sat in the bow, wringing out her dripping dreadlocks. Arden stepped toward her quietly, trying not to wake Talu.

"Uh, Ms. Dark Morning?"

The Selk only grunted.

"I saw you, uh, fighting last night."

A nod of acknowledgment.

"What were those things?"

"*Cachorros.*" Dark Morning spat into the water and offered no other explanation.

"Oh. Okay." After an awkward pause, Arden tried to figure out a way to segue into the question. He decided he'd better just ask. "Can you teach me?"

"Teach you what?"

"How to fight like that. With the staff."

The Selk raised an eyebrow. "Who do you need to fight?"

Arden thought of Steadman and his crew. "No one. I want to learn. To know."

"The staff is for protecting yourself and others," she said gruffly. "Not to pick fights."

"Yeah, sure. I know."

Dark Morning lifted her wooden pole from the bottom of the boat, examining its length. "You sure you want to do this?" she asked.

Arden caught his breath. "Yes. Very much."

Dark Morning turned her face away. "Fine."

Suddenly the wooden pole was between Arden's ankles. Dark Morning twisted it skyward, swiping his foot right out from under him. He saw the tree line turn upside down for a mere second before he hit the black water.

Arden struggled to the river's surface and spluttered.

Dark Morning sat in the bow of the boat, unruffled. "First lesson: stay alert. Lesson two tonight."

She turned and gave a sharp whistle, and from somewhere down the river the pink botos came leaping and splashing toward them.

Arden hoisted himself into the boat, dripping but smiling. She was going to teach him. He would learn to fight after all.

A shriek rang out from the curtained room.

"Oh gross, oh gross, I stepped on an eyeball! Oh, poor kitty, your— oh gross, it's all over ..." And then Talu's voice stopped. A second later she burst through the curtain, holding the second peeled grape.

"Arden, where are you?" she demanded.

Arden grinned. "Right here."

She turned his direction and threw the grape at him. It hit him in the shoulder with a splat—not a bad shot.

"You are horrible," she said, laughing, "terrible, the very worst!" She bent over to wipe the smashed grape off her bare foot. "I've got to hand it to you—that was well done."

"So we're even now."

"Even?" Talu tilted her head in his direction. "Absolutely not. I wouldn't sleep easy if I were you."

chapter 14

The Forty-Seven Warnings

Megan stood inside the cafeteria door, watching the rain against the glass and waiting for Bat. Her fingers wrapped around the small item in her pocket, and she smiled.

She had a way back in. Selena herself had given it to her.

"FriendMegan!"

Bat appeared before her in soaking galoshes and a raincoat that he'd put on backward.

"FriendMegan, I am going home today, yes?" he asked, his pale blue eyes earnest.

"Lower your voice." Megan glanced around the cafeteria lobby, but there were hardly any students around—not surprising on a cold, wet morning the weekend before Thanksgiving. She turned.

"Yes," she said. "I had a key all along. I'll explain later—right now we need to eat breakfast and get going."

After a hearty bowl of oatmeal (for Megan) and dry corn flakes with bacon, butter, and raisins (for Bat), the two climbed into the Toyota and headed back to Pequotsepos Bridge.

"Nara and Grakka and Mriv and Krea—they do not know where I am," Bat said as they slipped down the misty slope toward the river. "They will be worriedful for me."

"And I'm worriedful—I mean, worried—for my brother," Megan said. "What do you say we go find them?"

Megan reached into her pocket and pulled out the silver chain. A smooth, violet jewel the size of a walnut dangled from its end. A stray sunbeam broke through the clouds, and on the stone's polished surface dozens of tiny stars glittered.

"The Starstone," Bat whispered.

"Selena gave it to me to remember everyone by, and I've kept it all these years." She clasped the pendant in her hand, good memories rushing over her now. "But when I was in Woodshea, Amadrya used it to open a portal."

"Portal?"

"Like a door in the air. More like a rip, with Vindor on one side and my world on the other. Once it's open, all you must do is step through. Amadrya used the Starstone to create it."

"How?" Bat's blue eyes were wide.

"Like this."

Megan took the Starstone between two fingers, the chain swinging below it. She held it up just higher than her head, where the top of the door would be. Then she let go, just as Amadrya had done all those years ago.

As soon as she pulled her fingers away, the Starstone fell to the ground.

"No." Megan fished it out of the grass and tried again.

Again, the stone fell.

"*No.* This has to work."

Again and again she tried—holding it with one hand, both hands, above her head, at eye level, everything she could think of.

Each time the stone plummeted to the earth.

At last Megan sank into the grass, the back of her throat burning.

"I don't understand." Megan looked at the pendant that lay useless in her lap.

Bat put his hand on her shoulder sympathetically. "Maybe magic is more different in Vindor."

Megan sniffed. A cold breeze blew against her back, bringing with it cold drops of rain.

"Or maybe," Bat said, "The magic is more different in Woodshea than in the rest of Vindor. There are magicful places—maybe we can find one in the Mirror World, and the Starstone will not fail there."

"It's possible." Megan ran her hand through her hair, which grew wetter by the minute. "The problem is that in my world, we seem to have a severe lack of magic."

* * *

As the houseboat continued its way up the black river, Arden read through Megan's entries in the Book of Vindor and studied the hand-drawn map in the back. There sure were a lot of interesting places in Vindor.

And where he was now sure wasn't one of them.

The black water and dense line of trees continued endlessly, with no sign of human settlement anywhere.

He tried sketching the odd way some of the tree roots plunged directly into the river like tentacles. Other trees clung to mossy patches of soil on the bank, leaning over the river as far as they could. The roof of the boat hit some of them as it passed, which made the cat jump and arch its bony back every time.

Arden tried to draw the bizarre botos, but they were hard to catch a glimpse of beneath the black water, so he relied on memory. The drawing ended up looking something like a deformed beluga, which may have been an improvement.

Dark Morning could see the botos well enough that she could redirect them from time to time with her wooden pole. Besides that, she had spent the hours scowling silently—apparently her favorite pastime.

Talu had been quiet for most of the day—well, except for her torrent of giggles when Arden discovered a beetle mysteriously placed in his water canteen. Since then, she'd spent most of the day idling with the brown feather at the end of her staff and repeating some unintelligible poem to herself.

Arden sighed and leaned against one of the beams that supported the roof. The mummy cat glared up at him long enough to give him a dirty look and went back to napping on Talu's lap.

"What did I ever do to you cat, huh?"

Talu looked up in Arden's general direction and stroked the cat between the ears. "Snow White's sweet if you give him a chance, Arden," she said.

"Uh, no, I'm pretty sure that thing has a death wish on me."

As if on cue, the cat raised its head and hissed at him, baring its sharp teeth.

"Did you not hear that?" Arden asked.

"Hear what?"

"Never mind."

"I'm worried about him," Talu said. "I can't get him to eat anything."

"Undead creatures don't need to eat, Talu."

"He's so skinny. What if he's starving?"

"That cat is always staring at the water. I'm guessing he's watching for fish, and I'm sure he's able to catch them. He's survived this long."

"I guess so."

Arden leaned out and idly plunged his hand in the current, watching the tea-brown waves swirl over his fingers. "Dull days aboard the USS— what's the name of this ship again?"

"It's not a ship, it's a boat," Talu said. "And why would it have a name? It's not like it's going to come when you call."

"I dunno, but a ship's got to have a name. Ms. Dark Morning, what is the name of this fine vessel?"

The Selk only rolled her eyes.

Arden turned back to Talu. "Well, then, I guess it's up to me." He thought for a moment, then grinned. "I hereby christen this ship the *Bow to Your Sensei*. Get it?"

Talu frowned.

"*Bow*, like bowing to a teacher, but also as in the bow of a ship," Arden explained. "It's clever."

She shook her head. "You're very bored, aren't you?"

"You have no idea."

Talu ran her hand through her thick wavy hair. "Well, then tell me another story from Conny-tet-ut."

And so Arden told her stories about the Pilgrims, Sacajawea, the Underground Railroad, Sitting Bull, and whatever else popped into his memory. A disorganized history, for sure, but it was fun to tell, and it kept Talu in rapt attention.

And he glanced over his shoulder once or twice and saw Dark Morning leaning in, listening intently, though both times she quickly went back to correcting the botos.

"Tell me another one," Talu said after Arden finished the story of the Boston Tea Party.

"My brain is mush." Arden leaned back on the beam. "It's your turn to tell me a story about your people."

And so Talu launched into a long tale involving complicated sub-groups of the Nomads—people Arden couldn't quite keep straight. Windrose was one of the groups, but there were also the Wolfsbane tribe, the Blackmares, the Wildermusic tribe, and the People of the Fire Dance. Some half-tribes that had splintered off were thrown in, too, for good measure.

One theme was clear, though—the Nomads fought with each other *a lot*.

"Wait, hold up," Arden said at one point. "You're saying this chief led an armed raid against the Yellow Rock Tribe because the messenger forgot to wear shoes?"

"He didn't forget his shoes," Talu explained patiently. "He was *barefoot*."

"And the difference is …?"

"The Yellow Rock think shoes create an unnatural separation from the earth, so they won't cover their feet, except in deep snow. But the Brown Owl People think of bare feet as being disrespectful, so when they saw the messenger without shoes, they took it as the deepest insult."

"And so they launched an attack, no questions asked," Arden said.

Talu sighed. "That's the way it works, most of the time."

"So the Nomads spend all of their time getting offended and mad about random things."

"No, they're specific things." Talu closed her eyes and recited:

> *Fire People love horses above all;*
> *Do not refuse one as a gift.*
> *But goats they hate,*
> *Do not accept one when offered.*
> *The Yellow Rock abhor covered feet,*
> *Brown Owl People, uncovered.*
> *Brown Owl People also distrust smiles;*
> *Do not show your teeth when speaking.*
> *Wolfsbane consider plants a sign of weakness,*
> *Do not offer them berries or grain.*
> *The Blackmares—*

"How long does this list go on?" Arden interrupted.

"There are forty-seven warnings in all. But …" Talu swallowed. "I only know thirty-nine of them. I stopped learning them because I didn't think I'd ever need them."

"Need them?"

Talu touched the brown-and-white feather on the end of her staff. "All Peace Talkers have to know them, or they could end up in a dangerous situation."

"Wait—so what exactly is this Peace Talker job?"

"Talkers are there to mediate between feuding tribes. Sometimes they try to stop attacks before they happen." Talu's voice softened. "It doesn't always go well. I had a great uncle who was killed when one of his talks went badly."

"And after that you still want to do it?"

"Yes. Because it's *important*." Talu's good eye darted back and forth with conviction. "We spend so much time fighting and stealing from one another, and it's stupid. People get hurt. Tribes go cold and hungry during the winter. And all because people rush into a fight without stopping to listen or think first. Peace Talkers imagine a better way of life, a way where tribes help each other as brothers, not fight like children. Peace talking has been my dream since I was little. I cried for a whole week when my aunt told me no one would listen to me because—" She stopped abruptly, her face reddening.

"—because you're a girl?" Arden suggested.

Talu looked puzzled. "Why would that matter? Tribes with chieftainesses often prefer women Talkers. They don't always listen to them, but they say they like them better."

"Well, then why not you?"

Talu lowered her head, her shoulders slouching a bit. "Well, because, most of the tribes would see me and think that I'm ... that I don't do my fair share of work. I *do* though." She exhaled. "I work as hard as anyone else. They won't let me watch after the goats in the field, but I keep them washed and do double the work around the hearth-fire. And I watch the littles and tell them stories to keep them out of their mothers' way. And I carry the water and light the fires. I'm not a parasite. I'm not useless."

"Whoa now. Who said you were useless?"

Talu didn't answer, but Arden recalled her horrible grandmother. Maybe the rest of the Windrose people shared her sentiments.

He frowned. "Well, your uncle thinks you can do it."

"And so does Selena," Talu said quietly. "Selena believes in me— that's something."

"See, there you go," Arden said. He looked out onto the dark river. *Must be nice*, he silently added.

chapter 15

Don't Run

"So you guys hear about that nor'easter heading this way?" Orlando tipped a bottle of bright red habanero sauce into his bowl of salsa, sampled the mixture with the edge of a chip, and then poured some more sauce in.

"What's a norr-eater?" Bat tried to scoop salsa up with a broken chip, dripping most of it on the table in the process. Megan pushed a paper napkin in his direction.

"Big storm," Orlando said. "Like a cold-weather hurricane. Sometimes a blizzard even comes in."

Bat's eyes narrowed. "What kind of a lizard?"

"Oh, a real big one." Orlando winked at Megan. "Godzilla-sized. Comes on shore, stomps on hot dog stands, eats up boats."

Megan smiled. "He's teasing you, Bat. A blizzard is a snow storm."

Bat sighed in relief.

"Good to see you smiling, mi amiga." Orlando topped off his bowl with more habanero sauce. "That's the first time all day. The rain getting you down?"

"Something like that." She felt the weight of the Starstone still in her pocket, heavy and useless.

"Well, here comes something sure to cheer you up." Orlando leaned back as two waiters set a series of brightly decorated plates on the table, piled high with yellow rice, black beans, and plenty of crispy tacos.

Orlando thanked the waiters in Spanish and turned to Bat. "Mr. Shahck-re-ahck, I know you liked pizza, but here's something even better. Behold: before you are the best tacos on the planet. Dig in."

Bat took his words literally, and Megan tried not to watch.

"The best tacos on the planet, huh?" she asked.

"Oh yes," Orlando said between mouthfuls. "This place is little, but legit."

"Better than what your family makes?"

"Oh. We're Puerto Rican, not Mexican."

Heat rose to Megan's face over her blunder, but Orlando's grin put her at ease.

"Honestly, we're not much good at tacos, but my *abuelita* can make rice and beans that will make you weep with joy."

"Tacos!" Bat lifted his head up from his nearly-empty plate. "I love tacos!"

"Of course you love tacos," Orlando said. "Everyone loves tacos. Everyone except bad people, like politicians and supervillains."

"Supper villain?" Bat asked.

"You know, the Joker and Dr. Octopus. Lex Luthor is particularly known for his dislike of Mexican fare."

"He doesn't read comic books, Orlando—you're completely confusing him."

Orlando feigned concern. "Then as Bat's American Cultural Ambassador, I have failed. We must fill this void right away."

"What is a supper villain?" Bat asked. "Does he steal food?"

"No, even worse, if you can believe it. Supervillains plot the destruction of the whole world. They'll blow up the city, send a meteor crashing into the planet, press the doomsday button, all so they can get their way. But don't worry, Batman or Superman or Spiderman always stops them."

"Oh, like LadySelena."

Orlando wrinkled his forehead. "Who?"

"Never mind." Megan turned to Bat. "These are people from stories, from fables. They're not real. You don't have to worry."

The rain outside the window tapered off as they finished their meal. By the time they paid the tab, sunlight had broken through the ceiling of grey.

Megan excused herself to go to the bathroom. When she finished and went out into the parking lot, Bat and Orlando were standing by the car and Megan managed to catch the tail end of their conversation as she approached.

"So," Orlando was saying, "are you two a thing?"

"Oh yes," Bat replied.

"No," Megan said quickly. "We definitely aren't."

Bat looked up, confused. "I am a thing, and FriendMegan is a thing also."

"No Bat, he's asking if you and I are, you know, romantically interested." She turned to Orlando, reddening. "We're just old friends."

"Oh!" Bat seemed embarrassed, too. "No, no. FriendMegan and I are never in love. I am married. To not-Megan."

Megan almost dropped her purse. "What?"

"You're *married*?" Orlando asked.

"Yes, very married. You are not?"

"Man, I'm working on it as much as a poor college student can, but wow. What does your wife think about you coming over to America without her?"

"She doesn't know where I am," Bat said.

"Okay," Megan interrupted, sensing the conversation spiraling out of control. "I think she might not know where in the U.S. he currently is—I mean, he just got here, but she knows he's gone."

"No, she—" Bat quieted at Megan's sharp look. "Oh, I meaned, yes. What FriendMegan said. I get in the car now."

* * *

Beaches along the Blackwater's banks were harder to come by the farther up the river they went. Dark Morning found one at the end of a narrow U-shaped inlet that was too small for the *Sensei* to fit into. She fastened the houseboat to a tree some distance away, and Arden and Talu had to pick their way along the woody shore before they reached the sandy clearing.

The sun dipped toward the tree line, casting long shadows between trunks and sparkling on the water. Dark Morning swam out into the river and disappeared, probably looking for fish.

The two gathered firewood, and Arden watched Talu to find out her secret to getting a fire set up so quickly. Turns out she had a flint and iron in her bag. A few quick strikes of the stone against the iron ring and she had a spark going in no time.

Using a flint was kind of cheating in Arden's opinion, but he had to admit it was far more effective than rubbing sticks together.

Arden sat by the fire for a while after that, studying the way Talu had used dry leaves and bits of grass as tinder first, surrounding those with twig kindling, and then setting the bigger logs in a teepee shape over the whole. It worked beautifully.

Several moments passed before he realized Talu was nowhere in sight. He stood and looked toward the darkening woods. A narrow path cut between the trees, the grass and ferns worn away.

Wonder what kind of animal made that trail, he thought. He stepped cautiously into the woods, his senses alert.

"Talu?"

He followed the path a little farther.

"Talu, are you in here?"

He spied her up ahead, standing on her tiptoes and reaching toward the branches of an oak tree.

"What are you doing?" He came up beside her and peered into the dense branches.

"Snow White got up in this tree and I think he's stuck. Do you see where he went?"

"He's still back at the boat, Talu. He never goes far from the water. Look, we probably shouldn't be—"

The skin prickled at the back of his neck. He turned to spot a bit of movement beside a distant bush. Twenty feet up the path, a large, red-brown creature crouched, its yellow eyes fixed on them.

Arden grabbed Talu's arm, and whispered, "Cougar."

"*What?*" Talu's exclamation startled the big cat, which sat up, watching them now with curiosity.

It's sizing us up, Arden thought, his stomach going cold. *Deciding if we're worth eating.*

"Hey! Hey, get out of here, you big dumb cat!" Arden shouted, lunging forward a step. The predator turned its yellow eyes to him. Arden picked up a fallen tree branch, his hand trembling, and threw it toward the cougar. "Get out of here!"

Talu didn't speak or move, but Arden heard her gasping as she inhaled, much too fast.

Heart pounding, Arden desperately tried to remember the hiking safety tips he'd read about wild animal encounters. *Make loud noises. Make yourself appear bigger and more threatening than you are. Don't turn your back and run—that sets off its prey drive.*

Arden threw another branch and waved his arms like a crazy man. The cougar yawned nervously, displaying its long, lethal teeth.

"Talu, don't run." Arden took a step backward, praying this would work. "Just back up, make noise, try to scare it off. Whatever you do, *don't run.*"

Talu took a trembling step backward. Arden found a rock and threw it. The big cat glanced away, looking back up the path the way it had come.

At that moment, Talu screamed, turned, and ran for her life.

"No!" Arden shouted.

The cougar's eyes locked on her. It crouched again, raised its back haunches, and suddenly sprang forward, covering six feet in the leap.

Arden turned and scrambled toward the beach, his heart pounding in his ears. He could hear the huge cat land heavily in the dirt behind him, gaining on them swiftly.

Talu ran a few strides ahead, almost crying as she stumbled over roots and fallen branches. Arden's bare feet slipped on the mossy ground.

They reached the beach, kicking up sand. Arden glanced backward.

The cougar took another huge bound, its heavy brown paws landing close behind them.

One more leap and I'm done.

Talu sprinted toward the river, and Arden followed, desperate to reach it in time. He jumped over the campfire, then kicked his left foot back into the flames. His foot flung a burning log into the cat's face, and it let out a guttural scream.

Arden didn't hesitate, plunging into the dark water seconds after Talu did. By the time he was in up to his knees, the heavy water had already slowed him down. What had he been thinking? He realized in a panic that reaching the river didn't save them—in fact, it made their situation worse.

He glanced behind them and saw the cougar snarl, its huge teeth bared. It launched itself into the water and landed with a splash, then paddled toward them effortlessly.

He can swim.

There was no way they could make it to other side of the river in time. And if they somehow could reach the boat, the cougar could follow them into it.

Arden was in up to his chest now, swimming frantically. Talu flailed beside him, struggling to keep her head above the water. The huge cat was so close that Arden could hear it panting as it swam.

I am going to die.

Suddenly the cougar gave a chilling scream, splashing wildly. Arden continued swimming as fast as he could, then glanced back.

The cougar thrashed in the black water, flailing its huge paws. Before Arden could process what was happening, Dark Morning burst up out of the murky waves behind the cat. She looped her arms around its neck and flipped it onto its back. Arden got a glimpse of a knife handle plunged into the cat's underbelly before it disappeared under the water headfirst, its powerful back haunches kicking violently.

Talu gasped for breath. "What's happening?"

"Get on the boat!" Arden reached his arm out, clumsily grasping the side of the wooden ship. He dragged himself up and over the side, his clothes heavy and his limbs exhausted. As soon as his left foot touched the wood, he felt a searing pain, but he ignored it. He reached over the side of the boat and pulled Talu in as well.

"Where is it?" Talu's eye darted frantically toward the water.

"Dark Morning dragged it down with her. Why did you run?"

"Is she okay?"

The surface of the water bubbled and convulsed where Dark Morning and the cat went down. Arden couldn't see anything through the opaque water, but he doubted with that cougar's huge claws and teeth that the Selk would survive this. His stomach churned.

"We gotta get out of here or we're all dead."

He grabbed the rope that anchored the boat to the shore. If he could free the boat, the current might carry them away from danger. But he had no time to get on shore to untie it from the tree.

"Give me your knife," he ordered.

She fumbled with her pouch, her hands shaking. He grabbed the small knife and sawed the rope. The thick fibers hardly responded to the blade.

"Why did you have to run?" he barked.

"I—I'm sorry …"

Time was running out, but the blade couldn't cut through even the first coil. "You *never* run from a big predator—are you stupid? What's the use of even bringing you along if you're going to get us all killed?"

Talu cringed, drawing back as though he'd struck her.

Suddenly a figure burst up from the surface of the water.

Dark Morning.

She had two bleeding scratches stretching from her collarbone to her left arm, but they weren't deep. The cougar was nowhere to be seen.

"Where is it?" Arden yelled.

"Drowned," Dark Morning said flatly. She swam toward the boat and hoisted herself in.

Arden stared at her, dumbfounded. Dark Morning had taken down a cougar with nothing but a knife and her bare hands. "But how?"

The Selk wrung the water out of her sopping dreadlocks. "It was young. And small, as they go."

Something red-brown moved slightly under the water near the beach and Arden tensed. A moment later, the limp body of the cougar partially appeared on the sand. The black tip of its tail floated aimlessly on the current.

"It was young." Dark Morning's voice sounded husky, like she was about to cry.

Arden exhaled. Suddenly the pain across the bottom of his left foot nearly overwhelmed him. He threw himself down on a bench and pulled his foot toward him.

The arch of his foot was bright red and hurt something terrible.

Talu turned. "What's wrong?"

"My foot. I burned it when I kicked firewood at the cougar." Arden drew in a hissing breath. "I think it's bad."

"Let me see." Talu kneeled and put her good eye right near the sole of his foot. She reached out and brushed it gently with her finger. Pain shot over his skin so intensely that Arden almost kicked her in the face as a reflex.

"The burn's not bad," she said. "We'll get it in some water."

Dark Morning, meanwhile, stared at the limp body of the cougar washed up on the beach. A beautiful animal, tawny and well-proportioned, it now appeared serene and sad. Arden almost felt sorry for it—though far better it be dead than any of them.

"Should we leave it there?" he asked.

The Selk didn't answer, still watching the lifeless animal.

Arden grimaced as Talu's skirt brushed against his foot, but as soon as he dipped it into the bucket of cool water she set down, he felt immense relief.

"It's so still," the Selk muttered. "So still."

Arden repeated the question. "Are we going to leave it there?"

She looked at him, her expression almost afraid. "No, don't let the fish eat it. I'll bury it in the sand. I'll bury it where the little fish can't eat it. Not the little fish."

Dark Morning slid into the black water, muttering about the little fish as she swam toward shore.

chapter 16

The Bandit Queen

When Orlando dropped them off on campus, Megan led Bat to the campus library. A bitterly cold wind picked up as they approached the sagging white building, and Megan pulled Bat through the creaking doors.

The Edmund Fanning Library had originally been a home, built in the 1700s and restored several times before being converted to the school library. The cramped lobby had once been the home's foyer, and an oil portrait of a sea captain hung beside the makeshift circulation desk.

Megan stepped into the first room down the narrow hall. Rows of rickety shelves, heavy with books, took up most of what must have once been a formal dining room. In the middle of the room stood a couple of vacant tables where students could work.

Megan chose a spot where she could listen for the front door. Satisfied that they were alone and out of earshot of anyone, she turned to Bat.

"You're *married*? When did this happen?"

"Oh, years ago. We stealed Nara and all her brothers from the Pit. She was so, so thin with hunger, but she helped all the injuried right away, always asking to do more. She is the cleverest of all the goblins. She finded new ways to sneak around Masters, learning their passingwords and finding her way through their secret tunnels without light so they never seed her. She finded the smallest goblins, and the forgotten ones, and bringed them all back. Nara is bravest and cleverest and—"

The library door creaked open and shut again. Megan held up her hand to quiet Bat and waited as someone clomped down the hall.

A figure appeared in the room's narrow doorway—a petite girl in huge rubber boots.

"Oh … is this room taken?" She sounded so disappointed that Megan quickly motioned her in.

"No, you're fine. There's plenty of space. We were just leaving."

The girl's face fell. "I promise I won't bother you."

"No, that's not what I meant—please come in." Megan motioned to the far end of the table.

The girl sniffled and took her seat, avoiding eye contact.

Megan realized the girl wasn't quite as tiny as she seemed—she was only slightly shorter than average. But all her clothes dwarfed her, from her clunky boots to her baggy jeans to the sweater that hung down almost past her thighs. Over her head she wore a knitted red toboggan cap that completely covered her hair. She sat in the chair and laid an enormous leather book on the table. Pushing her large glasses up on her deep brown face, the girl pulled out a pen and began writing.

Bat stared at the girl a moment, his eyes wide. Megan was about to chide him when he blinked and looked away, apparently losing interest.

Megan wondered who this lonely student was, stuck on campus during Thanksgiving week. She turned back to Bat. "Keep your voice down. So you and Nara got married?"

"Yes," Bat whispered. "She is the Bandit Queen, and all of Ipktu loves her. I love her the very most, though." His forehead creased. "She does not know where I am. I am worriedful for her. I do not want her to be sad and full of scared for me."

"I'm sorry, Bat. I'm doing everything I know how. It's not like there's a book out there on the subject."

She paused. If Paracosmia had existed for as long as humans had been dreaming up worlds, surely she wasn't the only person in history to have ever traveled there. Maybe someone out there had, too.

And maybe someone else wouldn't have kept quiet as she had. They'd have wanted to tell someone—at least share their story online.

Megan pushed back her chair and stood.

"FriendMegan?"

"I had an idea. I'm going to Google it."

* * *

The evening grew darker as the sun set behind the trees, and a chorus of frogs took up chirring.

"Here," Talu said quietly. "Put this on your foot."

"Uh, that's a potato."

"I know. Put it on your burn."

Arden took the potato slice from her hand. He pressed the white flesh against his foot and immediately felt relief. "Wow, that actually works."

Talu turned and looked out toward the beach. Snow White slunk into her lap, and she stroked him absently.

"Are you okay, Talu?"

She ignored the question. "What's she doing out there?"

Arden squinted toward the beach. "Still burying it. She's been at it for almost an hour now."

"She probably doesn't want it to attract larger animals."

Arden frowned. "Maybe. But she seems to be putting a lot of care into it."

The Selk had, in fact, dug a grave in the sand, using only her hands and a small shovel. He had watched her chant something as she placed the knife and several fish in the hole with the big cat's body. At this point she had mostly filled in the grave, and now placed stones and charred branches from the dying fire over it. It seemed very much like a superstitious ritual or a funeral.

"I'm sorry about your foot," Talu said quietly.

Arden readjusted the soothing potato. "I stuck it right in the fire, but it only seems like the part that touched the log got burned. I don't know what I was thinking."

"You probably saved our lives." Talu swallowed. "Those few seconds the fire slowed it down—it would have made a big difference." Suddenly she let out a sob.

"Talu?"

"I'm so, so sorry. You're right, I *was* stupid." She hid her face in her hands. "I shouldn't have run—I almost got us all killed. I don't mean to be a burden to everyone. I'm not *trying* to be useless."

"Whoa." Arden straightened. "Who said you were useless?"

Talu lifted her head, her teary eye flitting over him.

And suddenly he remembered yelling at her. His heart sank. What exactly had he said?

"Talu—whatever I said, I didn't mean it. I was freaking out and in pain, and I would never have said that to you, but—" He fumbled and sensed that he was making it worse. "It's just that … I'm sorry. I shouldn't have said it."

"It's fine. I forgive you." But the heaviness in her voice had not changed.

Arden couldn't unsay the words, couldn't undo what Talu heard in them. Whatever he had said, she had believed that it was true.

I probably sounded like her evil grandmother. "I'm so sorry," he said again, knowing that it wouldn't help.

"It's fine." She attempted a smile. "Get a good night's sleep."

Arden lay awake for a long time, staring at the dim outline of the boat's ceiling, trying to process everything that had happened that evening. He could barely make out Talu's breathing through their curtain wall, and he thought he heard Dark Morning on the shore, shoveling sand back into the cougar grave.

Then suddenly his makeshift room filled with music—the crystal voice from the night before.

> *Twelve fathoms deep*
>
> *I lie asleep*
>
> *Who has drawn me here?*
>
> *They call me Moriana,*
>
> *Who draws my spirit here?*

Arden crept over to the curtains facing the shore and peaked out. He could see Dark Morning still guarding the grave, paying no attention to the voice. *She can't hear it,* Arden thought. *Talu can't either.*

Then he noticed movement on the opposite shore. Silhouetted in the moonlight sat the graceful figure of a long-haired mermaid. *It's her—the girl I saw at the cliffs.* He held his breath, afraid of scaring her away.

> *They call me Moriana,*
>
> *Who draws my spirit here?*

Slowly the mermaid turned her head toward him. He couldn't make out the face in the darkness, but he was sure she looked right at him. His heart leapt.

Before he could make a sound, she dove into the water and was gone.

* * *

Megan leaned back in her dorm chair and rubbed her tired eyes. She'd spent half of yesterday and all that morning searching the internet for something, anything about people crossing dimensions.

But she'd only found New Age pseudoscience websites, *Wrinkle in Time* fan fiction, and a step-by-step "transcendence" guide that at the end required you to order a dietary supplement.

She sighed. The most promising thing she'd come across was some sort of wormhole theory—which, given the unlikelihood of finding a wormhole in Mystic, Connecticut, seemed less than practical.

After all these hours, she hadn't seen so much as a tweet from someone who experienced anything like Paracosmia.

Megan glanced at the clock—already two in the afternoon. Perhaps the campus library would still be open. The Edmund Fanning was centuries old—maybe it had a room of old, weird books somewhere that had information that the internet didn't.

So that was her plan—hoping for a room of old, weird books. But it was the only plan she had, so she put on her coat and headed across campus.

Megan entered the musty old building and made her way down the rickety hall. She happened to glance into the first reading room as she passed. There, under the stern portrait of an old Puritan, sat the girl in the red toboggan cap and oversized clothing. Books of all sizes lay on the table around her, the piles reaching above her head. The girl had her nose buried in a particularly dusty tome, but she happened to look up and meet eyes with Megan.

Immediately the girl looked away, clearly embarrassed.

Megan stopped. "Hey, are you here for Thanksgiving too?"

The girl in the red cap fidgeted with her large glasses, glancing up for only a second. "Yeah."

Megan hesitated, then stepped into the room. "I live in Grace Palmer, second floor. Are you in Stanton dorm?"

"No, I live in Grace Palmer too." The girl shifted in her extra-large pink sweater.

"Really? I've never seen you around before."

"I guess I'm not that memorable."

Megan sat down at the table across from her. "That's not what I meant at all. My name's Megan."

The girl peered up from behind her glasses. "I'm Penny."

"It's good to meet you." Megan smiled warmly. "Hey, I've got to go work on, uh, a research project, but my friends and I are here all week. If you see us in the cafeteria, please come over and join us any time."

The hint of a smile played on Penny's thin lips. "Thanks. I might do that."

chapter 17

Unfit to Train

Arden awoke to a splash of cold water in his face. He spluttered and sat up, squinting in the dim light of early dawn.

Dark Morning scowled up at him from the water, her arms hooked over the side of the boat. "Get up," she ordered.

"Huh?"

"Did you want to learn how to fight, or not?"

Arden rubbed his eyes. "Yeah."

"Then get up."

Arden stood just as Dark Morning let go of the side of the boat and dropped into the water. He stumbled as the boat lurched with the change of weight, landing heavily on his left foot. Fiery pain shot up from the burn on his sole.

He hissed through his teeth, trying hard not to cry out. He wrapped another strip of cloth over the burn, hopped over the side of the boat and waded toward the shore.

Arden shuddered as he stepped onto the beach. Where exactly had Dark Morning buried the cougar? And were there live ones still lurking in the dark woods behind him?

"Here." Dark Morning tossed a bamboo pole at him, and Arden managed to catch it.

The Selk held her own staff out at an angle toward him. "Strike my staff."

Arden swung his pole, but before he could make contact the Selk moved her staff two inches out of the way. He stepped closer and tried again, barely missing. He clenched his fists around the pole.

Dark Morning held her staff out again, and Arden tried to strike it once more. The Selk dodged again, and then thrust her staff at Arden, lodging it in the small space between his wrist and his pole. She forced it down, twisting his arm and upsetting his balance. He landed face-first into the sand.

"Get up," she ordered.

Arden spat sand out of his mouth and got back on his feet.

"Now, block." The Selk swung her pole down at him.

Arden tried to swat it away but got his fingers smacked instead. But Dark Morning didn't stop. The blows came one after another. Some he managed to deflect with his pole, others stung him in the fingers or knee or foot. And even though he was tired, the Selk kept swinging.

Suddenly Arden recalled the alley behind the Wharton gym. He could feel Steadman's knee in his stomach, hear the jeers of Jay and Tyler as he curled up into a ball, trying to make himself as small as possible as the kicks and punches kept coming.

A tremor of rage moved up Arden's spine, and suddenly he lost control. "Stop!" he screamed. He swung his pole as hard as he could right at Steadman's face.

Only it wasn't Steadman. Dark Morning dodged the heavy blow aimed at her head and smacked the bamboo pole right out of Arden's hands.

She then picked up the pole and snapped it cleanly in half, tossing the pieces at Arden's feet.

"You are not fit to train." She turned to the black river and slid into the water, leaving Arden on the beach alone.

He sank into the sand, and a hot tear that he couldn't stop rolled down his cheek.

It wasn't fair.

Dark Morning should have been teaching him, not tormenting him. Not making him feel that terrifying powerlessness he'd become so familiar with. She'd pushed him too far.

He watched the sun rising over the black river and the tangled trees. The houseboat bobbed slightly in the current.

Talu had probably gotten up by now. Probably fussing over that silly cat. Probably feeling terrible because of whatever he had said last night when he freaked out.

What if Dark Morning was right, and he wasn't fit to train or to be a hero?

Maybe if he were stronger, he'd be the kid who lashed out at people weaker than him whenever he got mad. He didn't want to think about that.

He exhaled, blowing the tips of his red-brown bangs out of his face. He hoped they were close to that stupid library so he could find Korvin— and get out of here before he made anything else worse.

* * *

Megan shrugged off her peacoat and collapsed on her bed. Four hours of sorting through dusty old books, and not a scrap of useful information to show for it. Not even a hint. Every path she tried to follow into Vindor lead to a dead end.

A muted electric guitar riff played from the other side of the room.

Arden's phone.

She dove toward the red backpack and grabbed it. "Hello?" she asked breathlessly.

For a split second she had the wild hope it would be Arden on the other end. But it was Mom.

"Oh, Megan, hi. I hoped I'd be able to catch one of you before the reception cuts out completely. Is Arden there?"

"Uh, I'm not exactly one hundred percent sure where he is at the moment ..." Megan bit her lip.

"That's okay, I know you two are busy with all the camping stuff. Is he having a good time?"

"Oh, I think he's having quite the adventure." Megan winced. She hated fudging this way—but what was she supposed to tell Mom? That her son was trapped in an alternate dimension?

"Good." Mom sounded genuinely relieved. "I hate that we're split up over Thanksgiving, but I hoped this whole camping opportunity would be good for Arden. I think—" She lowered her voice. "I think some of the boys at school are giving him a rough time, though I'm hearing that from the faculty and not from him."

"Like he's being bullied?" Megan pressed the phone closer to her ear. "That's awful."

"I worry about him sometimes. He keeps things bottled up, and he won't talk—though he has a sudden interest in taking martial arts classes."

"He needs to protect himself?"

"I don't know." Mom sighed. "I would hope if they were actually hurting him I would know. But I'm concerned that he's less interested in learning defense and may be keener on offense."

He's going to try to join the war, Megan thought. *Please don't let him get himself hurt.*

"Anyway," Mom continued, "I hope this time away is good for your brother and gives him a new perspective. I know you've probably got limited phone battery, so I'll save the rest of my questions for when you come back. I just wanted to check in. I love you, Megan. Tell Arden I love him too."

Megan blinked away a tear. "I will as soon as I get the chance."

* * *

Travel that morning was quiet, with little sound except the whistles of birds from the forest and the lapping of waves against the creaking boat.

Dark Morning sat at the front as usual, scowling—also as usual. Talu had gone back to fiddling with the brown feather on the end of her staff while chanting under her breath, apparently trying to remember all the stuff that Nomads would fight each other over.

Arden found himself drawing in the Book of Vindor again. His "no one will notice one little doodle" had turned into at least three pages of sketches—of unusual trees, of the botos, of the fish he glimpsed beneath the opaque black water, and even a few sketches of Talu's wavy hair and

Dark Morning's clawed tail. He doodled absent-mindedly and was almost surprised to see he had finished a drawing of the cougar, its eyes staring up from the page, intense and almost sad.

He glanced up to see another set of feline eyes staring at him with the same predatory focus. They hadn't been there a second before.

"You creepy ghost cat—stop haunting our boat."

Snow White didn't blink. A shriveled paw shot out and snagged something in the binding of the book.

"Hey, cut it out." As Arden yanked the Book of Vindor away, a thin white ribbon appeared, drawn out by the cat's claw. Arden pushed the paw away, unhooking the ribbon, and he lifted the book out of the cat's reach.

Snow White made a raw "reaowww" of protest, then stuck his lean nose in the air and marched off, his whip-like tail flicking.

Curious, Arden put the book back on his lap and opened to the marked page. A white, five-petaled flower had been pressed between the pages next to the ribbon.

The page itself contained an entry in Megan's handwriting—the weird one about the end of her battle with the Shadow. She described a feeling of the world melting away around her, the clouds tearing apart to reveal a sky filled with stars which then proceeded to talk to her.

It had been a dream, obviously. Megan in a later entry had claimed it might not have been, but it *had* to have been a dream.

The way Arden saw it, if the world really had almost disappeared, everyone else in Vindor would have remembered it. People would be going around saying, "Hey, remember that time the world vanished, and the sky blew apart, and then it all came back? Crazy times, huh?"

He thought about asking Talu or Dark Morning if they remembered anything like that, but as he tried to come up with a way to word the question, a distant sound caught his attention.

A wooden, rhythmic pattern filled the air. At first, he mistook it for woodpeckers, but the pattern was much too complex.

"What's that sound?" he asked.

Dark Morning grunted. "Dembeyan drums. We're getting close to M'buk."

These drums sounded more like hollow wooden blocks and featured two or three of different pitches. The rhythm, though not exactly musical, was intricate and precise, with gaps of silence between each phrase.

As the *Sensei* traveled up the dark river, the sound grew clearer. Now Arden could hear a second set of drums, farther away, repeating each rhythm phrase beat for beat.

"Look," Dark Morning pointed ahead. "The gates."

chapter 18

The Gates of M'buk

Arden wasn't sure what he had expected the entrance to the Dembeyan Empire to look like, but he had not been expecting this.

On either side of the river stood two enormous towers of brown clay shaped like beehives, probably fifty feet tall. Huge logs projected from their walls like giant spikes, lined up in neat rows. Between the towers hung a huge gate of steel lattice, connected to a rather impressive pulley system. The gate allowed water to flow through, but blocked ships from traveling any farther up the river. Several people in long, brightly patterned tunics milled around on either bank.

"Toll collectors," Dark Morning muttered as she guided the botos to a marked docking station.

A man in a long, green robe covered in gold patterns stepped toward them. He smiled broadly, his straight, white teeth in bold contrast to his ebony skin. A second man followed, peered into their ship, and made notes in a heavy book.

"Welcome, welcome, my friends," the first man said. "And what brings a diverse group such as yourselves to the Dembeyan Empire?"

"We're going to N'gozi," Talu answered.

"Ah, N'gozi, the crown of the Empire! Have you ever been there, my dear?"

"No," Talu said, "but I've heard it's beautiful."

The man grinned. "More than beautiful—I guarantee you'll never see another city so grand and so cultured in all your days."

Arden smirked. *Try me—I've been to New York.*

"Do make time to see the observatory and the plaza—oh, and the many beautiful parks, of course. And what business brings you to the capital city?"

"We're going to the library," Arden said. "I have this letter from Selena that I need to give to the head librarian."

The man glanced at the letter in Arden's hand and nodded. "Is that so? Well, then I'll send the news ahead and I'll make sure someone is at the docks ready to meet you and escort you there—just a moment."

He stepped away from the dock and sat down in front of a hollowed log with three wide slats cut into it. He took a pair of smooth sticks and beat a complex rhythm on the log—the same sort of pattern Arden had heard in the woods earlier.

When he finished, Arden heard another drum in the distance echo the same rhythm, then a third one, farther away.

"There," the man said. "The message should be there within the hour."

So that's how it worked—like Morse code, with drummers passing the message down the line. Only it sounded a lot cooler than Morse.

Talu's eyes widened. "You can use drums to talk?"

The man grinned. "The Dembeyans can turn anything into language," he said proudly. "Now once you pay the toll, you'll be all set to go."

Dark Morning rolled her eyes and fished a few coins from her leather pouch, dropping them unceremoniously into the outstretched hand of the second man.

Dock workers used the pulleys to raise the huge metal grate, and Dark Morning directed the botos between the spiked towers and into Dembeyan territory.

The first man waved after them. "Best of luck to you. Enjoy the grand city!"

* * *

Bat stopped in the middle of the plaza, sniffing the air vigorously. For a moment, he leaned forward, almost crouching the way he did in his goblin form. Megan cringed.

His blue eyes narrowed. "I smell tacos." He took off in a scrambling run toward the cafeteria doors.

Orlando laughed. "I've never seen anyone run like that."

Megan shrugged, trying to be casual. How many times a day did Bat let something non-human slip through? Surely Orlando had started to pick up on these things. They couldn't keep up this facade forever.

But, Megan thought as she picked up her tray for the buffet line, what if they had to? She'd already worried plenty about what would happen if they couldn't bring Arden back, but what about Bat being stuck here? How could he make a life here, separated from his wife and his people and …?

"Something getting you down?" Orlando asked, balancing three yellow taco shells on his tray.

"Oh, I'm … having trouble with a project," she said, avoiding his eyes, and pretending to be concerned with selecting the right baked potato.

"I can commiserate with you there." Orlando grabbed a bottle of hot sauce. "I've been in the lab for days now and my cell samples aren't doing *anything*. They have the nerve to take a vacation when I'm here working hard."

They chose a spot and set their trays beside Bat's—which had twelve tacos lined up, one spilling seasoned meat onto the table.

Bat grinned up at them. "Dig in," he commanded, then proceeded to do so himself.

Orlando laughed. "This kid's appetite. Mr. Bat, how does your wife keep up with feeding you?"

Thankfully, Bat's mouth was full of taco, making his answer unintelligible.

Megan nibbled on a slice of bread, not feeling hungry.

"Um, excuse me, Megan Bradshaw?"

Megan turned at the soft voice to see the girl from the library. She wore a giant blue windbreaker and baggy jeans tucked into her white fuzzy boots. That same red toboggan cap was pulled low over her head, and she shifted under the weight of a leather satchel bag.

"Um, do you mind if I—?" Penny glanced at the empty seat beside Megan.

"Of course, please join us." Megan pulled out the chair and Penny set down her tray, piled high with three unadorned baked potatoes and a mound of French fries. She placed a mug of herbal tea beside her tray.

Megan motioned to her friends. "Penny, this is Orlando Ruiz and Bat, um, Shahck-re-ahck. Bat and Orlando, this is Penny ..." She turned to the girl in the toboggan cap. "I'm sorry, I don't know your last name."

"Chen," Penny answered.

The answer took Megan by surprise, and she glanced at the girl's dark skin and high cheekbones.

Orlando narrowed his eyes. "Your name is Penny Chen?"

Penny seemed to shrink in her seat. "Is something wrong?"

"No, nothing," Megan quickly said. She felt ashamed of herself—Penny could have been adopted, or the name could be another ethnicity beside Chinese. How rude had she been? "We're glad you could join us."

Bat looked up from his tray of decimated tacos, wiping his mouth with the back of his hand. "What is in the giant bag?"

"Books." Penny pushed up her glasses. "I, uh, do a lot of reading."

"On vacation?" Orlando asked. "Man, you're making the rest of us look bad! I'll bet you smoke everyone else in your classes though."

"I—" Penny glanced down at her potatoes.

Orlando smiled. "Nah, that's a good thing, Penny. You'll probably be everyone's boss one day."

And Penny cracked a smile.

Megan had to hand it to Orlando—he knew how to make anyone in the world feel at ease.

Orlando pointed to her tray. "So I take it you like potatoes."

The smiled disappeared, and Penny picked at her French fries with her fork.

"I'm not questioning you," Orlando said. "Just making conversation.

You do you, Penny Chen."

"Here," Bat said, "Have a taco. It changes your life away."

Penny wrinkled her nose. "No, thanks. I don't like them."

Bat turned to Orlando. "She doesn't like tacos," he whispered loudly. "Is she an evil supper villain trying to rule the world?"

Penny's eyes widened behind her glasses, but Orlando laughed. "No. Don't mind him, Penny. Bat's new to the area and doesn't understand all of the subtleties of American conversation."

Orlando chatted with Penny for a while, asking her questions about her major, where she was from and such, but most of the time Penny answered so quietly Megan couldn't make out what she said. Orlando didn't press, however, continuing cheerfully.

"Oh, FriendMegan!" Bat sat up suddenly. "Orlando is going to take me to a land of fish!"

"To a *what?*"

Orlando grinned. "I told him I'd take him to Mystic Aquarium. You should come, Megan. You and Penny both."

"I don't know. I'll think about it," Megan said.

They finished and headed out into the chilly but sunny afternoon. Penny paused at the cafeteria door. She pulled off her spectacles, tucked them in her bag, and put on an enormous pair of sunglasses that dwarfed her small face. She hurried away toward the dorms with hardly a wave goodbye.

Orlando rubbed his chinstrap beard. "Are you sure her name is Penny Chen?"

Megan looked up at him. "That's what she said. Is there something wrong?"

"I don't know. Thing is, I sat next to a Penny Chen in chemistry last year. But that definitely wasn't her. She was …"

"Asian?" Megan offered.

"I was going to say *taller*, but yeah, that too." He shrugged. "Must be two people with the same name."

"Yeah," Megan said, wondering what the chances of that were on such a small campus.

They walked down the campus sidewalk at a leisurely pace, Bat trailing behind to pick up rocks from the flowerbeds.

"Penny seems nervous," Orlando observed. "A bit socially awkward. Maybe she just needs some friends, like us."

Megan smiled. "You're a good guy, Orlando."

He grinned. "Tell that to Roz for me?"

The mention of Roz's name stung unexpectedly. Megan found herself mortified by the sudden rush of emotion. What on earth had gotten into her? She struggled to regain her composure and smiled. "I'll be sure to put in a good word."

"Gracias. Oh, and hey." Orlando turned to her. "You should come to the aquarium tomorrow too. It's supposed to be therapeutic, all those fish. And you, my stressed-out friend, could definitely use some fish therapy."

Megan tried to fend off a second wave of confused emotions. She really must have been stressed. "You know—I think that might be a good idea."

chapter 19

The Jewel of N'gozi

For the next few hours, Arden entertained himself by sketching the farms and villages he could see from the river. He sketched the rows upon rows of corn and beans planted in impossibly straight lines. He tried to capture the action of children in bright-colored clothing playing tag outside of houses shaped like beehives. He also spotted some kids sitting beside the water reading from scrolls—whether for fun or for schoolwork of some sort, Arden didn't know.

And always in the background played the sound of those wooden drums. He wondered about them even more now that he knew each was a coded message passed from village to village. The Dembeyans apparently had a lot of things to say.

"Is that the city?" Talu leaned over the side of the boat, her good eye darting back and forth. "I hear people talking."

"No, I think it's only a town." Arden lowered the sketchbook. "A crowded one, I guess. And it's got crazy barns with spikes sticking out, like giant Daleks. Or those old underwater mines."

Talu sighed and looked down toward the cat that that dozed in her lap. "The poor boy doesn't know how to use real words." She smiled mischievously. "He gets to the end of a sentence and gets nervous, so he makes some ridiculous ones up."

Arden grinned. "You got me. That's what I've been doing this whole time."

"How big do you think it is?"

"What, my ability to make words up?"

Talu tossed a pillow at him. "No, N'gozi. I've only ever sailed by it at a distance, and I've never gotten a chance to see it. I hear it's the grandest city in Vindor. My uncle says *ten thousand* people live there. Can you imagine ten thousand people, all living in the same place?"

"That *is* a lot of people," Arden agreed. In fact, it sounded extraordinary.

But what was he thinking? His hometown probably had triple that, and the nearby city of Hartford probably had a hundred thousand. And never mind the millions of people who lived in New York City alone.

But out here in the middle of nowhere in Vindor, ten thousand seemed like an impossibly large number, and Arden struggled to wrap his mind around that many individual human beings existing anywhere.

They sailed along the winding black river for some time longer, the rhythms of the wooden log drums growing louder as they went. Up ahead, the river curved sharply to the right. As the houseboat made the turn, Arden caught his breath.

"Uh ... Talu? Pretty sure we're here."

The city skyline before them was like nothing Arden had ever dreamed of. Tall, spiraling towers shot high above the tree line. Huge, stately buildings—dotted with windows several stories tall—stretched along the horizon.

The most striking thing about the place was the absence of straight lines. Everything was made of smoothed-out mud brick, the corners rounded, the buildings all a little curved and slightly tapering the taller they got. On top of that, nearly every surface was painted in colorful stripes and geometric patterns. The impression of the city was that of an ancient desert civilization with a splash of Dr. Seuss.

Dark Morning steered the botos toward the wooden pier along the dark river. The dock was crowded with tall people in brightly colored robes—men and women balancing heavy jars on their heads, bartering for goods at merchant stands, or conversing over long scrolls.

From out of the crowd, a handsome man stepped toward the houseboat. He looked to be in his twenties or thirties, and by the detail woven into the fabric of his long orange tunic, Arden guessed he was probably rich. An elegant young woman followed, dressed in the same orange with her dark hair twisted into a series of long, neat braids that extended halfway down her back.

"Ah, you must be the party from Alavar." The handsome man flashed a set of perfect teeth.

"How did you know?" Talu asked.

The young woman smiled, the sunlight glinting off her dangling gold earrings and playing off her smooth ebony skin. "We got the drum message an hour ago from the guard at M'buk. He told us of a Selk, a Tsuru boy, and a Nomad girl aboard."

"But he didn't mention how beautiful the girl would be," the man noted.

Talu blushed.

"Allow us to introduce ourselves," the young woman said. "My name is Uzimbe Ashana, and this is my older brother, Uzimbe Kwanu."

"I'm Arden, this is Talu, and that's Dark Morning over there."

"Pleasure to meet you," Kwanu said, but his eyes were locked on Talu. She didn't seem to notice, but Snow White looked up and hissed at him.

And for once, Arden agreed with the cat.

"The message said you were on your way to the library," Ashana continued. "It would be our pleasure to escort you there, if you are ready."

"Uh, yeah, we're ready," Arden said. He turned to Dark Morning. "I'm guessing we'll be back soon. I don't think it should take too long to find this Korvin lady."

Dark Morning crossed her arms. "I'm not going anywhere."

Arden stepped out of the boat and onto the dock, making sure he had Selena's letter tucked beneath his belt. The burn on the bottom of his foot flared up in pain, despite the layers of bandage wrapped around it. He grimaced and turned to help Talu, but Kwanu had beaten him to it.

Talu seemed surprised to find her hand wrapped inside of Kwanu's big, strong one. She nearly dropped her staff with her other hand, then tripped and practically fell out onto the dock.

"I've got you," Kwanu said, lifting her up and setting her on her feet. He paused for a moment, looking into her mismatched eyes. "Pardon my asking, but are you blind, sweetheart?"

Talu had turned bright crimson by this point. "Yes, well, I mean ... I can see some, I'm not completely, that is—"

"Don't be embarrassed!" Ashana said cheerfully. "It's nothing to be ashamed of! Why, one of our own council elders has been blind since boyhood, but you should hear him speak in the council! No one delivers a speech more eloquently than he."

Talu's face lit up. "Really?"

Kwanu smiled. "Of course. In N'gozi, physical disabilities don't bar people from reaching their full potential. Now if you'd like to take my arm, I can lead you on a tour of our grand city."

Talu nodded and took his arm shyly. Arden frowned, then followed Kwanu and Ashana. The pain of his burn subsided a bit, and he followed the tall siblings down one of the mud-brick streets toward the center of the city.

The city was almost too much for the eye to take in. People bustled by, each wearing colorful robes busy with embroidered patterns. Every available surface of every building had neat rows of hand-painted shapes and symbols: triangles, chevrons, diamonds, circles, or stylized images of spiders, fish, birds, and turtles. And over the sounds of laughter and conversation were always those wooden drumbeats, carrying hundreds of messages from one side of the city to the other.

"So you've never been to N'gozi, then?" Ashana asked. "Are you in for a treat—N'gozi is the crown of the entire Dembeyan Empire. Nowhere else in Vindor will you find more knowledge of medicine, or astronomy, or mathematics, or law, or history, or science. If you look over to the right—that big building with the dome roof is the famous observatory. And those towers are part of the great university, which draws students from the entire Empire to study. Oh, and look up ahead—there goes one of our esteemed professors!"

Arden squinted as he looked through the thick crowd of people.

"Where?"

"The woman in purple. It looks like she teaches mathematics."

"How can you tell that?"

"Because of the crosshatch pattern on her robe, of course," Ashana answered. "And purple is the color of a professor."

"Wait, so you can tell someone's job based on the color they're wearing?"

Ashana nodded. "The colors, the patterns of the print—every detail of a tunic tells you several things about that person."

Between the constant drumming, the busy clothing people wore, and—Arden guessed—the patterns painted on the buildings, everything in N'gozi represented a kind of message. It was busier than the neon advertisements up and down Times Square. The Dembeyans practically swam in communication.

Talu turned toward Kwanu. "What does your clothing say about you?"

"That my father is one of the head council members, and that our ancestry can be traced back many generations," he said proudly. "And also that I'm studying law."

"And mine says the same." Ashana motioned for them to follow her down a side street. "Only that I'm studying medicine. I just started this year."

"Wow," Talu said. "That sounds so important."

"Every job here is important," Ashana said. "You don't have to be studying something lofty to make a difference for the Empire. Every citizen in every city works in harmony to contribute to the glory of the Dembeyan people!"

"But don't the different cities ever fight over power or territory?" Talu asked.

"Oh, no. The cities of the Empire all work together because we know we depend on one another. And we have a system where we share leaders, so no one city's needs are ever ignored."

Ashana led them onto a broad boulevard, where people gathered in clusters around a man reading loudly from a scroll. Some of the people in the crowd began to debate the reader, and a lively argument followed, though Arden didn't catch the topic. They all seemed to be enjoying themselves, though.

Meanwhile, Ashana had launched into an eager explanation about the Empire's government system. She sure was the perkiest tour guide Arden had ever met. Her brother seemed to be listening disinterestedly, all while making a show of guiding Talu around obstacles along the street.

"Then each of those community leaders chooses someone from their own number to rule over the city," Ashana was saying. "And a handful of those leaders are chosen to come here to N'gozi, to help make decisions for the whole Empire. Everyone gets along well and works together!"

Arden seriously doubted that it always worked as smoothly as that. "What if the council decides it's going to run things their own way from now on and ignore what the people want?" he asked.

"But they wouldn't!" Ashana sounded so sincere.

"Right, but they *could*." Arden noticed Kwanu frowning at him, but he continued anyway. "What then?"

Ashana paused for a moment. "Well, that's where the king would step in, I guess. He's not involved in the government currently because we don't need him. But he will return at the first sign of the council violating the core values of the Empire, and he has the right to hold trial, depose the offending leaders and request the cities elect new ones."

Kwanu let out a strange laugh.

Ashana turned to Arden apologetically. "Some people, like my brother, don't believe the king exists—that he's more of an idea. In any case, we've done such a good job of ruling that no one's seen him in years, and I don't think anyone knows who he is anymore."

"How would you know who he was if he did come back?" Talu asked.

"By the blue eye, of course!"

Everyone Arden had seen in the city had brown or black irises, so it made sense to him how blue eyes would stand out. How this king would keep those hidden Arden wasn't sure—did they have sunglasses in N'gozi?

Ashana lead the party into a broad plaza, complete with sparkling fountains and large statues—not of military heroes, but of men and women holding scrolls, telescopes, protractors, and compasses.

A city that was super proud of its nerds. Arden had to admit it was kind of cool.

Ashana pointed to a building on the far end with an exceptionally tall spiral tower. "Up there is the Grand Hall where the council meets, and where public ceremonies take place. And across from that is the Great Library!"

The library building stretched at least three city blocks long and rose six stories high, with four narrow towers tapering high into the sky. And unlike every other building in the city, it lacked the busy painted patterns, instead gleaming in pure white.

"If N'gozi is the crown of the Empire, the library is the jewel," Ashana gushed. "Twenty thousand books and scrolls! Twenty thousand more maps and drawings and documents. Daily lectures on every topic under the sun. This is where you'll find the brightest minds in all of Vindor gathered."

"Wow," was all Arden could say. "So, uh, where do I find the head librarian?"

"At the main circulation desk, of course!" Ashana answered. "Here, I'll show you the way."

Kwanu cleared his throat. "I'm sure Talu has no interest in books or reading," he said. "Perhaps you would find the gardens more to your liking?"

It sounded like a backhanded insult to Arden. But Talu blushed and nodded.

"Excellent," Kwanu said. "We'll meet you back here in half an hour."

Before Arden could protest splitting him and Talu up, Kwanu whisked her away down a plaza sidewalk.

Ashana put her hand on Arden's shoulder. "Ready to see the world's greatest library?"

Arden sighed. Might as well get this over with.

chapter 20

Magic in the Water

Orlando Ruiz led his motley crew through the Mystic Aquarium parking lot—a little band of misfits that included Bat, who gaped wide-mouthed at the huge steel-and-glass roof over the ticket station, and Penny, who despite the overcast sky wore her sunglasses and carried her giant leather journal.

Actually, Megan realized, with her hasty excuses for her odd behavior, she probably fit well into the category of odd people that Orlando had picked up.

And yet Orlando acted completely comfortable in their midst, making sure each one felt like they belonged. Currently he chatted with the woman at the ticket counter, making her laugh over something.

Megan had never met anyone else so skilled at putting others at ease. She couldn't help but admire that in him.

Orlando waved them through the front doors and toward the main gallery. His espresso-brown eyes twinkled under the spotlights. "Come in, come in, my friends, to the amazing 'Land of Fish.'"

The four stepped inside the oversized room. The lights were dim, and among the darkened walls glowed tank after tank of living, swimming color.

Megan nearly ran into Bat, who had stopped right in the middle of the walkway. His mouth hung open as his blue eyes raced around the room.

Penny took off her sunglasses and stood transfixed by the giant coral reef display. She reached out toward it and seemed to be surprised when her fingers touched the glass.

Bat, meanwhile, ran up to the clownfish tank and pressed his nose against it.

Orlando chuckled. "Wow. You'd think those two had never seen fish before."

"I have not!" Bat peeled his face away from the glass. "I meaned, I have never seed fishes sideways before."

"Sideways?" Orlando asked.

"I have only ever seed the tops of fishes, in murky water. But this!" He turned to a tank where blue and yellow angelfish glided by. "These fishes are like pixies."

Megan cringed.

"Or like magic birds," Bat continued. "Oh! What is that?"

And he scampered off in the direction of a large, rust-colored octopus. Penny, meanwhile, stood mesmerized by the coral and swaying sea anemones.

Orlando beamed. "This is even more fun than I thought," he said to Megan. "This is like watching little kids on Christmas." He looked up at a huge wall of magenta jellyfish, pulsing and floating in slow motion. "But honestly, I can't help getting giddy at this stuff either."

Megan understood. She'd learned about tropical fish in elementary school and in high school biology, and then they'd seemed like nothing out of the ordinary. But now she couldn't believe that the creatures before her were real—the pompous spiny lionfish, the comical pufferfish, the hypnotic grace of the anemones.

She'd always thought that magic existed only in Vindor. But now, standing here in front of all this living beauty, she couldn't decide which place was more wonderful.

As Megan and Orlando moved through the exhibits, she noticed Orlando humming softly to himself.

His tone seemed right on pitch, and the tune clear—not the mumbling, indistinct sounds common to most people's humming. She thought she'd heard that haunting melody somewhere before.

"What song is that?" she asked.

"Hmm?" Orlando asked, still watching the sea turtle in front of them.

"What are you humming? It's pretty."

"Oh, just a little Puccini."

"Who?"

"You don't know Puccini?" Orlando clutched at his heart, feigning shock. "He's only the master of the melody. The king of opera."

"Wait a minute." Megan folded her arms. "You don't strike me as someone who likes opera."

"There's nothing else like it. When I was a kid, my aunt would blast Verdi and Wagner and the greats. I thought it was weird at first, but once I got past those warbly sopranos who give it a bad rap, I discovered the music is phenomenal. Opera's where you'll find some of the greatest melodies ever written."

Megan smiled. "I think it's cool that you're passionate about something that most people don't care for."

"I've never told that to any of my friends before." Orlando paused in front of a manta ray display. "I don't mind telling you, though."

Megan felt an unexpected twinge of sadness. She shook it off. "Don't worry, I won't tell Roz. Your secrets are safe with me."

And for once, Orlando didn't have a funny comeback. He shrugged and shuffled into the next exhibit room.

* * *

The huge doors of the Great Library gleamed in a vibrant blue, in contrast to the pure white paint over the building's earthen walls. Arden pushed the wooden doors open and limped inside.

The lobby was an immense room, with rounded stairways leading up to multiple balconies, all covered with that bright white paint. Swirls of blue decorated the floor where crowds of people bustled. Clusters of men and women stood talking loudly while a few men in unadorned white robes scurried by with heavy books in their hands or scrolls tucked beneath their arms.

Ashana pointed to a huge gilded table against the far wall, nestled between two curved staircases. "That's the main desk there. I'll introduce you to Oba Bwenye, the head librarian and—oh, Professor Gwijre!"

Ashana suddenly turned toward an older woman walking by—a professor, Arden guessed, based on her purple robe. "I'll just be a minute," Ashana called over her shoulder as she chased the professor down, leaving Arden standing in the middle of the blue-and-white swirled floor by himself.

"Sure, no problem," he said quietly.

How strange he must have looked standing alone in the lobby, the only kid in the whole room, looking out of place in the shirt, trousers, and straw sandals of the Tsuru people. No one seemed to take much notice of him, though, with everyone absorbed in their own conversations.

Ashana was nowhere to be seen—she'd probably chased that poor professor all the way to the end of the plaza by now. Arden shrugged and walked up to the huge, gilded desk alone.

A grumpy old man sat there with his nose buried in a giant book. He wore a long, white tunic with no pattern on it, and the hair cropped close to his dark scalp was silver.

Arden cleared his throat. "Excuse me."

The old man glanced up at him, then turned another dusty page of the book and said nothing.

Arden paused. "Um, sorry to interrupt you, but I have a letter for the head librarian. It's important."

Again, the man glanced up at him, then looked back down at the book.

"It's from Selena," Arden said.

The man extended his dark hand, palm upward, not taking his eyes off the page. "I'm the head librarian," he intoned.

Arden pulled the letter from his belt and placed it in the man's palm. The librarian withdrew it slowly, opened the seal deliberately, and read the letter at a pace so slowly Arden thought he would become an old man himself before he finished. For a head librarian, he sure was a slow reader.

Finally, the man sat up and looked Arden right in the face. His dark eyes bored into him so intensely that Arden almost wished he'd go back to reading.

"When was this letter written?" the old man asked.

"Uh, day before yesterday, I think." Arden did a quick calculation of how long it had been since Selena had sent them off. It seemed like a lifetime ago already.

"And where did you get it?"

"Selena gave it to me."

The man raised a silver eyebrow. "She handed this to you herself?"

"Yes."

"Humph."

The man leaned back in his chair and now turned the letter over, examining the blank side.

"Well," he said at length, "It's not a forgery."

"Uh …?"

"It's in Selena's hand, on Tsuru-made paper, which is typical of Alavar correspondence. And it was written recently, as you have indicated. But the contents make no sense to me."

"What?"

"This Korvin referenced here—I know her. Brilliant young woman. Dedicated scholar. I've taken a fondness to her and her serious approach to study, despite her somewhat odd Rikean ways. But she hasn't been here for weeks."

"Wait—what?"

"She told me she was headed back to Alavar—in quite a hurry, as I recall. It seemed that she had discovered something important in the Archives, but she had departed before I had a chance to ask her about it." The old man held up the letter. "So the nature of Selena's request leads me to the troubling conclusion that Korvin never told Selena of her plan to return, and—worse—that she disappeared before she made it back."

"Korvin is missing?"

"It would appear so." The man frowned back down at the letter. "I'll send out a distress alert and get a river crew searching for her—or whatever she has left behind."

Arden paused, trying to process. Korvin wasn't here. Their entire quest depended on this Korvin character, and she might be lost or even dead. Who would take over now and lead them into Nomad territory?

And worse, who would help Arden get back home? Selena had said that Korvin was their only key, the only one who might understand how to cross worlds, and—

"There's something else that doesn't make sense to me," the librarian said, interrupting Arden's thoughts. "I've never heard of this mist Selena writes about."

"She says it's attacking the eastern border or something."

The man shrugged. "I have never heard of anything like this in Vindor—I've never seen it referenced in the histories, and the latest foreign news reports haven't so much as mentioned it."

"Oh." Arden's shoulders sagged. "Well, thanks anyway."

"I'm sorry I cannot help you." The old man's voice sounded sincere.

Arden turned and stepped back into the middle of the grand lobby. So this was it. He'd have to go back to Selena completely empty-handed, with no Korvin and no new information.

He frowned. After everything that had happened on the trip, he wanted to at least do *something* useful. He glanced back at the gilded desk. He paused, and then marched back up to where the librarian sat.

The old man looked up. "Yes?"

"Could I see if I could find anything? I mean, about the mist," Arden said. "Selena described it to me. Maybe it's in the records, but you know, hidden, and you have to know what you're looking for to notice it. It's worth a shot, at least."

The old man closed his dusty book. "Well, I'm not going to turn away a young man who wants to study a topic he feels is important."

"I don't just *feel* it's important; it *is* important. At least Selena thinks so."

The old librarian rose to his feet, his height surprising Arden. "This way," the man said. "I'll show you the old Archives."

"Oh, wait," Arden said. "I'd better tell my friend where I'm going first."

The librarian sat down again. "I'll be here."

Arden limped outside into the grand plaza and spotted Kwanu and Talu sitting on the edge of a fountain. Talu was fairly easy to pick out from the crowd, with her caramel-colored skin, full head of wavy hair, and flowing skirt.

She sat awkwardly on the stone edge of the fountain, fiddling with the brown feather on the end of her staff as she listened to Kwanu going on about something. As Arden drew closer, the man reached out and patted Talu on the head, as though she were a child.

Arden clenched his fist and marched up to them.

"Talu, I need to talk to you."

Talu stopped slouching and looked up in Arden's direction. "Yes?"

Kwanu crossed his arms, the sleeves falling away slightly to reveal his muscular forearms. "There's nothing you need to say to her that you can't say to both of us."

What, do you own her? Arden almost said, but he eyed Kwanu's strong build and suddenly felt the need to refrain.

Arden turned to Talu. "She isn't here."

"Who isn't?"

"Korvin. The lady we came all this way to find."

Kwanu's eyebrow twitched but he said nothing.

"She left weeks ago," Arden continued. "We came all this way for nothing. Well, almost nothing. Look, I'm going to look through the library a bit, see if I can find anything about the mist. Do you want to help?"

Talu nodded, but Kwanu interrupted before she could get a word out.

"I doubt reading is Talu's strong suit," he said. "And Arden, I don't know how small you think our library is, but I think it's going to take you more than an afternoon to do even a rudimentary search." He stroked his chin thoughtfully. "I'll tell you what. I'll get your boat and your cabbie moved to the smaller harbor. It's quieter there than on the main river, and you can stay there overnight. I'll cover the docking fees for as long as you need. Now where did Ashana go?"

Arden shrugged. "She ran off after some professor, I think."

"Typical. That girl is hopeless," Kwanu said with laugh. "Well, you go to the library. I'll find Ashana and have her pick you up here at sundown—she'll show you the way back. Talu, meanwhile you and I can continue the tour of our city. That's definitely something you can handle, right, little lady?"

"Oh, yes, sure." Talu blushed and got to her feet clumsily, nearly tripping on her staff.

Before Arden could stop them, Kwanu had taken her halfway down the plaza.

Well, it looked like Arden would have to search the Archives without her help. He turned to go back to the gleaming white library.

How big could the history section be?

chapter 21

Penny's Secret

Megan sank onto a bench in the dark gallery room, her feet sore. They'd spent the last few hours walking through the aquarium, watching the antics of the penguins, gawking at sharks, and marveling at the Arctic belugas. Bat had insisted that they loop around again so he could revisit the octopus exhibit—a creature he had never encountered before.

Penny stood before the gigantic reef tank again, gazing at the colorful kingdom of tropical fish. She had her leather journal beneath her arm.

Why did she bring that huge book everywhere?

"So our friend Bat." Orlando sidled up beside Megan and kept his voice low. "I'm worried about him. Yesterday he told me he was a king."

Megan winced. How careless was Bat getting?

She feigned disinterest. "Did he now?"

"Yeah. Also, I'm not an expert on West Africa or wherever he's from, but it seems like he would at least know what an airplane does. I mean, even kids in the remotest jungles have some exposure to the modern world, but he acted completely freaked out when he saw one last night. Didn't he have to get on an airplane to come here?"

"That is odd." Megan pretended to be interested in the seahorse exhibit. "What do you make of it?"

Orlando sighed. "I don't know. The king thing worries me, like maybe he has some delusion or something. They wouldn't send a king as an exchange student, would they?"

He leaned against a pillar, his arms crossed. "I'm generally a live-and-let-live kind of guy, but there are a lot of things recently that don't add up. Like our friend Penny. I'm not trying to be nosy, but I looked her up in my yearbook and I noticed something weird. For starters, I couldn't find her at all, until I looked in the upperclassmen section. Turns out

Penny Chen is a *senior.*"

Megan glanced at her shy friend, who at that moment opened her huge journal and began taking furious notes as she watched the tank.

"Okay," Megan said. "I assumed she was a freshman, but I guess it's possible she's a senior. What else was strange?"

Orlando blinked. "About what?"

"About Penny. You said, 'for starters,' which made me think you found something else."

"Did I?" Orlando rubbed his sideburn. "I don't remember what I was going to say. She's a senior, you know."

"Yes, you already said that." Megan found this conversation strangely circular.

"Oh. Well, that was all, I think."

Penny closed the book and held it against her chest, as though trying to hide behind it. She clomped toward them in her boots and looked shyly at Orlando.

"I thought I heard my name." Her lower lip trembled. "Were you two talking about me?"

"Oh, nothing bad, amiga. We were just wondering if you're a senior."

Penny's eyes widened, and she clutched the red toboggan cap that hid her hair. "You think I'm *old?*"

Orlando smiled reassuringly. "No, not a senior citizen. Like a senior in school."

Penny relaxed and let go of her cap. "Oh, yes. A senior in school."

Orlando turned to Megan. "See, I told you. What do you say we drag Bat away from the calamari tank and go find something to eat?"

* * *

N'gozi's grand library had looked enormous from the outside—and that was before Arden learned about the several floors underground, too.

Oba Bwenye, the old librarian, had led him down a rough white stairway into the tunnel-like hallways of the Archives, illuminated by lamps of bronze and colored glass that hung from the ceilings. Branching off the halls were countless rooms, some only the size of closets, crammed with shelves of old books or wall cubbies stuffed with parchment scrolls.

Now Arden rubbed his eyes, sore from squinting in the dim light. He glanced at the oil lamp on the table—a kind of clay tea kettle with a sputtering wick coming out of its spout.

It was a wonder this whole place hadn't gone up in flames years ago. They could really have done with that heatless fire stuff that Megan had written about the Rikeans having.

He looked at the dusty tome in front of him. He'd browsed page after page of cramped script without finding anything useful—just boring lists of crops grown, ships built, and buildings repaired each year.

But at least he could read this one. Several of the books and scrolls he'd found at first were written in some sort of runes, others in hieroglyphics.

Arden sighed. He closed the book, picked up the lamp, and wandered to another room. He stood, staring at a precarious stack of scrolls taller than he was. He decided not to mess with it and turned back to the hallway.

"Feeling a bit lost?"

The lamplight flickered over the plain white robe of Oba, the librarian.

Arden sighed. "How do you find your way around this maze?"

Oba smiled gently. "For me, it's like finding my way around an old and dear home. Every room has meaning and memory, and the books and scrolls are like old friends. After being here so long, I find I prefer the company of books to most people."

So this guy probably needed to get outside more often.

Arden glanced down the impossibly long hallways. "Okay, Mr. Oba, where does the history section begin and end? Maybe that will help me find stuff."

The librarian extended his arms. "All of this floor is the history section, and the two floors beneath us as well."

"*All* of it? How much history do you need?"

"As much as we can get our hands on," Oba said. "The Archives contain the only history records in all of Vindor."

"What?"

"This is the only place in all of Vindor where you'll find any historical records," Oba explained. "That is, besides the odd journal here or there. But those never extend beyond a single lifetime."

Arden thought of the little library in Alavar. Yes, they had the Book of Vindor and a bunch of other volumes like it, but those only contained Selena's notes on stuff. He thought of the odd books about the Tsuru and how they'd left out information on when settlements were founded.

"How is that possible?"

Oba shrugged. "I wish we knew. The people of Vindor have no concept of their own history, even recent history. Ask your family back home what life was like during your grandfather's time—I guarantee they won't be able to name a single objective fact about their village."

"That's insane."

The librarian eyed him thoughtfully. "You know, you're the first non-Dembeyan ever to show interest in this topic—or to understand its significance." He paused. "No, wait, Korvin was keenly interested in this as well. She probably knows more about Vindor's history than even we do."

"Why's that?"

"Korvin is a Rikean, a people whose gift and main course of study is languages. She could read the documents that we can't—though what exactly she found in them, she never told me." Oba paused. "If you are looking for information about these mists, you might want to start with the books Korvin gathered—whichever ones you can read. She adopted a study room as her own down here. I'll show you the way."

* * *

A brisk wind picked up, rattling the remainder of the leaves clinging to the trees along the street. Orlando pulled open the heavy wooden door of Captain Ahab's Coffee and ushered Megan, Bat, and Penny inside.

The glow of old-fashioned lamps and the smell of freshly roasted coffee beans made Megan feel warmer immediately. The brass bell on the door clanged behind them.

Orlando crossed the shop's creaking floorboards to the large, wooden counter, where he ordered black coffee for himself and Bat. Megan ordered a latte.

The barista handed Bat a heavy ceramic mug, stamped with a whale logo. Bat sniffed the black liquid suspiciously and dipped his tongue into it, frowning.

"I need seventy more cents, miss." Megan turned to see Penny standing at the counter, staring at the quarters and dimes in her mitten.

A line of customers stood behind her, muttering, and the cashier didn't try to hide her irritation.

Yet Penny seemed unable to make a decision about the coins before her. She blinked back tears, clearly stressed.

"I've got it." Megan stepped up and handed the cashier a dollar. Penny looked up at Megan gratefully. She claimed her mug of steaming herbal tea and followed Megan to the table Orlando had picked out.

They settled into a booth by a large window, where they could watch the bay water churning in grey and white.

Orlando motioned to the waves. "This is from that nor'easter that's coming our way. Just the tip of it."

"Is it supposed to be bad?" Megan asked.

"Hard to tell. It's not supposed to arrive here until Saturday. The storm could go out to sea and leave us all alone. Right now, most of the worry is coming from shopping-mall owners, who are afraid the weather will scare away their Black Friday crowds."

Bat thudded his empty mug against the wooden table. He blinked. "I feel stronger."

"I told you, Mister Bat. Coffee is the great American secret."

"I feel very strong." Bat looked at his dark fingers, which trembled slightly. "Funny, but stronger. I think I can run very fast. Faster than a centaur, faster than a warhorse." Bat stood up on the bench.

"Bat," Megan said, "You can't stand on the furniture."

"But I *can* stand on the furnace-chur. Any furnace-churs in the world, no matter how tall!"

"Whoops." Orlando slid out from the booth and took Bat's arm. "Maybe I should have started him on a weaker roast. Come on, Mister Bat, we're going to go for a walk around the block."

"Can I go for a run?"

"Run as fast as you want, *amiguito*." He pushed Bat toward the door. "We'll be back in a few."

The brass bell clanged behind them, and Megan found herself sitting alone across from Penny.

"I guess he's never had caffeine before," Megan said.

Penny slurped her tea and stared out at the water.

"Too bad about that storm." Megan took another sip of her latte, struggling to make conversation. "But it doesn't sound like it will stop people from traveling home for Thanksgiving."

Penny didn't answer, staring at the waves through the window.

"Are, uh, you going home at all this week?" Megan asked.

Penny blinked back a tear.

"Hey," Megan said gently. "Is something wrong?"

Penny turned, her eyes brimming with tears. "I miss it," she whispered.

"You miss home?"

"Not home. The endless rolling oceans, and the beaches so pale they're almost violet." Penny spoke softly into her tea. "I miss the lights in the water—lights like the flashlight fish we saw at the aquarium, but smaller, better. And in the evenings when it was mild, the sea folk would come on shore. They didn't like the sunlight, but they would come in the evenings with stars above them and the little stars in the ocean around them, and they would tell stories …"

Megan perched at the edge of her seat, scarcely daring to breathe. "Sea folk—do you mean mermaids?"

Penny nodded, not making eye contact.

"Where did you see them?"

"Thalassa." The name was almost a sigh.

"I've never heard of that. Is it—?"

Penny stiffened and turned back to the window. "Never mind, I'm sorry, never mind. It's not real."

"It sounded real to you."

"It's a place I made up. It's nothing."

Megan leaned forward. "Just because you made it up doesn't mean it's not real. Where is Thalassa?"

Penny's dark eyes met hers, and she opened her mouth to speak.

But at that moment, the bell at the front of the shop clanged, and Bat and Orlando reappeared. Penny shrank into her large pink coat and didn't say another word.

Bat began chattering on about something, but Megan only half-listened.

Against all the odds, could it be possible that someone in Megan's circle of friends had also once been to Paracosmia?

chapter 22

The Atlas of Years

Arden had been reading for at least an hour in the cramped room where Korvin had once studied. He'd looked through the stacks of books and scrolls and found a few that were readable. He now skimmed a book that described the ever-shifting border designations within Vindor—not particularly interesting since he didn't know one of the landmarks it referenced.

His finger brushed against something silky. A thin white ribbon had been tucked between the pages of the book. A white flower, dried and paper-flat, slipped out of the book and fluttered to the ground.

As he bent to pick the flower up, Arden startled at a hoarse whisper from the hallway.

He spun around but saw no one in the doorway. Still the raspy whisper continued, hissing a string of words he couldn't quite make out.

Every muscle in his body tensed. Arden felt the need to run, to hide from whatever was coming for him. He became suddenly aware of how small and vulnerable he was down here, especially with his injured foot— virtually anyone could grab him and slam him against the wall, laughing while pressing a forearm into his neck as Steadman had done to him so many times. Arden could almost feel the desperate dizziness, see the corners of his vision darken as he struggled to breathe …

Footsteps sounded from the hall. His tormentors were coming for him, and with Arden trapped in this little room, there was nothing he could do to protect himself.

A figure in white appeared, thrusting the golden light of an oil lamp ahead of him.

"Be gone!"

Oba's voice rang out, surprisingly powerful.

"Be gone!" Oba seemed to be addressing not Arden, but the walls of the room. "Your power has been defeated—you have no business here."

Immediately Arden felt his heartbeat slow and his muscles relax, freed from the intense grip of fear.

Oba turned to him. "Was it bothering you?"

"Wh-what just happened?"

"Ah, that's right, I should have warned you about that. Remnants of something called the Shadow still linger in these halls."

"The Shadow?" His mind raced back to the frightening accounts in the Book of Vindor. "I thought it was dead."

"Ah, so you do remember it," Oba observed.

"I've read about it."

"I suppose you would have been a bit young to remember it for yourself." Oba looked thoughtful. "For some reason, the people of Vindor do remember the attacks of the Shadow, though even that memory seems to be fading."

"But I thought it was dead," Arden repeated.

"It is, for the most part. Banished by Selena at the Battle of Alavar. But weak remnants—shadows of the Shadow, you might say—still remain in places where it held the most sway, including these Archives." Oba set the sputtering lamp down on the table. "The strangest of these remnants was the Ice Chalice—a goblet with water permanently frozen inside, even when moved into direct sunlight. People were still coming to the library to gawk at it until recently, when someone stole it."

Arden shuddered. "Why would someone want that?"

"There's no understanding the minds of some people." Oba motioned to the book before Arden. "How is the search coming?"

"This is better, but I'm having trouble, uh, remembering all these place names."

"Geography is a sadly neglected art outside of the Empire." Oba picked up the lamp again. "Ah, well. I'll show you to the Map Room."

Arden followed him down the dimly lit hall. At one point he thought he saw their two shadows cast by the overhead lamps turn into three.

They passed several rooms stacked with books, not a single door over their rounded entrances—except for one with a huge iron gate over it.

"What's in there?" Arden asked, noticing three bulky padlocks and several chains. Beyond the iron bars he could see metal podiums in place of bookshelves, each holding up a single book.

Oba turned. "That's the Rare Book Room, where we keep a few volumes that are rumored to have, ah, less-than-explainable properties. Other people groups in Vindor might call them magic."

"Are they?"

"We are men and women of logic—but you'll notice we keep these books locked up and chained down—and we forbid anyone from touching them." A smile played at the corner of Oba's mouth. "We are human, after all."

"So why is one missing?"

The smile vanished. "What?"

"There." Arden pointed to an empty pedestal in the corner, a broken chain dangling uselessly.

"That's not possible!" The librarian pushed his lantern between the bars, frowning. "I'm the only one with a key to this room. No one should have been able to—and why the Arkheva, of all books?"

He turned to Arden. "The Map Room is two doors down to the left. You must excuse me—I need to look into this right away."

* * *

On the way back to Cove campus, Bat sat in Orlando's passenger seat, falling asleep. Apparently his first dose of caffeine had worn off suddenly and he was experiencing his first coffee crash.

Megan had opted for the back seat, where she could sit beside Penny, who wrote furiously in her leather journal.

Everyone had been silent since leaving the café.

But no … they'd had another conversation, hadn't they? An uneasy feeling crept over Megan. They had all been discussing something right as they got in the car, but try as hard as she could, Megan couldn't recall it now.

Penny put down her pen and leaned back, closing the book.

Megan spoke softly. "Do you mind if I ask you what you're writing?"

"Memories," Penny said. "I write them as fast as they come."

"Capturing memories is important," Megan said. "I sometimes wonder how much of our lives we lose to forgetting."

Orlando pulled his white car in front of Grace Palmer dormitory. Penny jumped out of the car as soon as it stopped and hurried toward the dorm without saying goodbye.

Megan got out, hoping to catch up with her. As she passed the driver's side, Orlando rolled his window down.

Megan stopped. "Thanks again, Orlando. This was a lot of fun."

"My pleasure, mi amiga. Hey, uh ..." Orlando readjusted the brim of his white ballcap. "You don't have any Thanksgiving plans, do you? Because you're welcome to come with me to my aunt's in Hartford. I'm just going up for the day—we'll be back here before eight. And the food is so good. You ever have squash flan? Or deep-fried pumpkin fritters? I'm telling you, Puerto Ricans do Thanksgiving right."

"Orlando, that sounds wonderful. Only ..." Megan glanced back up at the dorm door where Penny had disappeared. Time was running out to find a way to Arden, and her only clues were Mystic—and possibly Penny Chen. She sighed. "I'm sorry, I can't. I have to stay on campus to work on my, uh, project. I wish I could."

"Okay." Orlando's voice had an uncharacteristically flat tone.

And Megan realized how deeply she did want to go. "I'm not just saying that, Orlando. I would come if I could."

His brown eyes lit up. "Yeah? Well, next year then."

"What?"

Orlando turned red. "Nothing. We got to go. See ya."

* * *

Arden flipped through the oversized pages of the *Atlas of Years*. Each sheet of the yellowing paper stretched nearly two feet wide, with a huge hand-drawn map of Vindor and a strange date in the corner.

He looked at the last map in the book, tracing his finger over the path he'd taken. He'd started at the palace of Alavar, traveled down to the Selks' cliffs by the sea, then west to Shido, and then up the meandering waters of the Blackwater to M'buk and N'gozi.

The mapmaker had drawn outlines around each group of people: the Dembeyans, the Nomads, the Tsuru, plus those he'd only read about, including the Huntsmen and even the goblins of Ipktu.

He flipped to the previous map. According to the date at the bottom, it was only one year older. Not surprisingly, everything looked mostly the same.

He flipped to the map before that. Woodshea's borders were slightly smaller that year, but that was all.

Same for the year before.

Why waste time making a map every year? He flipped to previous years, taking them a couple at a time. The goblins had moved sometime during that period—he remembered Megan's notes saying something about that. Still not a good reason to redraw the map annually.

Suddenly he stopped. The map before him looked so drastically different that at first he thought he'd stumbled on an entirely different country. The mountains, rivers, and coastline kept the same shape, but the names had all transformed.

Alavar had been labeled as "The Ivory Tower," and the illustration showed only the single spire. Shido was called "Riverton," Woodshea was "Fairywood," and the entire Nomad nation had been renamed "The Vaeltaa."

Arden flipped back a couple more years to find the differences staggering. Alavar wasn't there, although a castle stood nearby with a giant stone bridge over the river. The Nomads—he assumed that was the group now named "Vaelletaan" referred to—lived in the mountains, not the plains. And he didn't see any trace of the merfolk anywhere.

Every single city and people group had been renamed. The borders between lands were completely different, so he couldn't tell who was supposed to be who.

He checked the date at the bottom of the map. This had been made *sixteen* years ago.

"Ahem." Oba Bwenye stood in the doorway, his lamp raised. "Miss Uzimbe is here to collect you."

"Mr. Oba, how long is a year?" Arden asked.

"Pardon?"

"Sorry, I know that's a weird question. But how many days are in a year?"

Oba raised a silver eyebrow. "Most of Vindor uses a 360-day calendar, but our mathematicians and astronomers determined some time ago that it's actually 365 and a quarter days long."

Arden looked back at the map. The book recorded normal years. How could this be possible?

"Is something troubling you?"

Arden shook his head. "I'm confused by these maps. Okay, so over the last ten years there have been a few changes—the goblins moved, the Tsuru added another city. Normal stuff. But look at this—once you go back any further than that, suddenly names are changing every year, and people are moving around fast. Crazy fast."

He flipped another page back. "This one says Shido used to be called Dragonville, and there are pictures of dragons all around. Did Vindor *lose* all its dragons in like two years?"

Oba leaned over the atlas, his forehead creased as he flipped back through the pages. "I have no memory of these changes," he murmured.

"But you would have been alive for all of this. This is only, like, twenty-five years."

Oba reached for another book, his brow creased. "Why don't I remember this? Surely the Empire hasn't changed ..."

"Knock, knock," said a cheerful voice behind them. Ashana stood in the doorway, smiling in the flickering lamplight. "I hope you don't mind, Oba Bwenye, but I let myself down here. Arden, are you ready to go?"

Arden turned to the librarian. "Can I come back tomorrow? I never did find anything about the mist, and I don't want to go back with nothing."

Oba nodded absently, his nose buried in an even larger atlas.

Arden took that as a yes. "Okay, see you tomorrow."

Arden followed Ashana through the streets of N'gozi, the setting sun turning the buildings orange and casting inky shadows from the towers. She chattered away about some professor's recent discovery, but Arden wasn't listening.

Why did people in Vindor move around so much? Why would they rename themselves every few years?

"And here you are!" Ashana had led him to a quiet street along the river, where a long pier lined the water. The familiar houseboat bobbed in the current.

"Thanks, Ashana," Arden said.

"My pleasure! Let me know if you need anything!"

Arden walked toward the *Sensei*, the burn on his foot hurting worse after the long walk. Dark Morning was nowhere around, but Talu perched on one of the benches, stroking the white cat.

"Is that you, Arden?"

Arden stepped into the boat. "Yeah. The library took me longer than I thought it would. How was your tour?"

"N'gozi is just—I've never experienced anything like it." She closed her eyes and sighed. "So many people, all working and living together in harmony—who would have thought such a thing could be possible? Oh, and all the things they *know* here! Kwanu told me how they look through a strange tube and see stars no one else can. And the grand speeches people give, and the medicines they have for all the sicknesses … Which reminds me." Talu pulled a small vial out of her pocket. "Kwanu said to put this medicine on your burn and it will heal much faster, because it's full of science."

"Full of science, huh?" Arden took the bottle and uncorked it. The liquid smelled strongly of flowers. He shrugged and unwrapped his bandage. He didn't see how perfume would help, but the potato had done a decent job, so who was he to judge?

"Hey, Talu?"

"Yes?"

"What does the name Vaeltaa mean?"

Talu shrugged. "How would I know? I've never heard of it before."

Arden looked at her. "What do you mean, you've never heard of it before?"

"Exactly that. Is it a N'gozi thing?"

"Uh, no. It's a Nomad thing. It's another name for your people."

Talu laughed. "You're making things up again."

"No, Talu, I'm serious." Arden frowned. "Your people used to be called the Vaeltaa—at least around the time you were born. What did your parents call themselves?"

Talu cocked her head. "We've always been the Nomads, as long as anyone can remember."

"What about living in the mountains? Does your uncle or anyone ever talk about that?"

"Mountains?" Talu looked almost offended. "Us? That's not possible. We're people of the open sky. We would never hide in caves—we need to feel the wind in our hair, or we feel trapped."

The boat lurched forward. Arden looked up to see Dark Morning hoisting herself into the ship, her dreadlocks dripping.

"Hey, Ms. Morning?"

The Selk turned to him, looking bored.

"Uh, I was wondering," he fumbled. "Where did you grow up? I mean, your people haven't always been at the same cliffs—"

"We've always been at the cliffs," she said flatly.

Arden thought back to the map without any mention of merfolk anywhere. "I mean, even like twenty years ago? You don't remember swimming there from somewhere else?"

"No."

None of this made sense. Were the old maps just completely *wrong?* How would anyone make that kind of mistake?

"Wait." Dark Morning closed her eyes, a pained expression on her face. "Wait. They were black."

"What were black?"

"The rocks. Not like the cliffs. So long ago. I remember the blood on the black, black rocks." Dark Morning looked away. "So black you could hardly see it, the blood."

Arden didn't know how to respond, but Dark Morning helped him out by going silent for the evening.

Arden helped Talu pat together some cold rice balls, a staple from their Shido reserves when they didn't have a fire. Talu worked quietly, apparently lost in her own thoughts as well.

How did she not know stuff from her parents' and grandparents' eras? Did her family never talk about their childhoods? And how could Dark Morning forget where she used to live?

Oba Bwenye had said that most of Vindor lived without history, but this didn't make sense. What was going on?

chapter 23

Thalassa Is Real

Megan lay on her bed, still in her sweater and jeans, staring at the ceiling. She'd stuck around campus all day, but no sign of Penny anywhere. She'd checked every room in the library.

The dorm had mostly emptied out the day before Thanksgiving, and Megan debated knocking on every door in the building to find her. But what would she say? Penny seemed reluctant to talk about Thalassa, and it wasn't the kind of conversation you could force.

Her cell phone buzzed. Megan reached over and glanced at the unfamiliar number on the screen.

"Hello, this is Megan." she answered cautiously.

"FriendMegan!" Bat's voice blasted from the other end. "Mr. Orlando, I can hear FriendMegan in the little box!"

Megan took the indistinct voice in the background to be Orlando's.

"Oh, this is very, very good," Bat shouted. "This is like the Rikean speaking tubes, but more magicful."

"Yeah." Megan held the phone a few inches from her ear. "You don't have to yell. I can hear you fine."

Someone knocked at her door and Megan sat up.

"Hey, Bat, can I call you back?" She hung up without waiting for an answer and opened the door.

There, dressed in baggy pink pajamas that clashed with her red cap, stood Penny Chen.

She cleared her throat. "I lied. Thalassa is real. And I can prove it."

* * *

Arden found himself back in the Archives early the next morning. Talu had declined to come—actually, she had been vague about her plans when he'd asked why.

Of course, there was a good chance that she couldn't see well enough to read—or maybe didn't know how. Megan had mentioned in the Book of Vindor that the Huntsmen didn't have a writing system—maybe it was true of the Nomads as well.

At any rate, he sat in Korvin's study room by himself once again. He leafed through the dusty tome before him—a Dembeyan account of Vindor's history. Based on some of the remarks in the entries, the author found the Tsuru, Nomads, and pretty much everyone else outside of the Empire to be kind of dim-witted.

And not a single line about the mist anywhere.

Arden flipped a few more pages and discovered another one of those silky white bookmarks, and a few more white flowers. The sentence at the top of the marked page read:

The Shadow has breached the boundaries of the Archives. It has taken the whole city now.

A chill ran down Arden's spine. He hadn't forgotten the terror of the Shadow from yesterday.

The next several pages detailed the havoc the Shadow had caused in N'gozi. First it froze the fountains in the plaza. Then it had begun to coat the city in black ice.

The account detailed how water rose up out of the Blackwater River, sliding along the streets, moving up the walls of buildings and freezing there. The ice moved slowly at first, building by building, pressing in toward the city center. Then it picked up speed. People had panicked, almost stampeding, and the ones not fast enough were frozen over by the black ice.

Megan hadn't written anything about this in the Book of Vindor. She probably didn't know it had happened.

Arden read on, his palms sweating. The ice got almost everyone in the end—only a handful of people escaped it by climbing into high spiral towers. The book's author had been one of these. The man's account read:

I looked out to a world of ice, terribly silent, impossibly still beneath a cold, blue sky. All at once I felt a terrible shudder in the air. I saw the towers of N'gozi sway and crumble. At first, I thought it must be an earthquake, until I realized with horror that the buildings weren't falling, but disappearing, brick by brick. They were being unmade.

The sky, too, was unmade. The blue unraveled, strip by strip, revealing empty blackness behind it.

At the time I had the distinct impression of dying, but now I believe that I, too, was being unmade. After some time—it's impossible to say how long—I miraculously regained consciousness. The sky shone blue once again, the towers of N'gozi stood tall, and all those who had been under the spell of the ice revived, unharmed.

But I cannot forget the terror of the unmaking.

Arden shuddered and drew the oil lamp closer to himself. As the light shifted across the page, he noticed another detail.

Someone had written in the margin with pencil or light ink. He squinted in the dim light and read: *Battle of Alavar. Date matches the B.o.V. account.*

And then, an arrow pointing to the paragraph about unmaking, and this note: *Megan Bradshaw??*

"What?" Arden's voice echoed in the empty room.

And then, strained voices came from somewhere down the hall.

"They sent *what?*"

It was Oba's voice.

"Yes, sir," someone else answered. "We don't understand it either."

"Not possible!"

Arden heard people running up the stairs. Curious, he took his lamp and followed them up to the lobby.

Chaos filled the giant room.

"What do they mean?" Oba Bwenye stood in the middle of the white floor, a surprisingly commanding presence. He pointed to a log drum at the top of a spiral balcony. "Ask them to clarify."

"Someone already has, sir. We are awaiting the response."

Arden now noticed the sound of drumming in the air, the same rhythm repeating over and over. Apparently, this was what had everyone in a panic.

"What does it mean?" he said to a man beside him. "What is the message saying?"

The man glanced at him, seeming to take notice of his Tsuru-style clothing. "It's from M'buk, young foreigner. The message says, 'Who are you? How did you learn our drum language?'"

"What?" Arden thought back to the man at M'buk's gate, the one who couldn't stop praising N'gozi. He was in charge of the messages, wasn't he? Why would he be confused?

The rhythm changed slightly.

"What does it say now?" Arden asked.

The man's eyes widened in fear. "They say, 'What is N'gozi? We have never heard of you.'"

* * *

Megan blinked at Penny, who still stood in her door. "Say that again?"

Penny looked her straight in the eye. "Thalassa, the ocean-world. I can prove it exists."

"Please, come in." Megan motioned to a chair and closed the door as soon as Penny stepped inside. She noticed the girl held an object, wrapped in a pale, pink pillowcase, under her arm beside the journal.

Penny slowly unwound the cloth, revealing a tiara like nothing Megan had ever seen. Broad white scallop shells, purple cowries, and pearlescent spirals were arranged into a breathtakingly beautiful crown, accented with pearls and tiny, pink sea stars.

Megan gingerly touched the diadem, heavy and smoothed by sea currents over what must have been generations. This was no costume prop.

"A mermaid gave this to me," Penny said.

"A mermaid in Thalassa," said Megan. "You've ... actually been to another world."

Penny laid the diadem in her lap, stroking one of the pearly spires. "Yes. And I'm only telling you this because ... because I can tell you've been to one too, Megan Bradshaw."

"You can?"

Penny nodded. "I can see it—that lonely look in your eye you get every once in a while. When you have a wonderful memory that you can't share with anyone, and it hurts."

"Yes," Megan whispered.

"I was fourteen when I went. Thalassa had been a daydream of mine, my vision of a perfect world. I always loved the sea. And then, one day, there I was. In Thalassa, with the mermaid princesses combing their hair on the shore, just as I had always pictured them. If it hadn't been so incredibly real, I would have thought it was only a dream. I stayed there for fifteen days."

Megan swallowed a lump in her throat. "I stayed in Vindor for twenty-eight."

Penny nodded. "I write it down, every memory. I never want to forget it. Not ever." She looked up at Megan. "Have you ever written anything about Vindor down?"

"No." Megan answered. "Well, I kept a journal while I was there, but I left it behind. I don't need one—the memories are all so vivid, I can't imagine forgetting any detail for as long as I live."

"It *can* be forgotten, though. That's why I write it down, every memory." Penny extended her hand and placed it on Megan's for a moment. The gesture was awkward, but it seemed genuine. "Writing helps with the longing, too. I can tell that you miss your world just like I miss Thalassa."

A tear slid down Megan's face—not from missing Vindor, but from the overwhelming feeling that finally someone understood. Ever since she'd returned to the real world, she'd longed for this—someone who could share her secret. Someone who wouldn't think she was crazy.

Someone who knew exactly how she felt.

Megan took Penny's hand and squeezed it in thanks, then paused. "Penny, I'm just wondering. Have you ever figured out a way to go back?"

chapter 24

Talu's Choice

Arden trudged back to the docks, the sun already sinking low. Another whole day of reading without a single mention of mist anywhere.

I am failing so hard at this.

The burn on his foot no longer hurt—the perfume "full of science" had worked.

The usually noisy streets were quieter tonight, all voices strained and tense. Apparently, the strange drum message from M'buk had freaked everyone out. Arden couldn't blame them.

He turned the corner and spotted the houseboat floating beside the dock. Talu and Ashana sat inside, chattering away.

Arden stepped into the boat and glanced at Talu. "Whoa."

The wavy hair on the right side of Talu's head had been pulled back in braids so tight that it showed her scalp.

Talu winced as Ashana pulled hard, trying to work a comb through the thick locks on the left.

"Your hair is so crazy!" Ashana said. "There's so much of it! But don't worry, we'll tame it yet."

Arden picked up a rice ball and sat on the bench opposite her. "How long have you been working on that?"

"Oh, about two hours already." Ashana grinned. "It will be worth it tomorrow, though."

Arden took a bite of the rice. "Why, what's tomorrow?"

Talu turned her head away from him—or at least as far as she could with Ashana yanking on her hair.

Arden narrowed his eyes. "What's happening tomorrow?"

Ashana smiled. "Talu and I are going to be sisters! Oh, think of all the fun we'll have together!"

"Sisters? How does that work?"

Talu murmured something.

"Uh, I didn't catch that."

"I said, Kwanu and I are getting married."

"*What?*" Arden almost inhaled a mouthful of rice. "Married?"

Talu fidgeted with her hands. "Yeah. Tomorrow."

"Are you *insane?*"

There was a long and awkward pause.

"Oh." Ashana cleared her throat. "I, uh, just remembered, I have another comb I wanted to use for you, Talu. Let me go get that, and then I'll come back." She squeezed Talu's shoulder and stepped out of the boat. "Sorry—it will only take a few minutes."

Arden waited until Ashana had disappeared down the street before turning to Talu again.

"Is this a joke?"

Talu fiddled with her skirt. "No." Her voice was soft, trembling. "Why would it be?"

"But he's like what, thirty years old?"

"I—I don't know."

"You don't know. What else don't you know about him?" Arden crossed his arms. "What on earth makes you think this is a good idea? Giving up everything to marry some creep you just met?"

Talu's voice quavered. "What do you mean, giving up everything?"

"I mean your whole future. Your home. Your dreams, Talu. Don't you dream about being a Peace Talker someday?"

Talu turned her head away. "That was always silly. I didn't want to admit it, though. It's stupid for me to think that my people would listen to someone broken like me."

Arden felt blood rush to his face. "Who ever said you were *broken?*"

Talu didn't answer. "But the Dembeyans—they respect me, despite my handicap. They *like* me, Arden. And if I marry Kwanu, I may be able to help bring peace back home, too."

"What are you talking about?"

"The Dembeyans don't like to see the Nomads fighting, either. There is peace here among the cities, and they want to spread peace. So Kwanu says they will send professional treaty-makers to the tribes to help them settle their differences. And I can be a part of that, because I know the tribes. I can help spread peace. It's the only way to get my dream."

"By marrying someone you don't even know? It's not worth it, Talu."

Talu stood suddenly, rocking the boat.

"What do you know, Arden? You don't know what it's like to be me. My people don't want me. What Windrose man would ever choose a blind girl for his wife? This is the one chance I have. The Dembeyans don't think I'm useless, unlike *some* people. And Kwanu respects me."

Arden shot to his feet. "No, he doesn't. Don't you see that? He treats you like a stupid little kid. He tells you what you like and what you don't without asking you! Is that what you want?"

Tears flowed down Talu's cheeks. "You're supposed to be happy for me."

"Are *you* happy for you?"

Talu sniffed and swiped at her eye, but she didn't answer.

Arden pressed again. "Are you happy, Talu? Do you love this guy?"

Talu hesitated. "Yes."

"You're lying." Arden's voice broke, and he felt that at any moment he might scream or cry himself. "You're lying, Talu, you're lying to yourself, and you know it. Don't do this. You're making the worst mistake of your life."

Talu scowled. "You don't know! It's *my* life, Arden. I can do what I want. Why don't you just leave me alone?"

She stepped over the bench and yanked the red curtain closed behind her. A moment later, he could hear muffled sobs.

Ashana reappeared, a long-spined comb in hand. "Talu, what's wrong?" Ashana gave Arden a dirty look as she rushed into Talu's curtained room. "What did he say to you? Come here. Poor girl!"

Arden picked up the cold rice ball from the bench and hurled it at the river. It hit the side of a cargo boat with a splat and slid down into the black water.

He leapt over the side of the boat onto the dock and marched down a city street at random. He didn't care where he went as long as he kept moving.

Couldn't she see how stupid she was being? Obviously Kwanu had talked her into this. He probably talked down to her to manipulate her, to convince her this was what *she* wanted when it was his idea all along.

But she wouldn't listen to Arden any more now, especially not with Ashana there. And by tomorrow it would be too late.

He thought about untying the boat in the middle of the night and have the current take them away, to get Talu out of here. But Kwanu could easily follow them, and the stunt would only make Talu mad. After all, this was still her choice.

Why did she have to be so stupid?

And why did he have to blow up at her? The sound of her crying had made him feel like the worst human in the world.

This was his fault. He had made them stay longer in N'gozi, on a naïve whim that he could find clues about the mist—a search that had turned up zero information. If they'd left right away, Talu would never have spent so much time with that creep and wouldn't be about to ruin her life.

Couldn't Arden do anything right?

To his surprise, he found himself in the city plaza—the Grand Hall with its spiral tower on one side, and the gleaming white library on the other. People were still coming and going out of the main library doors—the Dembeyans must not believe in closing hours when it came to learning.

Arden scowled and marched up to the blue door.

All right, you stupid library, you'd better give me some answers.

chapter 25

Vindor Recharted

Arden woke up with his nose buried in a book—literally. He lifted his head groggily and glanced around Korvin's study room, illuminated by the sputtering light of a single lamp.

He sat up and rubbed his scalp. It was always dark down here, so he had no idea what time it was or how long he'd been asleep.

Arden carefully poured more oil into the lamp, hoping he didn't ignite the whole room in the process.

On the left side of a table lay the small pile of books he'd managed to skim through before dozing off. On the right side sat a much taller pile still to go.

He sighed and reached for the next book in the stack—an atlas, similar to the one in the Map Room but much smaller. This collection of maps told the same story—people moving and changing their names like crazy for years and years, followed by ten years of relative stability. Then a bunch of blank pages, awaiting new annual maps.

A white bookmark peeked out from between some of these later pages. Curious, Arden opened to the marked spread.

A new map of Vindor, one he hadn't seen yet. The palace of Alavar still stood, as did cities like Elnat and Shido. But other changes to the map were drastic.

The Huntsmen territory had been renamed "Ravensblood." The oceanic territories no longer listed three types of merfolk, but only "Loray."

And the Dembeyan Empire was enormous.

The new territory stretched all the way to the northern mountains, with new cities along the Blackwater River that meandered throughout the plains of Gavgal.

This wasn't a record of Vindor's past. It was someone's plan for its future.

He leaned closer. In a remote corner of the plains, a tiny circle had been drawn. Arden squinted to read the label: "Nomad Allotment."

They're going to steal the Nomads' land and crowd them onto a reservation!

He moved the lamp closer and strained to read some of the other tiny notes. Beside the Tsuru territory, someone had written, "Military allies?" A different hand had answered: "Yes, but play rival lords against each other to keep in check."

There was something written by the cliffs where the Selks currently resided, too. His stomach went cold as he read it.

"The Graveyard Wastes. Uninhabitable."

Whoever made this didn't intend to chase the Selks out. They planned to massacre them.

The lower right corner of the map included a calendar date, and it looked like multiple parties had signed their names in red-brown ink. Only they weren't names at all, but various letters and symbols: A dark bird. A star-shaped flower. A messy letter M. And the ornate initials U.K.

Arden peered closer at the signatures. This wasn't ink—these people had signed in blood.

He shoved the book away from him, horrified. Whoever had made this map had been deadly serious. And considering they had tucked it away in a random book in a random Archives room, they probably didn't intend for someone like Arden to see it.

He reinserted the white bookmark between the pages, tucked the book beneath his arms and rushed for the door.

Oba Bwenye would probably know what to do. At any rate, he had to alert *someone* about this.

He hurried down the rounded hallway, then froze. Voices echoed down the hall.

Arden ducked into a room with rickety tables stacked high with dusty scrolls. He pressed himself against the wall, praying whoever it was didn't see him.

The voices drew closer, and the light from their lamps grew brighter in the open doorway.

The footsteps stopped. "Where *is* he?" a man's voice demanded.

Arden held his breath until his lungs burned.

"Give him a break. He's got a big day ahead of him."

"Yeah," said a third man. "He's giving up the bachelor life."

"What? I didn't think there could be a girl with blood pure enough for him."

One of the men snickered. "Oh, then you won't believe this. He's marrying a *Nomad*."

"An *ugly* one."

Arden clenched his fist.

"Stop lying."

"No, it's true. And he's doing it *today*. Within the hour, I believe. Wants to prevent her getting cold feet."

"But why? What on earth would he see in her?"

The second man lowered his voice. "The same thing Kwanu always sees. Opportunity."

"Huh?"

"Or the greater good of the Empire, if you want to put it more nobly. Which he always does."

"Or, if you want to put it economically," said the third man, "double the Empire's farmable land …"

"Not so loud," cautioned his companion.

The third man continued, his tone hushed: "Plus the strong possibility of gold in their bordering mountains. The Nomads are wasting the valuable land they exist on."

"A waste of space," agreed the first man. "By which I mean the people, not just the land."

They laughed.

Kwanu, Arden thought. *Uzimbe Kwanu. His initials are U.K.*

"The Nomads are weak, divided, and will eagerly sign any contract to spite their rivals—never bothering with the fine print until they're legally bound to it. The girl is the key to gaining the Nomads' trust, to starting our northern expansion."

"I'm sure next time we see Kwanu he'll be insisting we all find Nomad women to marry, to speed the process along."

"I'm all for the progress of the Empire, but *marriage?*" said the first man. "That's asking an awful lot from us."

"What are you worried about? You can always marry a real wife later. You know that's what he'll do."

They laughed again.

Arden's temples throbbed. Kwanu thought he could use Talu as a political prop, steal land from her people, and throw her away when he was done? Not if Arden could help it.

I have to stop that wedding.

Only he didn't know where the ceremony was. He couldn't go running through the streets, sticking his head in every window.

Think! Arden tried to recall the tour Ashana had first given them of the city. Of course—the Grand Hall with the huge tower. She'd said public ceremonies took place there, and knowing Kwanu, he'd settle for nothing less than the most prestigious building in all N'gozi.

The Grand Hall stood across the plaza from the library. Arden could make it in time.

Within the hour, they'd said. Maybe it had already started. He had to go now.

But Kwanu's three friends still stood in the hall, now arguing about some city zoning project. He couldn't appear now—they'd know he'd heard everything, including the secret plans to take over the Nomad territory.

Come on, he silently urged as two of the men were now debating precisely how wide streets should be and whether that would warrant a new building regulation.

Ugh, hurry up and pick something!

But he had the sinking feeling this conversation had only begun. Arden thought he might explode any second.

A chill ran down his spine. Stop a wedding? Was he insane? Why would anyone listen to a dumb kid like Arden? If he did manage to get to the ceremony in time, Kwanu would take one look at him and backhand him in the face. Or worse.

What was the point of trying?

Talu is, he thought, feeling the grip of cold loosen. It didn't matter if Kwanu beat him to a pulp. If he had the chance to save Talu from this nightmare, he'd risk it.

"Did you feel that?"

The men had stopped talking.

"I'm telling you, there's something still down here in these halls." The first man's voice trembled.

The wave of fear Arden just felt—that hadn't been nerves, it was that remnant of the Shadow. And it had found three new targets.

Arden clutched the atlas to his chest. He had a crazy idea that would either work brilliantly or get him in serious trouble.

Either way, it was his only chance.

He strained to hear the men's now-hushed conversation.

"Pull yourself together, Ogbe."

"But I *felt* it. Didn't you?"

"What are you afraid of?"

Arden swallowed, his heart pounding. Then, in the loudest whisper he could manage, he rasped: "What are *you* afraid of?"

One of the men dropped something on the floor. "D-did you hear that?"

"You can't hide from me, Ogbe," Arden rasped again. His forehead beaded with sweat as he peeled himself off the wall. *Don't see me, don't see me ...*

He kicked the room's rickety table as hard as he could.

Dusty scrolls crashed to the ground, their wooden rollers striking the stone in a confused clatter.

The men cried out, and Arden heard them scramble down the hallway. Arden waited a moment, praying all three of them had run, then dashed out of the room and sprinted the opposite direction.

"Hey!" someone shout behind him. "What the—? It's a kid!"

No! Arden pounded his feet against the smooth stairs, taking them three at a time.

"Stop him!"

Arden burst into the grand lobby, running past Oba Bwenye's desk. "What is the meaning of this?" the old librarian called after him. "Where are you going with that book?"

The men and women milling around the lobby now turned to him as he dashed by.

"He's stealing a book?"

"Stop the thief!"

Two men in white robes now blocked the open door up ahead. Arden clenched his jaw and didn't slow down. Just before he crashed into them at full force, he dove to the smooth floor and slipped between their legs.

"Stop him!"

The Grand Hall stood on the other side of the sunlit plaza, crowded with pedestrians at this time of the morning. Arden wove through the crowd, dodging between the narrow spaces between professors and doctors and everyone else in the crowd until the cries of "Stop, thief!" faded away somewhere behind him.

Being small and fast had its advantages.

He slammed himself into the doors of the Grand Hall, and they burst open with a bang.

In the center of an ornate lobby flanked by golden columns, Kwanu stood with a girl dressed in red. A semicircle of theater-like seats surrounded them, where proud elders in yellow robes sat. The grand Dembeyan council, Arden guessed.

Several younger people stood on either side of Kwanu, Ashana among them.

The girl holding hands with Kwanu was Talu, of course, but she was nearly unrecognizable.

Her hair had been completely braided, pulled away from her face, and piled up on top of her head with a golden tiara. Her face was made up with lipstick and rouge that were too dark for her, and an oversize red robe, embroidered with elaborate golden flowers, nearly swallowed her up. She looked small and uncomfortable.

Every eye in the room was on Arden now. "Stop the wedding!" he shouted.

"Arden?" Talu asked in a trembling voice.

Suddenly rough hands grabbed Arden's shoulders from behind. He struggled desperately as two guards pulled him toward the door. "Let me go—Talu, you can't marry him. It's a trap!"

One of the elders in gold stood and held up a hand.

"Young man, are you saying you have just cause to object to this wedding?"

"Yes!"

"Let him speak," the elder commanded.

The men released him, and Arden hurried to the front of the room.

"This man lied to Talu about why they're getting married," he explained breathlessly. "He plans to use her as a tool, to trick the Nomads into making treaties that steal their land."

"What?" Talu's voice shook. "Kwanu, that isn't true!"

"Of course not," Ashana piped up. "That's theft, and oppression, and it goes against everything the Dembeyan moral code stands for!"

Kwanu shook his head. "Don't listen to this child, your honor. You know how these Tsuru are. Besides, the boy has no proof."

"Yes, I do." Arden opened the atlas to the page with the white bookmark and held it up for the elder to see. "I found this in the Archives. It's a map that shows plans for the future. Here's the Nomad territory shrunk down to a tiny reservation, with new Dembeyan cities all around. *And* it's got Kwanu's initials on it. See? U.K."

"Is that so," the elder said, his voice strangely calm.

Arden turned to Talu, whose face had paled. Her good eye raced back and forth.

"Talu, I heard his friends talking. Kwanu sees you as a tool, a disposable one. He doesn't see this as a real marriage."

Talu turned to Kwanu, utter betrayal on her face.

But instead of assuring her, Kwanu pushed her into his best man's arms. "Keep hold of her."

He turned to Arden.

A swift dark blur, and the back of Kwanu's hand smashed into Arden's cheekbone.

Arden reeled, his vision going black for a second. He stumbled, grabbing onto an empty chair to stop from tumbling to the ground.

"Clever boy." Kwanu sneered. "Coming all the way here to rescue your little friend. To reveal my plan to the whole council."

Kwanu turned to the seated elders and held his hands up in mock surrender. "Well, my secret's out. My conspiracy's revealed, and now I'm done for. All right, which of you will do me the honor of punishing me for this evil plan? Who will stand against this crime of conspiracy?"

Some of the elders smirked and elbowed their neighbors.

Arden's stomach sank.

Kwanu turned back to him. "The problem with a conspiracy, little hero, is that it has to be a *secret.*" He smiled. "I got approval on the northern expansion three weeks ago."

"What?" Ashana shrieked. "You ought to be ashamed of yourself! All of you! That's not what our Empire is about. We use our knowledge to help the people around us, never to oppress them!"

Kwanu rolled his eyes. "Give it a rest, Ashana. That's not how the real world works. Never has been. Time you grew up, baby sister."

"Kwanu, you lying toad!" Talu struggled against the grasp of the strong young man who held her. "If you think I'm going to be a part of letting you cheat away our bright skies and open plains—"

"Oh, that ship has sailed, sweetheart." Kwanu pinched her cheek. "This whole arrangement would have been nice for you, thinking you were helping and all. But thanks to your scrawny friend, you're a liability to the whole project. I hope you enjoyed your plains and sky while you had a chance." He waved dismissively to the man who held her. "Lock her up somewhere until we figure out what to do with her."

"Kwanu, are you mad?" Ashana turned to the elders. "You can't let him imprison her without a trial—she's done nothing wrong!"

The elders only shifted in their seats.

The best man dragged the struggling Talu toward a back door. "Sorry, child, you're useless to us now."

"No!" A tremor of rage moved up Arden's spine, and he lunged at Talu's captor. "She is *not* useless. Let her go!"

But the man only kicked Arden in the ribs, sending him stumbling right into Kwanu. The would-be groom lifted his arm and struck Arden in the jaw.

He fell to the ground, spitting out blood. One of Kwanu's other friends kicked him sharply in the ribs again. Arden's side exploded in pain. Laughter, and then another man kicked him in the stomach.

It was worse than his worst nightmares. Steadman had nothing on the strength of these full-grown men. Arden could hear Talu crying for help in the background, but every time he tried to crawl toward her, the men dealt him a new round of blows, each hurting worse than the one before. Blood streamed from his nose and humiliated tears burned on his cheeks.

"Stop this at once."

Arden looked up through a swelling eye and saw a figure in white.

"Stay out of this, old man," Kwanu ordered. "This is official council business."

"Oh yes?" Oba Bwenye stepped forward. "Official council business now includes five grown men beating a teenager? You must have felt rather threatened indeed."

His strong hand wrapped Arden's, pulling him to his feet. Arden's whole body cried out in pain.

Kwanu's voice was deadly quiet. "Get out, old man. You don't belong here."

"Ah, but I do. Have you forgotten that the council meets in the Grand Hall precisely because it is a public place? All citizens are welcome to sit in on all meetings, as is our right as Dembeyans. Which is why the recent addition of guards has been so puzzling."

The head elder stood. "Bwenye, what is your business here?"

"Library business, as always. This boy took a book from the Archives, and I am here to retrieve it." The librarian picked up the atlas from where it lay on the ground.

"Leave that alone," the elder barked.

Oba Bwenye looked up at him. "Oh? The books of the Archives are my domain, unless that law has secretly changed as well."

He picked up the book, and none of Kwanu's thugs tried to stop him. For some reason, the old librarian had an air of authority.

"The white bookmark," Arden whispered. "Look there."

Oba Bwenye opened it to the marked page and studied it for a minute.

"Ah, so this is your game, then," he said quietly. "To take the progress of the Empire and instead of using it to prosper our neighbors, to suppress them."

"All of the council has agreed to it," Ashana said bitterly.

"Please." Talu's voice trembled. "I know my people fight. We act stupidly sometimes. But it is our *home*. And we are men and women like you."

"You are *not* like us," Kwanu hissed.

"Aren't we?" the librarian asked. "The Dembeyans are great men, indeed. But as soon as we fancy ourselves to be gods, we fall to ruin."

He peered at the corner of the map for a moment.

"These other signatures—they are not Dembeyan marks. Uzimbe Kwanu, which three foreign powers have you allied yourself with?"

A murmur riffled through the council.

"They didn't know that part of the plan, did they?" Oba smiled. "Keeping secrets from the council?"

Kwanu's mouth twitched. "Get out."

"As a citizen of N'gozi, you cannot cast me out from my own Grand Hall. That's the law."

Kwanu motioned to the council and his henchmen. "*We* are the law now, you fool. We won't listen to the lectures of a doddering old man."

Oba Bwenye bowed his head. Arden noticed the glint of a thin gold chain around his neck.

"If as elders you will not govern yourselves according the law," he said, pulling on the chain, "then as peasants once again you will be governed by a king."

Oba drew a golden medallion out from underneath his plain white robe. In the center a turquoise stone the size of a marble gleamed in the light.

Ashana gasped. "The Blue Eye!" She glanced once at her brother, defiance in her eyes. Before he could grab her, she dashed to one of the hall's windows where a log drum sat.

She picked up the drumsticks and beat out a loud pattern. "The king!" she shouted. "The king has returned to the Hall and the council is deposed!"

The air around the Grand Hall exploded with the new rhythm. Within minutes, all N'gozi would know. And the whole Empire would hear about it by lunchtime.

The doors burst open. Townspeople in clothing of every color streamed into the room, shouting questions and cheering.

Kwanu tried to make a run for it, but he couldn't push his way through the surge of people.

"Arrest him!" Oba cried. "His trial begins first thing tomorrow. And the elders must each be tried as well. Citizens of N'gozi, we will put this disgrace behind us and start over again."

chapter 26

Where Two Worlds Touch

Arden sat on the hard bench, groaning with every movement of the boat. His nose had finally stopped bleeding, and he rubbed that science perfume stuff on his bruises. The little bottle had nearly run out, and he wasn't halfway finished.

He gently rubbed his right eye and cheek. The skin felt warm and tight, and the swelling had worsened. Arden wanted to curl up in a ball and cry.

"Talu! Arden!"

He looked up to see Ashana, accompanied by Oba Bwenye.

Arden struggled to stand out of respect. "Mr. Oba! I mean, your kingness, sir." It didn't come out quite the way he expected. But then, neither had anything that had happened that morning.

Talu peeked out from behind the red curtain of her room, where she'd been hiding since they'd gotten back.

"Where's your medallion?" Arden asked.

"I have it with me. I hid it to travel here in peace." The old man sighed. "I never did like crowds. I'm already dreaming of the day when I can retreat again to the quiet of the library. But there is much work to do in the meantime."

He looked at Ashana. "But it seems we have a promising new generation of leaders coming up, so all is not lost."

Ashana bowed her head demurely, but Arden could see her smiling.

"At any rate," Oba said, "To the business at hand. I am here to see you off, and to give you a blessing and a warning."

"Huh?"

"First, the blessing. Young lady?" He reached forward and took Talu's hand. "Do not despair, dear one. Your heart will heal."

Talu sniffed and looked away. Just because Arden figured out that Kwanu was a creep didn't mean Talu hadn't felt shocked and betrayed. Her day had been much, much worse than Arden's.

"You are worth seven of a man like Kwanu. Do not forget this in your sorrow," Oba continued. "Rise from the ashes. Bring light to your people."

He turned to Arden. "And for you, the warning."

Arden squinted at him through his swollen eye. "Warning?"

"This morning the city of K'wambe went silent. No one there will answer our messages. Also, we've lost contact with a rescue party that reached the border of M'buk. The last message they sent mentioned the area was covered in an unusually thick fog."

"Fog?"

Oba shook his head. "I don't know what to think about this strange mist that's never mentioned in the Archives, but it makes me wonder. Ride swiftly north. Stay away from it. And if you learn more information, send me word right away. I fear our entire Empire may be in danger."

* * *

Thanksgiving morning dawned with a crisp frost over every tree and blade of grass. Megan helped Orlando scrape the white crystals off his car windows, surprised at how much she wished to go to his aunt's with him and Bat.

Megan had hesitated to let Bat leave campus when Orlando brought it up—especially since it sounded like Penny knew something about finding portals between worlds.

But Penny could still be shy and hard to keep engaged in conversation, and she clammed up whenever Bat was around. She'd agreed to help Megan look for potential doors back to Paracosmia throughout the day, and Megan didn't feel she could bring Bat along—and she definitely didn't want him wandering around campus unattended.

Megan finished scraping the back window as Orlando started the car to get the heater going. She turned to Bat, who was wrapped in two overcoats.

"Please be normal around the Ruiz family," she said quietly. "Don't mention Ipktu. Or your wife. Or that you're a king. Keep your mouth filled with food and talk about yourself as little as possible."

Bat nodded beneath his layers. "I will talk about feetball, then. Orlando says it's what his brothers talk of more than all things."

"Yes, sports are a great topic."

"I know all about it. First you take the skin of a pig, and then—"

Orlando honked his horn. "Mr. Bat, are you ready to experience your first and best-ever Thanksgiving?"

"Oh yes." Bat hopped into the passenger seat. "Bye, FriendMegan."

Orlando leaned out the window. "You sure you don't want to come?"

And Megan almost agreed on the spot—then remembered her task. "I wish I could."

Orlando tipped his ball cap to her. "Get lots done on your project. Adios!"

Megan watched the car as it disappeared down the campus road, then she turned back to Grace Palmer.

Penny sat on the steps, a maroon scarf looped several times around her neck and over her red toboggan cap. She peered out from behind her sunglasses. "Are you ready?"

Megan nodded, chattering against the cold.

"All right." Penny picked up her book satchel, the oversized journal among the books tucked inside. "Let's go find your brother."

Megan had told Penny everything the night before—about Vindor, the Shadow she'd defeated, and why she believed Arden was trapped there. Penny had listened intently, never interrupting. She'd told Megan she'd be happy to do whatever she could to help her find a way back.

As Megan drove to the bridge by the train station, Penny examined the pages of the books she'd brought along, pausing thoughtfully.

Megan parked in the train station lot and led Penny down the slope toward the river.

"Are you sure this is the spot?" Penny asked.

"This is where I found his bag, and where Bat seems to have appeared."

"Hmm." Penny dug through a compartment of her satchel and pulled out a large quartz crystal dangling from a leather strap. The grey stone had been badly cracked. For a moment it reminded Megan of the Smokestone—the crystal talisman that belonged to the Huntsmen girl Dagger, all those years ago.

"What's that for?" she asked.

Penny held out her hand, letting the stone dangle at the end of its cord. "There are weak places, where two worlds touch," she explained. "A crystal can sometimes detect them."

She walked in a circle through the frosty grass, slowly and deliberately. After a moment she took up the crystal and examined it.

"Well?" Megan asked.

Penny sighed. "Nothing."

"But there *was* a door here, somewhere."

"I don't doubt it," Penny said. "The thing is with these portals is that they don't stay in one place. Both worlds—this one and Paracosmia—are dynamic. Think of it as two pearls in a pouch, jostling against one another. At any given time, they're touching in different places. Only worlds aren't perfectly smooth, as it were. They're lumpy, like freshwater pearls. So some places …"

"Some places are more likely to rub than others," Megan finished.

"Yes, and at certain times the likelihood of them touching is amplified."

"That makes sense, I suppose." Megan paused. "How do you know this?"

"Oh. I, um, have been doing a lot of reading on it."

"Where? I've been searching for days and haven't found a shred of information anywhere."

"Well, I've been looking a lot longer than you. I've been looking for a way back to Thalassa since I was twelve." Penny held out the crystal again and headed for the underside of the bridge. "Let's keep going. Sometimes the portal shifts by a short distance."

They trudged through the cold, wet grass, tracing the river until it passed the train tracks and opened out into a small bay. Penny checked the crystal periodically, but never seemed to see anything.

"You said fourteen," Megan said after a few minutes.

"What?"

"You told me you went to Thalassa when you were fourteen, but a minute ago you said you were researching ways to get back since you were twelve."

"Oh." Penny paused, checking the crystal again. "Well, the truth is I was interested in all this before I went to Thalassa. That's what made my wish to get there so strong."

They walked in silence for a long time after that. A bitterly cold wind blew wet, salty air at them in a never-ending stream. The waves churned white, and Megan could see the boats in the marina on the other side of the bay bobbing up and down.

She hugged her coat closer and blew into her mittened hands. When they reached a small piece of sandy shoreline, Penny stopped.

The beach, abandoned on this cold November morning, offered a rickety wooden gazebo with one or two picnic benches inside. A long, wooden pier stretched over the coarse sand and then extended two hundred or so feet over the churning waves.

Penny stood looking out over the water for a long time, and Megan wondered if she was dreaming of Thalassa once again. The girl then turned and examined the pier and the gazebo.

"Oh!" Penny suddenly snatched up the crystal, cupping it beside her ear.

"What?" Megan asked breathlessly.

"For a moment, the crystal reacted. Then it stopped." Penny lowered her sunglasses for a moment to look out toward the restless waves. "There's something here, but it's faint and inconsistent. If it is a portal, we'll need a way to make the connection point stronger before it's of any use."

"Do you know how to do that?" Megan asked.

Penny pushed up her sunglasses and hoisted up her book satchel. "I'll figure it out."

* * *

The bulky houseboat made its way up the Blackwater River for what felt like three hundred miles, but it was probably more like six.

Talu had stayed in her curtained-off room for the entire trip. The white cat occasionally slunk out from behind the curtain to stare toward the water or make creepy chattering sounds at birds, but mostly he stayed in the room with Talu.

Comforting her, Arden hoped. He was sure she needed it.

As the sun set, Dark Morning directed the botos into a quiet bend in the river that formed a natural harbor between the river bank and a long sandbar. She released the botos, then turned to Arden.

"Meet me there," she said, pointing to the sandbar. "Bring a staff."

Arden blinked stupidly for a moment. "Wait, are you training me again?"

"Don't make me wait."

Arden winced as he stood. Two of his ribs sent stabbing pains through his chest as he bent over to pick up a spare pole beneath the benches. Surely Dark Morning would go easy on him today.

Arden waded through the shallow water and onto the sandbar, where the Selk sat, holding her wooden pole out in front of her.

"Strike my staff."

Arden stepped closer, trying to focus on quick movements instead of huge, easy-to-predict swings. But the Selk was still too fast for him, and his bruised legs hurt every time he tried to step forward.

"Don't leave yourself open," the Selk warned.

Arden swung again, but she flipped her staff around and struck him on the back, hard, knocking him into the sand.

He hissed through his teeth as pain shot through his ribs.

"Get up," she barked.

"Give me a minute, okay?" Arden struggled to sit up in the sand. "I just lost a fight this morning, I need—"

The Selk swung at him, the end of the pole stopping a mere inch from his nose.

"You didn't lose."

Arden blinked. "Of course I lost. Look at me! I didn't have a chance against those guys. They would have beaten me more if Mr. Oba hadn't stopped them. He's the one who won."

The Selk's staff sliced through the air again, and Arden recoiled. Then, gently, he felt the wooden tip under his chin, lifting his face so he looked right into Dark Morning's brown eyes.

"I heard what you did for that girl." Her voice was low. "She's safe and on her way home because of you."

The Selk pulled her staff back and turned to the water. "Rethink winning and losing."

Talu had made her way to the river's narrow shore and already had a blazing fire going by the time Arden made his way back. She'd removed every single braid from her hair, and her wavy locks were especially wild as a result.

Arden put a pan down over the fire and tossed in a piece of sausage from their stores.

"You okay?"

Talu sniffed and poked at the meat with a wooden spoon. "I'm managing." She glanced up in his direction. "How badly are you hurt?"

Arden stifled a groan as he shifted his weight onto his good foot. "Managing."

For a moment there was no sound but the sizzle of the meat in the pan.

Talu cleared her throat. "You warned me about him."

Arden didn't answer.

"But I wouldn't listen. I said I'd do what I wanted. I pushed you away. But you found me and tried to stop him anyway. And if you hadn't ..." Her voice trailed off. "Why?"

"Because you're my friend, Talu. And you were in trouble." He frowned at her. "You didn't think I could let him hurt you—you matter too much."

Without warning she caught him up in a bear hug, practically smashing every bruise he had. He resisted the urge to cry out in pain and let her hold him there, tears running down her face.

And despite his protesting ribs and the throbbing of his swollen eye, he realized he'd do it all over again if he had to.

Maybe being a hero didn't feel like standing over your defeated opponent. Maybe being a hero felt more like this.

chapter 27

Beneath the Blackwater

Megan and Penny talked long into the afternoon, trying to figure out the next step. The two primary problems to solve were strengthening the weak connection enough to support a portal, and then finding a way to open it.

"Isn't reaching it enough?" Megan leaned back against her dorm bed.

Penny shook her head. "This kind of door is typically locked. You need some sort of an object—a key of some type —to get through."

"Those aren't easy to come by, I suppose." Megan thought of her disappointing experience with the Starstone. "And once we do get into Paracosmia, we won't know where we are. We could end up in any one of thousands of lands."

"Right, but if this portal by the sea recently opened up to Vindor, I'd think it would still be connected there," Penny said. "It moved a short distance here, so I'd hope it only moved a short distance there as well. And the key itself—whatever that is—might influence where we end up."

"How do you know all of this, Penny?"

"Reading." Penny sighed, pulling her red cap farther down on her head. "Which it looks like I need to go do more of. Goodnight, Megan Bradshaw."

Megan turned in not too long after Penny left, but she tossed and turned for some time.

She was closer than she'd ever been to reaching Arden—tantalizingly close—but there were so many pieces to figure out, and so little time to do it.

Thanksgiving Day was now over. Mom would be picking Arden up on Sunday. That gave her and Penny a grand total of two days to get into Vindor, find Arden, and bring him home.

Megan awoke in the middle of the night in a cold sweat. She sat bolt upright, her heart hammering in her chest.

"Stay out of the water," she heard herself gasping. "Arden, stay out of the water!"

* * *

Arden woke up from his fitful sleep for the fifth time that night. Every breath he took sent pain shooting through the left side of his chest.

He wondered if his ribs were broken or just bruised. Probably bruised, since he could still walk around and stuff. But he had a feeling they'd be sore long after the rest of his injuries healed.

Wouldn't be so bad if I didn't have to breathe so much. He sighed, then immediately regretted it.

A sliver of moonlight appeared, filtering through a gap in the red curtains.

And then the voice.

> *Oh tell me, moon, if you can hear,*
> *Dreaming while under this spell …*

Arden sat up as quickly as he could. She was back!

Talu snored quietly in the room beside him as Arden pulled back his curtain and looked out to the Blackwater.

> *It's really her!*

At the far end of the sandbar, the mermaid had pulled herself onto a half-submerged log. Her long black hair fluttered in the breeze, and the moonlight dazzled on the part of her silvery tail above the surface of the dark water. She clasped her pale hands as though in prayer.

> *Where is the boy my voice can hear,*
> *Dreaming while under this spell?*

Arden glanced back toward Talu's room. "I'm here," he said softly.

The delicate face turned to him, moonlight glinting off tears pooling in her eyes.

Arden found himself overcome by the mermaid's beauty. He had an overwhelming urge to run to her, to touch her skin. He felt his face and ears turning red.

The mermaid didn't seem to notice. She stretched her arm in his direction, her eyes pleading.

Arden tiptoed toward the front of the boat, being careful not to rock it. Dark Morning was nowhere to be seen.

"Are you in some kind of trouble?" he asked.

Twelve fathoms deep

I lie asleep

And you have drawn me here.

Arden made the short jump from the side of the houseboat to the damp sandbar. His bare feet squelched in the sand.

"I don't understand. You're sleeping somewhere else? Then why can I see you?"

They call me Moriana

You draw my spirit here.

"Are you like a, uh, memory, or a projection?" He stepped toward her across the length of the sandbar.

With one arm the mermaid clung to the log, and with the other she held out a hand to him, her eyes pleading.

"What do you need me to do for you?"

Twelve fathoms deep

I lie asleep

And you must break the spell.

Arden knelt beside the submerged log. He reached out and took the mermaid's hand—soft and ice-cold.

She reached out with her other arm and placed it behind his head, drawing him into her. Her thin fingers ran through his hair, and she pulled him toward her lips.

A wave of hot emotion rushed over Arden, and he closed his eyes, leaning in for the kiss.

But her lips never touched his. Her fingers wrapped around the strands of his hair and she yanked violently.

Arden lost his balance and tumbled face-first into the river. Cold water filled his ears, his nose, his mouth, and burned in his lungs.

The mermaid shoved his face into the coarse sand below the surface, nearly crushing his nose. Arden flailed his arms and kicked, desperate to push her away. She threw her full body weight against his head and neck, smashing his face deeper into the sand. Tiny rocks scraped against his nose and lips.

Abruptly she pulled away, letting out an ear-piercing shriek that he could hear clearly though the water.

Arden pushed against the muddy bank and managed to get his head above the current. He took a spluttering breath and scrambled back up the sandbar, coughing so hard his lungs rattled and his ribs exploded in pain. He glanced back at the water.

The mermaid thrashed her tail and arms, wrestling with something pale and ghostly in the moonlight.

Snow White.

The cat perched itself onto the writhing mermaid's back, yowling and swiping its long claws at lightning speed. The claws dug deep into the pale skin. The mermaid twisted around and grabbed him by the neck, but Snow White slashed at her, drawing blood in three lines against her cheek.

"You horrid thing!" she screamed, flinging Snow White into the water.

A second later, the white bat-like ears reappeared above the surface, and the cat paddled its way right back toward the mermaid.

Two larger forms sped toward her beneath the black waves. Arden caught sight of a lumpy pink dorsal fin.

The mermaid took one look at the botos and dove, speeding down the river like a torpedo. The botos followed close behind.

"What is going on?" Dark Morning's head and shoulders appeared from under the water beside the *Sensei*.

Talu pulled back her curtain, rubbing her eyes. "Who screamed?" The cat pulled itself into the boat, looking more scraggly than usual, and jumped into Talu's arms. "Oh! Why is Snow White all wet?"

Arden sat on the sandbar, unable to make any words come out. Blood trickled down his lip.

Dark Morning pulled herself onto the sandbar and regarded his injuries with a frown. "What happened to you, boy?"

Arden pointed down the river. "There was a mermaid. The cat and the botos chased her off." He swallowed. "She, uh, tried to kill me."

Talu inhaled. "What?"

"There are no merfolk in this part of the Blackwater," said Dark Morning.

"She followed us, I think. I heard her singing back before we reached M'buk, but neither of you seemed to be able to hear it."

The Selk's dark eyes widened. "You had a Loray siren following you?"

"What's a siren?" Arden asked.

"Who sings sailor-drowning songs. Only males hear them." Dark Morning scowled down the river. "Why come so far inland?"

"She said she was under a spell," Arden said. "She kept saying, 'Twelve fathoms deep I lie asleep, my name is Moriana—'"

"*Moriana!*" The Selk splashed into the water and grabbed the side of the boat so violently that Talu nearly tumbled overboard. Dark Morning reached in and grabbed a bamboo pole with its end ominously sharpened. "Where did she go? I'll tear her limb from limb, I swear I will!"

Talu reached down and grabbed the Selk's shoulder. "Who's Moriana?"

Dark Morning spat into the water. "The Loray queen, who sends whole armies to kill my people. My husband lost part of his tail battling them, and maybe more since then." She shuddered. "I'll kill her myself."

Talu took hold of the mermaid's shoulder with the other hand, pulling her back. "But it *can't* be her, Ms. Dark Morning. If she's the queen, she'd be busy in her palace, ordering people around. She's far too important to wander all this way after some kids in a boat."

The Selk lowered her spear.

"The idea of the real Moriana coming this far doesn't make sense," Talu continued. "This is probably some devoted follower who's taken on the queen's name. Or a crazy mermaid who thinks she's something she's not. But not the real queen. Let her go. She's not worth it to us."

Dark Morning sighed. "Are you hurt, boy?"

Arden wiped at his bleeding nose with his sleeve. "I'll be fine."

"Get sleep," she said. "I'll guard until morning."

* * *

Megan woke early on Friday morning to a heavy rain beating against the dormitory roof. She opened her blinds to see the naked branches of the campus trees whipping around in the wind.

She dressed hastily, then stepped into the dim dormitory hall. Light peeked out from the crack underneath one of the doors. Megan paused beside it, straining her ears.

A muffled voice came from inside, with pauses that indicated she was hearing only half a conversation.

Megan couldn't make out the words—she didn't intend to eavesdrop on someone else's phone call—but after a moment she recognized Penny's voice.

Megan stepped back, waiting impatiently for the call to end. Had Penny discovered anything else in her reading? She was dying to know.

Penny sounded upset with the person on the other end of the call. Megan wondered what her friend's home life might be like. After all, she'd been left on campus during Thanksgiving. Was she not welcome at home, or did something about her family dynamic make staying alone at school the better option?

When the conversation seemed to have ended, Megan paused for another minute, then tapped gently on the door.

"Who's there?" Penny sounded startled.

"Penny, it's me, Megan. Is now a good time?"

"Oh, uh, just a minute."

A minute or so elapsed, and then Penny stood in the doorway. She wore baggy sweatpants and a hot pink sweatshirt with a kitten screen-printed onto it. Megan was surprised to see she wore the red toboggan cap even when in her pajamas.

"Come in. Sorry about the mess."

The room was dimmer than Megan had expected. The overhead light remained switched off, and blankets were thrown over the shades of the few lamps that remained. It took Megan a few minutes to get used to the low light.

The two sides of the room were a study in contrasts. The right side featured a bright pink bedspread and posters of pop stars and fashion models plastered over the walls. The other side was decked in navy and red, with Red Sox pennants, posters, and other team paraphernalia on every surface. Megan couldn't figure out which side was Penny's.

"I found something," Penny said. She plunked a heavy book onto her desk. "In here, somewhere."

Megan stood, trying to be patient as Penny proceeded to flip through the book's many pages. She glanced over at the nearby dresser, crowded with strange objects—a pile of books, the mermaid crown, the crystal, a polished stone, and a potted shrub. Shoved off to the side stood a photo frame labeled "Chen sisters." Megan frowned at the picture. The three girls in photo were all tall, thin, and definitely Asian. Could this be Penny's adopted family? And why wasn't she included in the photo? Perhaps another clue to her family dynamic.

"Something interesting?" Penny asked.

Megan quickly turned her attention away from the photo and feigned interest in the plant. "Oh, uh, is this oleander?"

"Huh?"

"The plant." Megan inhaled the sweet scent of the white flowers with their five showy petals each. "Our neighbor has one of these in her yard. She said it was called oleander."

Penny turned back to her book. "I don't know. I've always heard it called Starflower. Oh, here we go." The tome opened to a complicated chart involving constellations and two touching wheels that looked like Maya calendars. Penny jotted down several numbers, murmuring to herself as she pointed to various places along the circles.

Megan idly opened the book at the top of the pile on the dresser, surprised to find the paper as thick as parchment and yellowed with age. The script across the page was an unintelligible mess of squiggles and lines. Could it be Arabic? Thai?

"Are these from the Cove library?" she asked.

Penny looked up. "Oh, no, from a different library. They're mine now. There's a ton of material out there, though I've had to pull together a lot over the years."

Megan pointed to the strange script. "You can read this?"

Penny ignored the question, pointing to the chart before her. "Okay, so it looks like there are certain star alignments that affect the behavior of portals. But they won't be aligned right until ..." She traced one of the circles with her finger. "About a month from now."

"But we don't have a month!"

"I know." Penny frowned and reached for a different book. "I'll find a way."

chapter 28

The Dark Mirror

Talu had already started a breakfast fire on the shore by the time Arden managed to get up. He pulled back the curtain and stared out over the black water for a moment.

Suddenly the cat crouched beside him, appearing from nowhere. Arden looked down into the blue eyes.

"You saved my life, cat. You really did. Maybe I was wrong about you." Arden reached out to stroke one of the batty ears.

The cat bared its teeth and hissed. It turned its tail to him and sauntered away, thin nose in the air.

"Little stinker," Arden muttered.

Talu had a pot of rice bubbling over a small fire. "How are you feeling?" she asked as he trudged through the sand toward her.

"Managing. Where's Dark Morning?"

"Tracking down one of the botos that's still missing from last night."

Arden ladled some of the hot rice into a bowl. "That was impressive, the way you talked her down. I think she *could* have pulled that mermaid limb from limb." He thought of the cougar that had been five times the weight of the slender mermaid.

"I don't know." Talu nudged the campfire with a stick. "She has the strength, but she's weird about death."

"True."

"I think she lost someone. Someone important. Do you ever wonder why she's called Dark Morning?"

"Uh, because her parents liked the sound of it?"

Talu shook her head. "It's not a birth name. It sounds like a name people gave her after something major happened. But it doesn't make a lot of sense. Mornings are supposed to be bright and hopeful. Why is hers dark?"

Arden tapped the side of his bowl. "The idea of a storm, maybe?"

"Right. Or something new was supposed to begin, and it went badly. I suppose there's no way we can guess."

"What she said about her husband was interesting," Arden said. "I never considered her being married."

"She must worry terribly about him off fighting in that war with that wicked queen."

"No kidding."

Talu stepped away from the fire to empty the rest of the water from the pot into the river. Arden stretched his legs out in the sand, trying to soothe his aching muscles.

What Dark Morning had said about the Loray people wanting to kill the Selks matched what he'd seen on Kwanu's map. He recalled the section marked "the Graveyard Wastes" and shuddered.

Moriana ... the name Moriana began with an M. If the map illustrated her vision, then there was a good chance that Queen Moriana—the real one—could be one of Kwanu's co-conspirators.

But who were the other two? Who in Vindor would sign with a flower or a crow?

"Hey, Arden. Look at this funny stone I found!" Talu held out a broad, white scallop shell.

"It's not a stone." Arden sat up. "It's a seashell."

"You mean it's from the sea?" Talu's good eye danced.

"Yeah. How did a seashell get all the way up here?"

Talu drew the ridged shell close to her face. "My aunt says if you hold a seashell up to your ear, there is magic inside that lets you hear the sound of waves."

"Sorry, that one's the wrong shape. It has to be a spiral shell, I think."

But Talu already had it against her ear. She frowned. "I hear voices."

"Um, that's probably not something you want to announce, Talu."

"No, really. *Halls with boughs of holly ... Fa-la-la-la-la, la-la-la-la ... 'Tis the season to be jolly.* What's *jolly* mean?"

"What?" Arden jumped to his feet, wincing as he did so. "How do you know the words to—?"

She held out the shell to him. He took it and pressed his ear against it.

"See the blazing Yule before us, Fa-la-la-la-la, la-la-la-la, Strike the harp and join the chorus ... "

"Why on earth is this seashell playing Christmas music?" He turned it over. A flat black stone was jammed into the concave interior of the white shell. The dark surface was polished smoothly enough to be a mirror—but oddly enough, he couldn't see his reflection in it.

Arden tilted it toward himself. He could see some sort of light, but one not lined up with the sun behind him. It almost looked like the underside of a light bulb.

All at once, the light reflection vanished, and a woman's face appeared.

"Where have you been?"

The voice coming from the stone was as clear as day.

The reflection woman scowled from beneath her hood. "I told you I want the boy alive. If you betray me on this, Moriana, I swear—"

The face squinted up at Arden, and he realized with a start that she could see him, too. "Who are you?" the voice demanded. "Where did you get this mirror?"

Talu piped up. "We found you on the Blackwater. We thought you were a shell."

"Talu, no!" Arden clasped his hand over the black stone, blocking the face. He paused for a second, then lobbed the shell into the river. It landed with a *plunk* and disappeared beneath the surface.

"You threw it away?"

"I don't know what that thing was, Talu, but I think it belonged to the mermaid who tried to kill me. Whoever her friend was on the other side of that is not someone we want to find us."

He recalled the cold look in the mirror-woman's eyes when she said she wanted the boy alive. He shuddered. "Let's get out of here."

* * *

Megan sighed and switched off Penny's alarm clock radio. "When they finally do get around to reporting the weather, they don't give *any* new information."

Penny muttered something unintelligible, not looking up from her pile of books.

Rain lashed against the window, and something clattered onto the roof above them.

"That sounded like a big branch," Megan said. "I wonder if there are any updates online."

Megan retrieved her phone from her pocket, surprised to see she had missed a call. She pressed the voicemail button and listened.

"Hey honey, it's Mom," the recorded message started. "I'm guessing you're out of cell range right now. I wanted to check in and make sure you know about the big storm that's coming your way. I know the Williams said they had a weather radio, so hopefully this is old news for you. I know they'll make the right decision." Her mother's recorded voice paused. "Dinner at your grandmother's was fine but it wasn't the same without you two there. Boy, will I be glad to see you both on Sunday. Stay safe, okay? I love you, and I can't wait to see you soon."

"I love you, too," Megan whispered as the message clicked off.

A new and terrible thought hit Megan. She'd been so worried about what she would tell her mother if she didn't get Arden back by Sunday— but what if she couldn't get him back at *all*? What if she never reached him, never learned what happened to him, never heard his voice again?

She glanced down where Penny leaned over yet another set of charts. The chances of two normal girls breaking the barrier between worlds was such a long shot—probably near impossible.

Maybe Arden would return on his own, as Megan had—but then

again maybe he wouldn't. Vindor could be a dangerous world, and she had no guarantee that Arden would survive …

No. Selena will keep him safe.

But only if Selena knew he was there. In Vindor, Arden would be one teen boy in a world teeming with people. But to Megan and her mother, he was everything. Losing him would tear the fabric of their lives apart.

Megan wiped away a tear, then clenched her jaw. *Whatever it takes, Arden. I will brave anything to get you back.*

* * *

"The Yellow Rock abhor covered feet,
Brown Owl People, uncovered.
Brown Owl People also distrust smiles;
Do not show your teeth when speaking."

Talu had chanted to herself for most of the morning, sitting straight and tall as the botos pulled the houseboat farther up the Blackwater.

Many of the trees had given way to swaths of long green grass, and hills rose up and fell away on either bank of the river.

Arden had quietly taken up the Book of Vindor and tried to capture Talu's profile—the shape of her nose, the expression of intense concentration, the light playing off her thick, wild curls.

Talu furrowed her brows.

"Wolfsbane consider plants a sign of weakness, so don't … um, don't …"

All at once she leapt to her feet, sending the boat rocking. The Book of Vindor nearly slid off Arden's lap into the water, and he grabbed it just in time.

"What's wrong, girl?" Dark Morning glanced back from her place in the bobbing bow.

"It's a meadowlark!" Talu's face glowed.

Arden squinted toward the tangled tree line. "Where?"

"I don't know, but I heard it. The sound of home." Talu sighed. "Didn't you hear it?"

"I, uh, wasn't paying attention to the birds."

Talu sat back down on the bench. "You mean, you didn't hear the thrush singing earlier? Or the ravens calling?"

"No, sorry."

"You haven't noticed the birds this whole journey, have you?" Talu crossed her arms. "Don't you notice anything?"

"He does," Dark Morning said. "He draws things in that book."

Arden snapped the book cover closed, hiding the half-drawn picture of Talu. His ears went red.

"Really? What sorts of things?" Talu asked.

"Everything," Dark Morning said. "Trees. Flowers. Cities. Us."

"Let me see."

"No, it's nothing," Arden said.

But Talu reached over and snagged the book from Arden's hands. She opened to a random page and held it an inch from her good eye. "You made this?" she asked after a moment.

"It's not important."

"But it is, Arden." Talu lowered the book and leaned toward him. "To notice things so well that you remake them in lines is a great talent, and it shows you are an observant person, a deep person."

Arden cleared his throat. "You think so?"

"Yes," Dark Morning said abruptly.

Talu nodded. "You are capturing memories in this book. When you see these pages later, you will know exactly what you saw, even when your memories fade. This kind of thing is not something to be shy about. Art is a gift, and it is important."

She held the heavy book out to him, and Arden accepted it with a firm grip.

"Thanks, Talu."

The forests continued to thin out the farther they traveled, until only an occasional patch of pines or thorny shrubs took root among the stones and river grass.

Arden found himself looking out over stretches of plains with nothing to obstruct the view for miles. He noted with some uneasiness that anyone out there could just as easily see him and the boat floating along the river.

He was glad when Dark Morning eventually anchored the *Sensei* in a spot with hills rising on either bank.

With the boat secured, Talu leapt into the long grass and bolted up the hill.

Arden eased a load of cookware onto the bank. "Where are you going?"

But Talu didn't answer, her long hair and red skirt fluttering in the wind as she ran.

Arden jogged up the hill after her, wincing at the pain in his side. By the time he reached the top of the ridge, Talu stood with her arms stretched out and her head thrown back, grinning.

And Arden immediately understood why.

When they had talked about the plains of Gavgal before, he'd always pictured a featureless expanse of dry, yellow lawn.

Not so.

Thousands upon thousands of purple and yellow wildflowers danced among the long green grass. Here and there, tight ridges of pine trees stretched fifty or sixty feet high. They seemed to barely scrape the bottom of the gold-and-magenta sky that was somehow too enormous for Arden's mind to comprehend.

Illuminated in the orange light of the setting sun, snowcapped mountains dominated the western horizon, so huge Arden felt he could reach out and touch them.

Talu sighed. *"Home."*

A breeze rippled over the plain, setting the wildflowers bobbing in the ocean of grass. Talu stretched out her hands to the wind, her long curls tangling and untangling in a pattern so beautiful and wild Arden's pen would never be able to capture it.

"I didn't know I missed it this much." Talu reached down and grabbed a clump of yellow daisies and drew them to her face, inhaling deeply. "The open air, the free wind—and to think, I could have lost this forever."

She looked toward Arden, a tear glistening at the edge of her good eye. "I would have lost it all, if it weren't for you. Is it not the most wonderful thing you've ever experienced?"

"It's ..." Arden fumbled for words. "It's unreal. Everything's so ... and the mountains are so *huge*." He gazed at them again, marveling at how high they rose out of the surrounding landscape, straight and pointed like a set of dragon's teeth.

Talu nodded. "Those mark the end of Vindor, you know."

"Really? What's on the other side?"

"Your home—Outer Paracosmia. Well, I don't know if it's your land out there, or someplace else. I once dreamed of crossing the mountains and exploring it for myself, though now—" She closed her eyes and tilted her head back, letting the sunlight play across her nose and cheekbones. "Now I don't know if I'd ever want to leave this place again."

Arden held up a hand to block the sunlight, squinting toward where the gigantic range faded into the distance. "What's with that mountain?"

"Which one?"

Arden pointed. "That one."

"Um?" Talu laughed, her good eye flitting back and forth, and Arden realized his mistake.

"Oh, sorry." Arden had forgotten that Talu couldn't see much of anything out here—of this unbelievably beautiful landscape, she could probably only make out a few colors and shapes.

And yet she had clearly been experiencing more of it than Arden had. For a moment he wished he could stand in her shoes, to feel and sense everything the way she did.

He shook his head. "Sorry, there's a spot in the mountains way in the distance with a lot of black shadows over it."

"Black shadows? Oh, you must mean Furious Mountain."

"Come again?"

"Furious Mountain." Talu frowned. "It's not shadows, it's black soil that covers the entire area. It's the birthplace of the Blackwater River, which is why the water is so dark. The mountain is a frightening place, or so my uncle says. Hardly anyone goes there, on account of the evil spirit."

Arden raised an eyebrow. "The mountain is haunted?"

"Yes, there's a terribly angry spirit who lives there. All the oldest legends tell of a time when he got so raging mad, he turned the whole mountain to fire. Rivers of liquid fire—can you imagine, *liquid fire!*—flowed down the mountain. The grasslands burned down to the soil, and the smoke blocked the sun for a month. He's a *very* angry spirit."

Arden blinked. "Oh, wait. You're talking about a volcano."

"What's a volcano?"

"We have them in my world. They're like, mountains that blow up sometimes."

"Because of spirits?"

"No. Because of …" He paused, trying to remember how magma and tectonic plates worked. "It's because of … science."

"Oh." For some reason Talu didn't sound convinced. "Well, don't go there. The Blackwater will lead you right to it eventually, so we can't go too far."

Arden squinted through the light of the setting sun. "It must have been some eruption. Blew the whole top off."

Talu grabbed his hand. "Promise me you won't go there, all right? Even if it is just science in there, it still might get mad."

Arden laughed. "Okay, I promise."

They built a small fire on the sandy bank, using tufts of dry grass for kindling. Snow White paced along the shore as usual, never straying more than a foot or so from the river. Arden tried to offer him a piece of sausage, but the skeleton cat pretended to not even see it.

Arden sighed. "You're still a jerk, even if you did save my life."

Snow White purred, pleased.

"So," Dark Morning said, spitting out a fish bone. "Now what?"

Arden tossed a dry sprig of grass into the fire. "Well, Selena originally wanted Korvin to ask the different tribes if they know anything about the mist, plus make sure no one's gone missing. Obviously there's no Korvin, but Talu and I could try."

"Only from some tribes, though," Talu said. "Several of the tribes are enemies with the Windrose, so I can't talk to them."

"How do we know which tribe is which?" Arden asked.

"Colors, of course."

"Then what?" Dark Morning asked.

"If we work our way northward, we'll eventually find my tribe. They should be along the Bluewater Tributary somewhere. And then, well, I suppose that's where we say goodbye."

The word fell heavy on Arden's ear. He knew they'd all eventually have to part ways—he just didn't realize it would be so soon. His stomach sank. He didn't want to think about that.

"Then I take the boy back to Shido, right?"

"Yeah, I guess so," Arden said. Take him all the way back down where he'd have to explain to Selena that they had no Korvin and no real answers to anything. He sighed.

And then … well, Arden didn't know what would happen after that. Korvin was supposed to guide him back to the real world. With her missing, he didn't know what would happen next. It was strange—his old life seemed like a distant memory, and he'd hardly thought about home.

Arden leaned back in the sand and looked up at the evening sky, already strewn with glittering stars.

In so many ways, *this* felt like the real world, realer than his old life had ever been. He wouldn't mind staying here a good long while.

chapter 29

Children of the Open Sky

Arden woke at first light of dawn. He stretched lazily and parted his curtain.

Dark Morning sat straight and alert in the bow of the ship, her staff at the ready.

Arden rubbed his hand over his face. "What's wrong?"

The Selk glanced at him, then pointed at a tree on the bank where nearly two dozen crows perched. They sat silently, occasionally bobbing their necks or tilting their heads, but not making the usual racket that the crows back home did.

Arden swallowed. Every single one of them faced their direction, watching the boat.

He grabbed a wooden spoon and lobbed it at the tree. To his relief, the black birds spread their wings and took flight, croaking their disgust.

They circled a few times and then, one by one, landed back in the tree. Each one turned toward the houseboat once again, peering at it intensely with their beady black eyes.

Dark Morning turned to him, her face pale. "Untie the boat."

Arden obeyed, shuddering as he loosened the knot of the rope that anchored the *Sensei* to a tree. Dark Morning whistled for the botos, and within minutes the houseboat was moving upriver once again.

Arden cupped black water in his hands as the boat tugged along, trying to at least wash his face. As he brought one cupped handful toward his eyes, he caught a reflection of the sky above, and the silhouette of a silent raven gliding above them.

That afternoon, Dark Morning anchored the houseboat at a sandy peninsula. Beside it, a crystal-clear tributary flowed into the Blackwater, creating a strange swirling pattern of black and blue where the waters met.

"Tribes are almost certain to be around this area," Talu explained. "It's clover-bloom season, and everyone wants to bring their horses to graze."

Talu picked up her staff, gently running her fingers over the brown-and-white feather. She chanted a few lines under her breath, then turned to Arden and smiled with almost a forced cheerfulness. "Ready to go?"

She's nervous. It's her first Peace Talking gig, even if it should be an easy one.

He clapped his hand on her shoulder. "You'll be awesome."

A smile flitted over her face. "Thanks." She turned back toward the boat. "Kitty, want to come?"

Snow White sat on one of the benches and licked his leg.

"That lazy thing's never going to leave the boat, Talu. Let's go."

Arden and Talu headed east, working their way up and down a few green hills. The grass here was shorter and dotted with clusters of purple-and-white clover. Horses whinnied in the distance, and against the enormous blue sky, wisps of smoke rose from unseen campfires.

They crested a steep ridge, and below them, a caravan of fifty wagons spread out over the landscape.

The sturdy wagons had huge wheels, wooden walls, and roofs all painted in bright patterns. Speckled goats wandered among a dozen smoldering campfires, and in the distance clusters of horses grazed among the green clover.

"What colors do you see?" Talu asked.

Arden glanced again at the dizzying array of hand-painted wagons. "There are lots of colors."

"Of the banners, I mean."

"Oh." Arden looked at the flagpoles mounted to the wagon roofs, each bearing a huge cut of cloth flapping in the breeze. Most were a dull tan, but a few stood out in bright blue.

"Blue," he said.

"Oh, that's good. The Runningbrook tribe is friends with Windrose. They'll be happy to tell us anything we ask about the mist. Only let me explain who you are before you say anything; foreigners may not speak to the tribes unless vouched for."

Carefully they worked their way down the steep hill. Talu extended her staff and used the tip to avoid rocks and scrubby bushes, knocking off a few heavy heads of clover blossoms as she went.

But as soon as they reached level ground, she drew her staff vertically, holding it like a normal hiking stick. She stumbled over a stone and nearly tripped. Arden reached out to steady her, but she pushed his hand away.

"Don't. Please." With her free hand, she arranged her dark wavy hair so that it completely covered her bad eye.

She has to hide her disability, he realized. *Maybe they won't respect her if they know?* The thought made him angry.

The brown-and-white feather at the end of Talu's staff fluttered in the wind, and she touched it several times, as though reassuring herself that it was still there.

They approached a cluster of people standing in the center of the wagons. Some sat on horseback, while others stood with their arms crossed tightly.

Two men in the center argued loudly, though Arden couldn't catch the words. A few onlookers jeered or grunted in agreement, but the rest of the camp lay in tense silence.

Something definitely didn't feel right.

Arden turned to Talu, but before he could alert her, the taller of the two men turned sharply in Talu's direction and frowned. He wore a blue cap over long black hair.

He turned to the man he'd been arguing with, a balding fellow who held a staff of twisted brown wood.

"This is who you called for?" the man in blue asked. "A child, not even finished with her training? And who's the foreign boy?"

"I said I called for a Peace Talker," the bald man growled.

The tall man spat. "What a Brown Owl says and what a Brown Owl does rarely match up."

Talu stopped dead in her tracks, her good eye wide. "Arden," she whispered under her breath without turning to him. "What color are the banners?"

And Arden realized his mistake. Only a handful of the banners were blue, all in one section of the camp. The rest of the banners were light brown with a feather symbol.

The people in the crowd before them were clearly divided into two groups, and many had curved swords at their sides.

"Blue … and tan." He swallowed. "I'm sorry, I didn't know …"

Talu took a step back. "This is a tribal confrontation, we have to get out of here, we have to …"

"You, girl, come here," the man with the brown staff ordered. Talu closed her good eye, swallowed, and stepped toward him. Arden stuck by her side, glancing at his worn straw sandals. Which tribe hated shoes? He tried to hide his feet in the tall grass.

"I'm sorry, there's been a terrible mistake," Talu began, breathless. "I'm not the one you sent for, I just came to—"

"There's no mistake," the Runningbrook man in the blue cap said.

"But I'm not—"

The Brown Owl chief thumped his twisted staff on the ground. "Hear the grievances that the Runningbrook have committed against us!"

Talu stood stiffly, the fingers that gripped her staff turning white.

"Talkers mediate between feuding tribes," Talu had said. *"It doesn't always go well. I had a great uncle who was killed when one of his talks went badly."*

Sweat beaded on Arden's forehead.

"The Runningbrook have encroached on our feeding territory," the Brown Owl man declared. "They have purposely mixed their herds with ours."

"No one owns this valley!" one of the women in blue shouted. "We are free men and women like you."

The Brown Owl chief scowled at them. "Free to be thieves and cheats, you mean! We know how you work—you mix our flocks so when we sort them out, they may take the fattest and strongest for themselves and leave us with their sickly ones."

"False!" shouted the man in the blue cap. "These are lies the Brown Owls tell about the Runningbrook to all the tribes, so they may mistreat us. They have always been arrogant men who want to hold us down, to push us to the edges of the best lands, to lord over us."

"You have no respect for our solemn traditions. When we buried our great matron, you danced barefoot near our camp for a week, beating your drums as loud as you pleased!"

"You are not our chieftains. You may not command when we dance." The man in blue turned to the people around him. "Brothers, see how they seek to strip us of our honor, so they may make themselves our masters. See how they insult us with a blind and broken Peace Talker!"

Arden bit his tongue to stop himself from saying something that might get him and Talu killed.

"Now." The Runningbrook leader grabbed Talu by the arm and pulled her between the two groups. "What does the Peace Talker say? How may we be reconciled?"

"Tell us quickly!"

"Give me half a moment," Talu said. "How can anyone easily reconcile two peoples who are so determined to be angry with one another?"

The Brown Owl chief stepped in front of her. "Then you have heard it from the Peace Talker's own lips! There is no peace that can come between us. War is our only option!"

"You didn't let her finish!" Arden cried, but his voice was lost in the barrage of shouts that followed.

"Let there be war!"

"These Runningbrook must be taught a lesson!"

"We will burn the Brown Owl wagons to the ground!"

"Mark this day, we will not rest until they are scattered to the five winds."

Swords rattled. Arden grabbed Talu by the arm. "We've got to get out of here, *now.*"

But she pushed his hand away.

"Wait!" she cried. "You cannot declare war without the ceremony of commitment."

The crowd quieted.

"Ceremony?" the Runningbrook chief asked. "What is this you speak of?"

Talu straightened, standing tall. "Are you certain you want to go to war? Do you know what it takes?"

"Of course we do," one of the Brown Owls scoffed. "We know the weight of blood and honor and glory."

"Then you must prove it by the ceremony."

Arden hissed in Talu's ear. "What are you *doing?*"

She pushed him away and stepped forward. "You, chiefs of your tribes. Each of you must bring out the youngest child in your household."

A puzzled murmur among the people, and short delay as someone went running back into the camp.

What was Talu thinking? Clearly, she was making this ceremony up as she went. And based on the stern looks on the faces around him, Arden guessed he wasn't the only skeptic.

Finally, the Brown Owl People led out a boy of about three, a mop of wavy black hair over a grubby face. A moment later a Runningbrook girl appeared, six or seven, with blue ribbons braided into her hair.

Both chiefs shifted uncomfortably.

Talu turned to the Runningbrook people. "As you have noted, I am blind and cannot see the Brown Owl child. Can someone describe him to me? What color are his eyes? Does his face have innocence and wonder in it, or mischief? Does he have a strong look to him?"

"He seems healthy," one of the Runningbrooks answered reluctantly.

Talu knelt in the long grass. "What is your name, young Owlet Prince?"

The boy looked at her shyly. "Rinyu."

"And what are you the best at, Rinyu?"

His face lit up. "I run!"

Talu smiled. "Oh? Are you fast?"

"Very, very fast! I runned all the way to Big Ridge! I runned to the mountains and back!"

"That's good." Talu stood and nodded in the direction of the Runningbrook. "Don't you love to watch your children run free, beneath the huge sky, with the strong wind in their hair? I think there is nothing better than the boundless joy of children—little children who don't know there's anything to fear."

The Runningbrook chief nodded stiffly.

"And is this your child?"

"Yes."

Talu knelt in front of the girl. "And what are you best at, dear one?"

"I can sing!"

"Oh, singing is the best, even better than dancing. Will you sing for us?"

The little girl nodded eagerly, not bashful at all before the tense crowd. She gave a curtsy and launched into a song:

A little meadow-bird

High in a tall pine tree

He sings till all have heard

"Fly free, fly free, fly free."

It was a simple ditty with a repetitive melody. But apparently, it was a well-known song, for the Brown Owl boy ran up to her and joined in with a wavering voice:

I am that meadow-bird

I'll climb the tallest tree

I'll sing till all have heard

"Fly free, fly free, fly free"

The Runningbrook girl grinned and gave the little boy a huge hug. "Aw, Papa, look at him! He's so cute, isn't he?"

The chief looked away, but the girl insisted. "Isn't he, Papa? Isn't he?"

"Yes, love."

A stiff quiet hung over the camp. Somewhere a baby began to cry, followed by a mother's *shh*. A meadowlark took up a song in the distance.

One of the Brown Owl women stepped forward. "What is the point of all of this? What is this ceremony?"

"There is no ceremony," Talu said from where she knelt, her voice cool. "I wanted you to see their faces, to hear their voices. To see that their children are like your children and are loved just as much. But mostly, I wanted you to remember their faces."

Talu planted her staff in the ground and stood to full height. She scowled, a dark fire smoldering in her expression. "Because when the wagons burn, it is the little children who cannot get out in time."

She turned toward both groups of people, her voice low and powerful. "You have chosen war. Well, when you are dancing after the battle to celebrate the glory and honor and blood of your enemies, may these little faces appear to you. May you see them in the corner of your eye, hear these voices singing 'Fly Free' when you tuck your own children in at night—if you still have your own children. May their faces darken your dreams.

"But don't fear, for there is comfort! When you ache from the empty places around your hearth, you will say, 'There was no other way. For my enemies insulted me, and someone took my fat goat. Lighting wagons on fire and dealing out death at random was the only solution we could think of.'"

Talu's good eye trembled in anger.

No one answered.

Talu turned her back to them. "May you be happy in the path you have chosen."

"What is going on here?"

From over a hill, a woman in a long indigo skirt appeared, a white feather hanging from her staff.

The Runningbrook chief looked up, startled. "Who are you?"

The woman drew closer, her staff thumping on the ground in time with her heavy steps. "Did you not send for a Peace Talker?"

The Runningbrook leader glanced at Talu, and then back at the woman. "Oh, yes." He spoke in a metered, careful tone. "The Brown Owls have let their herds mix with ours. We need you to write a contract to determine a fair way to separate them."

The Brown Owl chief stepped forward, clearing his throat. "The Runningbrooks are noisy and disrespectful on our feast days; we need you to write us a contract to prevent this from happening again."

The Peace Talker blinked. "You're ready for treaties?"

The Runningbrook chief avoided her eye. "We want to be treated fairly, that's all. Surely you can make them do that."

The Peace Talker turned to Talu. "Who are you?"

"Talulaweyna of Windrose. I came here by accident, and I must be on my way." Talu sounded exhausted. Arden put a hand on her shoulder to steady her, and this time she didn't push him away.

"Very well." The woman regarded her thoughtfully. "I will pay the Windrose tribe a visit, Talulaweyna. I wish to speak with you further." She turned to the two tribes. "Now who will be swearing to this peace treaty? I need four from each tribe."

Arden and Talu marched over the grassy hills until Arden was certain they were out of earshot of the tribes. A crow cawed in the distance.

"Talu! You were *amazing* back there, absolutely brilliant!"

She looked in his direction, her eye flitting back and forth.

"I thought I had done it all wrong."

"Wrong? You literally stopped a war! How did you know that fake ceremony thing would work?"

Talu used her staff to guide herself around a scrubby bush. "I didn't know," she said. "It was a huge risk. But ..." Talu paused. "I have Kwanu to thank for that idea."

"Kwanu?"

"He didn't mean to teach it to me. But something he said at our wedding—I asked him how he could steal land from my people, since we are men and women like him. But when I told him that, he said, 'You are *not* like us.'"

"Who cares what that creep said? Don't let it bother you."

"No, it was *how* he said it that struck me: like a reflex, angry and frightened at once. And I realized, to some people the most terrible truth in all the world is this: everyone matters. Think about it—every single person you see has a life just as complex and important as your own."

Arden thought of the ten thousand people in N'gozi, each of them with childhoods, families, friends, memories, and dreams. He slowed his steps, the sheer weight of that thought pressing down on him. "Whoa."

"Most of us guess it must be so, even if we don't think much of it. But there are some people who are frightened of this truth and want to suppress it. Because it is so much easier to think of yourself as complex and in need of understanding, but others as objects in the way.

"I think this is what my people do," Talu continued. "We don't want to think of our enemies as having dreams and stories and children they love. It is much easier to think of them as just Runningbrooks or thieves or brutes who have no hearts, because then you may treat them as you please."

Arden worked his way up the steep ridge, his ribs aching. "So that whole thing with the children forced them to face that truth and draw their own conclusions. *Brilliant.*"

He stopped for a moment to catch his breath. "But next time, I'll try not to walk us into a war, okay?"

"I would appreciate that."

They sat down in the grass to rest a moment before resuming the climb up the slope, panting in the shade of some tall pines.

Talu sat up. "Arden, I don't hear any birds."

At that moment, a cold breeze blew down the hill, causing the hair on Arden's arms to stand straight up. He jumped to his feet, scrambled over the ridge, then stopped in his tracks.

Talu climbed up beside him. "What's wrong?"

Half of the green meadow before them basked in the afternoon sun as before. The other half, the part to the north, lay covered in a thick fog, as dark as a thundercloud. The surface of it shimmered slightly in the sunlight, dull like brushed pewter.

Arden's voice trembled. "I think—I think it's the mist."

"Where?"

"One whole side of the meadow is covered. And it's moving fast."

"We've got to warn the Brown Owls and Runningbrooks!"

"We don't have time." Arden watched the edge of the fog roll over a patch of blue flowers, obscuring them from view. He glanced toward the Blackwater River, its dark surface still sparkling in the sun.

"I think we need to run for it," Arden said. "If we go now, we should reach the boat before it blocks the path, and then Dark Morning can sail us out of harm's way."

"But the *people*."

Somewhere in the distance, a dog howled.

Arden exhaled, watching the edges of the fog bank swirl and coil as they claimed another few inches of the green grass. "Do you think we can get back to them in time, or are we putting ourselves in a trap?"

More barking and howling, closer now.

Arden frowned. "Wow. Is there a tribe that raises dogs instead of goats? Because that's a whole lot of noise."

Talu grabbed his arm, her fingers tense. "No one among the Nomads has that many dogs."

Arden looked back over the ridge. Within an instant, a long-eared hound appeared, its teeth bared. It sniffed and let out a howl that was answered by at least a dozen more.

Arden turned. "*Run!*"

He and Talu stumbled down the steep hill, tripping over rocks hidden in the grass. Behind them, a pack of snarling dogs followed in hot pursuit.

When the two reached level ground, Talu hiked up her long skirt, staff still in hand, and ran at a speed Arden didn't know she was capable of. A few of the leaner dogs broke from the pack and passed Arden, their sights set on Talu.

She bound over the meadows with long, graceful strides and was quickly a dozen yards ahead of him—heading straight for the wall of fog.

"Talu, stop!"

But the baying of the hounds drowned out his voice. He winced at the shooting pain in his side but somehow found the energy to run faster. "Talu!"

For a moment, Talu's dark hair and bright red skirt stood in stark contrast to the wall of metallic fog. The next second, she was gone.

Three dogs disappeared into the mist behind her.

Arden sprinted to the fog bank. "Talu!" He hesitated, then plunged into the fog himself.

chapter 30

Mist World

"I've found a way."

Megan sat up with a start from where she'd been dozing in the canvas Red Sox chair. "What?"

"The storm." Penny pointed to a complicated chart in one of the aging books. "It's a spiral in the surface of the world. It's strong enough to pull this world and Paracosmia together—but only for a few hours."

"When?" Megan asked.

"Tomorrow. Early. At the beach." Penny leaned back in her desk chair and rubbed her face. "The one last piece is the key. Which, it turns out, I may have half of."

"What?"

Penny reached for her satchel and dug through its pockets. "When I left Thalassa, the mermaid queen gave me two items. One was the crown, which you've seen. The other part has always been mysterious to me, but now I'm wondering if it's a clue." She continued to dig around in the bag. "It's a driftwood circle. Nothing particularly beautiful or fancy, but she gave it to me with the same solemnity as the crown."

Megan stood. "Wait—she gave you a wooden ring?"

Penny pulled out a small object and held it out. In her palm lay a perfect wooden circle, too small to be a bracelet and too large for a ring.

"I'm starting to think, based on my reading, that this is part of a portal key," Penny said. "But only part. And I don't know how it works."

"I do." Megan could scarcely breathe. "And I have the other half."

She reached into her jeans pocket, where the Starstone had been stuffed days earlier. When she held it up, Penny gasped.

The stars in the stone's surface sparkled weakly, barely visible in the dim light of Penny's room.

Megan held it next to the driftwood circle. "A perfect match."

"I don't understand," Penny said.

"When I was in Vindor, Amadrya—the elf queen—offered me a way back home. She took the Starstone, and then slid a plain wooden ring—just like this one—around it. I forgot about that part. The pendant reacted, and she could then open a portal between worlds."

Megan wrapped her arms around Penny in a hug. "This is the answer we've been looking for. This is how we'll get back into Vindor tomorrow."

Penny blinked. "We?"

"You're the one who's made this possible, Penny. I want you to come with me and Bat. It's an amazing world. And who knows—maybe Thalassa is nearby."

Penny smiled. "I think I'd be happy just to see Vindor. You're a beautiful person, Megan Bradshaw, so it must be a beautiful world."

* * *

A grey world surrounded Arden—cold, featureless, and constantly shifting. No matter which way he turned, swirls of nickel-colored fog obscured his view. Was he running in circles? Where was Talu?

A scream rang out behind him. Arden sprinted toward the sound. "Where are you? Are you okay?"

"Arden, help!"

Through the swirling mist he could make out the shape of Talu swinging her staff wildly in the air. Behind her a long-eared dog crouched, its teeth bared.

She doesn't know where it is.

Before he could cry out a warning, the dog lunged at her. Her staff flew out of her hand, and she fell to the ground with a thud, the hound latching onto her arm.

Adrenaline raged through Arden's body. He grabbed the staff and swung it hard, clearing it over Talu, but hitting the dog in the nose.

It released its grip, blood on its teeth.

"Get away from her!" he screamed. He swung the staff at lightning speed, forcing it to skulk backward. He leapt forward, placing himself between its bared fangs and the motionless form of Talu. Another dog appeared in the mist.

"You will not touch her again. Go!"

The second dog inched forward, growling.

Then the first one sprang at him. Arden's staff sliced through the air, knocking the animal to the ground. It yelped in pain and scrambled away into the fog. He whipped the staff behind him, making contact with another dog that had been sneaking up. The remaining dog watched him, then lowered its tail and backed away.

Arden waited, staff at the ready, but the dogs didn't return. He dropped to Talu's side.

She lay with the side of her face pressed against the ground, her whole body shaking. Her good eye flew back and forth faster than he'd ever seen it go.

"Where are they?" she rasped.

"Gone for now. We've got to get out of here."

"It bit me, Arden."

He glanced down at her right arm. Below the elbow, her white sleeve was wet with blood. His stomach churned.

"Is it bad?"

"Uh, no." He yanked his tunic off over his head and wrapped it around her bleeding arm, tying it as tightly as he could. "Just a scratch. Here, I'll help you up."

He looped her injured arm over his bare neck and helped her to her feet, wrapping his other arm around her waist. She took shallow, shaking breaths as she stood.

"Hey, Talu, we need to get back to the boat. You can do that, right?"

She nodded, still trembling.

Arden kept the staff in his free hand, hoping they wouldn't encounter more dogs. He concentrated on keeping Talu's arm elevated, above her heart, which wasn't easy to do with her being taller than him.

They trudged through the clammy grass together with awkward, halting steps.

"How badly am I bleeding?" Panic broke through her voice.

"You're fine, Talu." He felt his neck grow wetter. "I've got you. Hey, did I ever tell you the story about Batman? Okay, so this rich guy lives in a city called Gotham, and he spends his time beating up bad guys. But he doesn't want anyone to know it's him, so he wears a disguise that has this cape with wings on it, and …"

As he talked, he scanned the fog, praying they were heading the right direction and that the dogs weren't following.

"Also, he has this utility belt, which has all sorts of cool gadgets on in, like these boomerangs that explode, and …"

Her legs gave way beneath her, whether from shock or loss of blood, Arden didn't know. Either option wasn't good.

"Stay with me, Talu!"

He lifted her back on her feet. She took a few wobbling steps forward.

Please, God, please, we can't keep this up much longer.

The grey wall of fog before them brightened. Arden pulled Talu toward the light.

And suddenly the world around them was green and blue and gold again. Arden squinted against the intense whites of the snowcaps on the distant mountains. He glanced behind them to see the metallic wall of mist rapidly pulling away from them, retreating on the grassland. Somewhere ahead of them, the sunlight glared off a reflective surface.

"The Blackwater—it's just a little farther. Come on, Talu, you've got to stay with me."

She nodded weakly.

Slowly, painfully they worked their way up and down rises in the meadow. At the top of one ridge, Arden spied the red roof of the houseboat and steered their course that way.

His bare neck and back grew hot in the sun, except where Talu's damp arm lay. Her fingers felt so cold where they brushed against his shoulder.

They were almost to the boat when she collapsed to the ground.

"Talu!" he screamed, struggling to get her upright.

No response.

He looped her bleeding arm around his neck again, then put his other arm under her knees and lifted her off the ground.

Arden took a staggering step forward, sweat beading on his forehead. Then another step.

Every muscle in his body strained, and his side nearly exploded in pain. He took another step, and another.

"Dark Morning," he gasped. "Help!"

From beneath the black surface of the water, Dark Morning's dreadlocks appeared, followed by her stern face.

The Selk scowled up at him, then noticed Talu's still form.

Dark Morning screamed—a low, heartbreaking wail that reverberated in the air. The Selk swam like a torpedo to the shore and leapt out of the water, her clawed flippers gouging the sand.

She took Talu from Arden's arms, cradling the girl like a baby.

"There were dogs," Arden explained, panting. "One bit her on the arm—I think she lost a lot of blood."

"Light a fire. Boil water."

Arden obeyed, hurrying to the boat to grab the cast iron pot.

As he worked on the fire, the Selk held Talu close, murmuring in her ear. "Talu, stay here. Don't go. We need you. *I* need you. Don't go."

The white cat appeared out of nowhere, his bat-like ears pulled back in concern. He nudged his bony head beneath Talu's limp and dangling hand, purring nervously.

The fingers of her hand twitched, then stroked the cat's ears. Talu's eyes fluttered open.

"She's awake!" Arden cried.

The Selk exhaled, glancing gratefully into the sky. "Find a clean cloth," she ordered Arden. "Boil it. I'll fix her up."

* * *

As soon as Megan returned to her dorm room, she redialed the number Bat had used to call earlier that week. She had so much to fill him in on.

"¿*Aló?*"

"Oh, hi, Orlando, I didn't—" Megan stumbled over her words. "I mean—sorry, this is Megan."

"Ah, Megan, hi, did you, uh …" Orlando sounded as flustered as Megan. What had gotten into them?

"Sorry, Bat called on this phone earlier, and I didn't realize it was yours. Although I knew Bat doesn't have a phone, so I should have figured …"

"No worries, it's fine. Of course it's fine."

"So how was Thanksgiving?"

"Good. Great. Your friend Bat made quite the impression."

Megan's heart sank. "What did he do?"

"Oh, nothing bad." Orlando chuckled. "Have more faith in him, amiga. He behaved like a perfect angel, until the game came on. My brothers explained the rules to him once, and then, boy, did he get into it. By the end, Mr. Bat was jumping on the couch and questioning the refs, loud enough to make any Ruiz man proud. I think he likes football more than he likes pizza, which is saying a lot."

"It really is," Megan said.

"Speaking of which," Orlando said, "It's Friday, and I can't miss pizza night at Mistuxet. Wanna come?"

"What about the storm?" Megan glanced at the bending tree branches outside her window.

"Ah, it's nothing. Tomorrow's the day we have to batten down the hatches. Look, it's too late, because Bat heard the word *pizza* and he's drooling a puddle all over my carpet, so we're definitely going. Would you like to come with us?"

Megan smiled. "Yes."

"Great. We'll pick you up around six. Did you want to talk to Bat?"

"Oh—yes. Thank you."

"Here he is."

There was rustling on the other end, and then a loud clatter. Apparently, Bat had dropped the phone.

"Hello, FriendMegan?"

Megan rubbed her ear. "Not so loud. Look, Penny and I have a breakthrough on getting you back home."

"Penny Chen?"

"Yes, I can't explain right now, but we need you to meet us tomorrow morning outside our dorm, first thing."

"What have you broken through?"

"Shh." Megan hesitated, listening to the wind howl outside her window. "Please don't mention any of this to Orlando. Part of the plan involves … something a little dangerous, with us going out into the storm. It's all under control, but I don't want him to worry. Just meet us at the dorm tomorrow, okay?"

* * *

Dark Morning moved Talu into the boat and dressed her wound. Arden couldn't watch, opting instead to sit by the fire on the bank.

The sun sank below the mountains, attended by a fire show of magenta and orange clouds. The first stars of twilight appeared in the eastern sky.

Dark Morning lowered herself out of the boat, careful not to rock it. She pulled herself near the fire by Arden.

"How is she?"

"Fine. She's sleeping. It isn't deep. We'll keep it clean."

"Why did she faint on me back there?"

"Shock, probably. She'll be fine." The Selk hugged her thick, furry tail to her chest. "She'll be fine."

For a few minutes, only the crickets and river waves lapping against the side of the boat broke the silence.

Dark Morning frowned up at Arden, the firelight playing against her solemn face.

"Whose dogs were they?"

Arden blinked. "I have no idea."

"Cachorros? Or wolves, maybe?"

"No, these were like hunting hounds. But Talu said the Nomads don't have packs of dogs like that. I don't know why they came after us."

Dark Morning scowled into the fire.

Only she didn't actually look angry, now that Arden saw her this close. Yes, her eyebrows were furrowed, but the rest of her face seemed calm and thoughtful.

I've always thought she was mad, but maybe all this time she's just been thinking.

He opened his mouth, then hesitated, suddenly feeling an impulse to reach out to her. He cleared his throat. "So … what's on your mind?"

Her dark eyes widened in surprise.

Arden went red. "Just … wanted to ask. Not trying to be nosy. Sorry."

She turned away for a moment, her tangled dreadlocks obscuring her face. The crickets resumed their chorus.

"Sorry," Arden repeated.

"I was thinking," Dark Morning said softly, her face still turned away, "of how Talu reminds me of her."

"Who?"

"The girl I lost." Dark Morning lifted her face to the sky, her hair falling back to reveal the glistening spots on her cheeks. "My little one. She would have been about her age, if she'd made it past her second year."

Dark Morning turned and stared Arden right in the face. "And you. Your eyes remind me of my boy. When you came down the dock in Shido I saw it. Like my boy's. My sweet, sweet little boy, so still, so still."

A long silence fell, heavy as a weight on Arden's chest. Talu had been right about Dark Morning losing someone—but she hadn't guessed it had been twice. And whenever she saw Talu and Arden, or any teens their age, she'd think about what she'd lost—

"I'm sorry," he said quietly. "If I knew what to say to make you feel better ... but I don't. I wish I did. I'm sorry."

Dark Morning reached out and put her calloused hand on his shoulder. "It is enough."

Another long pause. Arden inhaled the cool night air, sweet with the scent of grass.

"How far did you carry her?" the Selk asked.

"I don't know. I was too worried about the dogs to pay attention. I used the staff techniques you showed me to fight them off, but I didn't get there in time." His throat ached. "If I had been there thirty seconds earlier, maybe this wouldn't have happened to her. If only I could have—"

"Things happen the way they do. No changing it. Don't punish yourself." Dark Morning looked him in the face again, her deep eyes piercing him. "There are two warriors. One fights only for pride and glory and the thrill of the battle. He lets anger rule. We Selks keep him in the caves. He is dangerous, unfit for war.

"The second warrior fights because he must, to protect people he loves. We put him on the front lines and make him a leader." She cleared her throat. "I was wrong. I thought you were the first, but you are the second. You're small, but you have a hero's heart. Never lose it, Arden."

Something deep within Arden stirred, welling up into his chest—a mixture of strength, confidence, and hope—and it glowed within him for a long time after.

And as the Selk dragged herself away from the fire and disappeared into the waves, he realized something else.

It was the first time she'd ever called him by his name.

chapter 31

The Coming Storm

The portly owner of Mistuxet Pizza approached the worn booth as the oddball group of Megan, Orlando, Bat, and Penny gathered their coats to leave. "Orlando," he said. "You're not staying on campus during this storm, are you?"

Orlando waved dismissively. "We'll be fine. Those dorms have been around since the Nixon administration. It's going to take more than a little wind to knock them down."

The waitress looked up as she took away the empty pizza plates. "Do you have bread and milk stocked up?"

"Oh, plenty. If by bread you mean corn chips, and by milk you mean frozen pizzas. We'll be feasting like kings, won't we, Mr. Bat?"

"You went home for Thanksgiving, though, didn't you?" The shop owner frowned. "Why would you drive all the way back to the coast?"

"No one in Hartford has pizza this good, and I couldn't miss my Friday tradition." He pulled on his puffy white jacket and nodded toward Megan. "Besides, someone has to make sure these kids stay out of trouble."

It's for us, Megan thought. *He drove all the way back to watch out for us.*

Orlando caught her looking at him and flashed a grin. She looked away, her face warming.

"We'll be fine," Orlando assured the owner. "I've got flashlights with batteries, and plenty of blankets. And we're not going to do anything stupid, like take a stroll out into the middle of the storm."

Megan winced and stole a glance at Penny.

But Penny fiddled with her journal, not paying attention. She'd been quiet and seemed almost on edge the whole evening. Probably the anticipation of tomorrow and all that she had to make sure went right.

The ragtag group stepped out of the warm restaurant and into the frigid air.

"Look!" Orlando pointed a gloved hand into the sky. Tiny snowflakes swirled in the icy wind. He grinned. "Ushering in the Christmas season."

By the time they arrived back on campus, an inch of white lay over the lawns. Orlando parked his car in front of Megan's dorm and stepped out, winking mischievously. "Hey, Mr. Bat, I have another American tradition to show you," he said, scooping a handful of snow into his glove.

Bat squeaked in surprise as the ball of powder splatted against his back. He quickly gathered up snow in his own hands and lobbed it at Orlando, who ducked behind the car.

Megan laughed and dodged a snowball headed in her own direction. Within minutes, everyone was covered in snow—everyone but Penny, who'd shrieked when a snowball almost hit her journal, then she'd hurried back into the warmth of the dorm.

Now Megan leaned back against the car, her cheeks and nose cold but the rest of her warm from running and dodging. Meanwhile, Bat was trying with some difficulty to catch snowflakes on the end of his tongue, leaping like a frog to try to meet them mid-air.

Orlando leaned on the car next to Megan, laughing and catching his breath. "I think he's going to have great memories of America."

Megan nodded, rubbing her cold hand. "Oh," she said. "I lost my glove somewhere."

"Is this it?" Orlando picked up a limp purple glove from a pile of snow.

"Thanks—not much use now, I guess." Megan put the wet glove into her pocket and rubbed her bare hand against the other, trying to warm it.

Orlando grinned and then, in an exaggerated voice, belted out something clearly from an opera: "*Che gelida manina, se la lasci riscaldar!*"

Megan laughed. "Is that Puccini again?"

"Yup."

"What does it mean?"

Orlando's espresso-brown eyes sparkled. "It translates to … 'What a cold little hand. Let me warm it for you.'"

And suddenly his bare fingers—strong and gentle and warm—wrapped around hers.

Megan caught her breath. Warmth flowed not only through her hand, but through her face and chest and her whole body. She looked up at him, bewildered. He smiled at her, looking shy and embarrassed himself.

Megan squeezed his hand back, her heart pounding. The moment swirled around her like the snowflakes, overwhelming her senses.

And suddenly she knew why her wish to go to Vindor had failed all those days ago, and why the words felt flat and lifeless in her mouth. She didn't understand it then, but she understood it now.

This is where she wanted to be, in this beautiful and strange real world with a magic all its own. This is where she belonged, in this life, this adventure.

Just one day, she thought. *One day to get Arden, and then I'm hurrying back here as soon as I can.*

* * *

"Are you sure you're okay?" Arden asked for the tenth time that morning.

"I'm *fine*." Talu sat beside the fire and patted her tightly bandaged arm. "I mean, it hurts some, but it doesn't have a fever in it."

"Yes, but are you sure?"

She nodded, a slight breeze playing through her wavy locks. "I guess I scared you yesterday, huh?"

"Yeah, a little. By which I mean Dark Morning and I were both freaking out."

"We were," Dark Morning called from the water's edge.

"Sorry." Talu ducked her head, looking sheepish. "I, uh, don't handle blood well."

"But I'll tell you what you do handle well," Arden said. "War talks! Dark Morning, did she tell you what happened with the tribes?"

The Selk shook her head and pulled herself closer on the bank.

"So we see this tribe—okay, well *I* saw them, that's important—and Talu asks me what color the banners are. And for some reason, I don't think tan counts as a color, so I just say blue. Turns out when we reach them it's two tribes, and they're ready to have a war, and they think Talu is their Peace Talker. And one side is yelling because the goats are mixed up, and the other side is mad because the other tribe dances without shoes on—"

Talu laughed. "Why would that make them mad?"

Arden paused, not catching her joke. "Uh, because they have this weird thing about shoes. Because they're Brown Owls. You told me that."

"Owls don't wear shoes, silly." She giggled.

"Not owls," he said slowly, "*Brown* Owls."

"Doesn't matter what color the owls are, they don't wear shoes. What is this all about, Arden?"

Arden looked to Dark Morning, her scowl of concern matching how Arden felt.

"Talu," he said. "Come on. You have that whole poem: '*Brown Owl People really like shoes, and they hate smiling. Wolfsbane think plants are lame.*' Okay, obviously I'm paraphrasing here, but you know what I'm talking about."

She frowned. "I don't understand. Who are Wolfsbane and Brown Owl People? Are they from your world?"

"Talu," Dark Morning said, "What's your clan?"

"Like, my family?"

"Yes, their name."

"Well, my father is Zoan and my mother is Ariandra, and my

grandmother—"

"No," Arden said. "She means the tribe. What do you call yourselves? As a group?"

"Uh … family?"

"Aren't you the Windrose?"

A flicker of recognition passed over Talu's face, then vanished. "I don't know what that is. It has a pretty sound to it, though."

Arden turned to the Selk. "How could she forget everything?"

"Wait, what did I forget?" Talu leaned forward.

"I'll check for fever." Dark Morning pulled herself toward the girl and pressed her rough hand against her forehead.

"I feel fine," Talu protested. "I don't know what you two are talking about."

How could this be happening? Talu had been so concerned with every detail of the tribes' quirks, and now she couldn't remember them at all?

And then Arden realized he'd already had a similar conversation with her back at N'gozi, when he'd asked about the name Vaeltaa and her people once living in the mountains as the *Atlas of Years* had shown.

And with Dark Morning, who couldn't remember where she'd spent her childhood.

In his mind, he heard the echo of drums. *"Who are you?"* the message from M'buk had said. *"What is N'gozi? We have never heard of you."*

It was the same pattern, over and over. People forgetting their identities and not recognizing that anything had been lost.

"Arden." Dark Morning sat on the bank with her arms folded. "Tell the story of George Washingstone again."

"Who's that?"

She scowled. "With the teeth made of wood."

"What?" he said, uncomfortable under her stern gaze. "I don't know who you're talking about."

"What is your home like?"

What did this have to do with anything? "It's—" He hesitated, drawing a blank. Then the familiar images came to him—the arched bridges and docks and crowded streets.

"I'm from Shido. My mother runs an academy there, and my sister went away last year to go to …" Another blank moment, and then the answer came to him. "To go to Alavar. Because she's Selena. Did you know that? Selena's my sister, but Mom and I live in Shido."

"No you don't," Talu piped in. "You are from Conn-en-en-tut. Where Paul Revere rode his horse in the midnight. Don't you remember telling us that?"

"Yeah …" Arden's head tingled. "But I told you, that's a legend, not a real story."

Dark Morning frowned at him, then at Talu. "The fog you went through—what was it?"

But before Arden could answer, cawing like strained laughter filled the air. He turned.

Countless black shapes beat through the blue sky, swooping right at him.

Ravens. Thousands of them.

And then a second sound—dogs howling.

"Stupid Selk!" Dark Morning cried. "Why did I stay here? Get in the boat!"

Arden grabbed Talu's good arm and pushed her toward the *Sensei*. Crows swarmed at them, their talons scraping against the red roof.

"Untie the rope!" Dark Morning shouted, diving into the Blackwater. She whistled for the botos, then grabbed the anchor rope and pulled the ship from the bank herself.

"Where are they coming from?" Talu ducked and tried to bat the crows away with her free hand.

"Hurry!" Arden shoved her into the boat, then jumped in himself.

As the boat pulled away from the shore, the hounds leapt over the bank snarling and snapping. The current caught the houseboat and sent it racing downstream, faster than they'd ever traveled, leaving the dogs barking in the distance.

The ravens, however, continued to follow, swooping down in turns.

The botos appeared beneath the dark waves, their long, pink snouts snapping at birds that got too close to the water.

Meanwhile, Snow White jumped onto the roof, growling. Arden heard the cat's claws scuffling, and a crow cawed out in pain.

The other birds backed off, following the boat from a safer distance. Dogs howled from either shore.

"What did we do to them?" Talu asked. "Why are they chasing us?"

"I don't know." Arden leaned over the bow, looking downriver to what lay ahead. The houseboat raced toward three dark shapes sitting on the surface of the water.

"Turn around! It's a trap!" he shouted, but Dark Morning's head was below the water, still pulling the boat. He yanked on the ropes. "Stop!"

The rapidly approaching shapes were canoes, he now saw, occupied by men in dark hoods. Wisps of smoke rose from something in their hands.

"Get down!" Arden leapt at Talu, pushing her onto the floorboards. He grabbed a wooden storage crate to shield themselves just as the volley of arrows hit.

One landed beside them with a heavy thud. In place of an arrowhead it bore a rounded black tip smelling of tar. A tiny flame licked at the end of it, then jumped to the ship's curtain.

Within seconds, the curtain was ablaze.

A second volley of arrows.

Talu screamed. "My skirt!"

Flames danced at the edges of the red fabric. Arden grabbed a sack of rice and whacked the edge of her skirt, trying to beat it out.

The boat lurched.

"Someone's boarding!"

Arden grabbed Talu and lifted her to her feet. "You can swim, right?"

"What?"

"Can you swim?"

"Yes, but—"

Arden pushed her toward the edge of the boat, her skirt still smoking. "Well, get ready to."

He shoved her overboard as footsteps thumped behind him.

A blinding crack of pain hit the back of his head, and everything went black.

chapter 32

The Sea and the Lake

Arden's in danger.

From the second her eyes opened, Megan felt in every fiber of her being that her brother needed her *now*.

The wind shrieked and whistled outside her window, and the frosty glass rattled. Undeterred, Megan dressed quickly and grabbed a bag with a few essential items in it—the Starstone most importantly. *Whatever it takes, Arden. I will brave anything to get you back.*

Penny waited for her in the chilly dorm lobby, wrapped up in a red coat and wearing a pair of heavy-duty work boots.

Droplets of freezing rain clinked against the door as Megan pushed against it, battling a fierce gust of wind.

The world outside was more grey than white. Trees bent in the wind, their boughs heavy with ice and snow.

"Where's Bat?" Megan shouted over the roar of the wind. "He's supposed to meet us here."

"We should go."

"Not without him." Megan wrested the door closed and dialed the number Bat had used to call her. No one picked up. "Hey," she said after the voicemail beep. "Bat, we're waiting for you, but we need to hurry. If you don't get this in time, meet us by the dock on the beach."

As she spoke, Penny jotted something down in her journal—probably last-minute calculations.

Megan glanced down at her hand, surprised to see she was holding her phone. She tucked it back into her bag and turned to Penny. "We need to get to my brother right away. What are we waiting for?"

"Nothing and no one. Ready?" Penny closed her journal and adjusted the lid on a pink thermos, releasing a whiff of a sweet, floral scent.

Megan forced open the door again, and the two of them made a dash for the blue Toyota, slipping on the sidewalk and fighting the wind the whole way.

Mercifully, the car started on the first turn of the key. Megan navigated the abandoned streets as well as she could, maneuvering around large tree limbs scattered along the roadways. After what seemed like an eternity, she pulled into a parking spot by the abandoned beach.

"Wow." Megan's fingers paused on her keys, reluctant to turn off the motor. "I've never seen the ocean like that."

Through the swirl of the snow and sleet, huge whitecaps churned on top of the grey sea. She glanced at the narrow pier where the portal was closest. A wave smashed over the rickety planks, soaking the wood and throwing foam ten feet into the air.

Megan hesitated. "I don't think this is a good idea."

"Do you want to save your brother or not?" Penny asked quietly.

Megan steeled herself and cut off the engine. "We'll make a dash for the gazebo and figure out the next step from there."

Penny placed the thermos of hot tea in Megan's hand. "You'll need this. To keep warm."

Megan nodded and pushed open the Toyota's door. A salty gust of wind nearly knocked her off her feet, but she dug her boots into the sand and struggled forward. Tiny crystals of ice prickled against her face, and she shielded her eyes with her sleeve. She hugged the warm thermos close to her body as her teeth chattered with the cold.

At last the two girls reached the gazebo, its wooden railings groaning in the wind. One side of the structure featured a battered brick fireplace, which provided at least some protection against the wind. Megan crouched on the wet floorboards and leaned against the bricks, taking a sip of the fragrant tea.

Penny, meanwhile, studied the cracked grey crystal.

"Well?" Megan asked as a shingle blew off the roof and bounced down the beach.

"It's here," Penny said, "But still not quite strong enough."

"But Arden needs me *now*. I don't have time to wait."

"There may be one way to amplify the connection," Penny said. "Worlds in Paracosmia are fueled by our thoughts and memories, right?"

Megan nodded, shivering.

Penny pulled out her leather journal and a pen. "Tell me everything you remember about Vindor."

* * *

The splash of a paddle and low voices pulled Arden back to consciousness.

His head throbbed and the world spun around him—at least, it felt like it did. He didn't dare open his eyes.

Where was he? How did he get here?

A rocking sensation came from beneath him. He lay on his back, he was certain of that now, in what felt like the bottom of a narrow boat. One of the black canoes, probably.

At least one other person sat in the canoe with him, paddling.

He opened an eye, carefully, to find the world around him entirely dark. *I've gone blind.* His nausea increased.

The rhythm of the oar hitting the water echoed, sending back high-pitched chirps from above and from every side. *We're in a dark cave*, he realized.

But why? And with whom?

He struggled to make sense of it all. Now he remembered the crows, the dogs, the flaming arrows. His heart lurched. Talu and Dark Morning—were they okay? How long had he been out?

Arden stayed perfectly still. The person paddling the boat probably wasn't a friend, and Arden didn't want to give away the fact that he was now conscious. If he were lucky, he might be able to jump up and dash away as soon as they reached land. That is, if his head would stop spinning.

At once, the chirping echoes stopped, and the dark world turned so bright Arden could see red through his closed eyelids.

He snuck a peek and saw open sky above, vibrant blue with wisps of white clouds.

The sound of the oars ceased, and the water lapped against some other structure. The person in the boat stood and pulled the boat against whatever it was.

"What took you so long?" The woman's voice was vaguely familiar, though Arden couldn't place it. "Is that him?"

"We found him with the Selk and the Nomad girl," answered the person from the boat. A second man grunted his agreement.

"Bind him there," the woman ordered.

Calloused hands grabbed Arden by the shoulders and legs and hoisted him out of the canoe. The pain in his head cut through him, and he couldn't tell which way was up. He tried as hard as he could to stay limp, to act unconscious, but his heart pounded. His only opportunity of escape was slipping away, and he didn't have the strength to run.

His legs dragged against a cool surface that felt like stone. The two men thrust Arden into a sitting position, shoving his back against a hard, smooth wall. Rough ropes wrapped tight around him, cutting into his arms and ribs.

And in the midst of the confusion, he remembered: his name was Arden Bradshaw, and he wasn't from Shido at all. He came from Hartford County in Connecticut, a world away, a place of highways and skyscrapers and computers and hundreds of other things that had never even been dreamed of in Vindor.

The rush of information hit him as with an electric shock, and his eyes flew open to the surreal scene around him.

Steep walls of rock curved around on every side, a perfect circle of crags.

I'm inside a volcano!

But down here in the crater, the air felt cool, not fiery. All around him stretched a jet-black crater lake, as smooth as glass.

Arden sat on a flat ring of speckled granite, maybe fifty feet in diameter, that formed a narrow pier in the center of the black lake.

Spaced evenly around the outer edge of the ring, twelve monoliths of black stone emerged from the water, pointed like jagged teeth. Arden had been bound to one of these.

The huge obsidian structures were polished to a reflective gleam, but as Arden looked, the black surfaces didn't reflect back the other monoliths, but different shapes altogether. Some of the blurred reflections seemed to move of their own accord.

The monoliths and stone pier surrounded an inner circle of black lake water. Rising from its tranquil surface stood a pillar of frosted glass, something silver sparkling at its base.

Arden struggled against the ropes that bound him to the monolith, but they held uncomfortably tight. No chance of running now—not that there was anywhere he could run to.

A woman in a black robe walked along the curved pier toward him, her orange hair brushing against the bow and quiver of arrows on her back. She stepped toward him slowly, methodically, something metallic in her hand.

The hairs on his neck rose. Arden struggled helplessly against the knots.

"Oh, you found him, did you?" The silky voice came from a dark-haired figure who emerged from the black water, hooking her arms over the edge of the pier several feet away from Arden. Her pale face bore three red scratches across the cheek.

The mermaid who had tried to kill him.

"No thanks to your botched job, Moriana," said the first woman. She was closer now, and Arden heard the metallic *shing* of a blade. He tensed.

"Are you going to kill him?" Moriana sounded bored.

"I'll thank you to mind your own business."

"You're not, are you?" Moriana flicked her silver tail beneath the water. "You're going to try some silly spell with blood because he's related to that girl. You and your backwoods superstition."

"Don't you disrespect the Ravensblood priestess!" scolded one of the hooded men who had captured Arden. "When Lady Dagger brings the Shadow to full power, you'll not want to be on the wrong side of her!"

"I'll take my chances." The mermaid yawned. "Korvin's going to be mad, you know."

Korvin? Had Arden heard right?

"Let her be mad," the woman in black said." I don't grovel to her the way you do. Besides, this boy is part of my payment."

"I thought the Ice Chalice was your payment."

"Yes, but I can't use it because it's holding *her*."

The mermaid paused. "I still feel like she's watching me. I can see those eyes glowing through the ice."

Arden glanced at the frosted pillar and noticed a dark shape in the center. Who did they have frozen in there?

He remembered Talu's story of the furious spirit that lived in the volcano and wondered if he'd rather take his chances with it than with these two.

Moriana swam toward one of the black monoliths. "Show me Korvin," she ordered.

The dark reflection shifted suddenly, revealing the shapes of rolling clouds and waves crashing against a shore.

"Still at the coast, looks like," Moriana called over her shoulder. "You may have a few minutes."

More metallic sounds. The priestess sharpened a bronze knife against a black stone.

Sweat beaded on Arden's forehead, the ropes still cutting into him. What was he going to do?

The sound of the sharpening stopped.

"Korvin's going to be mad," the mermaid repeated.

"Korvin can mind her own business," said the woman. "We're an equal circle of four. Well, three, now that Kwanu's failed. What makes you so eager to obey her?"

"Because she holds the key to all of my dreams," the mermaid said. "Well, not quite. My perfect version involves the Selks' disgusting bodies strewn out on the cliffs for the next decade." She giggled.

"You're a special kind of sick, Moriana."

"Quite a compliment, coming from Dagger Ravensblood, terror of Adræfan. I've heard what you do to those villages that resist you." The mermaid looked straight at Arden and grinned. "You should have let me kill you. This will be far worse."

The woman grabbed Arden's hair, forcing his head back and exposing his neck. She raised her bronze knife and smiled.

"Fa-la-la-la-la!" A shout rang out from the far side of the crater lake, followed by sporadic splashing.

Dagger let go of Arden's hair. "What by the bird—?"

From the corner of his eye, Arden saw Talu splashing along the surface of the black lake at a tremendous speed. The white cat perched stiffly on her shoulder.

"Fa-la-la-la-la-la, boughs of holly!" she sang.

A pink, paddle-like tail appeared behind her soaking-wet, red skirt. Talu was riding on one of the botos.

The hooded men grabbed arrows from their quivers, raised their bows and aimed.

Arden twisted against his ropes. "Talu, get down! They'll shoot you!"

"It's a season to be jolly!" she cried.

"Talu, no!"

Suddenly one of the guards plummeted backward into the black water with a splash. A second later a figure burst out of the water and knocked the other guard clean off the pier.

Dark Morning.

The Selk spun her pole at lightning speed, and in two swift movements, knocked the knife out of Dagger's hand and swiped the woman's feet out from underneath her. She pinned Dagger down, a sharpened end of her pole an inch from her pale throat.

"How dare you," Dark Morning spat. "How dare you hurt Arden, my …" The Selk stopped mid-sentence, glaring out over the black lake. "*Moriana,*" she hissed.

And like a torpedo the Selk dove off the pier into the water, rocketing straight for the slender mermaid queen.

Moriana shrieked like a little girl as Dark Morning leapt on top of her and drove her down. The two of them thrashed beneath the water.

Talu's boto swam up to the pier where Arden struggled against his ropes. Talu stumbled onto the narrow stone walkway and fished her knife from her pocket. "What's happening?"

"Dark Morning's gone after Moriana," he said as Talu sawed at the ropes with her small blade. "She's gone to—oh no."

"What?"

Underneath the surface of the lake, six or seven figures glided toward the struggling mermaids.

"Watch out!" Arden cried. "Dark Morning, you're surround—"

Talu gasped as a dripping guard grabbed her and lifted her into the air.

The woman in black stepped over Arden and wrenched the blade from Talu's grasp. "Stupid girl," she sneered.

Beyond her, in the lake, six silver-tailed mermen hoisted a struggling Dark Morning out of the water and onto the far side of the circle. White ropes like jellyfish tentacles wrapped around the Selk's body, and she writhed in pain.

Moriana positioned herself a safe distance away, fixing her black hair. "Don't kill her yet," she ordered. "This one deserves extra punishment."

"Let me go!" Talu kicked and twisted, but she was no match for the guard now tying her arms back.

"Don't bother, boys." Dagger sighed. "I have no use for her. Hold her down."

The two guards slammed Talu onto the stone pier and pinned her shoulders and legs down.

Slowly Dagger raised her bow and drew an arrow from her quiver.

"No!" Arden jerked violently against his ropes.

Talu's eye flew back and forth. Her voice trembled. "Arden, what's happening? What's she doing?"

Dagger pulled her arrow taut against the bowstring and planted her foot on Talu's midriff. Talu stopped struggling, her face going pale.

A smile played on Dagger's lips as she aimed for Talu's heart.

One of the guards looked up. "How's that cat doing that?"

Dagger's smile vanished. "What cat?"

Within the black circle of water, Snow White sat serenely, washing a batty ear with a paw. Just sitting on the surface of the water.

The cat's eyes shone blue, brighter than Arden had ever seen them.

Dagger whirled the bow around and let the arrow fly. The cat didn't flinch as it nearly grazed his ear.

"How did it get back here?" Dagger demanded, drawing another arrow.

Snow White yawned and stretched his lean body, sending ripples across the water where his paws touched.

Dagger's voice rose an octave. "Don't sit there, you fools," she screeched. "Shoot it!"

The guards glanced at each other, still pinning the struggling Talu.

"Forget the girl—shoot it. Shoot it now!"

As soon as they let go, Talu scrambled away, stumbling in Arden's direction. He managed to free a hand from the partially cut rope and grabbed her arm, pulling her toward him. She sobbed and gasped into his shoulder.

Moriana sat on the far end of the pier, crossing her arms. "Calm down, it's just a cat." She brushed the scars on her face as Dagger's guards took aim again. "If anyone should want that thing dead it's me."

"It's *not* a cat!" Dagger fired again, her hands trembling.

Snow White strolled across the surface of the water toward the icy pillar with the dark figure inside, taking his precious time as the guards released their arrows.

The first guard's arrow appeared to be right on target, but it plunged into the black water behind the white cat. The second arrow passed through Snow White's leg, disappearing with a splash.

The cat sauntered up to the frosty pillar and rubbed his bat-like ear against it, his blue eyes glowing.

Within the pillar, two blue lights appeared—a second pair of eyes.

At the base of the pillar stood a silver goblet. Snow White tapped it with a curious paw. It wobbled.

"*Kill him!*" Dagger screamed.

The cat looked toward her, his blue eyes transformed, glowing without pupils. He stretched out a skeletal paw, both defiantly and lazily as only a cat can do.

He knocked the Ice Chalice into the black water with a *plunk*.

The pillar crackled, and then burst into a thousand shards, revealing a blinding white light.

Arden shielded his eyes. In the center of the water a figure appeared—a pale, ghostly woman in a white gown that dazzled like new-fallen snow. Her blue eyes shone as the white cat twisted itself around the base of her long gown.

Eira.

chapter 33

Mists of Paracosmia

Eira threw her arms into the air, and immediately Arden felt his body stiffen, held by an invisible force.

"Who dares imprison me in my own chamber?" Eira's voice echoed off the sides of the extinct volcano.

Arden found he could move his eyes, and he looked from side to side. Everyone—Talu, Dark Morning, the Loray merfolk, Dagger, and the guards—had been frozen in place.

Eira stepped toward the pier, her footsteps sending ripples over the black water. "Moriana, the bloodthirsty queen. Dagger Ravensblood, cruel murderess, and your henchmen. And …"

Frowning, she stepped in front of Arden, who remained tied to the monolith. "Who are you?"

Arden felt his jaw and tongue loosen.

"We're not with them, ma'am!" Talu answered from beside Arden. "They caught my friend and we—the Selk and I—came up the Blackwater to rescue him."

"Ah," the spirit said. "Very well."

The immobilizing force released Arden, and the ropes that held him fell away. He stood to his feet.

He took Talu's arm and the two of them hurried around the granite pier to where Dark Morning groaned.

Carefully they pulled away the white tentacles, which squirmed and stung their fingers.

As soon as she could move, the Selk caught both of them in a bear hug, holding them close and sniffling.

"You two." Eira turned to the frozen Dagger and Moriana. "What have you done to my world?"

Neither answered. Dagger cursed under her breath, but Moriana grinned in a way that struck Arden as odd.

The ghostly woman stepped onto the pier and approached the closest black monolith.

"Show me Elnat."

The dark reflections on the surface of the stone shifted, revealing what appeared to be a cave. Eira paused for a moment, then went to the next stone.

"Show me Kavanna."

"Who is she?" Talu whispered.

"Eira. The spirit that guards this part of Paracosmia," Arden answered. "I read about her in the Book of Vindor."

The woman moved onto the next stone.

"Show me Woodshea."

"What's she doing?" Talu asked.

"I think she can see images of Vindor through the stones. That must be how she keeps tabs on them." Arden sat back. "Huh. From what I read, I guessed that she simply knew everything. Apparently not."

Snow White padded up the boardwalk, purring. He rubbed against Talu's skirt, and she stroked him.

But Arden could see a bit of the red skirt through the semi-transparent body. "He really was an undead cat all along."

"Then why can we touch him?" Talu asked.

"Maybe spirits can turn that on and off. I don't know."

Talu turned her head in the direction of the woman in white. "Excuse me, Ms. Guardian Spirit, is this your cat?"

"He's not mine," Eira said without looking away from the monolith in front of her. "He's been here longer than I have. He's connected to the river and does as he pleases."

"So that's why he doesn't eat," Talu said. "Or leave the water. He's a river spirit!"

Arden frowned down at the purring ghost cat. "If you're this ancient mystical being, why were you snotty to me this whole time?"

Snow White nipped at his hand.

"A cat's a cat." Dark Morning said, then she turned and frowned at the figure of Moriana. "She's smiling. Why does she smile?"

"I don't know, but it's kind of creeping me out, too," Arden said. "Oh! Guess what? I remember everything again. About George Washington and stuff—it all came back." He turned to Talu. "Do you remember, too? All the tribes and their fifty-seven rules?"

Her eyes widened. "Yes! It's all come back. But how?"

"I think it's this place."

"Where's my canteen?" Talu patted the side of her skirt, her hands searching. "If we bottle the water and take it to my people …"

"That's it!" Arden reached down to cup some in his hands.

Snow White arched his back and hissed.

"It's okay, kitty." Talu stroked the cat's back, but he remained stiff, his teeth bared. "Maybe we can't take it. The lake could be sacred."

"Hmm." Arden straightened and took a few steps toward where the spirit woman gazed into a monolith. "You're Eira, right?"

She turned, her blue eyes boring into him. "How do you know me?"

"I read about you in the Book of Vindor. Megan Bradshaw described you in some detail."

She frowned. "Megan's name is not supposed to be common knowledge."

"Let's just say I'm familiar with her. Look, we have a favor to ask you. People all over Vindor are forgetting everything. We think it has something to do with this weird fog. But if you would let us take some of this water, we think it could …"

Eira looked away. "No." The voice was heavy. "The mists of

Paracosmia must run their course."

Talu stepped forward. "But it's making everyone forget their history!"

"It is the way of our world."

"That's it?" Arden said. "We give up? I thought you were supposed to protect Vindor."

"I protect its people."

"That's the same thing."

Eira turned back to the monolith in front of her. "It isn't. I protect the people who live in this part of Paracosmia. I do my best to keep them thriving no matter what the land happens to be called at this moment. And it will not be called Vindor much longer."

"What will it be called?" Talu asked.

"That's up to the next dreamer."

Arden crossed his arms. "What's wrong with Megan?"

"She's growing up," Eira said, "forgetting the world she imagined as a girl. Every dreamer does. And our land cannot survive unless it is nourished by the thoughts and dreams and memories of someone in the Mirror World. When the one stream begins to dry up, the mists come in, clear away the memories, and a new dreamer's vision can take over."

Arden paused a moment to take all that in. "Vindor is ending?"

"But all our history," Talu said, "how can we just lose it?"

Arden frowned. "You already have." He thought back to the Atlas of Years and the ever-shifting borders. "Many times. You've changed your names and your homelands, and you never noticed. Everyone in Vindor has. Only the Dembeyans have ever mentioned it, and even they forget."

Dark Morning spat into the sacred black lake. "I hate it. It's cruel."

"You'll never know the difference," Eira said coolly. "Vindor has been extremely long-lived, since Megan's experience with this world has been so different. But in the end, they all forget."

"Well, bring her back," Arden said. "Make her remember again, and Vindor will be back to normal."

"*No.*" The spirit's voice echoed from the sides of the crater.

Arden blinked. "But you did it once before."

"And it was the most dangerous mistake I ever made. In my naiveté, I thought it would save Vindor from the Shadow. And it did, by a thread. But something far, far worse almost happened. The Shadow had more power than I knew. It took Megan down, and in that moment ..."

"The unmaking." Arden recalled the account from N'gozi.

"Unmaking." Eira nodded. "When a dreamer's memories are forgotten over time, the mists filter through, and it is painless. But when all memories cease at once ..."

She turned abruptly to the monolith. "Show me the land of Altheria."

The reflection shifted. At first Arden thought the stone showed nothing at all, but then he saw the tiny wisp of a cloud on a horizon.

Sand. Barren, featureless sand stretched as far as the eye could see, under a dark sky.

"This was a city."

Dark Morning gasped. "Where are the people?"

"Gone. Gone with the dreamer, who died unexpectedly and took all his dreams to the grave with him." Eira's voice softened. "Vindor is too dangerous a world for Megan. She must stay where she is safe, where we are safe. Go home, children. The mists will come, and you will forget all of this, and you will start new lives in peace. Leave me to deal out justice to these murderers."

Talu sniffled, and Arden put his hand on her shoulder.

"Well?" he said. "What about me? Do I go home now?"

"Go." Eira pointed at the Huntsmen canoe.

"Uh, it's going to take more than a boat to get me home." He paused. "You do know I'm not from here."

Eira's pupil-less eyes bored into him again. "How do you mean?"

"I'm not from Paracosmia. My name is Arden Bradshaw. I'm Megan's brother, from the Mirror World."

Talu's good eye widened. "You're from *where?*"

"That's not possible." Panic rose in Eira's voice. "All portals between the worlds are closed. I alone hold the ring keys."

Her hand went to a loop on her white belt and froze.

"They're missing."

And from the other side of the pier, Moriana laughed. "You no longer hold the keys, and the portals have been opened."

Eira whirled toward her. "What is the meaning of this?"

The mermaid queen grinned wickedly. "It means the circle of four has outsmarted the great Eira." She giggled. "I'm sorry, little boy, but your precious sister is in terrible danger."

chapter 34

The Door in the Air

The wind tore at the sides of the gazebo, loosening one of the boards from the railing. For a moment it seemed to Megan that the floorboards lurched underneath her feet, but a second later they felt stationary again.

"Penny, we need to get out of here."

Penny scribbled madly into her journal. "What else do you remember about the Rikeans?" she shouted over the howl of the wind.

"The what? I don't know what you're talking about. And we've got to find better shelter—"

The floor seemed to bend underneath her again, and at that moment a spasm of pain cut through Megan's stomach. She fought the urge to be sick.

"You don't remember anything more?" Penny pressed.

"About what?" Megan looked up to see her friend's dark skin and red toboggan cap blur into one another in a most disconcerting way. Megan grabbed part of the railing to steady herself as the floor seemed to move again.

"Are you all right?"

Megan shook her head, and her vision momentarily cleared. "Something's wrong. Everything feels like it's moving."

"It's probably the tea."

Another spasm of pain. "What tea?"

"The entire cup of oleander tea you drank." Penny pointed to an empty thermos on the floor of the gazebo. "You don't remember that either?"

Megan squeezed her eyes shut, trying not to panic. What was happening to her?

"I've got you." Penny took Megan's arm and helped her to her feet. "We'll walk slowly."

Megan staggered out of the gazebo and onto the sandy beach. The waves smashed against the shore, going blurry again for a moment.

Slowly, painfully, Megan followed the pull of Penny's arm. Boards creaked beneath their boots. The wind grew stronger, and the spray from the ocean felt bitterly cold against Megan's skin.

"Just a little farther," Penny said. "Do you remember why we came out here?"

Megan struggled to connect her thoughts. "It was very important ... it's about Arden ..." But she couldn't recall the conversation.

She fought against the wind as she stumbled along the wooden pathway that seemed to warp and rock beneath her.

"Wait a minute." Megan lifted her head to see churning grey waves smashing all around her. The beach was a hundred feet behind them. "Why are we on the pier? We shouldn't be out here."

"The portal is out here," Penny said. "It's all under control. Do you need to sit down for a moment?"

Megan nodded, shaking. She crouched down, her fingers clinging so hard to the edge of the boards that it hurt.

"I suppose this is far enough," Penny said. "Do you remember what this is for?" She reached into her satchel and pulled out a pendant with a large purple stone the size of a walnut.

Megan couldn't remember ever seeing a piece of jewelry that beautiful before.

"Do you know what this is, Megan Bradshaw?"

Megan cringed at a new wave of stomach pain. "I don't know."

"Good." Penny carefully laid the purple stone onto the pier. Tiny stars danced over its surface.

Suddenly Penny's heavy boot came down on top of it with a sickening crunch. She lifted her boot slightly, then kicked the damaged pendant out into the crashing waves.

Megan looked up at Penny, bewildered. "Why—?"

"I don't need yours." Penny pulled out a second pendant, with a pearlescent stone gleaming as softly as the moon. Her lips curled into a smile. "I have Selena's new one. How do you think I got here from Vindor in the first place?"

In her other hand, Penny held up a circle of driftwood. She released it, and to Megan's amazement, the ring remained suspended in the air.

Penny slipped the Moonstone pendant into the circle, and immediately it shone with a dazzling white light.

"By the way," Penny said, "The crystal is just a rock, and there's nothing magical about this place. The key to Vindor works anywhere— this is just extremely convenient." She paused. "But you don't remember what Vindor is, do you?"

The word sounded vaguely familiar, like something half-recalled from a dream.

Penny shook her head. "You spent two hours telling me everything you knew of this world you dreamed up—in fact, I have it all written down here."

She held out the oversized journal. "Funny thing about this old book—the Arkheva, as it's properly called. I mentioned I capture memories here—but not *my* memories. Anything I write in this book ceases to be remembered anywhere but here. Didn't you wonder why you and your friends have been so forgetful lately?

"I know, Megan Bradshaw. Right now, you can't remember any of it—your long-lost friend Bat, unable to explain how he got here. Your realization that your brother is trapped in another world."

Her brother? Had something happened to Arden?

"All painstakingly researched and orchestrated over the past several months." Penny frowned. "And then a lot of last-minute improvising once I got to this insane world of yours. But it all paid off, with your sudden willingness to give all your memories away to a stranger promising a way back in."

"You also don't remember drinking the poison tea that I made especially for you. I jotted that one down too."

Another wave of pain. Megan tried to rise and realized with panic that her legs were too weak to cooperate.

Penny took the chain dangling from the suspended pendant and yanked downward. Over the howling of the wind a tearing sound rang out, as though Penny were ripping apart the fabric of the air.

Megan's vision blurred again, but for a split second she thought she saw mountains and a smooth, dark lake.

Penny slowly pulled off the red toboggan cap. Long hair fell to her shoulders, hair whiter than the icy sky around them. "I am Korvin, the new and final Guardian of Vindor." She held up the journal. "The memories that nourish our world and control its destiny—these memories now belong to me. We are free to control our own fate."

She stepped closer to where Megan sat helplessly on the pier. "Vindor doesn't need you anymore, Megan Bradshaw."

Penny put her heavy boot on Megan's chest. "And neither do I."

A swift shove, and with a lurch the pier disappeared from beneath Megan. For a second the entire world turned to grey nothingness, and then a heavy wave crashed over her head, forcing her under the water.

She couldn't move her arms and legs, couldn't tell which way was up, and couldn't get to the surface. Wave after angry wave beat her down as her lungs screamed for air.

Megan remembered vaguely that this—the icy water, the helplessness—had been the way she once thought she'd die, but she couldn't recall why.

Then the waves smashed her into one of the pier's heavy support poles, and she inhaled sharply. Salt water rushed into her lungs, burning like fire, as her body sank beneath the icy water and onto the cold sand below.

* * *

"What have you done?" Eira's voice thundered through the crater.

And then a different sound, as though someone were ripping fabric.

Between two of the black monoliths a thin grey light appeared, widening for a moment to reveal dark clouds and angry ocean waves.

A young woman, dressed in a red, buttoned coat, stepped through the sliver of grey light. Her long hair fell in snow-white waves over her shoulders, and she held an oversized leather book.

"Who is she?" Dark Morning whispered from where she crouched beside Arden and Talu.

And at once Arden remembered. He'd seen that face before—in the train station back at Mystic. She'd tapped him on the shoulder, asked him strange questions, and scribbled something down in that leather book. She did this several times, eventually chasing him down to the river. How had she just vanished from his memory until now?

The white-haired girl stepped onto the pier and retrieved a pendant from the air as the grey tear sealed up behind her. A ring of ash stood suspended for a moment, then crumbled into powder.

She surveyed the circular dock and frowned in Arden's direction. "Dagger and Moriana, you had only two responsibilities: kill the bait, and keep the meddling spirit contained. I confess I'm disappointed in you."

"It's not my fault!" Moriana squeaked.

The girl sighed softly. "Oh, well, it doesn't matter now."

"Who are you?" Eira demanded.

"My name is Korvin. I'm your replacement." She held up the oversized book. "And if I were you, I would stand down."

And to Arden's surprise, Eira took a step back on the lake.

"Ah," said Korvin, "you know what this is then."

"What have you done?" Eira hissed.

The girl stood up straighter. "I have released Vindor from the tyranny of the mists of Paracosmia. No longer is our world controlled by the whims of mere children in another world. We now possess the memories. Vindor is free."

"What did you do to my sister?" Arden's voice broke.

Korvin ignored him. "Please unbind my companions."

Eira stretched out her hand, and at once the suspended figures around the pier moved freely.

Moriana flexed her silver tail and dove into the water, her head and shoulders reappearing above the surface a moment later.

Dagger picked up her bow from where it had fallen and drew an arrow from her quiver.

"Thank you, Korvin." She pointed the arrow right at the white-haired girl. Her henchmen did the same. "Now if you don't mind, I'll be taking that book from you."

"Dagger Ravensblood, that's not nice." Korvin stuck out her lower lip. "After I let you be part of my plan, how would I know that you'd turn traitor as soon as you had the chance?" She paused, thoughtfully. "Oh, right, but I did know that. Megan Bradshaw told quite a few stories about you, all running along that same line. And I have the memories here."

"What is that to me?"

Korvin opened the large book and carefully tore three pages from the binding. "You can't survive without these memories of you," she said. "Don't you know that?"

"I will not hesitate to kill you, Korvin. Give me the book of power."

"It doesn't have to be this way." Korvin held out the three pages. "You are doing such a good job bringing the Huntsmen nation into order. You can be their queen, as long as you don't rebel against me."

"I take orders from no one."

Korvin sighed. "And you never will again."

She released the pages from her hand. The three paper sheets fluttered down and landed on the black surface of the lake.

Dagger gave a strangled gasp. Her black dress and orange hair lost definition, the colors bleeding into the background of mountains and lake.

And as the ink smeared on the waterlogged pages, the image of

Dagger Ravensblood washed away, like sidewalk chalk in the rain. In a moment, all that remained of her was a faint orange smudge where her hair had been.

A stunned silence followed, broken by the sound of the Huntsmen's weapons hitting the stone. The guards fell to their knees, covering their faces.

"Effective." Moriana tossed her long hair. "Serves her right, the arrogant witch."

"Korvin." Eira's voice trembled. "You do not understand the power you wield."

"But I do. Trust me, I've done a lot of research." Korvin closed the book. "Don't be afraid, Eira. I will use it as a tool for good. We will bring Vindor out of chaos and into order and enlightenment. Imagine, every city as advanced as Elnat and N'gozi. Wars and tribal rivalries in Gavgal and Adræfan will cease. Vindor will have peace."

Talu stood. "That's not peace!" she cried.

"Shh!" Dark Morning pulled Talu down beside her, clapping a shaking hand over her mouth. "Don't speak."

The back of Arden's throat burned. So this was the girl who'd dedicated herself to studying in the Great Library, the one Selena and Oba had trusted much. She had used her knowledge to create a weapon of death that no one could stand against.

And if those were Megan's memories, what had happened to Megan?

Moriana flicked her tail carelessly in the water. "This is all inspiring, Korvin, but you have a promise to keep."

Korvin sighed. "You have such unpleasant tastes."

"Do this for me and I'll be loyal to you forever. You know I will."

"All right." Korvin opened the book and tore out several more pages.

Moriana swam up eagerly to one of the black monoliths. "Show me the Selk cliffs."

The reflection on the stone shifted, revealing the sea cliffs teaming with moving figures.

"Ooh, wait." Moriana pointed to Dark Morning. "Make the fat one watch."

Before Arden could react, hands burst out of the water and grabbed Dark Morning by the tail, yanking her off the stone ring and beneath the black water.

"No!" Talu screamed.

Several mermen guards then pushed Dark Morning, wrapped in those paralyzing tentacle ropes once again, onto the pier in front of the monolith.

"Make sure she can see." Moriana swam up to where Dark Morning writhed. "Ready to watch the end of your brutish race?" She flashed her perfect teeth in a wicked grin.

Dark Morning ceased struggling and looked Moriana right in the eye. She spat in the queen's face.

Moriana screamed. "You vile thing! How dare you! Korvin, kill them all!"

And as if in slow motion, Arden felt his bare foot against the stone pier, propelling him forward. One, two, three, four running steps and he had reached Korvin.

She noticed him only at the last second, entirely unprepared.

Arden snatched the pages from her hand and wrenched the leather book out of her arms. He held onto them for dear life as he shoved Korvin into the water and continued running along the circle.

Ahead, Eira rushed forward to meet him, her hands outstretched to take the book.

A cold hand wrapped around Arden's ankle. Moriana.

He tried to kick her away, but the force threw off his momentum. His other foot hit a wet spot on the stone path, and he pitched forward, plunging headfirst into the black lake.

The Selk pages and the entire book of memories splashed in with him.

chapter 35

The Weight of Memory

Arden panicked beneath the dark water, trying to right himself. The book grew heavier in his hand, water soaking into the pages and the leather binding growing slick.

It slipped from his fingers and sank into the black water.

Arden dove after the book, kicking desperately. His lungs screamed for air as he descended deeper, his hands flailing forward into the lake that seemed to have no bottom.

The loose Selk pages drifted by his face, now disintegrating blobs of pulp.

His fingers brushed the book's spine once, but it wasn't enough. The book of memories disappeared into the inky blackness forever.

He turned to the wavering light above him and kicked his way to the surface. He spluttered and coughed, treading water in the center of the circle.

Not a soul remained on the stone ring.

He could see faint smudges of color—white where Eira had stood, brown where Dark Morning had been tied, red from Talu's skirt.

Within seconds, even those residual colors faded into nothing.

"No!" His cry echoed off the crater walls, the only sound in the place.

He splashed over to the circular pier and scrambled toward the nearest monolith. "Show me the cliffs!"

The dark reflection shifted.

Ocean water broke against a barren, featureless beach. No sign of life.

He struck the rock with his fist. "Show me N'gozi!" The image shifted again. Beneath a dark sky, sand dunes stretched as far as the eye could see.

"Show me Shido! Show me Alavar! Show me Gavgal!"

Desert after desert after desert.

Arden sank to his knees, hot tears coursing down his face. Ten thousand people once lived in N'gozi. Two dozen tribes once wandered the plains of Gavgal. The cliffs had been teeming with Selks.

And with one clumsy move, he'd killed them all.

A lonely wind whistled over the edges of the volcano.

His friends were dead. Talu ... was dead. She'd never be a Peace Talker now. He'd never hear her laugh again, never see the wind play through her wild curls, never see her eyes light up the way only hers could.

And it was all because he had failed her.

He let out a sob. "Talu, Talu, I'm sorry. I didn't mean for this to happen."

"It's all right."

He spun around.

There, her red skirt and black hair fluttering in the wind, stood Talulaweyna of Windrose.

He stood slowly. "T-Talu?"

"I'm here. What's wrong?"

Arden threw his arms around her.

She felt as real and as solid as she had ever been. He pulled back and looked at her. "But how? You died!"

"I did *what*?"

"You vanished, like Dagger. How did you get back?"

Talu's forehead creased. "I—feel like I went somewhere for a moment, somewhere far away. But then—I heard you calling my name. And now I'm here." She closed her eyes for a moment, letting the wind rustle through her hair. "Where's Dark Morning?"

Arden turned to the empty spot where the Selk had been tied. "Dark Morning? Can you hear me?"

Nothing.

Arden stared at the spot, wishing her back with all his strength. He could still picture her ever-serious eyes, her tangled dreadlocks, the strength in her arms and clawed tail.

And a moment later he realized he wasn't just visualizing her. The actual Selk sat upon the dock, blinking in confusion.

Arden turned to the black monolith. "Show me the plains of Gavgal."

Once again, the black stone reflected only sand dunes. But this time as Arden concentrated, tiny sprouts pushed their way out of the ground. They grew tall within seconds, wildflowers bursting from their tops like fireworks while snowcapped mountains amassed behind them. Two meadowlarks flew across the reflection, lodging in a towering pine, while herds of horses and goats wandered around a circle of Nomad wagons.

"It's all coming back!"

Dark Morning dragged herself toward another black stone. "Show me the cliffs!" she cried.

Arden, meanwhile, ran to the next monolith. "Show me N'gozi! I need to see the white library, the Grand Hall, the people in their ridiculously patterned robes, the docks, all of it!" As he spoke each detail, it took shape in the reflection before him.

Dark Morning shouted at her monolith. "Show me the cliffs!"

Arden paused to watch the bustling central plaza, filled with citizens of the great city. He exhaled. Everyone seemed to be going about their scholarly business, completely fine.

"Show me the cliffs!" Frustration rose in Dark Morning's voice. "Give me back my people!"

Talu touched Arden's elbow. "You try, Arden."

Arden stepped up to Dark Morning's monolith, which reflected only that barren shore. But as soon as he got closer, huge cliff faces rose from the sea, dotted with caves. Figures darted beneath the surface of the foaming water. Lounging on some of the rocks below were those little girls weaving spiky flowers together, just as he'd seen that morning long ago.

Dark Morning threw herself at the reflection, kissing the images as tears streamed down her face. "They're all there. My people are there, all of them alive." She wiped her eye with a fist and turned to Arden. "Why didn't it show when I asked?"

Talu clapped a hand over her mouth. "Arden's making it."

Arden frowned. "What?"

"It's not all reappearing on its own. Vindor is coming back because *you* remember it."

"That doesn't make sense."

"Yes it does. Eira said Vindor couldn't survive without the memories of someone from the Mirror World. And now that someone is you."

"Huh?"

"You're from the Mirror World," Dark Morning said. "*You* are the memory book now."

"Bring them back, Arden." Talu's voice broke. "Bring everything back."

"But I can't remember *everything* in all of Vindor!"

"You have to try."

Arden swallowed and turned to the monolith.

"Show me Shido. I need to see its marketplace, the bridges, the garden, the teahouse. Now show me the docks. I need to see the Blackwater River, stretching all the way from the sea, up through the forest, then through the plains. Show me ..."

And Arden called up every detail of Vindor he could remember— every city they'd passed, every tribe Talu had named, and cities like K'wambe and Elnat and other places he'd only read about.

And as he named them, the details burst out from the empty deserts.

He spoke until he was hoarse. At last he sat down on the stone pier, utterly exhausted.

"You've done well," echoed a familiar voice.

Eira stood before him on the water, the white cat rubbing against her gown.

"I guessed on some of the places," he confessed. "Like, I don't know anything about Mauritius, except that there's white marble and centaurs live there."

"It is enough," Eira said. "The people have returned, and that's what matters. Vindor always fills in its own gaps. If details have been changed, no one will ever know the difference." The spirit sighed. "Vindor owes its continued existence to you. Today and for as long as you remember it."

The words fell like a weight on Arden's shoulders. "You mean, I have to *keep* remembering it?"

"The burden is now yours, Arden Bradshaw. For as long as you remember us, you keep the mists at bay. Now we must prepare for you to go."

"Go?" A lump formed in his throat. "But—I can't go now. My friends are here. And besides, I have to get back to Alavar, and see Shido again, or at least get one more glimpse at the mountains, and—"

"You cannot stay here, Arden Bradshaw."

"I'm not ready to go!"

"That doesn't matter. This is not your world, and balance must be restored."

"But ..." He grasped at straws. "I need the Book of Vindor. If I'm going to remember all this place, I need to have my sketches and Megan's notes. We'll take a quick trip back to the boat, or whatever's left of it, and..."

Eira held out her hands and the beat-up Book of Vindor materialized in her grasp. "This?"

"Oh, right. But I also—"

"You cannot delay this. Now say your goodbyes."

Heart heavy, Arden knelt beside where Dark Morning sat. "I don't know how to thank you for all you've taught me."

She took his face in her hands. "You saved my people. I can only dream that my son would have grown up to be like you. You have a hero's heart within you, Arden."

After a long moment, she let him go. Arden sniffled.

The cat wound around his feet. "Oh, it's you," he said. "So long, Ghost of Gollum. Stay creepy." He patted Snow White on his bony head, and for once the cat didn't hiss at him.

And now Talu stood before him, tears in her eyes. "Don't go."

"Apparently, I don't have a choice."

"Where is the Mirror World? Can I visit you?"

"I don't think so, Talu. I think this is goodbye for good." He swallowed. "I wish I could watch you bring peace to your people. You're going to be the best Peace Talker the Nomads have ever seen, you'll see."

She threw her arms around his neck. "I swear by the west wind and the sun and the whole sea, I'll never forget you, not ever!"

"I'll never forget you either, Talu."

And as he took the heavy Book of Vindor from Eira and stepped into a ring of swirling light, he hoped with everything within him he'd be able to keep that promise.

* * *

Slowly, slowly, the nickel-colored fog began to clear. The feeling of floating gave way, and Megan sensed that she now lay on something solid and soft and warm.

Around her swirled the sounds of sneakers squeaking, high-pitched beeping, and voices—including a familiar one.

"Mom?" she murmured.

"She's awake! Oh, thank God, she's awake. Megan, Megan you're going to be okay."

Her mother squeezed Megan's hand—a hand wrapped in a bandage with a plastic tube taped onto it.

Now more people had gathered around Megan—someone touched her head while someone else pinched her wrist. She squinted beneath a harsh white light.

I'm in a hospital, Megan thought. But try as she might, she couldn't figure out what could have put her there.

"Megan."

She looked up to see her brother. Why did he look so sad?

"I'm all right, Arden," she said, though she was only guessing at that. Meanwhile, the last of the fog cleared from her mind, and she sensed that something important had slipped through her fingers forever.

The next few hours involved a flurry of questions from all sorts of people Megan had never seen before.

"Do you know anything about oleander?" a man from the police department asked her.

"It's a bush." Megan rubbed her fingers over the cast on her wrist. "With star-shaped flowers. Our neighbors have one."

"Yes, it's fairly common, but also highly toxic. We found unusually large amounts of it in your system. Do you remember what you ate last?"

"I had lunch in the cafeteria, with Roz and Celia and … what day is it?"

The more information that the police and hospital staff gathered, the less sense it all made. Megan had lost over a week of memories— the entire Thanksgiving break—even though the doctor in charge of the poison center had never heard of oleander causing that.

She and her brother had not gone camping as planned, though the reasons for this were unclear. At the end of the week, an acquaintance had received a strange voicemail from her. He drove out to the beach during the worst of a major nor'easter and arrived just in time to see her fall off the pier. He risked his own life to pull her from the water, administered CPR, and called an ambulance.

But no one could explain the mysterious poisoning or what drove Megan to go out in the storm in the first place.

Other details didn't add up either—the conflicting stories of where Arden had been and the severely bruised rib and concussion he couldn't account for.

When her hospital room finally cleared of strangers, Megan leaned back against her pillow, wondering if she'd ever make sense of it. She couldn't believe an entire week and a half of her life had simply vanished.

But it seemed that something else was missing, too—some deeper part of her.

"Knock, knock." A young man entered the room. Megan didn't know much about Orlando Ruiz, except he was a sophomore science major of some sort, heavyset and typically quiet.

And that he had saved her life.

And that for some reason her heart leapt when she saw him.

He shuffled into the room, wearing a heavy-duty bandage around his head. Apparently, he'd gotten some nasty scrapes himself pulling her from the stormy sea.

"I don't know how to thank you," she said as he sat down.

"Relax. It's what friends do for each other." A cloud passed over his expression. "I know you don't remember it, but we *are* friends."

"I know," Megan said. "I can't remember, but somehow I know."

"Hey, Bat wanted me to give this to you." He placed a piece of gravel in her hand. "He said it was his 'most indignant rock.' Boy, am I gonna miss that kid."

"What?" Megan asked.

"Yeah, weirdest thing—he wanted to come here and make sure you were okay, but he said a blue-eyed lady had come to take him home. Gave him only a few minutes to say goodbye. I've gotta be honest, Bat's story never made any sense."

Megan frowned. "Who's Bat?"

Orlando paused. "You know, your foreign exchange student friend. From that place no one's ever heard of … what was it, Ipnu? Ipktu?"

Megan shook her head. None of it sounded remotely familiar. "I don't know who you're talking about. I've never heard of a country by that name."

Orlando buried his face in his hands. "Oh, I really wish you hadn't said that, amiga. That makes two people I remember that no one else has heard of."

"Two?"

"I don't suppose you remember Penny Chen—or at least the girl going by that name. When Bat and I drove up to the beach—I got the message you left for him and got worried—she was with you on the pier. She pushed you in, Megan. I have no idea why she would, but I saw her do it, right before she disappeared into thin air. Literally disappeared into literal air."

He sighed. "The police think I imagined her, you know, with me getting bonked on the head and everything. The real Penny Chen was in Boston the whole time—and it turns out she *is* a senior, and tall, and nothing like the girl we hung out with. Although she did tell me someone broke into her room over vacation, moved her stuff, and wore her clothes.

"Everything about Bat and Penny's stories were bizarre, now that I think of it," he continued. "It's like when you have a dream, and everything makes sense until you wake up and see it's all ridiculous." He rubbed his bandage. "I overheard the nurses who fixed me up discussing whether I should have a psych evaluation."

"You are not crazy." Without thinking, Megan reached over and squeezed his hand.

A few seconds later she realized she was holding hands with some guy she hardly knew. Warmth rushed to her face, but Orlando looked up at her and smiled shyly.

He squeezed her hand back. "You know what, Megan Bradshaw? I think if you and I stick together, we're gonna be just fine."

chapter 36

Vindor Unbound

Arden leaned over his sketchbook, amazed at how smoothly the graphite pencil glided across the paper. It was much easier to wield than the ink quill he'd grown accustomed to, and he'd already filled two pages.

Mr. Malanati had let him sit in on that afternoon's art club meeting, and as the other students finished up a painting project, Arden was allowed to try out some of the classroom supplies. He'd gravitated to the pencils.

"Arden, what is this?"

Arden turned around to see Mr. Malanati behind him. Instinctively he tried to cover his drawing up.

"Don't," the teacher said. "Did you do this just now?"

Arden nodded. Several of the other students gathered around him.

"That's cool," one of the boys said.

Before him spread the huge mountains of Gavgal, rising out of the plains like dragon's teeth. A pair of meadowlarks flew toward a ridge of pines.

"What's that?" A girl pointed toward a circle of Nomad wagons.

"It's a, uh, old-timey camp thing."

"Are you drawing this from memory or imagination?" asked Mr. Malanati.

Arden paused. "Both."

"We have a competition in February," Mr. Malanati said. "If you're willing to work, I think you'll have something worthy of entering. You need to work on perspective a bit, but you have an observant eye."

"Thanks. I'd like to give it a try."

"Excellent. I hope to see you here on Monday. And give my best wishes to your sister."

As the club members packed up their supplies, Arden gathered up his sketchbook, backpack, and battered hockey stick and stepped outside into the cold afternoon air.

"Hey, Pansy Garden."

Arden knew he'd have to face this eventually. He tensed, feeling the heft of the hockey stick in his hand.

And then he had an idea. The center of gravity was a bit different, but in many ways the hockey stick was similar to the bamboo pole he'd trained with. A few practice swings and he'd probably be able to figure out how to manipulate it just as fast.

He quickly reviewed what Dark Morning had taught him about balance, defense, and not leaving himself open for a blow.

About how a real warrior viewed conflict. And what it meant to be a hero.

And his hand relaxed against the shaft. He propped the hockey stick against the side of the art building and stepped away from it. He turned to face his tormentors with empty hands.

Eric Steadman had almost caught up to him now, with Jay and Tyler trailing him.

Arden was shocked at how, well, *normal* Steadman looked. After facing a cougar and a mob of grown men, some high school student didn't seem nearly as threatening. *He's a kid like me. I wonder why he stood out in the cold all this time, waiting for me to come out.*

What was Steadman desperate to prove by pushing smaller kids around? Rumor had it that Eric's dad was a rough guy. Maybe Steadman hung around campus because he didn't want to face home, and he bullied smaller kids because that's how he was treated. Arden felt sorry for him.

Steadman slowed as he approached. "Why are you looking at me like that?"

"Like what?" Arden asked.

"Like the way you were just looking at me. Don't you disrespect me." Steadman stomped toward him, but Arden forgot to flinch.

"Did you come from art class, Pansy Garden?" Steadman sneered.

"I did, actually."

"Oh, goodie. Let me see your book full of sissy drawings."

Arden shrugged and pulled his sketchbook out. "If you want to see it, that's cool, but I haven't added much since you last looked. I had a busy vacation."

"Oh." Steadman looked at the sketchbook, unsure. Apparently, he hadn't been expecting that response.

Arden turned to Jay, who lingered in Steadman's shadow. "Hey, Jay, I heard you got a new dog over Thanksgiving."

Jay's face lit up. "Oh yeah, a German Shepherd. He's got a black mask over his eyes, so we call him Zorro. He chases my mom's cat, but cats are creeps, so I don't care."

"Oh, I watched the creepiest cat over Thanksgiving," Arden said. "He looked like a dead Egyptian mummy and made the ugliest sounds. I'm pretty sure that cat was haunted."

Tyler guffawed.

"Don't you laugh at him!" Steadman's voice had a note of desperation. "You only laugh when I say you can."

Jay and Tyler exchanged a glance, and Tyler rolled his eyes.

"What did you do over vacation, Eric?" Arden asked Steadman.

"That's none of your business," he snapped back, his face going red.

"You don't have to talk about it." Arden hoped Steadman wasn't trying to cover up something unpleasant. "Well, I got to get home. My sister came back from the hospital last night, and I want to check on her." He smiled. "Nice chatting with you guys. Same time tomorrow, I assume?"

Steadman opened his mouth, but nothing came out.

Arden passed the three boys and retrieved his unused hockey stick from the wall. *Thanks, Dark Morning*, he thought as he headed home.

Megan sat propped up on the living room couch, chatting on the phone. She looked surprisingly cheerful for someone with a broken wrist, a badly sprained ankle, and nasty bruises all over. And after having her stomach pumped, she had just started eating solid food again.

She laughed into the phone. "I never would have guessed that Orlando Ruiz was such a huge Elvis Presley fan! Oh, hey, my brother got back. Hold on a minute." She lowered the phone. "Hi, Arden. How was art club?"

"Good. You feeling okay?"

"I'm feeling great." Megan grinned. "Oh, you mean the cast and all, don't you? Well, not the best, but I'm on the mend."

"Hey." Arden hesitated. "Uh, I met an old friend of yours the other day. She had a funny kind of name—what was it? Oh yeah—Nikterra."

He watched her intently, hoping for a flicker of recognition. But Megan only shrugged.

"I don't know anyone by that name. Did she go to Wharton?"

Arden's heart sank. But with the book with all her memories in it destroyed, what had he expected?

"No," he said. "She didn't go to school around here."

Megan resumed her conversation with her friend as Arden shuffled down the hall.

Arden's heart ached to tell her all about Vindor—to share his life-changing adventure with a sympathetic ear. But the whole thing was too fantastic for anyone to believe. Megan was taking psychology courses now, and with no reference point for Vindor of her own, she might question his sanity.

Now Arden understood why Megan had kept her own adventure hidden from him for so long. And he forgave her. Keeping something like that to herself for all those years couldn't have been easy, and he could only guess how hard it would be for him down the road.

At least Megan was free of that now. Maybe it was better this way.

He went to his room and opened the Book of Vindor to where he'd sketched the plains of Gavgal. He laid down the drawing he'd done in art club and compared them, looking for any detail he might have misremembered. He knew he didn't have to get every part exactly right—Vindor would simply adapt to any changes without anyone blinking an eye.

But if there was one place in the world he wanted to keep perfect, it was those wild, open plains. For Talu.

He worked quietly for some time, correcting the silhouettes of the mountains. Then in the foreground he drew a familiar figure, the wind blowing through her wavy black hair. At the end of her staff he added a white feather.

Bring peace to your people, he urged.

"Where'd you get that book?"

Arden turned to see Megan standing in his doorway, leaning on a crutch.

She pointed to the Book of Vindor. "That looks antique. Where did you find it?"

Arden sighed. "You wouldn't believe me if I told you."

Megan hobbled across the room and picked the volume up. Her brow furrowed as her fingers traced the silverwork along its binding and cover. She seemed curious but gave no sign that she recognized it.

Now she examined the hole in the front cover—the jagged tear that pierced through most of the pages as well.

"It's damaged," he said. "I don't know how that happened."

"Dagger's arrow," she murmured.

"Huh?"

"Dagger shot at us." She spoke so softly Arden could barely hear her words. "If the book hadn't absorbed the blow, it would have killed Bat. At least, that's what Nikterra said." She blinked and shook her head. "What did I just say?"

Arden held his breath, hoping against hope.

Megan opened the book, flipping a few pages. She stopped. "This is my handwriting."

Now her eyes flew over the text, and she turned the pages so fiercely Arden thought she might tear them. "Bat and Nikterra," she murmured. "The Huntsmen and the Rikeans, and Boath and Resh ... I remember— but it was a dream, wasn't it?" Megan sank into a chair, poring over the pages of the book for a long time.

"It was real," she said at last, her voice breaking. "This is what was missing—the part of me that I lost. It's all coming back as I'm reading it, the faces and cities and—" She looked up at Arden, wide-eyed. "*Where* did you get this?"

He leaned over and opened the book to the section where his sketches began.

She clapped a hand over her mouth. "You've been there. You know about Vindor. All my life, I wanted—and now—"

"Now we're both keeping it alive," he said.

"Alive?"

"Eira told you that your dreams and memories shaped Vindor, right?"

She closed her eyes. "Yes, I remember that now."

"Well, she told me that Vindor only exists *there* as long as it exists in the mind of someone *here*. You forgot it, but my memories kept it alive. Apparently, it must be someone in the Mirror World who thinks about it—it doesn't matter who. So now we both remember it. We'll keep Vindor going as long as we do."

Megan leaned back. "That's a lot of responsibility for two people."

Arden looked at Book of Vindor in his sister's lap. "It's too much for two people," he murmured.

Megan smiled gently. "I think together you and I will be up to the task."

"No," Arden said. "Why should it be just us? We could write a book."

"Huh?"

Arden pointed to the Book of Vindor. "You remembered everything because it was written down. What if we wrote a book? Or two books—one about your adventures, and one about mine."

"Arden, no one would believe it."

"They don't have to *believe* it. We pretend it's fiction, we make up an author name, we get it out to readers. They'll think it's just a made-up place—"

"But they'll be imagining Vindor too."

He nodded. "Even a handful of people thinking about Vindor, dreaming about visiting it for themselves, would keep it alive long after we forget it."

Megan struggled to her feet, using her crutch for support. "But Arden," she said. "All those new dreamers—they'll change it."

"Let them," Arden said. "Let them add new heroes, new places, new adventures. That kind of change is what Paracosmia thrives on. Vindor will keep growing, unbound, for years to come, and the mists will never be able to take it away."

Megan struggled to her feet and hobbled toward Arden. Solemnly she held out the battered Book of Vindor, and Arden took hold of it.

"It's in our hands, Arden," Megan said. "Let the new chapters begin."

"Let us go forth, the tellers of tales ... Everything exists, everything is true, and the earth is only a little dust under our feet."

—Yeats

About the Author

In addition to being a fantasy author, Emily Golus has also been a scriptwriter, a puppeteer, a magazine editor, a blogger, a Good News Club teacher, and the "cool aunt" to three nieces and five nephews. She lives in Upstate South Carolina with her woodworking husband, an awkward cat, and the world's most talkative baby.

A New England transplant now living in the Deep South, Golus is fascinated by culture and the way it shapes how individuals see the world around them. Her fantasy works are filled with diverse and complex people who are unwillingly united in times of great danger. Golus aims to write stories that engage, inspire, and reassure readers that the small choices of everyday life matter.

Vindor Needs Your Help!

If you enjoyed *Escape to Vindor* and *Mists of Paracosmia*, you can help get it into the hands of more readers by leaving a review on Amazon and Goodreads. Many people rely on these sites to decide whether to try a new book, so your words can make an impact!

For additional content about Vindor and its peoples, including detailed illustrations and an interactive map, visit WorldofVindor.com.

You can also visit EmilyGolusBooks.com to learn more about world-building and how you can meet the author in person.

Finally, and most importantly: dream on, my dear world-making friends!

All my love,

Emily Golus

CPSIA information can be obtained
at www.ICGtesting.com
Printed in the USA
BVHW030809271221
624878BV00005B/88